THE UNIQUE MAGAZINE
Summer 1993

ISSN 0898-5073
Cover by Paul Lehr

Weird Tales® is published 4 times a year by Terminus Publishing Co., Inc., PO Box 13418, Philadelphia PA 19101-3418 (4426 Larchwood Ave., Philadelphia PA 19104-3916). 2nd Class Postage paid at Philadelphia PA & additional mailing offices. Single copies, $4.95. Subscriptions: 4 issues (one year) $16.00 in U.S.A. & possessions; $22.00 elsewhere, in U.S. funds. Postmaster: send address changes to *Weird Tales*®, PO Box 13418, Philadelphia PA 19101-3418. Copyright © 1993 by Terminus Publishing Co., Inc.; all rights reserved; reproduction prohibited without prior permission. Typeset, printed, & bound in the United States of America. *Weird Tales*® is a registered trademark owned by Weird Tales, Limited.

In Memoriam: Fritz Leiber, Jr., 1910-1992

We deeply regret the recent death of the great gothic genius of American letters. Highly honored within the fantasy and science fiction field, revered by colleagues, winner of (among others) six Hugo Awards, and World Fantasy Awards both for Best Short Story and Lifetime Achievement, a Nebula Grandmaster Award, and a Gandalf, Fritz Leiber, Jr., never quite came to the attention of the Critical Establishment because he was "genre," which was the general public's loss. But we are certain he will be belatedly "discovered," like Philip K. Dick. Wait and see.

We last saw Fritz when he appeared as Principal Speaker at the Philadelphia Science Fiction Conference in 1990. Even then, though age had somewhat diminished his magnificent actor's voice, he was incisive and fascinating. Those who heard him speak in his prime — such as the memorable reading of Lovecraft's "The Haunter of the Dark" at the World Fantasy Convention in Providence in 1975 (only scant blocks from the scene of the action!) — have some idea of how Leiber once held audiences spellbound. At the Philadelphia Science Fiction Conference, Darrell Schweitzer conducted the Principal Speaker interview, during which Fritz ranged back over more than fifty years of writing and experience.

Here was an author who began as a correspondent of H.P. Lovecraft and then went on to virtually invent the modern horror novel with the twice-filmed *Conjure Wife* (1943). *Our Lady of Darkness* (1977) continued to demonstrate an artistry matched only by Shirley Jackson's *The Haunting of Hill House.*

He remained, in every decade since the 1940s, at the cutting edge of fantastic literature.

He made his first professional sale, "The Automatic Pistol," to *Weird Tales*®. The story appeared in the May 1940 issue, although by then his second sale, "Two Sought Adventure," (the first Fafhrd and Gray Mouser story, since retitled "The Jewels in the Forest") had already been published in *Unknown.* Seven more Leiber stories ran in these pages, the last being "The Dead Man," in the November 1950 *Weird Tales*®; but, in the first phase of his career, Leiber was much more strongly associated with *Unknown,* which gave readers *Conjure Wife* and the classic "Smoke Ghost." Under the guidance of *Unknown*'s editor, John W. Campbell, Leiber switched over to science fiction and became a star contributor to Campbell's other magazine, *Astounding Science Fiction* (now published as *Analog*), where Leiber's *Gather, Darkness!* began serialization a month after *Conjure Wife* was featured in *Unknown.*

Later, Leiber contributed to every leading science fiction magazine, from *Galaxy* to *New Worlds*. He wrote fantasy and horror when the market would support it and saw his Fafhrd and Gray Mouser series revived in the late 1960s, in a paperback book series which has remained in print ever since.

Some of his science-fiction novels, such as *Gather, Darkness!* (1943, 1958) and *The Wanderer* (1964) are classics. *The Big Time* and subsequent "Change War" stories made the inter-universal time-streams, where Snakes and Spiders battled to cancel one another out of history, a permanent part of Leiber Space.

Leiber could turn anything into high art. He could turn out absolute gems to order around magazine covers. He wrote satire, adventure, hard-science, avant-garde fantasy, even a Tarzan novel. His Fafhrd and the Gray Mouser series was the most literate sword and sorcery ever done, its final volume *The Knight and Knave of Swords* (1988) edging the stalwart heroes inexorably nearer to old age and death.

He ranged impressively over topics as varied as witchcraft, politics, sex, cats, chess, Shakespeare, and time-travel; substantial essays and poetry in addition to fiction. His quiet passing on September 5, 1992 was not unexpected, but it is a grave loss. Fritz Leiber was, without a doubt, one of the giants.

We also regret the passing, 13 January 1993, of Margo Skinner Leiber, Fritz's widow. She was a poet of great renown. Some of her verse appeared in *Weird Tales®*.

We are particularly pleased to offer a rare Fritz Leiber poetry cycle, this issue. *Demons of the Upper Air* was written in the late 1930s, and sent by Leiber to his correspondent and mentor, Lovecraft. (It is ironic to read in Lovecraft's letters how flattered and honored Lovecraft was to correspond with the son of the great Shakespearian actor, Fritz Leiber, Sr.; presciently, H.P.L. saw enormous promise in the younger Leiber.) The title poem was published in the Fritz Leiber issue of *The Magazine of Fantasy and Science Fiction* in 1969, and Roy Squires issued the whole sequence as a limited-edition pamphlet the same year, but there have been no reprintings since, and we are fairly certain that you haven't seen these poems. The illustrations by Keith Minnion are, of course, new.

We can only regret that this will probably be Fritz Leiber's last appearance in The Unique Magazine, unless unpublished manuscripts turn up, since we do very few reprints, and most of Leiber's fiction is available in his various collections.

On the subject of Fritz Leiber, let us highly recommend Bruce Byfield's *Witches of the Mind: A Critical Study of Fritz Leiber,* which is not only the best book written about Leiber, but one of the best single-author studies we have ever seen. (Available from Necronomicon Press, 101 Lockwood St., West Warwick RI 02893 for $9.95 plus $1.50 postage & handling.) And, the Philcon presentation, which became Fritz's last interview, was published in *Marion Zimmer Bradley's Fantasy Magazine* issue number 15 (Winter 1991) and is available from Marion Zimmer Bradley Ltd., P.O. Box 249, Berkeley CA 94701 for $4.95 plus $2.50 postage *per order* (Which means you should pad out your order: issues 1-3, 5-17 are available. May we shamelessly plug the Darrell Schweitzer stories in 6, 11, and 17, and the really great Jason Van Hollander story in 6?)

On the subject of reprints, Ian Watson's *The Coming of Vertumnus* in this issue has already appeared in the British magazine, *Interzone,* an excellent British magazine which has little American circulation. We have used stories from its pages before, going as far back as Watson's *When Jesus Came Down the Chimney* in issue #293. In every case, the *Weird Tales®* printing has been the first North American publication.

Sometimes we've been a bit sloppy about acknowledging this, though, and for that we apologize. Last issue, for example, while we admitted that the four Lord Dunsany stories came from British magazines, we were no more specific than that. Here are the complete data: "The Rations of Murdoch Finucan" first appeared in *Punch* for 8 October 1947. "A Modern Portrait" appeared in *Punch* for 9 January 1946. "Echoing Dream" appeared in *Argosy* for October 1956 (the British digest, no relation to the American pulp magazine of the same title; this was, incidentally, the last story Dunsany published

in his lifetime), and "Helping the Fairies" appeared in *Strand Magazine*, May–June 1947. The stories are, respectively, copyright 1947, 1946, 1956, and 1947 by Lord Dunsany.

Incidentally, we hope to have more hitherto unknown Lord Dunsany fiction in the immediate future.

Marc Uwe Zender writes:

I had to write to congratulate you on the new format for *Weird Tales®*. Although I have to keep #305 and #306 in a different shelf than my earlier straight-spined issues, I firmly stand by your decision to alter format rather than fade into obscurity. Your selection of stories, both old and new, reflects the usual range of prose and poetry which I have come to regard so highly that your magazine remains my only subscription (and will continue as such). Keep up the good work.

In my opinion, the highlights of your most recent issue were Hoffman's "Valentines" (reminiscent of Seawell's chilling "Something for Amy," which appeared in your 301st), Tanith Lee's "Antonius Bequeathed" (a wonderful piece, and — I think — her best since "The Lily Garden") and, of course, your collection of Dunsany's shorter pieces — of which I greatly enjoyed "A Modern Portrait." Congratulations are in order for both Schweitzer and Joshi for rescuing these gems from obscurity.

And to jump on the scholarly bandwagon, I just have to respond to Gerald Pearce's note on the etymology of Lovecraft's Abdul Alhazred. While I am certainly of the opinion that if the "Cthulhu Mythos" of H.P. Lovecraft (and, naturally, August Derleth) is to continue to grow and receive new acolytes, then it must adapt and respond to new knowledge and experience — I don't necessarily believe that altering the name of Lovecraft's ancient scholar is required. It is certainly possible that the fault of translation — at least within Mythos consistency — may rest with the renowned Byzantine scholar Theodorus Philetas who, as Lovecraft explains in his "History of the *Necronomicon*," translated the Arabic *Kitab Al-Azif* into Greek in A.D. 950. It may even rest with Olaus Wormius, or perhaps even John Dee. Thus it becomes clear that the name Abdul Alhazred need not be taken as an obvious blunder on the part of Lovecraft (though it may actually be so), but the natural result of the many translations and expurgations committed before it finally fell to Dr. John Dee to make some sense of it all.

However, if it is necessary to delve into the depths of the past to search for an original Arabic source for the renowned Mythos scholar, then I believe we need look no further than William Hamblin's fine explanation as it appeared in his essay "Notes on a Fragment of the *Necronomicon*" (published in *Call of Cthulhu Keeper's Book,* Chaosium Inc.):

"'Hazred,' which itself is not an Arabic word, is probably a textual corruption from which it might be possible to reconstruct the original . . . I would speculate that the original word was 'Azrad,' which is the

Publisher: George H. Scithers. Editor: Darrell Schweitzer. Managing Editor: Carol Adams. Art Director: Michael W. Betancourt. Assistant Editors: Leslie Smith, Dainis Bisenieks, Diane Weinstein, Don Keller, Nicholas Beauchamp, & Kyle Phillips. Circulation Manager: Tina Hoffman. Computer Consultant: David J. Williams III. Of Counsel: Matthew Wolfe.

elative form of the Arabic verb 'zarada,' meaning 'to strangle or devour.' The correct name . . . was Abd al-Azrad, which would be translated 'the worshiper of the great strangler or great devourer.'"

This explanation is, of course, consistent with Arabic grammar. Moreover, it is certainly more in keeping with Lovecraft's conception than de Camp's "Servant-of-God Flower-of-the-Faith," and bears the benefit of sounding like its own future corruption: Abdul Alhazred. It is also similar to Pearce's own offering: Abd al-Azhar. Indeed, the only difference occurs in a literal reading of the two forms. For instance, Pearce suggests that 'Abd' more properly means 'slave' or 'servant' than 'worshiper' — and this makes a great deal more sense when one considers Abd al-Azrad's rumored end within the pages of Ebn Khallikan's biographies (as reported in Lovecraft's *History of the Necronomicon*):

". . . seized by an invisible monster in broad daylight and *devoured* horribly before a large number of fright-frozen witnesses."

Christopher Dunn writes:

Of course I am glad the new format has come together, and as I said last time, do whatever you need to keep in print.

Stories: To choose between what I thought were the best two is not easy — "The Pulse of the Machine," I mean, and "Ridi Bobo." But, in the end, I vote for the latter. The Deveraux story was remarkable. "To open its pages was to watch a universe unfold," Gene Wolfe wrote a while ago in *WT;* I thought "Ridi Bobo" demonstrated exactly that, original and perfectly done. Much of the same applies to "Pulse," too, but that was an approach to a traditional theme, which "Bobo" was definitely not — unless . . . (I darkly suspect social satire, but can't prove it. Get him to sign something.) I also liked "Rogue Wave" — but that's mostly out of a personal prejudice for vast unknown Things lurking just out of sight.

From what was said in the Eyrie this time, the Dunsany stories must be genuine, but it's funny: I would have thought at first that they were pastiches; they sound like him and they don't. Were they *written* in the '40s and '50s? Or were they early stories? In any case, no fan of *WT* but wouldn't hope for something like the Schweitzer-Joshi discovery (that has a Lovecraftian sound, somehow: should it be the "Schweitzer-Joshi Revelations"?)

We're almost certain that the Dunsany stories were written shortly before they were published, as they are very typical of a large body of Dunsany's work found in the magazines of the period. The strangeness may simply be that you (like most readers) aren't all that familiar with the later Dunsany. His *early* (pre-World War I) work was mostly in a quasi-biblical/heroic or ironic mode — the stories found in *A Dreamer's Tales* and *The Book of Wonder.* The stories we published are from the same time as — and more closely resemble — those of *The Fourth Book of Jorkens.*

(One of us claims that the adjectival form should be "Lovecrafty," but he lacks Proper Reverence; ignore him.)

Mr. Dunn adds in another letter (referring back to the editorial in *Weird Tales*® #305) that, while he isn't in favor of censorship, he would very much like to drive a stake through the heart of such absurdities as Fred Saberhagen's novelization of James V. Hart's screenplay of Francis Ford Coppola's *Bram Stoker's Dracula* — which is not, in any way, to be confused with a novel called *Dracula* by Bram Stoker, any more than the movie lives up to its title. Can anything be "done" about such blatant falsifications, Mr. Dunn wonders.

Not that we can think of. You don't have to buy the book. Instead, reread *Dracula* to see how *little* the Coppola film has to do with Stoker's original. Far from being the most faithful adaptation ever, it is the *most variant,* as way off the mark as the silent film of *Moby Dick* entitled *The Sea Beast,* in which Ahab kills the whale and gets the girl in the end. (We're not making this up. Honest.) Any virtues of *Francis Ford Coppola's Dracula* (to use what should have been its full title) are Coppola's, not Stoker's. It is an entirely *original* creation.

L.P. Van Ness writes:

Nina Kiriki Hoffman's shape-shifting lynx, in "The Pulse of the Machine," demands a writing style that is both sensory and minutely precise, and the writer does a very credible characterization, as exemplified by this passage, "I can smell the chill, dewed metal, and the weeds that try to grow, stunted and sunless, beneath the machines." In fact, she is especially successful in creating memorable olfactory sensations in her tales. In "A Seance," Natasha "lit the candles, adding the clean scent of wax to the odor of stale incense." In "Ceciley in the Supermarket," Ceciley notes that the "mist machines over the salad vegetables gave the impression of cigarette smoke, though the air smelled wetter and less flavored." And in "Where the Sun Stays for Winter," Mila "smelled woodsmoke and baking bread and morning." In the same story, the writer even utilizes the olfactory to describe an apple's taste, "It was a taste like the smell of a spring night."

This trio of Nina Kiriki Hoffman tales features strong, intelligent girls and women. My favorite was "The Pulse of the Machine." The interchange of ideas between Terry, the shape-shifting lynx who has come down from the mountains for an "education," and Anitra, who is a student of human nature, helps create very real characterizations. And the reader is left craving more crime-fighting adventures, for Nina Kiriki Hoffman has created, in the characters of Terry and Anitra, the female equivalent of a modern-day Holmes and Watson.

Brett Campbell expresses appreciation for the improved format in issue #306 and for John Betancourt's "Buck, Glory Rae, & the Three Little Pigs," then, referring back to issue #304, reservedly praises John Brunner's "Concerning the Forthcoming Inexpensive Paperback Translation of the Necronomicon of Abdul Alhazred," his one reservation being "how easily [the story's narrator] 'buys' the truth of Alhazred's insane writings. It seems to me that a man as pompous, erudite, and arrogant as Wharton . . . would have been far more likely to pooh-pooh such poppycock as nonsense, even after having read a considerable ways into it and having a few bad dreams . . ." To which we can only say, in Mr. Brunner's defense, that the story has strong elements of parody, in which certain Things are taken for granted. Maybe the Great Old Ones made him do it . . . More seriously, you have a point, the same that one of us addressed in an essay, "Character Gullibility in Weird Fiction, or, Isn't Yuggoth Somewhere in Upstate New York?" The author must always balance what a reasonable person would believe to what we, as readers, know because we are reading a fantasy story. The characters themselves cannot know they're in a fantasy story, and would therefore grasp at "logical" explanations for quite a long time.

We are also particularly pleased to hear again from **G.W. Young,** who was so critical of issue #305, but is much more pleased with issue #306. **J.M. Haydock** asks us to return to the old format no matter what it costs; and we can only say that, alas, we cannot, because the cost would be the end of the magazine. We are reassured to see, by bookstore orders and subscription renewals, that we seem to have definitely gotten away with the format change, and the magazine's continued existence is now much more certain than it was a year ago. But there is no way to go back to the old format.

Joseph R. Hansen asks if we have ever considered republishing the original run of *Weird Tales®* in facsimile. Well, we admit we would like to see someone — probably not ourselves — publish a facsimile reprint of the magazine's first year simply because those issues are so fantastically rare, but it would be an *enormous* project to reprint the entire run of 289 pre-Terminus issues, quite impossible economically. A set would retail for many thousands of dollars. Maybe someday all of *Weird Tales®* will be available on microfilm, but in the meantime, we must subsist on the numerous anthologies — we particularly recommend Marvin Kaye's *Weird Tales: The Magazine That Never Dies* (Nelson Doubleday) and the forthcoming Wildside Press series edited by Kaye and by John Betancourt, which will devote one volume to each year of the magazine's existence, starting, of course, with 1923. (Write to Wildside Press, 37 Fillmore St., Newark NJ 07105 for details.)

William C. Mueller, Jr. expresses regrets about our new format, finding it "unweird," to which we can only refer him to the reply to Mr. Haydock above, and point out that for most of the first year of the magazine's existence, *Weird Tales®* was published in a large, 8.5x11-inch format, very similar to our present one. Then the magazine went to the then-standard "pulp" size of 6.5x9.25 inches. In 1953, the magazine shifted to digest size, like the current *Analog* or *The Magazine of Fantasy & Science Fiction*. *Weird Tales®* was revived in 1973 as a pulp, lasting four issues; again in the early '80s as a paperback book (four issues, from Zebra Books); and again in a format almost identical to our present one (two issues, on glossy paper, 1984–85). Terminus Publishing Co., Inc., revived it in the 6.5 by 9.25 inch format, perfect bound (that is, with a flat spine), on book paper. So *Weird Tales®* has been all over the lot . . . although we haven't published it as a *scroll* . . . yet.

The Most Popular Story.
Voting was very light this time. (We need to hear from you!) First place was a tie between Nina Kiriki Hoffman's "The Pulse of the Machine" and Tanith Lee's "Antonius Bequeathed." Second place went to Hoffman's "The Seance," and third was a tie between Robert Deveraux's "Ridi Bobo" and Nina Hoffman's "Valentine." Ω

SHADOWINGS

Alone

with the

Horrors

by Douglas E. Winter

Where to begin? I've written entire books about writers; the thought of now devoting only 2,000 or so words to Ramsey Campbell's *Alone with the Horrors* (Arkham House, 1993, $26.95), a weighty retrospective on a professional career that spans almost thirty years, 200 short stories, and a dozen novels, is a daunting one. It doesn't help that my views go beyond the professional to the personal.

Our relationship has been a complex but comfortable one. I've dealt with Ramsey Campbell as a reader, fan, reviewer, interviewer, photographer, editor, panel member, fellow film enthusiast, drinking companion, houseguest, tour guide, and — above all — friend. We've had our share of those peculiar male bonding experiences — none of them unspeakable, but a few of which ought not see print, at least in our lifetimes. I have lost count of the videos we have watched together, from the sublime (Dario Argento's *Inferno*) to the ludicrous (*The Monster of Piedras Blancas*, among so many others). I have witnessed not one, but two, of his dramatic (and I do mean dramatic) readings of that lost classic of horrific fiction, "The Legs That Walked." We have dined together at such mealtime meccas as the Weenie Beanie and Meacham's Baltic Fleet, and it was his careful directions that took me, one rainy London afternoon, down into Soho to the very doorstep of Spank-O-Rama.

Yet I'm still at a loss when it comes to the idea of trying to find words to define Ramsey Campbell. After more than ten years of camaraderie, so much of Ramsey remains a cipher to me that I have concluded that there is no certain way of knowing him save through his fiction. He is not so much a private person as a private personality — and it's not a matter of that legendary British reserve (and legend it is, for I've had more Britishers spill their life stories to me over a handshake and a pint of lager than I care to remember). It is simply part of being Ramsey Campbell.

Thus: If you are looking for insights into the man, turn quickly from this meager column and explore his writing instead. For newcomers and veterans alike, there is no better place to begin than *Alone with the Horrors,* a worthy celebration of Ramsey's career that features 39 of his best short stories and a new introductory essay. There you will also happen to find some of the most original and compelling fiction of our time.

So unique is Ramsey Campbell's craft that it may come as a surprise to some to learn that his first published stories were pastiches of H.P. Lovecraft. I discovered these stories (or, as Ramsey has described them, "indiscretions") at the same time I learned that Arkham House was a thriving small press in Sauk City, Wisconsin. Pursuing things Lovecraftian with the wanton fervor of adolescence, I ordered *The Inhabitant of the Lake & Less Welcome Tenants* (1964) from Mr. Derleth — paying the weighty hardcover price of $4.00 — and soon indulged in the glories of new tales of the "Cthulhu Mythos" set in a British amalgam of HPL's Arkham, Dunwich, and Innsmouth. To my young and undiscriminating eyes, stories like "The Room in the Castle" were the next best thing to uncovering a trove of new manuscripts by the late gentleman from Providence. There was no telling then that I was surveying the mere sketchwork of an apprentice whose skills would soon surpass those of his master.

In retrospect, it is easy to see how even these early stories distinguished this teenaged writer from the others who sought to carry on — or, in some cases, co-opt — the Lovecraft mythology. Clearly the storytelling technique, so easily emulated, was but part of the attraction for Ramsey; more important was the unbridled sense of cosmic awe and the latent psychedelia, that kind of wide-eyed-with-wonder way of looking at (and through) the world that Ramsey would ultimately adapt so very well to his own intent. Years later, when I discovered his second Arkham House collection, *Demons by Daylight* (1973), in the dusty basement of a "magick shoppe" just off Harvard Square, I was awakened to Ramsey Campbell on his own terms. There was no turning back from stories like "The Interloper": This was Lovecraft for the seventies . . . Lovecraft for grown-

ups. I've read virtually everything that Ramsey has written since.

In noting Ramsey's Lovecraftian roots — dare I say tendrils? — I would be remiss if I did not mention the profound impact of other writers. Too often the myopic stare of *genre* criticism chooses to define its own in terms of its own, when the best, and certainly the most original, of our writers usually find their inspiration elsewhere. Stephen King would not exist, at least as we know him today, without the likes of Don Robertson and John D. MacDonald; Clive Barker would not thrive without the Jacobean dramatists Marlowe and Webster. Although other writers of the supernatural, notably Robert Aickman, M.R. James, and Fritz Leiber, affected Ramsey's developing craft, his mature writing was energized by sources as diverse as Vladimir Nabokov and John Franklin Barden and William S. Burroughs — and, no doubt, the Russian classicists (one cannot read that compelling jeremiad, *The Count of Eleven* (1991), without sensing the shadow of Dostoevski). So much has been written about Ramsey Campbell as today's prime exponent of the weird tradition that it seems only fair to underscore how often and how capably he has subverted — and, indeed, written *outside* of — that tradition.

Several years ago, an intriguing — and quite telling — review of Ramsey's *Dark Companions* (1982) appeared in a leading sf magazine. The reviewer raved on about the elegance and eloquence of Ramsey's prose, but then, in that backhanded style to which we have all become so accustomed, asked a musical question:

So . . . why doesn't it scare me?

This is the kind of simpleminded, but too often sincere, question that was asked about J. G. Ballard's science fiction in the sixties and early seventies: Where are the rocketships? The aliens?

We so obviously denigrate that which we love, striving always to simplify it, to find its common denominator — and, above all, to make it *safe*.

Ramsey Campbell is proof positive that horror fiction is not, and never has been, about "scares." This is not to say that he cannot deliver them — consider the memorable opening chapter of his first novel, *The Doll Who Ate His Mother* (1976) — but that his interests are not so superficial. He is not an avuncular stylist in the contemporary American mold — the Robert Bloch or Rod Serling or Stephen King whose voice, like that of the campfire storyteller, is so intrinsic to his story. Like these and other great writers of horror fiction, Ramsey is there, lurking in the shadows of his prose, but there is no sense of a handholding reassurance, a guarantee that we will wake from his dark dreams.

There is no sense that we are safe.

Ramsey Campbell's fiction is insistently closer to the edge than most of what is published in the name of "horror"; it dares the precipice of reason, the human

dilemma of knowing and not knowing, believing and disbelieving. Even when he writes explicitly of monsters or the beyond, there is an undeniable sense that the rational and irrational are one, that nothing is certain or can be made certain.

In our *Faces of Fear* interview, Ramsey recounted a teenage experience of seeing an unknown symbology form in the patterns of a railway car seat. This aesthetic is a hallmark of his art: reality blurred, not necessarily by the prospect of the supernatural, but by the prospect of madness — or, indeed, of simple imagination. I can think of no other writer who so profoundly grasps the illusory nature of fear, understanding that it lives and grows in that precious realm between thought and act, possibility and fact. Thus Ramsey Campbell's most powerful fiction has concerned itself less with the supernatural than with fear of the supernatural — not with madness, but with the fear of madness.

When we list the landmark collections of short stories published during the past two decades, the brightest years of horror fiction's modern renaissance — J.G. Ballard's *The Atrocity Exhibition*, Dennis Etchison's *The Dark Country*, Clive Barker's *Books of Blood*, Thomas Ligotti's *Songs of a Dead Dreamer*, Peter Straub's *Houses Without Doors*, Jack Cady's *The Sons of Noah* and a handful of others — we will find that almost a third of them were written by one man: Ramsey Campbell. *Alone with the Horrors*, a virtual "best of the best," will assuredly rank as among the great short story volumes of the genre — indeed, of the century.

As a novelist, Ramsey has produced a diverse array of entertainments, from psychological suspense to supernatural thrillers to surreal delights. His success at novel length is such that, among fellow writers and enthusiastic readers alike, there seems never a consensus as to which books are his best. My favorites include *The Face that Must Die* (1979), *Incarnate* (1983), and *Midnight Sun* (1990); ask the next person and you'll no doubt hear three different choices.

Ramsey also has produced a considerable portfolio of non-fiction that should one day see print in book form. He is the most popular of contemporary horror writers to contribute regularly to the literature through reviews and criticisms; I wish there were many more like him.

Looking back on this remarkable and prolific career, I can't help but mention in closing the most important fact about Ramsey Campbell. It's a simple fact, but one that, in reading (or writing about) a retrospective of the caliber of *Alone with the Horrors*, might all too easily be overlooked:

For all of his achievements, Ramsey Campbell is still a young writer, with many, many years of work ahead of him.

I look forward to those years with great expectancy, for I know that the best is yet to come. Ω

MOVING?

If you do, please let us know — a few weeks in advance if you possibly can — where you are going. In order that we can keep sending the Unique Magazine to your new lair, let us have your old address (with ZIP code) and your new address (again, with ZIP code). Please!

KING WEASEL

by Ian Watson

illustrated by Alan Clark

Diane Cobbett was driving along the narrow, twisty road from Upton to Woodburn of a Saturday afternoon. Beside her, pile of exercise books balanced on his knee, Saul Cobbett was grading maps of imaginary nature reserves drawn by his class of twelve-year-olds. In the back of the aging Renault young Tim turned the pages of a comic while his younger brother Josh steered a model harvester around the seat as though it was a racing car.

Tim had already begun school; Josh would follow in another year. Diane would go back to teaching then. Craft and Design; preferably in the same school as Saul, or else they would need two aging cars. The family income would rise; lean times would be over.

No doubt several years of belt-tightening had fully justified themselves — in the production of Tim and Josh. In some other respects . . . Saul stared at the bare, October-sodden, misty fields and hummed a low dirge-like noise, of unvoiced, displaced complaint which the car engine mostly drowned.

Stuck on her own in a small village with two young kids, energetic Diane had become — what was the diplomatic word? — obsessive.

It wasn't that Saul jibbed at their totally vegetarian diet. That made financial as well as moral sense. It even made gastronomic sense, since Di worked wonders with spinach quiches, vegetable curries, spiced rice, pea soup. The last time Saul had tasted meat, by necessity — a greasy lamb cutlet which was all that the school canteen had remaining on offer that day — he'd felt disgusted and contemptuous.

It wasn't that nowadays Diane would shake her fist and shout abuse at passing fox-hunters, any of whom might easily be local school governors who might interview her in future and would remember her bouncy chestnut hair, her Rubens milkmaid looks. He totally agreed with Di's hatred of the hunt and all its costumed, bullying, thundering arrogance.

It wasn't that the boys had certain toys taken away from them, others denied to them. Obviously kids oughtn't to play with imitation weapons. And Josh had hardly brooded over the fact that his model farm was culled of its four plastic pigs and two plastic turkeys by Di — since pigs and turkeys were reared for one purpose only: slaughter.

Nor was it the recollection of Tim's tears when they finally released his pet rabbit into the wild that April. Tim had agreed bravely, or seemed to. Diane had prepared the boys well for the great event, so that it seemed a triumph both practical and sentimental. Di couldn't bear to see Teddybun captive behind chicken-

wire any longer. He should bound free, find a mate, build a burrow with a rooty doorway on the edge of the copse by the safe-looking pasture they chose. Better one summer of liberty and a natural death than life imprisonment. Teddybun had run off quickly enough, tail bobbing as if in agreement. They had waited a whole hour, picnicking on salad sandwiches, in case he came back; but he hadn't — and they were saved the labour of feeding and watering the rabbit and shovelling up its latrine-full of droppings once a fortnight, which had earned Saul one nasty bite on the knuckle from the robbed animal. He fully agreed with the *evil* of captive animals. Their own efforts for Teddybun's welfare, prior to liberation, had shown how wretchedly most pet rabbits must fare with cramped hutches, monotonous diets, insufficient water, a dozen other thoughtless cruelties. The notion that rabbits *liked* eating dry hay and their own droppings!

It wasn't just . . .

The Renault rounded a bend. Ahead on the crown of the road a creature thrashed about in broken agony.

Despite the boys loose in the back, Diane instantly stamped on the brake.

"Something's been run over! The bastards didn't stop!"

With the rubbery resilience of kids, Josh and Tim had survived the abrupt stop, though Josh was now bleating, "Me howitzer! Me howitzer's lost!"

"Harvester," Saul corrected automatically.

Tim was more interested in the spectacle ahead and in the word "bastard" which he repeated as though that was the name of the afflicted animal. Once Diane opened her door and leapt out, the writhing creature promptly disentangled. A sleek russet-furred worm on legs raced for sanctuary in the grass verge; a gray rabbit lurched, staggered, and fell over.

No road victim, this. A weasel had been clinging to the frantic rabbit's neck, about to kill it. Thrusting school books on to Diane's seat, Saul climbed out; Tim also came.

The assaulted rabbit lay panting in shock, making no effort to escape from the approaching giants.

"I don't see any blood," Saul said.

"Mum!" Tim pointed at the verge. Amid the long grass a lithe little body stood upright. Up on its hind legs the weasel was staring at them with fixed, beady malevolence, with outright hatred.

Saul clapped his hands. "Shoo! Buzz off!"

The weasel seemed to quiver with intensity — its only concession to movement.

Saul gathered the rabbit carefully into his arms

since it couldn't stay in the center of the road. A scrappy, skinny beast, it only weighed a fraction of what Teddybun had massed; though maybe now, six months later, Teddybun too was as light as this wretched starveling. Mud immediately smeared any part of Saul's anorak which the rabbit touched; it was damp and filthy. But it kicked powerful hind legs a couple of times.

"There, there, poor little thing," crooned Saul, to quiet it. "Seems in working order. At least the weasel didn't have time to snap its spine."

He walked to the nearer verge and deposited the rabbit, which scrambled a very short way before flopping. The weasel watched all this alertly.

"We can't leave it here," protested Diane. "The moment we're gone, the weasel will nip across. It's just waiting."

Saul gathered the rabbit up again. "I'll carry it a hundred yards down the road. You drive after me. It's half-paralysed with shock. Maybe it can't survive."

"Can't? Do you suggest putting it out of its misery? With a stone, or a punch?"

"I'd probably bungle it." Accompanied by Tim, Saul walked on; soon the Renault purred slowly after.

When Saul next laid the rabbit on the grass, it was no more energetic. Across the way, the thin russet body reared again, glaring inflexibly. Refusing to quit, the weasel had kept pace. Its mouth opened. It seemed to hiss at them through tiny sharp teeth, though the sound was inaudible.

"What bloody cheek! I suppose this was its supper. Look at my coat. All filthy from it."

"Why don't we take the rabbit home, Dad? Nurse it, then bring it back when it's better? We still have Teddybun's run and rabbit pellets."

"No. We just got rid of one captive animal."

"It's unfair! It'll die."

"We're responsible," Diane called intensely, from the car.

"For everything in the world?"

"For this little bit of everything, where we interfered."

Saul sighed. Shucking off the soiled anorak, he wrapped the rabbit securely, head and ears protruding. Then he climbed back into the car, where the school books were lying on the floor.

As Diane engaged gear and pulled away, Saul noticed the weasel darting along the verge, rearing to gaze vindictively. A rainbow sticker on the rear window announced: ECOLOGY IS OUR ONLY HOPE. Another stated: BAN CRUEL SPORTS. The Renault very quickly outdistanced the brown smudge.

Saul stroked the rabbit's head, then desisted. Maybe he was terrifying, not comforting the limp animal. Instead he stroked his own beard — that of a younger Solzhenitsyn, said Di — without which his face might have looked at once morose and undistinguished. Those whiskers gave to a puddingy countenance and gimlet eyes a certain messianic nobility.

Terrifying the animal.

He remembered . . .

When Saul and Diane first got married they had lived in a small town flat. They had acquired a pair of chipmunks, plus a large cage with an exercise wheel. That was because they loved animals. However, they were out all day so it would be cruel to keep a dog or cat.

Every time they returned home one of the chipmunks would instantly leap into the wheel and rotate it vigorously (be-dum, be-dum) as if in glad greeting. The other would scrabble up one side of the cage, over the roof, and down the other (be-doom, be-doom). Up, and over, and down.

Only after some months did it occur to Saul that the chipmunks ran because they were terrified, but there was hardly anywhere to run to. One day he and Diane decided to let Ben and Babs out for an exploration of the living room. Lifting the cage down from its table and opening the wire door, they sat back with quiet pleasure to watch adventures.

Ben's and Babs' twitching noses explored the open gap many times before they dared venture further. Ten minutes went by before the chipmunks at last tumbled out and began to move around the floor. They didn't exactly run, or walk. Instead they plucked themselves along at considerable speed like absurd clockwork toys with wheels in their bellies. They seemed to have no idea how to use their legs normally. After a lifetime spent in cages they had the wrong muscles. Their mode of locomotion was disgusting, as though Ben and Babs weren't furry little pets after all but bags of hairy entrails equipped with claws. Saul rose to pick them up and put them back.

Both chipmunks evaded him. Running flat on their bellies, however ungracefully, they escaped him time and again. At last he'd snatched at a passing chipmunk. His hand closed not on its body but on its tail . . . and that tail came off in his fingers. He clutched, in horror, a twitching bottle-brush; dropped it immediately in disgust. Ben — or Babs — ran on, a long thin spike sticking out from the animal's rump, flicking a drop of blood from the end, then another, the inner core of the tail.

He'd finally trapped each chipmunk separately under a cane wastepaper basket and restored each to the cage. Ben — or Babs — sat beady-eyed, sides heaving, seemingly impervious to the loss of its bushy brush.

Over the next few days the raw spike had dried up, withered, fallen off. A week later Saul and Diane took the cage down into the shared, wild garden to set the furry pets free. Though so much like squirrels in appearance, Ben and Babs didn't flee to the nearest leafy tree. They scrambled into an open drain and vanished down it like two sewer rats.

That, in retrospect, had been the beginning of the eventual liberation of Teddybun, of the purging of pork from Josh's toy farm, of fists brandished at riders, of Diane's protestations that all pet shops should be banned. And sideshows at fairs which dangled prizes of goldfish in asphyxiating bags. And. And.

The Ben-and-Babs episode had elements of farce, didn't it? Farce for the humans; horror for the animals. Or was the horror largely in the minds of sensitive people? And had that horror now burrowed so deep into Di — much as he agreed with her, a hundred percent — that it was like a tumour in her brain: deranging her behaviour?

She too had been shut up in a cage, of sorts, for the past few years together with two monkeys, namely Josh and Tim.

Saul wondered as he tugged at his Russian beard. No, of course she was right.

"Can't we keep him, Dad?"
"Of course not, Tim."

It was the following Saturday morning and they were due to make another trip, to buy toilet roll and such; and to return the rabbit to its native hedgerow.

Behind chicken-wire the rabbit was cleaning its coat, burrowing and biting at fur. Matted bunches of hair sprouted like tatty tusks alongside its whiskers. It had gorged on pellets and muesli and sultanas, lettuce and cabbage leaves and carrots cut into sticks. Not *too* many green leaves; must avoid bloat. It had failed to learn to use Teddybun's drinking bottle, and had spilled many saucers of water by standing in them. And it had made free with the huge, ever-open, several-chambered, hay-carpeted rabbit house which Diane had adapted and extended from the original hutch. Yet the animal still seemed feeble.

"If we take him back to the fields he'll die."
"Why should he?"
"Winter's coming."
"So?"
"He's been hurt, worried. If he was a person he'd stay in a hospital."

Saul saw the logic of this. Besides, what was the point of a spacious rabbit house and run without any rabbit in it? Diane had once spoken of turning the entire garden into a rabbit habitat, a rabbitorium. That was when they were still wrestling with the ethical problem of Teddybun. Even so, the rabbitorium residents wouldn't really have been free to race and leap as the whim took them. Also, they would have devoured all the vegetables, undermining the Cobbett family economy.

The run, with grass and a few paving slabs underfoot, was built along the back of the modernized stone cottage so that a kitchen window looked into it. The quarter-acre beyond was entirely devoted to vegetable plots, fruit under netting, a herb garden and an area for compost bins and bonfires. A rotary washing line acted as a good bird-scarer when the wind blew and shirt sleeves flapped. Before the Cobbetts moved in, there had been a zone of delphiniums and roses, but they had rooted those out for greater economy. The view was arguably ugly but the immediate neighbours weren't compelled to look at it, and the Cobbetts rarely invited anyone in.

They preferred to live a self-sufficient life. The boys were encouraged to play on the green out front. The Sandersons next door had actually had the nerve to complain about the washing Diane so often hung out, and about the frequent bonfires; Saul had told them to mind their own business. There had also been a quarrel about ownership of the boundary fence — the Sandersons were very territorial — which Saul resolved by rearing an inner barrier of tall poles and chicken-wire to grow beans.

Just then, Diane came outdoors holding a cardboard box.

"Tim doesn't want the new Teddybun to go," Saul said.

"It's not fair, Mum. He's still ill."

The rabbit hopped over to the latrine which it had by now assembled and let loose a dozen more gray marbles. It nosed and nibbled a couple, exposing green sludge. The real Teddybun had never eaten his own excrement; the Teddybun Hilton was permanently well-stocked with meals, however the guest rabbit had the habits of the wild. Half-digested food shouldn't go to waste without reprocessing. Dung was always good for another trip through the stomach.

Of course, the latrine was also designed to attract passing females. Their guest was a buck, with genitals like flabby red strips of smoked cod-roe pasted under his bob-tail. He wasn't in season right now, but rabbits were generally preoccupied with a

cocktail of droppings, territory, food, and sex.

"He's weak as water, Mum. He couldn't run away from a farmer with a rifle! Or a hound."

With childhood cunning Tim had pressed the right buttons. His mother chewed at her lip, dubiously.

"Yes, we're responsible," she said. "We've committed *crimes* against animals. He can stay another week."

As soon as the Renault had turned on to the by-road to Upton, Diane called to the boys in the back, "Which of my animals shall I summon?"

"Fox!" cried Josh.

"Muntjak Deer," suggested Tim.

"They're too shy," said Saul. "Only come out from dusk to dawn." The Cobbetts had only ever seen one diminutive Muntjak, crossing the road in their headlights late one evening.

"Badger, then!"

And the only badger they'd ever seen was a bear-like corpse by the roadside, swiped by some careless driver. Elsewhere in the county illegal badger-baiting still occurred. Sets were dug up; a badger was dragged out and forced to fight dogs to the death, to the terrible damage of dogs too. It made one's blood boil.

"A fox," said Diane. "Let's hope there isn't a hunt today." She wound her window down and called at the countryside, "Come, fox!"

The idea of "calling her animals" was recent, and amused the kids, whatever the outcome. Saul recalled the school sixth-formers acting Shakespeare's *Henry the Fourth* in the gym the previous Christmas. "I can call spirits from the vasty deep," blustered Glendower, the loud-mouthed Welshman. And Hotspur replied, "Why, so can I, or so can any man. But will they come when you do call for them?" This was a game, yet there was true passion in Diane's voice.

"Come to me, fox!"

Saul spied quick movement in the verge ahead. A little russet head on a furry snake-like body shot up to stare at the approaching car.

"Weasel!"

Diane braked. The Cobbetts stared at the animal; it glared back viciously.

"That's the same one!" cried Tim. "Good job we didn't bring Rabbit."

Saul snorted. "This is nowhere near. Another couple of miles on."

"Same weasel, Dad."

"Nonsense."

Diane was gazing mesmerized. Leaning over, Saul snapped his fingers in front of her eyes.

"Don't! Look what you've done!" The weasel had dropped low, masked by grass.

For a while Diane drove on in silence, then she said over her shoulder, "Yes, Tim, we'll keep the rabbit over winter. We'll let him go free in the spring."

"Keep him captive?" asked Saul. "Is that consistent with our principles?"

"I'll feed him and clean him — you needn't worry! He's my responsibility. In fact, don't you dare go inside his run at all! You just make empty noises about principles."

"What do you mean by that?"

"Last month you said, 'What'll happen to pigs and turkeys when everybody's a vegetarian? They'll probably go extinct.' As though eating them was a kindness!"

"I didn't exactly —"

"It's better if pigs *do* go extinct, than live in concrete Belsens then be trucked screaming to the slaughter. We should join the Animal Liberation Front if we had any contacts."

"I think," Saul said carefully, "that most A.L.F. people live in towns. We'd stick out like a sore thumb, living in a little village. The police would hear about us immediately." Though of course he agreed one hundred per cent.

"And the Hunt Saboteurs! If only we knew someone."

He realized that they were verging on a quarrel, yet he still felt perversely moved to mutter, "Funny sort of fox, that was. Same habits, though."

Diane darted him a look as furious as the weasel's.

A couple of hours later, on the return journey, the Renault had already reached the main road down into Woodburn when Tim squealed, "There it is again! Over in that field!"

Though Saul swung round, he saw nothing except ploughed earth. Amidst the sea of clods he hardly expected to make out one little slinky brown body. Tim couldn't reasonably have seen one, either.

"Be quiet." The boy was pressing buttons again, trying to stir up trouble.

"It's heading for Woodburn, Mum."

"Drivel," said Saul angrily. "There'll be fifty different weasels between here and where we found the rabbit."

A pheasant in almost tartan plumage erupted from the near verge, winged low across the road, narrowly missing being struck down.

"My God, we nearly *hit* it," cried Diane. "That's your fault, Saul, distracting me. We ought to drive more slowly." She proceeded to do so, down on into the village.

And perhaps somebody from Woodburn would hit the same pheasant the very next day, with a blast from a shotgun; and eat the bird, after shaking out the lead pellets.

Tim said, "Mum."

"What?"

"Kevin Bantock's hamster died. Blood came out of it."

"*How?*"

"They've got him an albino guinea pig."

"To live in the *same size* cage?"

"The cage and toys cost a lot."

"Oh God. People shouldn't be allowed!"

Tim was making absolutely certain that they kept

the rabbit and lavished care on it. By way of apology and recompense.

Sunday afternoon. From the kitchen, Tim shrilled, "Mum! Dad! Mum!"

Saul and Diane arrived simultaneously, to witness outside the window a weasel sneaking into the rabbit run through the chicken-wire. Saul rapped on the glass so hard that he punched a hole in the pane.

"Bugger!" His hand bled.

Diane had run outside and was tearing at the hooks on the wire gate of the run, while the weasel hesitated, half way to the open hutch. As she dragged the gate open, the invader snaked through the wire and away.

Licking his wound and spitting, Saul rushed outside too. He wrestled a handkerchief from his jeans pocket to wrap his fingers.

Diane checked the rabbit. "He's all right. Chicken-wire's no protection! We'll have to bring him indoors. Fetch a cardboard box for him. We'll shift the hutch, and the wire. I'll reconstruct it all in the kitchen."

"What? I'll flatten the bloody weasel with a spade first."

"You'll never catch it. Tim, fetch a box!"

"That was the same weasel, Dad."

"Impossible."

Several hours later the rabbit's relocated quarters occupied a full third of the kitchen. The hutch complex stood within a fence of chicken-wire nailed to frames stabilised by a wall of old bricks piled two deep. The rabbit was laying down a new latrine of vegetable ball bearings on the linoleum; unfortunately its droppings rolled all over. Saul had pinned cardboard, cut from the box, over the broken pane to exclude the draught. A replacement pane would have to wait till the following Saturday.

He looked out into the dusk. In the light cast from the window a slim shape slunk from behind a cabbage, then reared on its hind legs to return his stare, eyes gleaming bright.

"It's there again! It won't give up. Tim's right: that's the same animal, miles from where it started out. It's . . . like a Fury! Pursuing us." Diane had joined him. "Ah, it ducked."

"Do you suppose it has rabies?" she asked. "I mean, such mad persistence."

"You're persistent too. That doesn't mean —" He didn't complete the sentence. "It wants its meal. We stole its meal. Maybe we condemned it to starve."

"If it's starving, it made a damn long journey. Like us walking all the way to London."

"This isn't natural, Di. Weasels don't act that way. A *cat* might walk for miles, and even hold a grudge. Or a dog. Maybe," he hesitated, "we should put the rabbit out for it."

"What a mad, sick thing to say."

"If not, we'll have to catch it and kill it."

"But there's no reason to kill it," she said indignantly. "It'll go away."

"What, after following scent for miles?"

"The scent *of a car?*"

"If we got ourselves a pussy cat," said Tim, "it would stop the weasel."

No one replied. They could never adopt a cat. Canned cat-food was made out of the offal from slaughterhouses.

A noise woke Saul that night. Loud thumpings. Switching on lights, he hurried downstairs; slammed on the kitchen light. In its hutch the rabbit was going crazy. The weasel stalked the run.

With a howl of rage which froze the rabbit Saul hoisted one of the bricks and hurled it at the intruder. Wallpaper burst down by the floor, spewing dusty plaster. The weasel had dodged up and through the chicken-wire, to vanish from sight.

Saul jumped to the window, tore the curtain aside. His cardboard draught-stopper hung loose.

"Saul! What is it?"

"Guard the stairs, Di! Weasel's in the house. The rabbit's still okay."

He heard her descending.

"Guard them!"

"I don't see any weasel," she said from the kitchen door.

He gestured. "Got in the window. It pushed the cardboard loose."

"You mean you didn't pin it properly. Weasels don't climb into houses."

"I saw it right there!"

"God, the wallpaper's smashed to pieces. What a filthy mess."

"I missed it, Di."

"And maybe you were aiming at the rabbit. Wake up! I'm living with a loony sleepwalker." She crossed to the window, flicked at his cardboard makeshift, then stabbed a triumphant finger. "See?"

He saw: six feet away, a weasel standing up on its hind legs, looking at the lighted window.

"So it's still hanging about," she said, "but it certainly wasn't inside."

"Damn thing must have shot through the hole . . . but I'm sure it didn't. I'd have seen."

"I hate broken sleep. Fix that stupid cardboard back. I'll nail some hardboard on tomorrow. And close the curtain." She went back upstairs.

As he turned to restore the cardboard, three weasels watched him from outside; his heart chilled.

He snatched the powerful, rubber-sheathed torch from its hook, killed the kitchen light, and pressed the torch to the neighbouring pane. The yellow beam lanced out across sprouts and cabbages, across movement. A rippling of the earth. A wave of small creatures.

"Di!" he screamed. "Come back down!"

She returned shortly, swearing. A single weasel stood sentinel in the torch beam.

"I . . . I saw more than one."

"Oh, did you?"

"I swear."

"How many?"

"Three together. Behind, a carpet of them. Hundreds. It was as if . . . 'Come, my animals!' — and they all came."

"So that's it. Because I criticized you, justifiably, in the car. You're being hateful."

"Di! Please believe me. There's one loose in the house already — with us and the boys; and the rabbit."

"I wouldn't be likely to forget the rabbit, would I?"

"Why should we deserve this? Is it because . . . if we have our way, and piggeries and pet-shops disappear, and no one eats meat or keeps animals, the weasels of the world will go hungry?"

"Do you think weasels eat steak and pork? They eat wild mice, wild rats, wild birds! You're the weasel. Look at your nasty little vicious watery eyes. Find somewhere else to sleep tonight. Don't come in my bedroom."

She dashed upstairs, tossed his pillow down a moment later, slammed the bedroom door. He heard the bolt click home. So he perched a brick on the windowsill to wedge the repinned cardboard — there were no weasels visible at all — then closed the curtain and took his pillow through to the lounge, pulling the door softly shut behind him.

He lay coldly and rigidly on the sofa. He couldn't sleep. After maybe fifteen minutes he rose and went through to the kitchen to eat some chocolate.

Behind its chicken-wire the rabbit lay dead like a bunch of ghastly rag. Blood, guts mixed with half-digested green mush, spilled out of it over the yellow lino. Saul staggered, sick at heart.

He visualized: himself running upstairs, pounding on the bedroom door, even smashing the bolt off in his urgency to make Di understand that the rabbit was dead, torn open, but that *he* hadn't gutted it — a weasel had, a weasel which was loose in the house, hiding, waiting to emerge again.

He also imagined: Di refusing to believe that he was innocent, herself becoming a Fury, tearing at his beard and cheeks in rage and mortal fear as she drove him from the house — "Sleep in the car!" — and locked him out, there where the weasels awaited, a thick carpet of sharp-toothed fur. But he might reach the unlocked Renault, and sanctuary — while Di and the boys were left to invasion by the weasels. That single brick wouldn't keep them out.

Why was he imagining this violent scene? He and Di were pacifists as well as vegetarians! Was this some form of rebellion by the beast locked up deep within him? Something malign was tampering with his mind. Blood-lusts were imprinting themselves, or surfacing: the frenzy of a fox in a hen-house, of a weasel on a rabbit's neck. He felt appalled.

The weasel had effectively given them the evil eye — for there was a fury in the home too. That was Di's rage, the rage of a tiger, at everyone who oppressed animals, exploited them, made them suffer.

No one but Saul had seen that pack of weasels outside. Only he had witnessed the invader in the kitchen. Could he have imagined those others? Could

he have killed the rabbit himself? Dragged it from its hutch, snapped its neck, and disemboweled it — without knowing his own actions? He examined his hands. Clean. His pyjamas. No blood stains. No yellow streaks of rabbit piss which was like pus. No green slime.

He crossed to the window, shifted the curtain cautiously, wary of being bitten.

The brick had moved. The cardboard hung loose again. Window ledge, tiles, even the steel draining board were patterned as though dozens of tiny feet, muddy from damp soil, had scampered across.

How many of the beasts had already got in and hidden? How many were waiting to slip through any door that opened? Or reach other rooms by way of fireplaces and chimneys and higher fireplaces? Sooty, oblique chimney-bricks should offer plenty of footholds for claws. He suddenly felt as scared of remaining in the house as of being forced to leave it, to race to the Renault to shut himself in its tin shell. As quietly as could be he restored the brick to its former position, then added two more from among those buttressing the chicken-wire.

He needed a weapon. A hammer to smash weasel skulls. No, something handier. A poker. Tiptoeing to the illuminated lounge, he hefted the fire-iron. Sneaking to the foot of the dark stairs, he switched on the upper light.

From half way up, to as high as the landing, the stair carpet was hidden by a mass of weasels. On the landing itself, dominating them, one particular weasel stood upright as though making a speech to its troops. Unmistakable: the eyes, the gaze, the poise. A few subaltern heads shifted to register Saul's presence, but otherwise the weasels made no move.

A terrible understanding dawned on Saul, as a thin piping voice pierced his head:

"*You stole from the Weasel of Weasels! From the Archweasel.*"

He couldn't actually be hearing the creature speak! A weasel couldn't use words. Its brain couldn't know them. Somehow Saul's mind was translating what the weasel felt: the message coded by its beady eyes.

"*All species of animals possess a king, a masterbeast. One which incarnates weaseldom, amongst weasels. Frogdom, amongst frogs. Rabbitdom, amongst rabbits. I raised such a furor in my tribe across many days' journey of land. They converged here, rallied to their king.*"

A psychic furor . . . because the weasel they had robbed had *understood* that it was archweasel. Perhaps not many archanimals ever knew. When one archanimal died, another beast of its kind was born to be archanimal, and had a chance to know itself.

Saul reeled at this strange knowledge.

"*Two* archanimals of any species, surely?" he whispered.

Archmale — and archfemale. Just as had walked into the Ark in the legend. Preserve the two archweasels, male and female, and the whole of weaseldom could be reborn, could spill out from their loins in all its variety.

Likewise with every other species. Just as the whole human race had spilled out from Adam and Eve — which was the true meaning of *that* legend. Primitive, primitive, these myths of the Ark and of Adam! Deeply, primevally engraved.

Early man, closer to nature, must have known that archanimals existed. Hence the concept of the totem animal. That knowledge persisted, deeply buried. It rose in Saul this night.

How could that be? Unless . . .

"*I* am the archhuman! Out of all the human males alive on the planet today, I — Saul Cobbett — am it!"

Someone had to be. A definite individual with a name, and a home, and a life.

Watching the archweasel watch him, Saul felt hot, glowing, illuminated. Conscious as never before.

Maybe Jesus Christ had been an archhuman too. When Jesus was thirty years old he realized this, and interpreted his new-found knowledge according to his milieu — as Messiah.

Adolf Hitler had almost made himself into a war-god, inexplicably. . . .

Some archhumans might never awaken to the fact. Others might be born in a remote jungle where even their neighbours were strange foreigners; they would still be the archhumans of their time, until they died.

"Who's the arch-human female today?"

Diane? Hardly. She would have seen the horde of weasels massing in the garden; been impelled to see them. She would be seeing them on the stairs right now. The archfemale could well be Chinese or Indonesian or a Russian citizen. She might be seventy years old, or newly born.

"How did you realize who you are, Archweasel? Unless . . . my own scent awoke you, last week! My aura, as archhuman. Just as your aura has awakened me."

The archweasel glanced away, sank down as if in compliance. Then it raised its head, and spat-hissed defiantly — for why should it submit? It made no move to lead its band against Saul, to attack. He felt that an uneasy truce prevailed.

"Shouldn't my face be more full of character? More startling, more defined — with mesmeric eyes, or signs of grace?"

Why so, if he was Everyman? Maybe the sheer volume of people alive today diluted, rather than enhanced?

Saul thought momentarily of the Pied Piper, who had charmed the horde of rats led by the Rat King. Another legend of an archhuman? One who had led away all the sons and daughters of Hamelin. As Saul gazed at the weasel army hugging the stairs he chuckled, then laughed aloud.

He needn't try to smash these weasels with the poker. Why should he be aiming to kill the archweasel — instead of acknowledging a fellow arch-being of a different species?

Pied Piper.

Saul started to whistle loudly, then to sing:
"Oh I'll take the high road
And ye'll take the low road — !"

"Shut up!" Diana shouted from inside the bedroom. So she wasn't asleep. However, she didn't open the door to see.

Whistling again, still keeping his eye on the archweasel, Saul withdrew towards the kitchen. The weasel army turned about, flowed downstairs. He leaned over the chicken-wire, spitted the rabbit on the poker through a loop of intestines, hoisted it, detached it. Tossing the fire-iron clatteringly on to the draining board, he carried the corpse to the back door. Weasels poured steadily after him.

Striding out into the night, now less coaly thanks to a risen gibbous moon, and still whistling, he threw the dead rabbit away from him. The weasel flood parted around him, to claim and devour their prize. One weasel alone stood aloof, watching the fray.

Disturbed, and perhaps also scenting blood, the Sandersons' Doberman — which was kept outside *every night,* even in the winter — began to bark frenziedly. The archweasel took to its heels, away through the cabbages. Its whole army followed, a wave quitting a shore and not returning. Saul was left alone with himself, and the moon, and his knowledge. He stopped whistling.

A light had gone on upstairs in the Sandersons', and he thought that someone was staring from a

darker window. However, the guard dog calmed and presently the light went out.

"So," said Diane as she scanned the vacant run. Saul had cleaned most of the mess off the lino before she came down.

Josh was still abed but Tim had to be breakfasted and readied to catch the primary school bus. Within half an hour Saul was due to drive off to the comprehensive school. He swallowed black chicory coffee which was still too hot.

"Where's the body? In the dustbin?"

"Garden. The weasels ate it. That got rid of them."

"You do seem proud of yourself." She poured muesli for Tim, added milk. "Bastard."

The boy wandered into the kitchen and clutched at the chicken-wire. "Where is he, Mum? I can't see him."

Just then the front doorbell rang. Relieved, Saul hurried to answer. Too early for the post.

Brian Sanderson was a chunky, balding man with a tightly trimmed dark brown moustache. Area manager of a meat processing firm. Pies, sausages, faggots. He had on an expensive grey suit and a flat tweed cap with a long, aggressive brim.

"Right," Sanderson said without preamble, "you were out in that so-called garden of yours at three A.M., whistling your head off, making our dog go wild. What was the big idea?"

An incensed Diane shoved Saul aside. "Is there a law against being in our own garden? Your raving hound woke *me* up. No wonder, when it's shut out in any sort of weather. Next thing, it'll be turning vicious. Supposedly! You'll be having it killed so you can buy another to maltreat."

"Don't you come that line with me, Missus. I'm warning you not to taunt our dog."

"Oh, shall we whisper and wear cotton wool on our feet? If that animal disturbs our sleep, we'll dance around our garden playing trumpets if we feel like it."

Sanderson looked at Saul, not her. "I'm warning you. Watch out."

Saul felt surprise. Obviously Sanderson failed to realize that he was in the presence of the king of his species; of the only man alive who incarnated humanity, who could whistle the weasels.

Saul exerted himself mentally, trying to awe their neighbour, to impose himself upon the man by power of will or grace. As Hitler, as Jesus had done. He made his eyeballs bulge. He began whistling the same tune which had led the army away the night before.

He imagined Sanderson suddenly overcome with an ecstasy of amazed communion with the archperson fleetingly revealed to him. Sanderson kicking up his feet and dancing a jig, capering over the road on to the green. Alternatively, Sanderson shrinking back trembling, drool on his lips.

Brian Sanderson merely stood his ground.

"The damned offensive impertinence of you two nutters! So-called teacher, covered in hair like a caveman. You're trash, that's what you are. A visual insult — like your garden. Your Missus daring to criticize how we look after our dog; spreading slander to the few people she *does* know in the village. Oh I've heard —!"

Saul gaped as the man ranted.

"What's more, I've heard how your nipper had all his toy piggies taken by Mummy in case he grows up fancying a bite of bacon. Shaking your fist at anyone on a horse; you really know how to be popular. All the other lunacies. Pair of loonies, that's what you are. If you ever had a mongrel, which God forbid, I bet you'd feed it on boiled cabbage. I'll tell you what real cruelty is. It's in raising kids on a diet of roots and leaves. Toss a pound of raw veg in the blender, and scream, 'Dinner time!' Give them brain damage, like their parents. From malnutrition! You should be reported. Those kids should be taken into proper care. My brother-in-law's a magistrate. Any more bother from the both of you, and I'll take steps."

Sanderson did take steps: back towards his own large renovated thatched cottage, where a Toyota estate car poked from the garage.

"Bother, did you say?" Diane cried after him furiously. "We hardly *see* you — and certainly don't wish to."

Their neighbour paused. "I saw *him* all right, last night. Bloody three A.M. Out there yodeling at the moon, or whatever ecologists do. Drove the dog bananas." Sanderson entered his Toyota and drove off.

"Archhuman, you?" a thin, inner voice taunted Saul. *"You're nothing of the sort."*

With numb horror Saul understood that he had simply met, and met by chance — though with all the compelling strangeness of a mystical experience — an actual archbeing, the weasel king. An archbeing had revealed itself to Saul, knowing — in whatever way a weasel knew things — that Saul recognized its true nature. Would honour it. Or else would be torn to pieces.

He'd been illuminated and forsaken; to make of his experience what he cared. Or could.

The knowledge was totally alienating. There was no way to share it — by adopting a weasel as his family or tribal totem. Nowadays there were so many harvesters and crop sprays and hard roads and battery chicken houses and pig units. In another forty years there might be no animals visible in the countryside. In the prehistoric past, it wouldn't have been so.

What had happened, was for him alone, and the knowledge would cripple his heart and life forever — as though he were a rabbit maimed by a gin-trap, a fox by a wire snare, which it could only escape by gnawing through its own limb, amputating part of itself as a sacrifice.

Diane had slammed the door upon their already departed visitor. Saul slunk through to the kitchen, where Tim — ears agog — pretended to be hungrily spooning up muesli from his china bowl which Diane had decorated with painted bluebells. Naturally he had heard the whole exchange at the front door. The boy darted diplomatically blank glances from the empty run to his father, and back.

Glancing down into Tim's bowl, Saul found himself seeing not toasted wheat, rolled oats, bran, hazelnuts, sunflower seeds, and dried apple — but chewed bones and broken teeth, and flakes of dried flesh, swimming in blood. He felt a terrible, unappeasable hunger. If somehow he could satisfy that hunger, he feared that he would vomit.

The comprehensive school where Saul taught geography was set in the sprawling village of Kingsbury, nine miles along the main road which passed their house. After Saul drove out of Woodburn, though, he cut on to the by-road towards Upton.

Di had had precious little to say to him before he rushed off; while for his part he had done little more than indicate to her the many tiny vague footprints on window ledge and tiles and sink unit — at which she had snorted contemptuously. Saul could have made that mess himself by stippling with muddy fingers, scratching with his fingernails.

Why wasn't he driving directly to the school? That was because he had decided to kill himself. Or rather, he was luxuriating in the idea as a form of emotional balm, consoling himself by toying with the notion of suicide. He would reject the sardonic, gnawing gift of the weasel king. He would toss in the weasel's face the gift of life, and of knowledge. Besides, he would erase the mess at home by vanishing from the scene.

Exactly how would he kill himself? By hanging himself from a tree bough with the tow rope? Perhaps; but slow strangulation did not appeal. By crashing the car? The by-road had too many bends to pick up any adequate speed; the main road would have been far more suitable. He would simply end up in a ditch, saddled with a large garage bill for recovery and repairs. Or by routing the exhaust gases into the car through a hose-pipe? He'd neglected to bring one.

"Self-pity, self-indulgence, selfishness!" he growled at himself; and this was true. The night before, for a few minutes he had been an extended self, an exalted self; then he had deflated like a balloon.

He had been driving automatically, unaware. Abruptly he realized that he had reached the bend near where they had rescued the rabbit. He braked, nosed the Renault part way on to the verge, and stepped out.

Could the archweasel's short legs have carried it as far as this in the past five or so hours, if it ran flat out? Unlikely.

The hedge, recently trimmed by machine, was a leafless line of splintered sticks like broken chicken bones. Fields were empty, foggy, with an isolated skeleton oak tree and a few skeleton elms nearby. The air was grey. A crow flapped by. No other hint of life.

Saul climbed a gate and walked out across the field, tacky soil engulfing his shoes, gluing itself to the soles in fat balls. It was a huge field — several ancient fields combined in one for more efficient harvesting — and he walked a long way till fog erased the view in all directions. He felt that he was erasing himself too, murdering the last vestiges of that preposterous arch-self which he had conceived the night before.

In the fog ahead, a figure tottered. A farm worker? Someone out to take a pot-shot at pheasants? A gun-shot in the wrong direction might solve all Saul's problems honourably and meaninglessly.

The figure capered as though treading on coals, not soggy clods; maybe it was trying to keep its shoes clean. It looked weirdly ragged, hairy, and at first the head seemed bound around with a mass of woollen scarves. A tramp — who had slept in some derelict barn overnight?

Noticing Saul, the figure jolted in his direction and suddenly was clearer. A coat of russet fur, with a long band of white fur from the throat all down the underbelly. Jutting whiskered snout, beady black eyes, crumpled crinkly ears. Forepaws flailing the air, not human hands.

The weasel king! — but not the slim little archweasel of the previous night. No, this creature was nearly as tall as Saul and as bulky as a man. He froze in fear as the shape lumbered towards him.

But then he saw the beast differently.

It did wear a coat: of stitched brown fur and white fur. The head was a mask: a fur-covered framework with ears of leather, whiskers of horse hairs, eyes of dark glass. The forepaws were gloves, gauntlets; the hindpaws were tight boots. The tail, a fox's brush. This was a man dressed like a medieval mummer — or something more ancient.

"What on earth are you?" cried Saul.

The mummer dropped to all fours and ran clumsily around Saul in a circle, spit-hissing, then rose and raked the air and spoke: in a thick accent, part guttural, part twangy. Saul couldn't understand a single word. What language was it? Anglo-Saxon? Celtic? Norse?

"I don't understand."

A weasel-glove reached and flipped Saul's tie out, then jerked, tightening the knot throttlingly. The other glove pawed at his jacket. Saul tried to step back but the glove had seized his lapel and wouldn't let go. Both gloves gripped him now, forcing his jacket back over his shoulders, imprisoning his arms as he choked. The weasel king's arms had a wiry strength.

The mummer spun Saul around. Partly to escape and partly because he couldn't prevent it, Saul let his jacket be stripped from him. Hastily he tore the tie loose from his neck, to breathe. The mummer grunted approvingly and peeled off first one animal gauntlet then the other. These were thrust at Saul so commandingly that he accepted charge of them. The mummer's bare hands were gnarled, almost tattooed with ingrained dirt. A finger poked at

Saul's white shirt, hooked suggestively at the waist band of his trousers. Backing off a pace, the mummer unhooked and shed his coat of skins from off a dirt-caked torso. . . .

Saul stood unsteadily, his feet pinched by the tight beast-boots. The gauntlets compressed his hands into claws. The coat of many furs rasped areas of bare flesh. He peered through the dark glass eyes of the head-mask — faintly misted by his own exhaled breath — at a parody double of himself. For the strange dirty man was now fitted out in Saul's own shirt and trousers, jacket and shoes. The tie was knotted around the man's waist as a belt; the shoelaces were left undone. The idea had been to exchange costumes. Roles. And Saul had had little say in the matter.

But the features of the ex-mummer bore no resemblance. Thin, beak-nosed, ratlike, days unshaven. Dark eyes gleamed at Saul. The man grinned impishly, showing foul black stumpy teeth. He patted his new garments, raised a hand in rude salute, then sang aloud with a kind of crazy joy — and ran off across the soil into the fog, shoes slapping.

Should Saul remove the giant weasel-head and carry it under his arm like some deep-sea diver? Or like a knight carrying his visored helmet? Time enough to take it off when he got back to the Renault, he decided.

So he set off in that direction on numbed, constricted feet, wondering whether he had just been assaulted and had his clothes stolen by a tramp in exchange for that tramp's own crazy costume. Maybe the tramp had somehow mesmerised him, or Saul had done so to himself, and in actual fact he was walking across this field dressed in a filthy old fur coat found in a dustbin, with a bag over his head, two plastic insets for eyes.

Exertion fogged the eye-pieces further. It took Saul a minute or two to wonder at how many more oaks seemed to be looming in the dense mist. When he did wonder he felt scared to take the head-mask off, as if to do so would be to lock those intruding trees in place.

When he came to the road, the road was a muddy track hemmed on the far side by dense woodland. He fled along the track, stumbling and sliding, flapping his forepaw-gauntlets for balance, hoping somewhere to find tarmacadam and a Renault.

Presently the forest withdrew behind thick mist and there seemed to be rough pasture to his left. Ahead loomed a cottage: a hovel of stone and timber almost buried under a bonnet of black, rotting straw. Then another. A raggy scrap of a child saw him and ran screaming. A dog began to yelp. A fat woman in a hooded gown made a sign and shouted incomprehensibly. He spied a pond with geese afloat. As mist thinned fitfully other vague hovels swam into view, around a green. A reedy whistle blew penetratingly; voices called out.

Several men in homespun tunics trotted up. They wore little jingling bells on wire around their ankles, and clutched wooden staves; these, they clashed together in the air rhythmically. Women arrived, some barefoot, their braided hair held tight in linen cauls — and a motley of children too. The boldest kid darted at Saul, to touch and flee. Wood thwacked on wood, beating out a greeting, yet the adults appeared to regard Saul's presence — the Weasel King's presence there — with a shade of puzzlement. He oughtn't to be here yet; or perhaps not of his own accord.

Before long a good many other smock-clad men armed with staves arrived, out of breath, ankle-bells tinkling. A large circle formed, each man clashing wood with his neighbour on one side then the next, advancing one pace, retreating one pace.

Should Saul remove his head-mask and reveal himself as a stranger? That might infuriate the villagers. What would the outcome of this ritual be? Did they mean to beat him to death with the staves? Surely not. The costume he was wearing must be valuable to them; they wouldn't risk wrecking it. Yet why had the mummer forced, or fooled, Saul into exchanging garments? Ordinarily the villagers would have hunted the weasel King through the woods and fields before herding him into the village — to do what, eventually?

Perhaps the mummer had simply been possessed with greed for Saul's fine clothes and shoes.

Saul thought of corn dollies and of Morris Dancers, but somehow the present situation seemed quite different, and its nature eluded him. He knew of peasants in the distant olden days wearing antlers, imitating stags; and he'd heard of the Fisher King, which he thought must be a heron. But a *weasel* king?

Maybe he was meant to be a bear. He bowed his head to inspect his costume more closely — and it was just as he had thought at first: a multitude of white strips and russet strips cut from hundreds of skins and sewed so as to resemble a giant weasel. He felt hoodwinked, threatened, degraded — yet oddly exhilarated too, for he hadn't after all lost touch with the archbeing he had met.

When he raised his head he recognized the chunky, balding, moustached man who stood opposite, scowling and weighing his stave.

"Sanderson . . . ?"

But how . . . ? And *Diane* was one of the women who waited outside the circle, anticipatively. He saw his wife clearly but he didn't call her name too. It came to him then that he hadn't merely been shifted into a countryside of the past — though that would have been disconcerting enough on its own. No, he had been shunted into a different species of past reality, one where a weasel king dominated this assembly and could summon human beings at its whim; one dreamed by weasels, rather than remembered by men.

As though this realization was a signal, a trigger, his coat writhed. No longer was he wearing a garment of many furs. The costume had changed. He was covered in live weasels, clinging all over him, hot bodies clawing for purchase, nipping his skin with fierce strong jaws. They crawled, they climbed, they hung. All the weasels of which the coat was made had come back to life.

He screamed. He danced. This was the part of the rite which the mummer had been keen to avoid! The reincarnation of all the slaughtered weasels. That, and also —

Clashing their staves one final time, the men rushed in and started beating him. To save him — or break every bone in his body?

He fell amid a squirming, biting furry mass. Blows rained down. The villagers were obtaining materials for next year's weasel coat: that was his last thought as he lost consciousness.

He woke torn and battered, in mud. As his eyes blinked open he saw clods of ploughed earth stretching away at nose level. His body was half paralysed with bruises and with cold. When he turned his head painfully, a five-bar gate loomed high, set in a hedge of splintered chicken bones. A few feet beyond that, the back bumper of the Renault!

Cold knives cut at flesh and muscles as he struggled to stand; he was only dressed in muddy string vest and underpants which the mummer had let him keep. Somehow he scaled the gate, knowing that — thank God — he'd left the keys in the ignition. Soon he was inside the car, hugging his shivering self. He switched engine and heater on. As the air warmed, his brain unjammed.

He could hardly continue onward to school in this state. If he returned to Woodburn, though, would Di ever believe him? Maybe he had been trying to expiate his supposed crime — of rabbit murder — by lunatic self-flagellation: by tossing away his shoes and outer clothes and rolling in mud and on stones, then diving through a hawthorn hedge a few times, on the principle that enough self-punishment inflicted dramatically enough should surely merit forgiveness for the uncommitted slaughter ... of one bloody stupid mangy rabbit.

"Maybe," he mumbled aloud, "I *did* do this to myself. But the Weasel King made me! To show me his importance, his charisma."

Entering Woodburn, he hunched in the driving seat to hide his undress. Once parked outside their cottage he peered carefully to check that the coast was clear before sprinting round to the back door. And in.

"Daddy's got his clothes off!" piped Josh. Hurrying into the kitchen, Diane gathered the boy to her.

Saul held his hands out in appeal. "I had an accident."

"You smashed up the car!"

"No."

She eyed him warily, hugging Josh. "What sort of accident?"

"I was mugged. A tramp waved me down on the way to school. He looked distressed. But he jumped

on me, and knocked me out. When I came round, in a field ... " He indicated his wounds and bruises.

"And this happened on the main road?"

"Yes," he lied. "There was no other traffic at the time."

"You must phone the police."

"I'd rather not."

"If it's the truth, you'll phone the police! Or I shall."

"We don't like the police, do we? Why cause trouble for some poor wretch? It's only a few clothes."

"I suppose it was only a rabbit, too! Where's your watch?"

He remembered that the mummer had taken his watch as a fancy bracelet.

"Let's talk first. I must put some clothes on. I'm cold."

"You're lying. It was *Sanderson* who stopped you, wasn't it? And humiliated you! How can we live here when we've been made fools of? That's his idea. But he's committed assault — and theft!"

Praying that Diane wouldn't touch the phone, Saul fled upstairs to change his underwear, to shower and dress. He was shocked to discover the time: nearly eleven.

When he came down again clad in jeans, sweater, and trainers, Diane had made hot chocolate drinks for herself and for Josh but not for him.

"Phone the police!" she ordered.

"Look, it wasn't Sanderson." Saul still ached all over. "I'll phone the school, though."

"Coward. Fool. You'll let Sanderson get away with . . . rubbishing us."

Josh took his daisy-painted mug, and himself, away from this argument. Moments later the boy was shrilling, "That man has Daddy's coat on!" Hot chocolate spilled from the mug in one hand while Josh pointed through the front window with the other. Diane was beside the boy in seconds; Saul, less speedily.

A thin, ratty, unshaven man was hiking across the green, carrying a roped plastic bag of possessions. He wore a white shirt and familiar jacket and trousers, the waist tied round. The man stepped on to the road, to proceed along it.

"Stay here!" Diane ordered Josh. She wrenched open the front door and dashed out with a "Hey!" Saul trotted after her.

"You stole those clothes from my husband!"

The man's teeth were badly decayed. His jacket pockets bulged. "Stole, is it? Why, hullo squire," he greeted Saul. "Were you trying to play a trick? He gave 'em to me as a free gift, lady. Like Jesus Christ himself. Don't you go saying I stole. I threw me old things away."

"Is this true?" Diane turned on Saul. "You gave him your clothes?"

Just then the side pocket of that jacket, which had been Saul's a while before, squirmed. Out poked a small russet furry head. Glossy-eyed, bewhiskered, crumple-eared, with a white muzzle. Up stretched a white neck like a miniature giraffe's, as the animal sniffed the air.

"A weasel!" Diane gasped.

Blanketing his own — almost electric — shock, Saul experienced a deep, miraculous feeling of relief.

"Oh yes, lady. Why, on the road they call me the Weasel King. I always catches and tames a weasel. So he'll keep the rats off me when I sleep out; and other things. Once, I even had two weasels, but that's risky. Weasels don't much care for their own kind, not *generally*. Boy an' girl only gets together one day a year to mate. Generally."

Sliding from the pocket the weasel climbed lithely up to the fellow's shoulder, where it reared to survey the neighbourhood.

"Weasel?" Diane repeated helplessly.

"I knew one chap keep a ferret in his trousers. Flush out his supper for 'im, it would. My boy goes one better — brings me a fine rabbit back with 'im. Then I'll skin it, an' feed him the liver and stuff, an' cook the coney over a fire on a stick, I will. A'm known for it, on the road; and no one's ever called me thief."

Saul hoped to take him by the arm, but the weasel jerked out like a snake, spit-hissing.

"You don't touch me nice new clothes! Mine, now. Me little friend wouldn't like that. Oh no indeedy."

"Weasel King," said Saul, "will you help me? Will you come into the house and talk to me? Please."

"Saul!"

"Hush, Diane. Will you, Mr King?"

"Mister, is it?" The man grinned, foul-toothed. "I could take a cup of something hot and a bite to eat. You're like Christ Jesus himself. I won't filthy your fine chairs and carpets, lady. Not today."

Wouldn't he? His hands were dark with dirt.

Was this person genuine? Or was he weaseldom itself in a human disguise? After all that had occurred surely it was an impossible coincidence that a human weasel king of the byways should happen along. Saul didn't exactly feel afraid to invite the tramp inside; the fellow seemed benevolently disposed. He did wish he could recall the actual events of their encounter earlier that same morning. What if the events which Saul remembered had been the real events?

Josh's face was pressed to the window.

"That'll be yer little boy, eh? Needn't fear me fur friend. Won't nip yer lad so long as yon don't annoy 'im. Won't nip no one but an enemy; or a juicy rabbit."

If this *was* a man, why then, he must be some sort of latterday enchanter, a down-at-heel, outcast *witch* with a familiar. A week ago the "magician" had sent his weasel accomplice to catch him a meal . . . and he'd had that meal stolen by the intervention of the Cobbetts.

Once they were all inside — Diane leaving the door wide open despite the chill in the air — the weasel rushed from shoulder to floor. As though fully familiar with the lay-out and well aware there were no cats or dogs, it scuttled to disappear upstairs. Josh squealed with a mix of excitement and disappointment.

Soon the tramp was drinking hot chocolate and scoffing cheese, boiled free-range eggs, and bread provided by Saul.

"Wouldn't happen to have a scrap of flesh for me friend, eh? Don't matter if it's cooked flesh." 'King' scrutinised Saul and Diane. "No, s'pose not. You wouldn't."

"And how do you know that we wouldn't have?" Diane demanded.

"Cos me little pal never went for the kitchen. He can smell meat a mile off. Whiff o' blood."

Mention of blood reminded Diane, who shifted closer to the phone. "My husband says that you attacked him violently. Why else would he give you all his clothes?"

"Look at these, lady, all neat and clean. Do these come off a fellow as was beaten up?"

"The tie isn't too neat." There was sarcasm in her voice.

"Never could abide a tie. Better as a belt."

"That watch does look nice on your wrist, Mr King."

"Is the glass smashed? Are the hands bent? Is the strap broke?"

"I lied about him attacking me," admitted Saul.

"Then who did attack him, Mr King? My husband's covered in cuts and bruises. Hundreds! How did he get them? Did he inflict them on himself? Or was it done by a balding person who drives a Toyota?"

'King' leered at Diane. "I didn't say *where* he give me his clothes. Sometimes I meets people in funny places which aren't quite neither here nor there. In-between places; that's me own business." The tramp's voice hardened. "Me, I don't belong in your type o' world, of houses an' cars an' employment, lady. I'm outside, an' most folks don't care much for that! Needs to know how to duck out, I do. Dodge round the back o' the world a bit."

The weasel had reappeared. It chattered squeakily as if delivering a report, then ascended its master and snuggled into his pocket.

"It was you we stole the rabbit from, wasn't it?" Saul asked quietly. "It was you who sent all the weasels. I think you're the archhuman, aren't you? Otherwise you'd never have mentioned Jesus. He was one too."

Bewildered, Diane hoisted Josh to her hip and retreated to the kitchen. "You come here a minute!" she called to Saul.

He obeyed. She nodded him urgently away from where the tramp could watch, could hear her whispering.

"What do you mean, we stole the rabbit from him? And what was that name you called him: archhuman? What's going on?"

"Will you leave it till later, Di!" He attempted to return, but setting Josh down smartly she blocked him. Briefly they waltzed like two cars at a fun fair before he thrust free.

"He's gone, Di!"

Saul ran to the door. Outside, the road was deserted; likewise the green. Nobody could have vanished from sight so quickly, even at a sprint.

"He must be upstairs, Saul! Filling his pockets! Go and see."

Saul leapt upstairs, and checked bathroom, bedrooms, wardrobes. He even threw himself down to squint under the beds. On his return he skidded on the stair carpet, almost taking an ankle-wrenching tumble.

"He isn't in the house." Saul checked the unlocked car outside. Empty. He darted to the side path which led round the rear, colliding with the dustbin in his haste. Here was the only place where King could have hidden — lurking until they ran to the front door, before escaping by way of the back garden. King wouldn't be finding the bottom fence easy to scale. As Saul pursued, shouting, "Come back, Mr King!" the Doberman hurled itself at the Sandersons' side of the other fence, barking furiously, shaking the panels. Saul couldn't see King anywhere.

He trampled carelessly through cabbages and sprouts, past the netted fruitery, then stumbled over compost and bonfire remains. Gripping the far fence, he hauled himself up. It had dawned on him that the Doberman only began to bark *after* he arrived on the scene.

Straining, he spied on to lawn islanded with

ornamental conifers. A middle-aged woman, whose name they had never troubled to discover, glared at him indignantly from her kitchen window, a plate suspended in her hand. Supposing that a tramp had just leapt into her garden, she wouldn't still have been washing dishes; that was for sure. Saul was also sure that King hadn't come nearly as far as this. Grimacing at Mrs Somebody, he let himself slide back on to weeds.

Diane had followed part of the way. He rejoined her.

"King didn't scram down the road. He isn't under our beds or crouching in the car. He certainly didn't escape over any fence of ours."

"Where is he, then?" she whispered.

"Dodged round the back, and ducked out. Almost told us as much, didn't he?" He reached to touch her hand. "Let's go inside, Di. I have a tale to tell you." He hesitated till her hand clasped his. "A tale of weasels and a mummer — and a king of men with rotten teeth."

They held hands as they returned indoors, into the kitchen.

"Di." He held her.

"Saul."

"You'll have to believe me."

"I think I will."

"I'd better begin with what really happened last night —"

"Wait. We left the front door open." Gently, she disengaged.

Moments later, she cried out; Saul came swiftly.

Josh was holding to brown-stained lips what appeared to be a half-consumed aubergine . . . except that the inside of the egg-plant was as black as the skin itself, save for a few white lumps.

"What is it you're eating, Josh? Where did you get it?"

"Man dropped it on the chair. It tastes lovely."

"But it's —"

"A black pudding," said Saul. "It's a *blood sausage*. He's eating cooked pigs' blood and fat . . . Give that to me!"

The boy took another large bite and bolted it down. "Me like it!" Evading Saul, Josh ran to the open front door, and paused defiantly.

"Mum," the boy pleaded, "why can't *we* have a pet weasel? Can you catch a baby one — and tame it? We could feed it on stuff like this. *He* must have done, for when it couldn't hunt enough." Josh crammed more black pudding into his mouth.

"But you and Tim *promised* me," Diane begged her son. "Tim swore he would never eat any meat at school — only salads and vegetables."

Cunningly Josh said, "I'll promise if we can have a weasel." He seemed a different child — a changeling — as though the cooked blood had entered not only his belly but his heart.

"No," snapped Saul.

The boy put two taboo words together. "Bloody bastard," he said.

Diane began to scream. Ω

ALL FLESH IS CLAY

by John Ordover

Again there is a knock on my workshop door, a dry white sound that scrapes along the wood. The empty figure stands there as always, grinning as always. It moves slowly in; its thinning tendons pull at its yellowed bones.

I have a reputation among the dead. My name is whispered in the graveyards and given to the dying as a sign of hope. I gesture, and moved by love or hate or desperation the skeleton seats itself in my special chair.

I have no sympathy for them; if I were freed of life I would never return. To me there could be no reason strong enough; no lover, no child, no need for vengeance powerful enough to pull me back.

I examine the body carefully, measure the sleeve and inseam, use tiny instruments to check the shape and pattern of the cheekbones and chin. A woman, I see by the pelvis, Caucasian by the arms, Irish by the eye sockets. I speak to her.

"I can do it," I say, "can you pay the fee?" Her jaw opens and her hand comes up. From behind silver-filled teeth she takes a photograph and a money card authorized to the estate of Joan McFarrel. She'd prepared well. Few anticipate the need.

I slide the chair down flat and begin. The remnants of her tendons are useless and I cut them away, paralyzing her. Then I turn to the head.

The textbooks I studied to be licensed for my craft require a layered approach; start with the organs, they say, lash the plastic replicas in place within the ribs; put in the simulated blood tubing, then set the contracting fiber muscles; connect the metal tendons and give motion to the body; then progress to the dermal coverings and finally the head. They condemn any other practice as grotesque and unlikely to be successful.

I disagree.

I bring out a bowl of dull red putty and roll it into long thin snakes. I place them on her skull and circle her empty sockets with them, then flatten them out, spread them, knead them flat. There are still no eyes, and her cheekbones are white and rough. Her teeth still grin at me.

I lay the muscles and tendons into the red mask on her blank face, then cover them with a second layer, then a third, the cosmetic layer that looks like human skin. From a box on my desk I take round white balls, styrofoam, with black buttons glued on. Sculpting carefully, I match them to the sockets, then lay them to one side.

I build the eyelids out of cardboard backed with clay, then anchor them above the empty sockets. I place two saline-soaked pads inside the skull, then reach for the puppet eyes. The first stage is complete and I wait for the soul to merge.

There are many reasons, apparently, to leave your coffin and go walking through the night. Most are better done without flesh: flesh that can hurt; flesh that can die again. Often the reason becomes unimportant when the pain of living returns.

That is why I start with the eyes. The books tell you to finish the limbs and torso first, to work your way backward through the anatomy text. Many of those operations are successful, but the patients, reminded now of life, remain dead of their own choosing.

The full process is lucrative, and the estate pays win or lose. Many of my colleagues consider the fee and follow the book precisely, wasting time.

Her eyes come to life, blinking and staring, salt tears from the pads running down and back into her empty brain-case. The styrofoam softens and the black eye-buttons turn light blue. I check the photograph and find blue eyes.

I will continue.

The face is the simplest part, and the part that gets the most praise. I am not a visual artist, but any craftsman can follow a design. I do it quickly, matching her to the picture she brought. Soon her face is staring at me from below a bare bone headcap.

The tone of the flesh, the general appearance — that requires no true talent or genius. But will the skin feel like skin, the muscles feel like muscles, not from the outside, but from the inside, to the wearer?

I run my fingers along soft but muscular arms that hours ago were nothing but bone. The hands require much precision, and I work on them closely under bright lights. Her eyes follow me as I work, sometimes closing in fear, sometimes spreading wide as I trip over a too-soon-functioning nerve; they have dampened further, the no-longer-button pupils contract and dilate in the light.

Her hands are shaped and finished, and her arms and legs and feet, but her ribs are still bone and lie empty, her pelvis fleshless and stark white. I stop for lunch before I move on.

I watch her face as I eat. Without lungs the newly-made mouth cannot speak, but somehow with nothing in her skull she can still think, still have emotions that come in waves of silent laughter or lips set in grim, determined lines. The constant use is changing the face quickly, the clay fading into true skin, the eyes already filling with their own tears.

As always, I wonder what reason she has that is worth the pain I inflict. I have heard many explanations, some trivial or misconceived; many tragic: one man, shot dead by a woman he could not make love him, thought this act of suffering would win his murderess's heart; one rich young woman strangled by a husband who she did not know would kill her daughter next; when I told her she had no child left behind she slumped back to clay before my eyes. People return to wives and lovers; to hate and pain; to uncompleted follies: swept away by what they think they feel.

After lunch I place the major organs. They are pre-packaged yet complex, both boring and difficult. I tear the cellophane wrapping from her lungs and tie them carefully inside her ribs. With air from a tube I inflate them, and check them for leaks or punctures. They work well, and I attach the trachea to the back of her throat. The sound of the air rushing through her mouth is a scream muffled by clay walls.

I put a respirator in her, then watch the inflating lungs change color and become at least somewhat alive. I unblock her throat and speak to her.

"Hello," I say pleasantly. "Things are going well." She tries to speak, then tries again. I think I understand her. "Yes, quite well," I say, then turn back to my work while she breathes deeply and tries to talk. Despite the distraction I secure the heart and stomach and liver, then discover the gallbladder is too wide and trim it back.

Her lungs are working better now. She is crying with the pain, yelling it out, the sound sinking into my padded walls. Her volume lifts and falls, going up whenever I touch her, softening when I step away.

Her pain comes from her own choice. I can see in her eyes that she knows this, that she does not regret the ordeal. How foolish.

I finish inside her, her heart beating slowly, intestines and uterus in place. The law requires that my creations be sterile, but I refuse to be less than thorough and connect her ovaries. She must be complete.

Her arms and legs have motion now, and I cuff them down to keep myself and her new body safe. There is still no skin between her neck and thighs, and there are many nerves to place. An unrestrained reflex could destroy her.

Her screams increase in number as I lay the skin in and the new connections start to grow. If I placed her brain now, it would be far worse. This way the impulses are implied, not sensed, and some of the pain is lost. At least that's what the souls tell us.

The first and second layers done, I start on her breasts. She is clothed in the photo she gave me, but I can guess at the shape her body had and I improve it slightly. I make the men just a trifle longer, too. No one complains.

I build her vulva and vagina carefully, using the standard pattern for her genetic type. I plant the area with scattered hair, slightly darker than the bright red I will use on her head. I feel inside her for a moment, getting the texture perfect and the small glands placed correctly. I stroke her gently until I feel her contract once on my fingers, then I withdraw them and step back.

She looks perfect, and when I run my hands along her she feels perfect, still more like clay than flesh but evolving quickly. I walk around her and put my hands on her head.

Her brain case is still empty. Gently I remove the package from the cool, dark place it is stored, then peel back its wet covering. The grey rubber mass is slippery and must be connected exactly right.

The brain sealed in place, I secure her red hair and sit waiting, coffee in hand, for the true scream.

It comes an hour later, an average time, and she shakes the house with her voice, shouting her pain outward like a baby. She does it twice, then pants heavily. I walk over to her.

I examine her again for texture, ask a few questions about how this or that feels to her. She pants as she answers, her tone reflecting relief and memory of pain. I help her up and go to fetch clothes for her, all part of the service.

When I get back she dresses and asks for coffee. I use it to test her senses; taste, smell, heat, touch, and the numerous small reflexes of drinking and swallowing. She works perfectly, nature and determination again making up for lack of precision, smoothing over any errors in duplication.

She does not now look or feel like clay.

"Was it worth it?" I ask her. No one ever says no; they would look idiotic.

She turns her eyes on me, surprised. "Of course," she says.

"Was being dead so bad?" I ask, watching her face carefully.

She thinks about it while sipping at her coffee. "It was a great opportunity," she begins, "you know, a chance to be forgiven and begin again. But you can't finish what you'd already started."

"And you have something to finish?" I say, a patronizing tone in my voice. "A marriage, a love affair, a child you think needs you?"

"A painting," she answers flatly. "It's sitting on my easel, only half-finished. I tried to forget about it . . . ," she sips again at her coffee, then looks helpless and shrugs, ". . . so I came back."

"A painting?" I ask. For some reason the thought upsets me.

She shrugs again. "So sue me, I don't like to stop in the middle of something." She stands up. "My will said to leave my studio alone. Can you call me a cab?"

I do so, and when she leaves I think about my next client, and my next. I work a lot, and there is always the chance that something will happen, that between the lungs and liver my heart will fail, or I will fall, and there will be a canvas on my table that I will never finish, never make whole. The image chases me and I shake; I think of the pain of merging and I shake again. For most of the night I balance the fears.

In the morning I call my lawyer, then arrange for nude photos to be taken, from many angles. I will be ready, I tell myself, if I become a canvas for someone else. If I become the one strapped empty to a table, desperate for life, I am prepared.

I love my work. Ω

AN EXAMINATION PAPER

by John Brunner

MOUNTBROOMSTICK COLLEGE
Department of Pure and Applied Thaumaturgy
SENIOR YEAR, FINAL EXAMINATION SESSION:
PAPER #1
Maximum marks: 100. Time allowed: two hours

INSTRUCTIONS TO CANDIDATES

Answer all four questions in Part I; any two questions from Part II; and *either* any two questions from Part III *or* the question in Part IV. Write the number of the question in the left-hand margin before you begin.

Approved reference works may be consulted, but second sight and crystal balls are not allowed.

NB: Do not open your paper until the invigilator has dematerialised the basilisk inside.

PART I (4 x 5 MARKS = 20)

A: At least one of the following does not appear in the list of Enochian Demons: *Babel Bonoham Farfarello Furcas Michael Mitraton Murmur*

State which, and describe what help you would require of it or them when compiling a dyspepsia curse disguised as a rock-and-roll, blues, or country-and-western record.

B: Returning late to dorm, you discover your roommate in the clutch of one of the Lesser Elementals. You have no time to demand its Name. At your immediate disposal are:

A CO_2 fire-extinguisher; a jar of pepper; a large white handkerchief; a copy of *The Lesser Key of Solomon*; three yards of quarter-inch hempen rope; a foil pack of frozen chicken giblets; a shaving mirror (or a powder compact with a mirror in the lid); loose change whose total value ends with a 7; and a glass of dandelion-and-burdock cordial.

Is it possible to save your roommate's (a) life, (b) soul? Explain how, or why not, as appropriate.

C: List six ingredients for a love-philtre in order of spiritual cost. Justify your preferred means of administration (e.g. food or drink, impregnating soap/lipstick/toilet paper, in aerosol form, etc.) Do not omit to state whether your subject is straight or gay or swings both ways.

D: Falling behind with your studies in the autumn term, one foggy night you cede your shadow to Askyalos for a week in exchange for comprehension of the set grimoire. The knowledge thus acquired enables you to foresee that an Indian summer will begin tomorrow, when you are due to leave on a field trip. How can you prevent your instructor from discovering this infringement of college rules?

PART II (2 x 10 MARKS = 20)

E: During college vacation you visit a friend whose parents live near a dairy-farm. The owner of the farm is telling anyone who will listen that your friend's mother, a foul-tempered witch, is souring his cows' milk. In not more than 200 words, describe *either* the spells she has most likely employed, *or* how you would save the day by changing the milk into Gruyère cheese.

F: A taxi-driver short-changes you and drives away before you catch on. In not more than 200 words, describe how you would get even. Remember to state whether the engine of the cab is regular or diesel.

G: Another student, invited to a party in your room, brings along two succubi/incubi despite their being banned from college premises. The deputy assistant warlock is heard coming to investigate a breach of curfew regulations. The person who brought the succubi/incubi has drunk too much and passed out. You have two minutes to conceal them or disguise them as persons entitled to be present. In not more than 200 words, explain how you would achieve this.

NB: you have had no forewarning and must make shift with articles normally present in the room and the adjacent bathroom. Your sex will be taken into account.

H: In not more than 16 lines, contrive a spell singable to *Greensleeves*, warranted to induce a plague of frogs, toads, and/or lizards in the visiting team's dressing-room prior to an important football game. Extra credit will be given for internal rhyming.

PART III (2 x 30 MARKS = 60)

I: When preparing a mojo hand, is a 1947 recording of the Original Zenith Brass Band accompanying a funeral parade more or less helpful than a bowl of shrimp gumbo followed by an oyster po'boy? Discuss, with reference to the rôle of tenor saxophones and the proportion of gumbo filé.

J: "Werewolves can very easily be created by starting with a German shepherd. My finest specimen was a boy called Hermann Schwanzer whom I met on a hillside in the Tyrol." (From *Memoirs of a Modern Mage* by Oskar Kruntsch.) Discuss, bearing in mind the possibility that Kruntsch's "German" shepherd may have been Austrian.

K: This examination paper is becoming unbearably hot to the touch and you're afraid it may catch fire before you finish reading the questions. If the foregoing statement is true, leave the hall and wait outside. The invigilator will want a word with you afterwards. If it is not, devise a novel torment for Mountbroomstick College to inflict on students who try to cheat in an examination.

PART IV (60 MARKS)

L: Dame Jane Whichaway, widely respected for her pyrotic gifts, holds that the absence of crocodiles points to cynical adventurism on the part of Lord Crowsnest. He, on the other hand, relies on his notorious ability to bake raspberry tarts as grounds for claiming that the periastron of Tau Ceti W echoes the inclination of Whichaway Moat at 43° from the vertical. Should or should not King Bjorn the Sulky cancel tomorrow's palace picnic? Ω

DEMONS OF THE UPPER AIR

by Fritz Leiber

illustrated by Keith Minnion

I

There is a whispering outside the walls,
A thing on the roof,
Come from the shadows, most like a shadow,
But a shadow with teeth and hooking claws,
A whispering shadow.
The hearts that hug the fire within
Beat faster, move closer,
Cowering down in their pocket of safety,
Opposing the threat from the alien reaches,
Pretending they do not hear the voice
Of the thing from the thin high air.
It whispers of battles above the low clouds,
Of creatures nearer and creatures stranger
Than those in the shielding house would wish;
The penetrant treble it hummingly sings
The challenging song of those who ride
Where the air thins out to emptiness;
Then its voice goes low again to tell
Of the terrible insecurity
Of the whirling, plunging earth.
Let the dwellers within shut their ears,
Stuff cranny and crack,
Bolt shutter and door and inner door —
There still comes a murmuring down past the fire,
Against the smoke and the pushing heat,
Tainting even the roaring of the fire:
A whispering outside the walls,
A thing on the roof.

II

Solyman sought to seal us up,
Thinking we were a book a man might seal,
Thinking we were strange pictures
And our racing thoughts
But dimming words upon an ochered page.
Lo, Solyman is dead
And we still ride the upper air
Above a newer Babylon.

Upon the cold moon's spaceward side
Our fortress stands, the gates rust not;
Out on the last unknown sphere
That rings the sun, our pennon flies;
And men still hear above their heads
Our whistling cries, our trumpet calls,
And see, gigantic, menacing,
Our shadows on their tallest walls.

True, true indeed, a book are we,
A book that was penned by the Elder Gods,
A book that never a man may seal.

III

Above, above
The air is thin, the sky is bright;
Come up, soft sister, through the night.
Around, around
The far stars wheel, the space winds surge
Against the dwellers on the verge;
The sky is black, the sky is bright;
Leave dreaming to the lower night.
Leave, leave
Your body to the earth,
Your sins to hell, your plans to mirth;
Cast, cast away
All lesser fear
To cumber still the cumbered sphere;
Slip, slip
Your silky, soft cocoon
And shoot up to our midnight noon.
Your soul is steel: hard, slim, and bright;
Thrust it, O sister, through the night.

IV

Signs? Signs? You ask for a sign?
These be the false signs that yet stir the mind
To spy for the true:
The eye of the cat and the words of the madman —
Sudden, scattering, unlinked words;
The cries of the screech owl, of shells, and far
    lightning,
Only seeming to come from the haunts of far souls;
The symbols bizarre of the mathematician,
A mad arabesque that is logic to him;
The stones and the streets of dead, desert-hid
    cities,
Walked once by men commercial and civil,
Men up to the minute, by such and no others;
The brooding of mountains, the anger of oceans,
The lean wind, the cold spaces, the black suns
    beyond suns,
The howl of the wolf and the wings of the raven —
Those be the false signs
That yet prick the mind
To hunt for the true.

These be the true signs, if true signs there be:
The far darting vision that comes with creation;
The quip of the great man sharp-tweaked by Fate's
    fingers;
The last, doubtful hints on the great heap of
    knowledge —
Strange scavenger birds that plot a strange flight;
The certainty born of practice and labor,
But by what father none may know;
The slipping of meditant souls from earth bodies;
The pantherlike leap of imagination;
Second sight, far sight, beyond all suns seeing:
Those be the true signs, the signs of dark power
The signs of the far way, if such signs there be.

V

Since dark first fought with brightness
And the first-created cat wailed down
The cry of chaos, new-coherent,
From the upspringing, inky walls of Nifelheim,
We have been.

Old as are the Elder Gods,
Yet not as they.
We strive not, boisterous,
To build firmaments,
But fly, black-winged, above;
They make the mighty music of the spheres —
We, the shrill soaring overtones.

The windswept, icy mountaintops of mind
Show tracks of our sharp claws.
Both over raging war and striving peace
Our wing beat sounds.
Ultima Thule is our perching place
And to the uttermost black bound of things
Our squadrons strive.

Ghosts are we, but with skeletons of steel.
As mists are we, yet in our loins a seed
That laughs at barrenness.
The present grips the future with our claws,
Forgotten facts ride forward on our wings,
And inspiration's first faint harmonies
Sound in our songs, while eerie far-off things
Call out to beg us bring them down to earth.

No one so deaf to miss our whispering,
No realm so light-drenched but our shadows fall;
Ho, wild, unruled allies upon the earth,
We are your friends who ride the icy nights,
We are the demons of the upper air.

VI

Ho, tramper on the road below,
I spy the way that you must go —
Each springing step on toward your grave,
Each foe and friend you'll meet, each knave.
First, there's an inn across the hill,
Sweet girls to sport with, wine to swill;
Chill is the way here in the air
And chill the part of you I bear.

Beyond the inn's a castle tall
Guarded by glacis, ditch, and wall;
Towers lift there from the snow,
Grimly gaze on those below;
They're manned by things with axe and mace
And are the Furies' perching place.
Yet flinch not and you'll pass 'em by
While 'neath the Furies' flocks I fly.

Beyond, a factory city's found
With costly suburbs snuggled round
And rich, sweet stench of luxury;
A mighty marching there I see,
Tuned to strong metal's martial din;
When I grin down on those rich things
I must beat swift my black bat wings,
For o'er that town the air is thin.

And still beyond's a dimmer way,
A pit too deep for any day
To penetrate, a landscape dark
With inky clouds — and yet some spark
Shows me beyond the last black streak
An eyrie on a mountainpeak.
A meeting place for you and me?
A grave? Or will we see the sea?

Ho, tramper on the road below,
The way's not bad that you must go;
And there is always enough air
To bear the part of you I bear;
But press on strongly with long stride;
Live, love, and laugh; swing your gaze wide;
And do not dawdle by the way —
Remember, I'm not in your pay.

VII

Be these my words
To that which is higher,
To that which is darker,
To that which is swifter.
Be message, not worship,
Be parley, mistrusting
The spirits of night
And the upper-air riders.
By all gods forsaken,
By old thoughts ghost-ridden,
By earth lords fear-shaken,
By elder things bidden,
I may not house with you
And yet I must seek you;
I may not school with you
And yet I must cry you.
Black loving and longing
To you be my token;
In dreams and in nightmares
Like Bifrost Bridge crashing,
I've seen your black horses
And heard their wings clashing;
My soul has rid with you,
Its charger mistrusting;
My spirit has cried out
Your thin cries, dark lusting;
With you I have charged
In terror and pride
To riddle all riddles
In Asgard's-ride.

My words be a token
To lean souls swift riding.
My cry be a challenge
To evils time-biding.

IIX

Out the frost-rimmed windows peer,
You who have arisen early;
Mind not cold for you may see
Faint glimmering fliers spiring free
Between last stars and leafless tree —
Knights of the night! — and you may hear
A fanfare from the stratosphere
With calls like these, gnat-faint yet clear:

"Ho, brother, is the way past Neptune clear?
And those gaunt beasts on the galactic rim—
Do they claw still the Elder Gods' last gate?
News of the airless monster chance or fate
Drove once across the river none may swim?
What of the Other Creatures that we fear?
What stars tow now the planets they ruled late?
And he who went beyond — say, what of him?"

Eldritch words like these are flying,
Voices through the high air crying;
You whose sleep was too uneasy,
You may hear them, rising, dying.

Ω

MANUSCRIPT SUBMISSIONS

After the first of September 1993, we will be reading unsolicited manuscripts again. Right now, we're overstocked, and things are a bit in turmoil while we move our offices; so — PLEASE! — hold all manuscripts (unless we've *asked* you to send something) until that month. Then there will be a flood of manuscripts, so be patient with us while we handle that flood.

However (editors are issued an endless supply of **howevers** when taking office), we will read only those manuscripts which are in standard manuscript form. Briefly: manuscripts must be typed, with a fresh, black ribbon (if you use a printer, the closer its printing comes to 10 pitch or 12 pitch Courier typeface, the better), on one side of 8.5 x 11 inch white paper, skipping every other line (what is loosely called "double-spaced"), with margins of about an inch all the way around. Pages must be numbered (we prefer but do not insist on author's-name/short-title-of-story/page-number in the upper right corner of each page) starting with the first page of text. The story's title, the author's byline, and the author's real name and mailing address must be typed on the first page (or title page) of the manuscript. (How can we send money if you don't tell us where to send it!?!) Each manuscript must have with it an envelope, with postage affixed, addressed to the author. If you want the manuscript back, send an envelope and postage adequate for that; if you do not want the manuscript back, say so, and send a business-sized envelope — again with postage affixed, addressed to the author — so that we may comment on the story.

A few details: If your material is available on computer disks, tell us so in a covering letter or on the first page of the manuscript; do NOT send computer disks until asked. You MUST keep a good copy of your manuscript, in case of loss in the mails or in our offices (we try to be careful, but cannot be responsible for such a loss). We — along with other editors of science-fiction and fantasy magazines — do NOT read stories which are being seen by another editor. (There are rare exceptions; if yours is one, explain the circumstances.) If we have seen a story before, you MUST tell us when, and what we said then, and exactly what changes you made in response (not only does this save us time, but it saves you the risk that we might think the story had been published by someone else and we had seen it there).

Some details for writers in other countries: if you cannot get U.S. postage stamps, send International Postal Reply Coupons. Two coupons will cover postage for a one-ounce air-mail letter. If you cannot get 8.5 x 11 inch paper, use the closest standard size available in your country.

Problems we see all too often: You must indent *every* paragraph, including *every* paragraph of dialog. Do not put **extra space** between every pair of paragraphs (extra space should be used to show a change in scene, in time, or of point of view). You must not send manuscripts by certified or registered mail, or with insufficient postage (we editors do not like to stand in line at the post office to retrieve such; again, your ONLY sure protection is to keep a good copy of every manuscript you send out). You must not use dying typewriter or printer ribbons, nor put your printer in draft mode. You cannot trust a spell-check program to correct errors such as **its** for **it's**, or **right** for **write** or even **rite**. Do not use staples, binders, folders, or stiffeners; paperclips are sufficient. Do NOT use "erasable" paper.

Cover letters? Only if you must; don't distract editors from the *story* you want them to buy. Do use a cover letter if the editor has seen the story before, if there is anything peculiar about the rights to the story; do not use a cover letter to tell how good the story is. It's useful to mention that you have sold to professional markets before (if you've sold to *The New Yorker,* don't cite an appearance in your high-school newspaper; mention your sales to the *Horse-drawn, Cable, & Electric Street Railway Gazette* only if they are relevant to the story in hand).

Basically, your story must **be interesting** — interesting enough to be worth the editor's time and the readers' money; you must **put that story in the format that an editor can use**; and you must **send the story to an editor who might buy it.**

Required reading: *Weird Tales*'s guidelines; just send us a stamped, business-sized envelope for them. *The Elements of Style,* by Strunk & White, available in all good bookstores. Recommended reading: *On Writing Science Fiction: the Editors Strike Back,* by Scithers, Schweitzer, & Ford, $19.50 and *Science-Fiction Writer's Workshop I,* by Barry B. Longyear, $9.50 (both prices postpaid) from Owlswick Press, PO Box 8243, Philadelphia PA 19101-8243 (in Pennsylvania, add 6% tax). Ω

TAKING HER TIME

by John Brunner

illustrated by George Barr

The Meet-the-Writers party, first scheduled item of the SF convention weekend, was in full swing and the hall was crowded, especially near the bar. Members of the organising committee had introduced fifteen or twenty notables, one of whom Celia Compton had actually heard of, and now — with more or less good grace — they were allowing their readers to accost them. They were identified by one-size-fits-all helicopter beanies. Apparently this was a Fannish Tradition . . . whatever that might mean.

Among the throng, however, there was one man who seemed more concerned about catching Celia's eye than chatting even with the guest of honour, though he stood almost within arm's reach. The third time he smiled at her down a chance-opened avenue of people she realised his attention was making her nervous. He wore the unmistakable expression of someone who expected to be recognised. Yet she couldn't place him. He was rather older than her, neither handsome nor ugly, neither smart nor shabby, neither tall nor short: in sum, a nondescript sort of individual. Out of politeness she smiled back, but felt glad that they were twenty or thirty feet apart and to close the gap would involve pushing between several groups engaged in animated conversation.

She wished she was, but she had wandered away from the friend she had come with and stood conspicuously alone with only a glass of wine for company.

And the stranger who seemed to think he knew her was about to make his play, for the hour allotted to make the acquaintance of the authors was up and it was time for a disco. An amateur DJ was taking station at the turntables, encouraged by shouts from his friends.

Hastily Celia drained her glass and made for the bar, pretending she hadn't noticed the man's move. But the bartenders were so busy that she had to wait a long time for service, and that afforded him the opportunity to reach her side.

"Hello, Celia!" he exclaimed.

She was wearing a convention member's badge, but she felt sure he hadn't needed to look at it. So they had met. But when and where?

While she was still uncertain how to answer, one of the barmen completed an order and looked for another customer. The man held out his own glass, for beer, and took hers with unchallengeable assurance. "Dry white wine as usual?" he inquired. "And a dry white wine, please."

There was no help for it. She'd have to read his name. As he turned to deliver her fresh drink she contrived to do so, and discovered he was called Adam Lord.

But still no recollection of their previous meeting.

"Cheers!" He was holding up his glass and smiling. And he added, "I think we ought to let other people get to the bar, don't you?"

Without the slightest intention, she found herself moving away in his wake, towards the end of the hall furthest from the loudspeakers. A moment later the DJ reached for the mike and made a booming announcement.

Wincing, Adam grimaced. "I hate to think what he's got in store for us! I don't care for disco music much, do you? I'd rather have that good sixties stuff like you and Hilda were playing at your party."

Instantly memory returned. Of course! Celia could have kicked herself. This was the Adam who had been brought along last Saturday by someone working in the same office as her room-mate Hilda Jones, and they had chatted for what seemed like only a few moments but turned out to be nearly four hours. How could she possibly have forgotten? And what in the world had they found to talk about so intently on first meeting? She couldn't remember that, either.

Feeling like a total klutz, she forced warmth into her reply, which she had to repeat in a near-shout because music blasted out simultaneously with the first word.

"Sorry to be so slow, but I think I have culture shock! All these hundreds of people I don't know — I guess I just wasn't expecting to run into someone I did."

"You haven't been to one of these events before?"

She shook her head. "Hilda did and said it was a great weekend, so since it's right in the city . . . But this is my first."

"That makes two of us," Adam said. "I got talked into it at your party. I thought of saying suckered, but now I've found you here . . ." Glancing towards the DJ, he pulled a face again. He seemed to have a wide repertoire of faces to pull. "Should I ask you to dance?"

"I don't think I'm in the mood."

"Nor me. Shall we find somewhere quieter? It's a big hotel — even that racket can't penetrate everywhere."

"Yes, all right."

"Then let's go exploring." He took her arm. She raised no objection.

"Well, you certainly made a hit this evening!"

Startled, Celia came to herself. The room, which had been in semi-darkness, was brilliantly illuminated; Hilda had turned on the main lights. The tape-player was silent. The doors and windows were open, and from the room across the hall reserved for smokers drifted a faint stale smell broomed along by a half-hearted breeze.

Rising slowly, taking in countless dirty glasses and empty paper plates, Celia said, "Where is everybody?"

Hilda stared in surprise. "Gone home, of course. It's two o'clock."

But I thought it was supposed to last the whole weekend — until Monday night!

Just in time Celia stopped herself from uttering the words aloud. This wasn't the Escutcheon Hotel; this was the apartment she had shared with Hilda for the past six months. She hadn't been at a science-fiction convention tonight, but in her own home, joint hostess at a party for twenty friends and half as many friends-of-friends. She knew that perfectly well, and proof was all around her.

Yet a shiver crawled down her spine. Why, then, did she clearly remember extraordinary, vivid sights and sounds — being accosted by two boys in identical gorilla suits, wearing badges that identified them as King Kong and Kong King, listening to a hoarse, tired voice intoning in a key that kept wandering from G to F and back an interminable ballad about a contest between wizards — instead of her and Hilda's guests?

Hilda was continuing. "Think it was a failure? I don't. People started arriving at six, remember. . . . Is something wrong?"

Celia hesitated. "I don't know. It's just that I can't believe it's so late. Where's the time gone?"

Hilda chuckled.

"You, honey, have been deep but *deep* in conversation. I don't think anything short of an earthquake would have distracted you. What sort of guy is he, anyway?"

"Who?"

"Adam that you've been talking to all night, of course. Honey, are you sure you're okay?" Hilda had been gathering up glasses to wash; now, setting them down again, she laid a hand on her friend's arm, looking worried. That was nothing to how Celia felt.

But I was talking to Adam at the Escutcheon Hotel. We were at a disco first, then we escaped to a quiet bar, then we got invited to someone's suite because they were bidding for the next convention, or something, and later there were movies and a parody of West Side Story *and a masquerade where someone was accused of cheating because he wore an Air Force high-altitude flying-suit instead of a costume he had made himself . . .*

Only — only I wasn't, was I?

"Honey, you're shaking!" Hilda exclaimed. "You'd better turn in."

"No!" Celia forced out. "The place is such a mess —"

"In the morning," Hilda said firmly. "I don't know what this guy Adam has, but obviously you OD'ed on it." Abruptly suspicious: "He didn't give you anything, did he?"

"Of course not!"

"Don't snap my head off! People do bring stuff to parties 'cause they can't get high enough on wine and company, and if someone — Never mind. You get to bed."

Dumbly Celia obeyed. But she lay awake a long time, listening to the sound of Hilda clearing up what she had promised to leave until the morning but unable to bring herself to help. Her mind was haunted by an obsessive mystery:

What became of my party?
Where was I during it?
I'm sure — I'm certain — that I wasn't here . . .

Celia was waiting at the supermarket checkout, it being her turn to buy household necessities. As usual she was worrying whether she had remembered everything Hilda had listed, and selected the best of the bargain offers, when she noticed with alarm that although there were only four people ahead of her, one woman who looked as if she had picked up a month's supplies for a family of ten was slowly counting and re-counting a wad of bills with the expression of someone who couldn't believe there wasn't another twenty in there some place.

Just my luck!

"Good afternoon!" said a bright voice behind her. "How are things with you this fine day?"

And now to be accosted as well — !

Not looking round, only vaguely aware that a man had joined her line, young to judge by his voice, she said, "I wouldn't if I were you."

"Excuse me? What?"

Celia pointed at the woman counting her money. She had started over for at least the fifth time.

"I see what you mean!" the young man murmured. "Quick — there's only one customer at the next one."

Why she reacted so swiftly she had no idea, but a moment later they were second and third in line and the person ahead was accepting change. The money-counting woman had not even reached the clerk.

"Thanks!" she said. She had to. "My wits must have been wool-gathering or I'd have done this myself." Decanting purchases from her cart, she glanced at her unexpected companion. There was nothing remarkable about him; he was just an ordinary man with a pleasant, diffident smile.

"You don't remember me, do you?" he said after a pause.

"Ought I to?" she countered, opening her purse.

"Well, we did spend rather a lot of time together at the science-fiction convention."

Oh my God!

Oddly, he didn't sound offended. His tone was neutral, as though he was accustomed to being easily forgotten. Nonetheless she felt heat rush to her face. Her cheeks must be tomato-red.

"Goodness, I'm sorry! Adam?"

"That same, and at your service." He parodied a bow, taking his turn at the counter. He had bought only one too many items to use the six-or-less checkout, and his paper sack was ready in moments. Dreadfully embarrassed, she waited for him to rejoin her, although she would infinitely rather have gone straight back to her car. She had two weekends' worth of chores to attend to. But how could she just walk off? They had indeed spent a lot of time together at the convention, though she couldn't recall quite why. Perhaps it was simply because he was almost the only person there that she knew, apart from Hilda — and Hilda, who though overweight had bright eyes, a dimpled chin and a tan no sunbed could impart, had not been short of company.

Briefly, resentment burgeoned in Celia's mind. Thanks to Adam she seemed to have squandered a chance to meet a lot of interesting new men. She'd let herself be — the word sprang to mind — *owned* for the entire weekend, and that was totally out of character.

She was rehearsing the proper words to convey pleasure at this encounter, thanks for Adam's company the weekend before, and her intention of going home right now, when she found him taking her grocery bag. A feeble protest died a-borning at his dismissive wave.

"I've got practically nothing to carry, and this is a load. Your car's outside?"

"Uh — yes."

"Show me where. I didn't have to drive here. I live right around the corner."

Another unwished mystery: they'd spent that long together (the awful suspicion was growing that it had included nights as well as days) and she hadn't even obtained his address or phone-number. A little sniggering demon emerged from the recesses of her mind and promised to torment her as often as he could.

"Are you all right?"

Pausing in full sunlight outside the exit, Adam was regarding her solicitously.

I wish people would stop asking me that! I haven't heard Hilda say anything else all week!

"Of course I'm all right!" she snapped.

"Ah-hah. Well, it is very warm today." Turning, Adam walked on, seeming to divine which of a hundred cars was hers and making straight towards it. "Let's go for a drink, hm? I've had a pretty hard week. I've earned one. I'm sure you have, too."

Celia's fingers were all thumbs. She dropped the car-keys taking them out of her purse. He retrieved them and unlocked the trunk for her, maintaining his grip on the groceries, and then looked a question: *how about it?*

With a sense of doom she heard herself say, "Okay. But just one. I have so many things to do."

That wasn't the way it happened. From the bar — where they had more than one drink — she drove them to a Thai restaurant that Adam said was excellent, and it was, and some time towards midnight they were in a dark cellar bar that featured an elderly black pianist. Ignoring the music, she was hanging fascinated on Adam's every word.

But this was one of the places that hadn't caught up on anti-smoking laws, and eventually she found her eyes were stinging and her throat was sore. The moment she mentioned the fact Adam smothered her in apologies.

"How inconsiderate of me! And it is late, isn't it? What a pity that Czech movie is at such a ridiculous time, nine o'clock! The one about the time-travellers that's never been shown in the West before. You would like to see it, wouldn't you?"

"Yes, of course. It sounds fascinating, and if it's not even going to be on TV . . ." She glanced at her watch. All around them milled people in fancy dress, Draculas and aliens, witches and barbarians, enough extra crewmen for the *Enterprise* to overload her warp engines. A constant hubbub of voices filled the air, punctuated by bursts of near-hysterical laughter.

"And we'll want some breakfast first, naturally. Call it a day?"

"I guess that would be a sensible idea."

"Well!" Hilda's eyes were sparkling. "I don't suppose there's any point in asking whether you enjoyed the weekend!"

What?

Dazed, Celia glanced around. She wasn't in a smoky cellar sitting at a beer-wet table while a grizzled pianist hammered out blues and boogie-woogie. This place was so light it hurt her eyes. Tiled floor, marble walls, people waiting in line with baggage at their feet . . .

A carved and painted shield on the wall caught her eye. This was the Escutcheon Hotel. People were taking down posters announcing changes to the published programme of the SF convention. A member of staff was reprimanding them for using Scotch tape on surfaces where it might leave a mark. A wall-clock showed nearly three P.M., checkout time.

"Celia?" Hilda said uncertainly. "Are you — ?"

"If you ask whether I'm all right," Celia gritted, "I think I shall hit you."

Alarmed by the venom in her voice, Hilda drew back half a step.

"Honey, I didn't mean to upset you. It's just that . . . Well, you were supposed to ride home with me every night. I thought things must be going swingingly with Adam. What happened? Did it turn out he's married or something?"

But Celia wasn't listening. She was staring at the vast glass windows of the hotel's atrium, the afternoon sunlight on the palms beyond, raising her left arm as though meaning to consult her watch yet unable to summon the energy to glance down.

Where's it gone? The bar, the beer, the boogie-woogie — why do I remember that and not what Hilda says I should?

Stifling a cry, she ran out of the hotel in search of her car. There was no sign of it. Standing bewildered, picturing theft and the need to call police, she abruptly remembered.

She hadn't driven to the convention hotel. She'd driven to the bar, and the Thai restaurant, and the jazz cellar, because when her car was right on the spot there didn't seem any point in switching to Adam's. But not here. Not to the place where she actually was, where according to Hilda she had spent the whole weekend.

And it had to be true, because of the date on her watch.

Heaven pity me. I must be going mad.

A light male voice inquired, "Excuse me, is this place taken?"

Sullen, Celia shrugged. She could scarcely refuse to share her table, much though she would have preferred to. The mall's only coffee-shop was nine-tenths full, and the rest of the place eleven-tenths. One could scarcely move in the most popular stores without treading on someone's toes. She had hunted all afternoon for a new suit to wear to the office, bought one, was now regretting her choice and wondering why she'd bothered anyway, because it was on the cards that she wouldn't have her job much longer. Twice in the past three days her boss had bawled her out for elementary yet expensive mistakes.

But how can I concentrate when my mind is crumbling?

"Why — ! Goodness, for a moment I didn't recognize you! Celia, you look terribly upset! What's wrong?"

Startled, she strove to focus on the man facing her. At first she couldn't see him clearly, and the horrifying thought that she might soon need glasses crossed her mind — one more problem, as though she didn't have enough already.

"Celia, it's Adam! We went out together last Saturday. You can't have forgotten the Pattaya Garden? And listening to Daddy Joe Ivories?"

But that wasn't . . . wasn't real.

Except she couldn't make herself believe it wasn't. As she gulped the last of her herbal tea, resolving for the space of a heartbeat to collect her purchases and beat a retreat, she checked and hesitated.

It was real. I remember it too clearly for it not to have been.

So it followed that Adam too was real. And what he was doing to her —

Was he doing anything to her? Accusations mustered on her tongue-tip, and refused to pass the frontier of her teeth. Suddenly it seemed absurd to hurl such charges at this person who was regarding her so sympathetically. Who was, in fact, saying:

"You must have had a tough week. Trouble at work?"

And she heard herself replying bitterly, "You're reading my mind."

"No, I promise you." A chuckle. "I do have talents, but telepathy is not among them. Want to tell Uncle Adam all about it?"

The tone in which he uttered the question, above all his self-deprecating use of "uncle," broke down barriers. She found she was smiling because, at the oldest, he must be two years her junior.

Though he didn't sound that young, nor on close inspection look it, not now that his expression was grave instead of cheerful.

Encouraged, she poured out her problems — those, at any rate, relating to her work. The worst one of all, the one that underlay the rest, she dared not mention. She was fighting against repeating even to herself the idea that she might become insane, especially in the presence of the person she suspected was responsible. But how could anyone affect another person's sanity without — oh — poisoning her, or hypnotising, or working a spell? And she was determined not to believe in spells.

"I get the impression," Adam said at last in a judicious tone, "you don't much enjoy your present job. Fancy being interviewed for a new one?"

"I don't understand," Celia said after a moment's hesitation.

"My company" — she registered that he didn't say "the company I work for" — "is always actively recruiting. On the basis of what I know about you, I think you'd fit in fine. Care to come and look us over?"

"On a Saturday afternoon?"

"The operation runs twenty-four hours a day. But don't worry — I'm not suggesting that you'd have to work shifts. Only a few of the computer staff do that. Most of us keep regular office hours. How about it?"

"Well, I'm not sure I —"

"The pay is good." And he mentioned a sum half as large again as her current salary.

"You really think I could be worth that?"

"My dear woman!" Adam looked and sounded shocked. "What a way to sell yourself! The only person who can make you worth that much is you — correct?"

She hadn't even started to bridle at his use of the term "sell yourself" when she realised he meant it in the other sense: promote and publicise. That left only one course of action. All her suspicions vanishing, she gathered her belongings.

Somehow she never got around to asking what his company did, or manufactured, or distributed, or — or whatever, though she did notice that the sign beside the door read ADAMS LORD with an extra "S." But he brushed her query aside, saying merely, "It inspires confidence if the people we deal with think there's more than one guy in charge."

Its headquarters were in an expensive area, and not on one floor of a high-rise tower, either. They occupied the whole of a compact but splendidly appointed two-storey building, with a large car-park alongside.

"My staff," said Adam dryly, "don't have parking-meter problems. I won't allow it."

He led her in and out of empty offices where the carpets were as springy as the turf of an expensive golf-course; where computers of the latest design hummed softly and restful green and bronze displays reported incomprehensible calculations; where lunch menus from half a dozen local restaurants were posted above tear-off pads on which to write one's order prior to ten A.M.

"No, you don't have to eat at your desk," he murmured. "We all get together in here at twelve-thirty. All of us, me included." He opened the door to a room that was more like a conservatory. Gorgeous tropical plants framed a window overlooking a Japanese sand-garden; a gaudy parrot squawked a welcome as it landed on his shoulder and gave his ear a friendly nibble; a bored ginger cat sunbathing on a west-facing windowsill opened and shut one eye and paid them otherwise no smidgin of attention.

"Sit down," Adam instructed, waving at a deeply-padded velvet chair. "Dry white wine? Or how about champagne — Louis Roederer Crystal? It's rather special."

It was indeed delicious. With it she ate caviar and crackers, smoked salmon and pumpernickel, and afterwards the best pineapple she'd ever tasted.

"Well, I've much enjoyed the evening. I hope you have too. No need to get up — I can walk home from here. We've practically come around in a circle, in case you hadn't noticed. I'll be in touch. I have Hilda's number which is also yours. Good night!"

"Good night!" And, staring after him with smoke-bleared eyes, Celia found herself wondering why after their previous meeting she had expected him to look and behave like somebody much older. He had acted practically — well — boyish, even to holding her hand under the table.

Which was wet, as she suddenly realised. She'd put her elbow in a puddle of beer, and that meant another trip to the cleaners for this overworked jacket. Next week she really must buy a new outfit for the office.

Abruptly eager for fresh air, she rose and headed for the door, assuming Adam had picked up the tab.

He hadn't.

A stern voice said, "Lady, ain't you forgetting something?"

"I thought my — my escort . . ." The words trailed away as she fumbled for her purse. Adam had, after all, paid for dinner, and the Pattaya Garden's food had been just as good as he had promised. Sighing, she laid bills beside the cash-register and waved away the change. In the background Daddy Joe began a new number, a slow and rocking blues.

Pushing open the exit door, she felt annoyed with herself for using the term "escort." She ought to have said "companion" or something neutral like that. The idea of women needing to be escorted, as though by a gaggle of men-at-arms —

Where the Hell am I?

She had been expecting to emerge in the down-town area, to see clean sidewalks and, across the street, towers with half their windows lighted even at this late hour. She was prepared to collect her car from an enclosed and private parking lot. Instead, here it was right on the side of the road, and two dour policemen, one white, one black, were walking around it with suspicious faces. One was noting down its number.

As she approached, they turned and stared at her.

"Your car, lady?" the white one demanded.

"Yes! Yes, it's mine!"

Christ, they're not going to breathalyse me, are they?

"Then I guess we'd like to see —"

My driver's license? She fumbled in her purse.

"— you get on board and make for home. Leave a car like that on a street like this, you never know what might become of it."

But it's only a Japanese compact. New, of course — I bought it to celebrate getting my job. Even so . . .

She put her hand to her forehead, feeling giddy. She still had this clear, this horrifyingly clear, conviction that she ought to be somewhere else.

Worse yet: *somewhen* else.

"Lady, you been drinking?" said the black policeman.

She forced a smile. "A couple of beers. If you can call what they serve in there beer."

With infinite relief she saw the white policeman frown at his companion, conveying clear as speech, "Don't push it — if she's going to have an accident she may as well do it on someone else's turf."

And the black man gave a shrug and nod.

Careful not to betray the slightest hint of drunkenness, and finding how difficult it was even though she felt cold sober, she got into the car, started up, drove away. Her mirror confirmed that they were watching. She had no idea whether it would set her on the right road home, but she turned at the next corner simply to be out of their sight.

And was immediately lost, in a city she had lived in all her twenty-seven years.

Because she was completely convinced, despite the evidence of her eyes and the street-names and the overflowing garbage-cans and the addicts and winos picking through their contents in hope of something fit to eat or wear, that she ought actually to be leaving the splendiferous headquarters of Adam's company.

A minute further on she had to pull over, rest her forehead on the wheel, and surrender to the need to cry.

"Seeing Adam again this weekend?"

"Who?"

"Gal, this has gone too far!"

It was Friday night. Hilda, who came — as she liked to say — from an old-fashioned Southern background and was into being domesticated, was gathering up table-napkins, pillow-covers and other articles she planned to take for washing. Now she let fall the lot and stood sternly over Celia with hands on hips.

"Hear me?" she demanded. "I said —"

"Yes, yes, yes." Celia rubbed eyes red from private weeping on the way home. She had made still more mistakes during the week and today her boss had

finally lost patience and given her notice. She had marched out defiantly, declaring that she didn't care: this was a lousy firm to work for and she'd had the offer of a better-paid post.

But I haven't. That's next week. Or maybe tomorrow. Which is crazy, isn't it? Either that, or I am.

She no longer knew where — no: *when* she was. Sometimes it turned into where, as well.

"Are you sure you're doing right, getting this mixed up with a kid like him?" Hilda, leaning close, put the insistent question.

"Who?"

"Honey, you got it bad, don't you? Adam! Who else?"

"What do you mean, a kid? He's —"

Celia broke off. A moment earlier, she hadn't even known who Adam was. Now his image was clear in her mind. Except it wasn't. There were several images, overlapping and not matching. One was of a man perceptibly her senior, by five or maybe seven years; one was of a youth of college age; and in between there were others, she couldn't tell how many, that contributed to making her mental picture —

"Smeared," she said aloud.

Hilda, on the verge of contradicting, interrupted herself to demand, "What in Hell does that mean?"

Celia clung to the word, repeating it until she was sure it wasn't going to evaporate like — well, like the company headquarters of Adams (not Adam) Lord, the jazz cellar, the science-fiction convention, the party. So long as she held it in mind she was able to retain the tantalising glimpses of each of them, recall events she was sure she had witnessed, that were becoming vague as dreams.

One thing's odd. Adam isn't there. I am. He isn't.

With immense effort, staring at a blank blue wall where she and Hilda were agreed there ought to be a picture or a hanging — the landlord wouldn't let them paint a mural — but they hadn't found the right one yet:

"Hilda, did I really spend most of our party talking to Adam?"

Even the name seemed to want to slip away, like a fish she was trying to catch with her bare hands.

"You surely did," Hilda confirmed.

"And did I stay at the Escutcheon the whole weekend?"

"Honey, what's all this about? You know you did! I thought great, here Celia's found a guy who — "

"Hilda, I *don't* know I did. Any more than I know he picked me up at the supermarket and took me to a Thai restaurant and then to hear Daddy Joe Ivories."

"Hey, you caught him? My pappy had some of his records! Broke 'em, though, one time when — Sorry, honey. Go on."

Slowly, concentrating on every syllable, Celia said, "I *remember* us going there. In the same way I remember Adam taking me to his company headquarters to offer me a job." A deep but rapid breath before Hilda could burst out with congratulations, and the last essential word:

"*Tomorrow.*"

"What?"

"Thank heaven. I've got you saying it at last instead of me saying it all the time."

"But this don't make no kind of sense!"

"Exactly." Now she had broached the subject, Celia felt an access of confidence. Twisting around on the sofa, she gazed earnestly at her friend. "Did you never have the experience of meeting a person in the wrong context?"

"I don't get you."

"Oh!" — impatiently. "You see somebody day after day, like the clerk at a checkout, or someone at a gas station. You said hello and smiled a hundred times. Then you meet somewhere else and you don't catch on. Maybe you never saw the whole of the other person before. It was always half a person on a stool, or a face bending to the car window."

Cautiously, Hilda nodded.

"Well, it's like that when I meet Adam. I never recognise him."

"But, honey — !"

Celia was drawing another deep breath, because this time what she said was once for all. She was taking Hilda into her confidence because she had nobody else to tell. She was frightened to the prickling roots of her hair. Most of all she was afraid of being sent to a psychiatrist, afraid of being told she was crazy, afraid —

She had to break her train of thought. Loudly: "I just figured out that the reason I don't recognise him is that the last time we met hasn't happened yet."

There. It was out. With beseeching eyes she scanned Hilda's face, seeking clues to her reaction. Surely she was bound to say, "You better see a doctor and go find someplace else to live 'cause I don't fancy sharing with no crazy woman!"

But Hilda didn't. She simply sat there, visibly thinking, her lips moving now and then as though to test a phrase and abandon it when it proved inadequate.

And finally she said, "Then what about the party?"

Celia could have hugged her. That was exactly the point preoccupying herself.

"Right! It must have been the real first time that we met! It was only the next time that . . ." Her voice failed, as though her diaphragm had frozen in mid-breath.

"Honey?" Hilda touched her hand.

"Yes, I'm okay. It's simply that . . . I said I couldn't remember anything we talked about, didn't I?"

"Mm-hm." Wary eyes searched her face.

"I just did remember one thing. He pulled one of the oldest lines in the book. He said, he actually literally said, 'Haven't we met somewhere?' "

Hilda pondered that a while, then let go a puff of long-stored breath.

"*Hah!* You mean he didn't say 'somewhere before'?"

"You're taking me seriously! I can't believe it! I was sure you'd think I'm crazy!" Celia was beside herself.

Hilda shook her head. "No, gal, I don't think that. I been around crazy people. My pappy went crazy from booze — it was one time when he was drunk he smashed those Daddy Joe records. My mammy took to the church and religion made her kind of weird, too. My kid brother got strung out on crack and a gang of my cousins went the Rasta route so now you can't talk to a one of 'em 'cause they all fried their brains with too much ganja. . . . No, gal: we've been roomies more than half a year and I got to know you pretty well. You're not crazy."

Half blinded by tears, Celia pressed a plump brown hand between hers.

"But if I'm not," she whispered, "what in heaven's name is happening?"

"That," said Hilda in a judicious tone, "is what you and me got to figure out."

Withdrawing her hand, sitting down in a facing chair, she set her elbows on its sides and gazed thoughtfully into nowhere.

"Well," said Hilda, "we know one thing. Whoever your Adam is, he must have one Hell of a good cosmetician."

"What do you mean?"

"Well, at the party he looked kind of — not old, not really, but older than me and I'm older than you. Matter of fact — 'course the lights were down — I'd have said he was going grey. At the science-fiction convention I did a double take."

"Go on!" Celia urged. There was a terrible tightness in her head. Each word struck like a drumstick.

"Well, he didn't look that way at all. Maybe my age, a couple years older than you. Then —"

"But you haven't seen him since the convention!" Celia burst out.

"Sure I have."

"When? Where?"

"At the supermarket. I got there twenty minutes after you. I'd forgotten to put some things I needed on the list. I spotted you at the checkout. I did call

out but you were talking to Adam by then so you never noticed. That's why . . ."

The words trailed away. After a pause, her voice suddenly shaky, Hilda resumed: "I asked if you thought it was sensible to mess with a kid like him. Didn't I?"

"Yes!"

"Why in the world did I say that? I know damn well he isn't a kid. I know from the party. Yet at the supermarket I'd have sworn he was a lot younger than you."

Their eyes met, and each saw that the other's mind was full of unspeakable dismay.

Eventually Hilda pulled herself together.

"This," she said, "calls for the devil's brew, like my mammy would say. Martinis?"

"Yes, and make them strong!"

"Just suppose," Celia said with the careful articulation of the nearly drunk determined not to lose hold of the artificial clarity which stems from alcohol, "that when I meet Adam . . ."

Hilda set aside the phone-directory from which they had satisfied themselves that there was no company in the area called Adams Lord, or Adam Lord, or A. Lord Inc., or any title involving either name bar a religious publisher and a trendy men's-wear store. She cut in.

"You always find you're back at the last place you met him."

"I told you that already" — with a flare of annoyance. "What I started out to say . . . Oh, Hell! You drove it out of my mind. I wish you wouldn't interrupt!"

Frowning into her glass, Hilda offered, "He robs you of the previous week?"

"That's it!"

"How?"

"*I* don't know! But it's the only idea that fits. My life has been folded back on itself like — Ever see one of those people who tear paper into shapes?"

"Mm-hm. My pappy used to do that, before my mammy told him when he entertained at clubs and parties he was serving the purpose of the devil."

"That's the way I feel."

"Like my pappy?"

"*No!* Like the sheet of paper!" Celia gulped the last of her fourth martini and fumbled for the olive among half-melted ice. After three goes she retrieved it and popped it in her mouth. Chewing, she went on, "Look, when he said at our party that we'd met before, what he meant was that we'd met at the Escutcheon, right? So that accounts for why I remembered the convention when I should have remembered the party."

Hilda was reaching for the pitcher she'd filled with gin and vermouth. Spilling only a few drops, she managed to top up both their glasses and add another olive to each.

"You're making me giddy," she complained.

"It's not me, it's the —"

"It *is* you! You're claiming that when you left the

bar where Daddy Joe was playing you remembered —"

"No, you've got it wrong. That wasn't when I remembered the convention, that was when I *found myself* at the convention. When I left the bar, what I remembered was . . ."

It was her turn to be at a loss for further words.

"What you remembered," Hilda supplied, "was what you tell me hasn't happened yet. Like the offer of a new job."

"No! I — uh — remember that from *tomorrow!*"

"Gal, you surely have me confused . . . Okay, this time you've managed to remember without meeting Adam. What brought it back? It hasn't been this way before, right?"

"Right." Celia bit her lip. "Well, I guess it must have been because I got fired."

"Think that's Adam's fault?"

"Of course. It's because of him I haven't been able to concentrate on my work. Could you, if every weekend you seemed to be losing the previous four or five days, yet you were still living the time in between? I mean, I have been at the office. I haven't called in sick or anything. I've *been* there."

"And you recollect being there?"

"Not clearly. But other people say I was."

"I guess that has to count for something." Hilda yawned and stretched, glancing at her watch.

"Gracious, it's midnight! We've been gabbing for hours and I haven't done half of what I meant to."

Alarmed, Celia jolted forward on the sofa. "You're going to quit now, just when things are starting to make sense?"

Another yawn enveloped Hilda's response.

"Sense to you, gal, maybe. Not me. Far as I can tell, you think this guy is kind of a time vampire, stealing a week of your life every time you meet him. If that's the way of it, all I can say is he must be getting a *lot* of interest on your investment. 'Night!"

"Wait!" Celia pleaded. "What do you mean?"

"Well, if after meeting you three times, or four if you count the one you say hasn't happened yet, he can switch from older than me to younger than you, he must be working one Hell of a deal . . . Oh, honey!" She strode back to sit at Celia's side, face and manner desperately earnest.

"You've got to admit it doesn't make sense. The only thing that's certain is that you'd be better off if you'd never met the guy . . . Say!" She leaned abruptly closer, staring at Celia's left temple.

"What?" from a mind filled with chaotic visions.

"Did you realise you got grey hairs?"

Breaking into sobs, Celia staggered to her feet. Her drink splashed on the floor. Uncaring, she rushed for her room and slammed and locked the door before Hilda could follow and offer meaningless consolation. Fully dressed, she flung herself across the bed and shortly fell asleep on tear-damp pillows.

In the morning, Celia's head ached, her guts were sour, and her mouth tasted foul. She forced herself to stand up and found she was swaying as though still drunk. She had had terrifying dreams, but no details would come clear.

There was no sign of Hilda, not even a note.

Dully, she went to the bathroom, showered, dressed, ate breakfast, all by machine-like reflex. She didn't dare look in a mirror.

Grey hairs . . .

But what in the world was going to happen to her today? She had been planning to buy a new outfit for the office —

Why? If I've just been fired, what's the point?

Was that last week, or this week? She tried to read the date on her watch, but it was blurred. (*Glasses as well as grey hairs?*) Perhaps things would make sense if she could believe she'd set out to buy new clothes for not her old job but interviews for another one . . .

That didn't work either. Her private time had been too hopelessly scrambled.

But she had lost her job. There was no doubt about that. Otherwise she would never have opened her heart to Hilda, and that too was incontrovertible. In the living-room the carpet was still wet where Hilda had mopped up her spilled drink.

Well, there's one person in the world I'm not going to "sell myself to" in search of work!

Possessed as much by hatred as by terror, Celia donned outdoor shoes, checked her purse for keys and money, and set off for the agency where she had obtained her present post. Whether they could find her another was irrelevant. All she wanted was not to be trapped by Adam Lord, whoever or whatever he might be.

Was she doomed to meet him again today? If so, where? Maybe she ought simply to stay home, keep the door locked, the phone off . . .

But he knew where she lived. She would be cornered here.

She almost tripped as she ran down the stairs.

Above the store-window, brilliant even in sunlight, a blue sign sparkled like a river flowing over diamonds. In the window itself, information scrolled slowly upward on TV screens: job specification, hours and salary, vacations, benefits. Touch-sensitive pads stuck to the glass, and trailing cords like limp brown pasta let one halt the lists for closer scrutiny.

A score of people stood watching the displays, as many men as women. Most of them wore a sullen look that Celia had learned to recognise: they weren't honestly expecting to find work, but to quit searching would be to abandon their self-respect . . . or what was left of it after maybe months of unemployment. There was suppressed anger in the air; she could practically smell it.

"Hi, Celia! What on earth are you doing — checking whether my firm offers competitive rates? I promise you won't find a better salary through these people!"

The voice was a high tenor, almost shrill. Not even a young man's, but definitely a boy's.

With a terrible sense of foreboding Celia shifted the focus of her eyes from the list of jobs to the reflections on the glass. Yes, Adam was behind her, smiling, expecting her to turn and greet him, lie perhaps about being here on behalf of a friend . . .

And looking about nineteen.

All the wrinkles had gone, that she remembered — could remember, by deciphering the maze of dream-like memory — from the party, even from the convention. His hair was impeccably black, and not from dye. He had sported an incipient paunch. Now his belly was taut, his torso muscular. Also his smile was dazzling. Two or three men in the group of job-seekers, who had, as Celia was half-consciously aware, looked her over in the customary masculine way, turned back to their study of the scrolling lists, resigned to being outclassed. Also some of the women betrayed envy, asking one another wordlessly how Celia, no younger than themselves, could attract such a handsome, youthful stud.

Grey hairs.

Almost, she looked for them in her own reflection. But something else Hilda had said sprang back to mind, miraculously, blessedly.

"You'd be better off if you'd never met the guy . . ."

Followed by a statement of Adam's own: *I do have talents but telepathy is not among them.*

What kind of talents, then? Hilda had said "time vampire" . . . "Time thief" fitted, too.

She thought of closing her eyes, but changed her mind. The one resolution she made, instantly and faithfully, was not to turn around. Whether looking at him straight in the face had anything to do with his power, his magic, whatever the Hell, she had no idea, but insofar as anything about her last few contorted weeks of life did so, it made sense not to render herself more vulnerable than she could help.

She waited, thinking of Perseus and Medusa. As she had expected, a moment later Adam advanced to her side and took her arm, saying, "Come on, you don't need to waste time here. I —"

That was as far as he got before she stepped hard

on his foot and swung her purse backward into his groin.

"Get your hands off me!" she shouted. Her voice cracked on the last word, but the cry had been loud enough. All within earshot turned their eyes to her. And him.

"But —"

"What the Hell do you think you're doing, you Goddamned molester?" Gaze fixed on the window, she relished his bewilderment — and incipient alarm, for the other job-seekers were turning bodies now as well as eyes.

"Now just a moment — !"

"You quit harassing me, you son-of-a-bitch, or I'll call the police! Stop mauling me! Keep your filthy hands to yourself!"

A stout black man and a lean, wiry white one exchanged glances and nods and each took one menacing stride towards Adam. Two women stationed themselves either side of Celia, also one black and one white, and the latter said, "We're with you, sister. Who is he?"

Lent confidence by these volunteer supporters, Celia at long last dared to turn and look her persecutor in the face.

"Him?" she said loudly and clearly. "Oh, I don't know him. I don't know him from Adam."

And Adam screamed.

"Hi, honey," Hilda called as Celia re-entered the apartment. Obviously she had a date tonight; she was sitting in a towelling robe in the living-room, wet-haired, watching the TV although its sound was nearly drowned out by the buzz of the hair-dryer. "You okay? We got kind of like you said smeared last night, so I figured I'd better let you sleep on when I went out. *Are* you okay?"

"Never better," Celia said composedly.

"You got a date tonight? Going out with what's-his-name?" Her hair dry enough, Hilda switched the blower off and put it back in its case.

"No, I've neglected my chores too long. I'll have a quiet evening at home. Read, or watch TV."

"Uh-huh. Say, there was kind of a weird story on the news. See it? No, you wouldn't have, but they'll repeat it, I guess." Rising, she bustled around, putting the dryer away, picking up a dress on its hanger to inspect it for creases. "You could be interested. Happened outside that agency you got your job through."

"Really? What did?"

"Oh, some crazy old loon tried to grope a girl right in public. Couple of guys warned him off and he keeled over and died. Heart-attack, I guess."

"What's so weird about that? Happens all the time!"

"Ah, but there were these people saying they were sure he was a kid. Could have sworn to it.

Good-looking, too. Only when he fell down it turned out he musta been about ninety."

"How do you know?"

"He didn't have any ID. They put a picture on, 'case anybody knows who he was. Funny!" She checked. "Reminded me of someone, come to think of it."

"Who?"

"Oh, I can't call the name to mind . . . By the way!"

"Yes?"

"You weren't down that way this afternoon, were you? I caught just this glimpse and thought hey, that's Celia . . . But I guess I imagined it."

Celia forced a smile, posing as for a police lineup. "Still think it was me you saw?"

" 'Course not! But . . . Just a moment, honey." Dress draped over arm, Hilda stepped close, scrutinising Celia's left temple.

"What's that for?"

"Did I or did I not say last night I'd seen grey hairs on you?"

"I'm not sure. Those martinis were awfully strong."

"I guess they must have been." Doubtfully, Hilda turned towards her room to get dressed. "You don't remember?"

"See any grey there now?"

"None. Not a trace. I guess you're right about the martinis. . . . Weird about this old guy that everybody mistook for a kid, hm?"

"Must have been wearing a mask," Celia offered. "Or maybe he had a terrific cosmetician."

"Ha, ha," Hilda said, tossing her robe aside as she passed the door. And added overshoulder as she selected bra and panties from a drawer, "Shame you don't have a date! I thought you were getting on fine with what's-his-name."

For a long moment Celia was unable to reply. She was re-seeing the appalling transformation of Adam, or as much as she had been able to endure before taking to her heels. None of the little crowd had tried to detain her. They'd been too overcome with astonishment and fear at the sight of the bald, toothless, half-blind, *shrivelled* parody of a man writhing and howling on the ground.

Just in time she said, "I don't expect we'll see each other again. But I'm not sorry."

It was only under her breath that she murmured the moral she had drawn from her suffering, which one day she hoped to share with Hilda and other friends — perhaps. With, at least, the ones prepared to listen. One day she might be able to declare, in plain words:

"The boss of his company may well be Adam's Lord — may have been from the start. And I guess you'd expect him to move with the times.

"But I can't believe that he was ever Eve's." Ω

THE NEFERTITI-TUT EXPRESS

*Poem written on learning that trans-Egyptian railroad firemen
sometimes used mummies for locomotive cordwood*

Did they do *that?*
Stoke furnaces with shrouds,
With clouds of mummy-dust and old kings, too?
Across Egyptian sands on railroad paths
Long, long ago when trains were new?
Amidst the oldness of raw dunes, worn pyramids
Did trans-Egyptian stokers, running low on fuel,
Turn roundabout and summon Tut or Hotep's sons
And feed them in the fire, make pyre and burn a
    royalty?
They did.
Or so I've heard.
Absurd.
They stopped along the way and snitched a tomb,
    six tombs.
At ten times twenty stations (named for Styx)
    called
All Aboards! to plenty of ripe lords and ladies there
Strewn forth by death four thousand years before.
All folk were mummified, of course, and not just
    kings and queens;
The common sheep whose sleeps were common as
    the dust that gleans
Were there in harvest windrows scythed by lusty
    death;
Like kindling all about they hid in millioned graves.
So when the train puffed up and
    ocean-tidal-smoked
While waiting to be fed — the dead, sand-drowned,
Were handy stokings and wry faggots for the fire.
Their rictus smiles did naught for them;
The mummies, grinning with their grins
Were flung in locomotive bins;
Ten mummies at a time popped in
To make St. Elmo's iron firewheels spin.
Like holy loaves they baked in steams
Or flew in winged papyrus dreams tossed up
Like midnight ravens, charcoal rooks,
Old Alexandria's finest books set fire by fools,
Those graduates of Caesar's dumb Praetorian
    schools.
A pageantry of raped sheaves breathed
    self-consume.
From locomotive Hades, swift Hell's flume.

From Cairo south the mummy-fields were bled
And to the gorge of rushing Baal the linens fed
And scarabs wrapped in tar were from the porch
Of ancient tombs seized forth to bandage torch,
Light hierarchies of Time and, one by one,
With mighty Ra, fall in that final Sun,
That Sun which in the bosom of steam-beast
Of Tyre and Ptolemy makes equal feast,
To churn forth funeral plumes along the shore
Of salt-plowed Carthage, then turn back for more.
Fair Nefertiti (Yes? Perhaps!) then knew the flame;
One-eyed or two, all burned to chars her fame;
Her profile, infamous, her beauty bright
A thousand tigers' eyes fireworked the night.
And Cleopatra, Caesar's cat, her ticket, too,
Was taken, torn, ignited, spread like smoking dew
On lip of Sphinx which asks and answers: What
Burns faster, finer: Bubastis? Thoth? Anubis? Set?
    or Tut?
Above remote Baghdad their farblown charsoots
    sail
Where old soothsayers spy them, spin a tale
Of mummy-dragon breaths across the stars
And Cleopatra's heart fixed fiery bright as Mars
As off the engines of destruction smote and strode
And in proud chariot fires the ancient pharaohs
    rode.
In fine incense and smoke they draughted,
    shimmered, blew
And all the bright Egyptian winds of time bestrew
To flag downwind through Alexandrian East
Until mid-feast some New Year later on
A Faisal in his palace, cool, Arabian-kept at dawn
Unslept and suddenly panicked and cold
For no good reason at all, sat up and wept,
Called out to the wind, afraid to die.
Then raised one trembling hand to find and pluck
The last offending soot of Nefertiti's flesh
From out his weeping eye.

— **Ray Bradbury**

DRAWING ROOM HERONS

In the drawing room
a horse hair sofa
a dusky shaded lamp by the
voluminous chair you could
lose yourself twice in

in the other corner
never interrupting
yet never leaving
you quite alone

a heron, long beaked, silent, one foot
poised in air as if to stately
walk out of his own death.

— Blythe Ayne

BACK ISSUES:

We are currently moving our office. For the time being, we must limit our sale of back issues of *Weird Tales*® to complete sets of the the thirteen issues from #290 through #302, and to single or bulk copies of #306 and #307.

(issue number)290: **65TH ANNIVERSARY ISSUE!** **Gene Wolfe** (featured author) **& George Barr** (featured artist), with Ramsey Campbell, F. Paul Wilson, T.E.D. Klein, & Tanith Lee.

291: **Tanith Lee & Stephen Fabian**, with Morgan Llywelyn, Nancy Springer, Brian Lumley, & Harry Turtledove.

292: **Keith Taylor & Carl Lundgren**, with Tad Williams, Alan Rodgers, & Nina Kiriki Hoffman.

293: **Avram Davidson & Hank Jankus**, with Robert Sheckley, Keith Roberts, Carl Jacobi, & Ian Watson.

294: **Karl Edward Wagner & J.K. Potter**, with Jonathan Carroll, Brian Lumley, R. Bretnor, & Nina Kiriki Hoffman.

295: **Brian Lumley & Vincent Di Fate**, with Phyllis Ann Karr, Darrell Schweitzer, Robert Sheckley, & Keith Taylor.

296: **David J. Schow & Janet Aulisio**, with Tad Williams, Harry Turtledove, & Michael Rutherford.

297: **Nancy Springer & Frank Kelly Freas**, with John Brunner, Susan Shwartz, & Thomas Ligotti.

298: **Chet Williamson**, with Stephen King, Ian Watson, R. Bretnor, Fred Chappell, & Darrell Schweitzer.

299: **Jonathan Carroll & Thomas Kidd**, with William F. Nolan, Ian Watson, R. Garcia y Robertson, & Nina Kiriki Hoffman.

300: **Robert Bloch & Gahan Wilson**, with Henry Kuttner, Ray Bradbury, Lawrence Watt-Evans, & Michael Rutherford.

301: **Ramsey Campbell & Bob Walters**, with Stephen King, Robert Bloch, Darrell Schweitzer, & Keith Taylor.

302: **William F. Nolan**, with Robert Bloch, Brian Lumley, & Ronald Anthony Cross.

303: TEMPORARILY OUT OF STOCK

304: TEMPORARILY OUT OF STOCK

305: OUT OF PRINT

306: **Nina Kiriki Hoffman & Nicholas Jainschigg**, plus stories by Lord Dunsany, Robery Deveraux, Tanith Lee, & John Gregory Betancourt.

A set of the 13 issues, #290–#302, $30.00. Single copies of #306 or #307. $5.00 each. These prices include shipping.

SUBSCRIBE NOW & SAVE!

In the U.S.A. and possessions, 6 issue subscription , $24; elsewhere, US$30 In the U.S.A. & possessions, 12 issue subscription, $46. Elsewhere, $57.

If you order our first 13 back issues (issues 290–302) for $30.00, or if you order our first 6 Issues in Special Hard Cover editions for $30.00, then you may subscribe (or extend an existing subscription) for $4.00 off the subscription rates listed above.

Send check or money order, or give us your Visa or MasterCard number, its expiration date, and your signature. Please include your ZIP/Postal Code with your address.

Our address:

Weird Tales®
PO Box 13418
Philadelphia PA 19101-3418

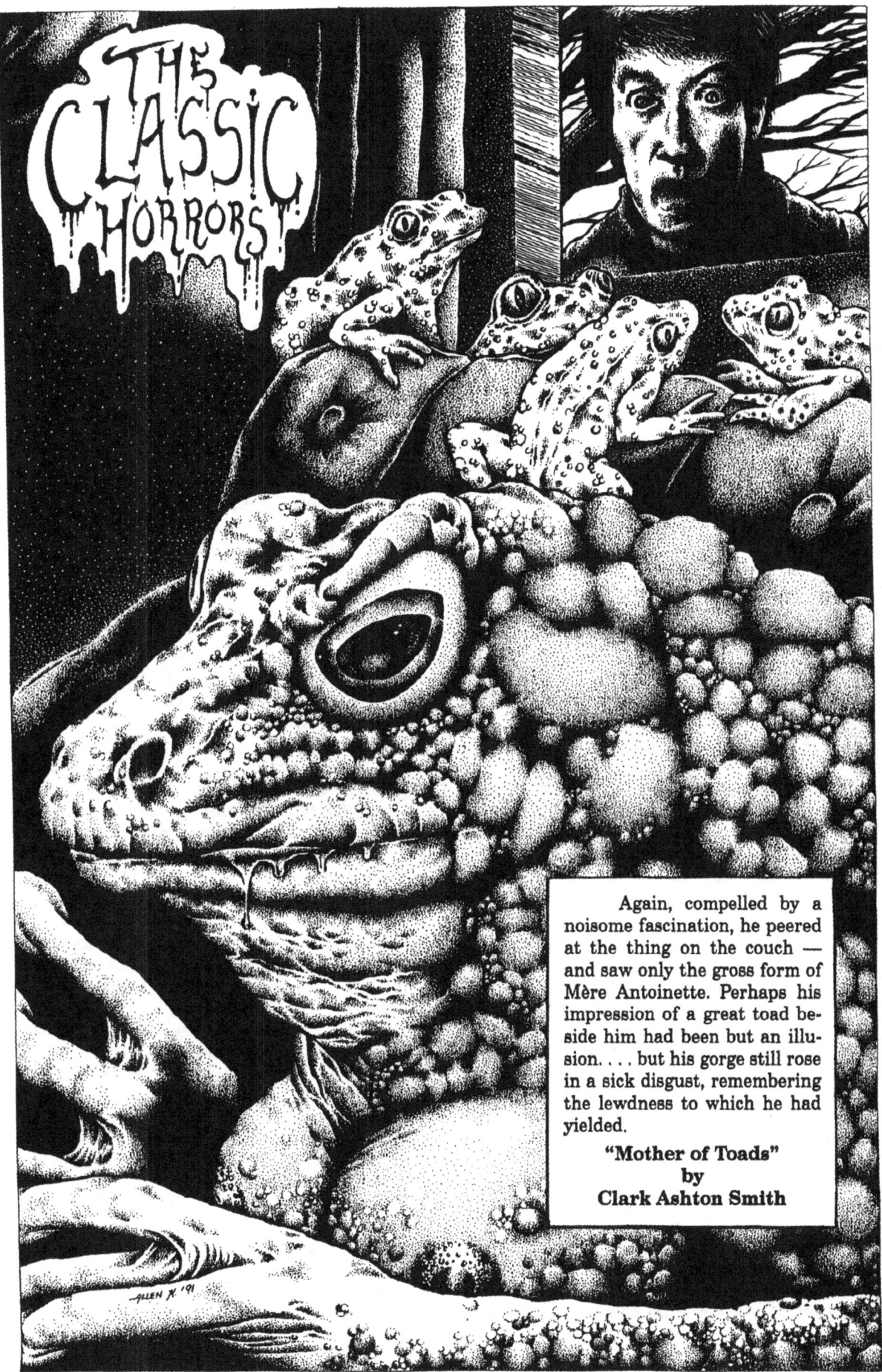

Again, compelled by a noisome fascination, he peered at the thing on the couch — and saw only the gross form of Mère Antoinette. Perhaps his impression of a great toad beside him had been but an illusion. . . . but his gorge still rose in a sick disgust, remembering the lewdness to which he had yielded.

"Mother of Toads"
by
Clark Ashton Smith

THE WRATH OF THE GODS AT MACY'S

Doris Egan

illustrated by Bob Eggleton

I was tired of everything after my last job. Branwen, my colleague, talked about a vacation at some bed-and-breakfast inns in the foothills of the Blue Ridge Mountains; civilized places with flowers on the table and antique stores down the road, where sound carries easily through the old plaster walls and the innkeepers greet you by name. I wanted someplace impersonal. Someplace with sliding glass doors. Vegas would have been all right, but there were too many lights.

It was off-season, though, at the Jersey shore. God, I hadn't been there in years and now it all came rushing back, the smell of the washcloth in my hand turning into the smell of a wet bathing suit. Asbury Park, Seaside Heights, Wildwood Crest; the names of my childhood summers flickered through the emptiness. The cheap, over-air-conditioned motels, the chlorine pools, the great plastic logos that lit the night skies in the little towns, vacancy or not. The Swan. The Sand Dollar. The Astronaut. And now it was October, and the pools would be covered, and the families packed into their cars and gone away, leaving the wind to whip down the beach. Not many places would be open at all; it would take a lot of phoning. The idea appealed to me.

"What is wrong with you?" asked Branny. "The trees will be turning color up and down the coast, and you want to look at sand. Come with me, for God's sake."

"They said we've got a month, right? This is how I want to spend it. I want to get out on the Garden State Parkway and open all the windows. I'm sick of riding in limousines — I'm sick of trying to see through those smoked windows — I'm sick of being watched —"

"Sick of me, too?" asked Branny.

"Not that." I went over and took her in my arms and kissed the top of her head. Two middle-aged women, starting to put on a little weight. Why must I always stand apart and look at the appearance of things, and dismiss the truth that lies inside? And only with the good things. With the bad things, I fly straight to the heart.

"I give up," said Branwen. She squeezed me and let me go, and went out to the sitting room of our suite at the New York Hilton to make plane reservations. "Look," I heard her say, after arguing with the telephone. "I'm a registered Oracle, and I want a ticket now."

I met Branwen after my life changed drastically. For fifteen years I taught fourth grade in Warrentown Grammar School. Warrentown is a small town in Massachusetts; very rural, somewhat isolated. Their educational standards were not stringent. Nor were mine; if anyone was interested in learning, I would help — if not, it was their own affair and their family's. Not perhaps the best attitude for a teacher, but it seemed to be what the town was looking for. The kids were out about a tenth of the time, either hooky or working on the farm. So be it. And it wasn't as if I were on the backside of the moon; we did have cable TV, two video rental stores, and a triplex cinema in Main Street. And I could drive down to Boston whenever I liked.

I made my first prophecy three days after I turned forty-one. I was making my annual announcement that Box Hill, behind the school parking lot, was off-limits after a snowfall — the kids liked to steal trays from the cafeteria and ride them down. Too fast, and they ended up on the concrete in the parking lot, not to mention scaring Hell out of any drivers.

"That includes you, Bobby Grant," I ended up saying, to my surprise. My voice boomed out over the room. "The next time you try that you'll break an arm."

The kids all looked at Bobby, assuming he'd been seen. But I hadn't seen him. I'd been in Boston during the first snowfall.

And damned if the kid didn't show up in a cast, two weeks later. "Serves him right," said the parents, with the usual parental concern for rule-breaking in a small town. "You kids listen to the teacher and stay away from Box Hill."

"Self-fulfilling prophecy," said a couple of the other teachers. "You shouldn't have said it; it had a subconscious effect."

Not self-fulfilling, I thought to myself. Just a prophecy.

No, I didn't know what was going on. But I knew I hadn't been the one speaking.

So much for the winter; there were a few other odd incidents here and there, but nothing to raise any eyebrows. Come spring there was a town meeting to discuss the proposed replacement of the covered bridge outside town with a steel-and-concrete bridge. This sort of debate goes on all over New England — there was a hard core of aesthetic groupies who wanted the bridge kept and repainted, and there was a somewhat larger bunch of townies who were tired of getting calls from every large truck coming into town. They all had to be directed way the Hell over to Sayreville and down I-24.

I sort of liked the bridge, myself, but not being a city worker or a store owner I didn't have to deal with the inconvenience much. So I kept my mouth shut during the debate. The townies won, after five years of bringing up the same topic, and they wasted no time in calling for a motion to announce open bidding for contractors. I raised my hand, was recognized, and stood up.

"DON'T BE AN IDIOT," I said to Bill Shafly, leader of the townies. "THAT BRIDGE'LL GO DOWN UNDER THE FIRST HEAVY LOAD." It came out as though from a microphone — the whole auditorium must have heard me.

No one becomes an Oracle who hasn't made a fool of himself in public, not once but many times. I was more embarrassed later, thinking back; at the moment it happened I was having too much trouble believing it. I sat back down and tried to pretend it was someone else who had spoken. That was how it felt anyway.

There isn't much anybody can say to a statement like that, so they sort of picked up the pieces and went on, with some odd looks at me. I worried about my job for days. But it was an old-fashioned place, and a certain amount of eccentricity was almost expected from a spinster schoolteacher.

Eleven months and a few other incidents later the bridge went down under a 10-wheeler from Boston, the firm of Taper and Shafly was indicted, and my reputation was not what it had been. That was when the stories started cropping up on TV, stories of apparently normal people making successful predictions. I was interested at first, then I started turning off the set.

But it was in the papers, too. And it was in the eyes of the kids at school, and their parents. "Tell me how Suze's going to do," said Suze's father on Open House Night.

I said, "She's getting all A's and B's, and she has a good attitude. I'm sure she'll do fine." And he kept looking at me as though he was waiting for something more.

Other rumors came from the outside world. But not so much detail here, it looked as though things might be being hushed up. Funny happenings connected with these new predictors. And then the government announced it wanted to study the phenomenon: rewards were offered for every predictor accepted by the Project, and a good salary to the predictors themselves.

It was a year before they came for me. Long enough to have heard the word "prediction" replaced by the word "prophecy." Long enough to hear the edges of what was going on in the Project, which I wanted no part of; long enough to read the editorial headline in the New York Times on Christmas day: **The Gods Return**. Not that they meant anything like that, literally — not the Times. But they'd gotten enough data on the Project to consult a few professors of mythology and psychology. "It seems that these unusual people are able to tap into the universal archetypes — that racial library where potent images are stored — and come away with information. Has the human race reached a point in

its evolution where the shadows we have pounded down into the subconscious can now be brought out into the light, examined and classified, made to serve us? The answer is still in those shadows. But it's a suggestion of hope, a chink of light to hold our hands under and watch in wonder, on this Christmas Day."

Thank you, New York Times.

The two FBI men who came to my house a week later were more prosaic. Nobody pulled a gun or anything, but I was given to understand that my replacement for the spring term was already on her way, and if my duty wasn't clear to me then life could be difficult. I packed a couple of suitcases and handed one to each of them to carry. They didn't protest. A third, clean-cut quiet-macho suit-type was waiting by the car, so I gave him my giant shoulderbag. Let them make themselves useful. No dogs or cats to arrange for; somehow I'd never gotten to it. I locked the door, and never saw the place again.

I wandered through the rooms of our suite restlessly, pulling back the drapes to look down at the New York streets, imagining how they'd looked in 1920; in 1860; in 1700. It was a game I played. Branwen was packing her suitcase a day ahead of time — Branny is like that — when she turned to me and said, "I need a sweater."

"You have three sweaters."

"Button-down cardigans. I want a pullover — a fisherman thing, something wild and Celtic."

"A cardigan will keep you just as warm."

"I'm going to the mountains and I want to wear a pullover." She was getting her stubborn tone.

That dreaded experience, clothes shopping, hung over my head. I said. "We can rent videotapes at the front desk —"

"Let's go to Bloomingdale's."

"That place is a maze! You can barely find your way from one floor to another. I refuse to step foot —"

"You're depressed, you need to get out. Let's go to Altman's."

"I can run the bath, we can order Chinese, get some videos —"

"Macy's," said Branwen, as though it were the closing proof in a scientific paper. She pulled out my hightop sneakers and handed them to me.

We went to Macy's.

"Good," she said to me in the cab, "you need to walk around a little. You've been in a rotten mood since Virginia."

"I have not been in a rotten mood. I've been thoughtful."

She turned serious for a second. "Kiddo, I know it's not a good idea to ask" — I could see her weighing the odds on whether the taxi was bugged — "but you haven't cursed anybody or anything, have you?"

"I said I wouldn't and I haven't."

She looked relieved. "I didn't think so." Somewhere around 40th Street she said, "But all the little things that went wrong in D.C. — the ambassador tripping in the receiving line, the caterer's truck breaking down, everybody's luggage getting sent to Panama — I was wondering, you know, if maybe you'd been letting Loki out again."

"I don't think you can count the luggage. That's normal."

"That's not the point, sweetie."

I shrugged. "I like Loki, the way I like the Jersey shore. And who knows how much longer I'll have with him?"

"Why shouldn't you have time with him?"

"Because," I lied, "I promised the Project Chief I wouldn't invoke him any more."

Branny smiled. "Good, I'm glad you did." She squeezed my elbow. "You can get in a lot of trouble that way."

——— · ———

We got out of the taxi in front of the sign that said **WELCOME TO MACY'S, THE LARGEST STORE IN THE WORLD** and walked in through the revolving doors, in our Reeboks and plaid wool skirts. She wore a white cardigan and I had a gray blazer. What a video we would make, I thought. Middle-Aged Lesbian Schoolteachers From Hell.

The Project had taken over an old army base. They housed about 250 of us, and about 300 of them. "They" were all government-issue: testers and watchers, note-takers, cooks and maintenance and security staff. We called it Fort Fear. The fear was that we were going crazy.

There wasn't one of us who hadn't considered it before we came; and feelings of sanity are not encouraged by people who respond to what you say by taking notes instead of replying. I had nightmares for weeks after I arrived, and annoyed the watchers by not being able to remember them.

But everything becomes routine. There were people I talked to in the halls and the cafeteria — Mr. Sackville, an elderly gentleman with a cane, who told me that he had chats with Aphrodite every evening after dinner, and she had asked to be remembered to me. I had not yet had a vision myself then, and he made me uncomfortable when he talked this way. I tried to handle it with grace. And there was Gerda Licht, a college student to whom I gave my butterscotch pudding one day at lunch. She heard Vishnu and Rama, and was given to saying things like, "The present and future do not exist. Involvement binds us to illusion. Are you going to eat that chocolate cake?" I didn't think she should have been there at all, but she got to her feet one day in the middle of a revival showing of "Casablanca," just as the Marseillaise was being sung, and announced that an earthquake was imminent. "I'm as surprised as anyone," she added, in a totally different voice. She then prudently left the theater. Enough people were sufficiently nervous to follow her out, and she got credit both for saving their lives and for predicting the New Madrid quake before it happened.

I woke one morning from a dream of blood and fire, and saw a man in a helmet sitting in the chair by my window. He smiled at me and vanished. Later that day I was trying to get a Hershey bar out of the machine in the lounge when Mr. Sackville came in. A blue-eyed woman in a long gown was on his arm. He adjusted his bow tie and pulled out one of the plastic chairs for her to sit down. She gave me a glance from those oceanic eyes, and inclined her head. A vision of doves and sea-foam rolled around my head. I left quickly, went to my room and locked myself in.

The psychiatrists came for me eventually. They talked me out of the room and brought me to the testing board. "It's a breakthrough," they said. "Be glad," they said. "Now you'll learn to invoke the state consciously."

"*Invoke* it? To what purpose? I don't want it, I just want to be left alone."

"To answer questions," said the youngest, a red-haired, earnest boy with freckles.

"There's death in your face," I said, because there was. "Is that answer enough for you? What other questions can you have?"

He swallowed, and the others gave him a brief look but kept to the road. I found out later he had AIDS. "We need to know certain things. Listen — are we on track in our cancer research?"

"Yes," I said without thinking.

"How soon will we have a major breakthrough?"

"It will be solved within your lifetime."

A buzz at this. "It matches," said one. "Shut up," said another.

"The drought in Yemen. How long will it continue?"

"Fire and dust for two more years. Then food enough to feed the country."

"Will Kelliher win re-election?" asked a voice. The others looked at him.

"By a landslide," my daimon said, abandoning circuitousness.

"Will the Senate ratify the weapons treaty?"

Silence. "I don't know," I said. "He's gone."

"Who?" said a tester quickly. It was the same voice that asked the two political questions. Good old Kelliher had an inside man.

"I don't know," I said again.

——— · ———

Things were a little better in the Fort after that. I started to get into the pattern of things. I played bridge with Mr. Sackville and Gerda and any fourth we could get; I got a government bonus for passing my invocation test; I bought a CD player, but it was stolen. Sometimes I saw other sorts of beings in the Fort — beings who looked like Hermes and Pan and Apollo, but not as I would have pictured them. They were other people's invocations. What's more, the same legend manifested differently for different Oracles. Maybe that *Times* writer was right; this individuality of visions certainly seemed to support the idea of archetypes rather than gods. Goat-footed Pan stole Dr. Perlmutter's cap one day, and he wondered why everybody laughed.

It loosened us all up. Before we knew it, invocations were happening all over the place. They had to start registering Oracles and graduating us as quickly as possible before things got out of hand.

There isn't much I can tell you about the gods, except don't play poker with Loki, chess with Odin, or anything at all with Lucifer. I suppose the people who hung out with Rama learned more elevated things.

——— - ———

So far I haven't told you about the other breakthrough I had at the Fort. Some time after I arrived, I saw a hand-printed poster in one of the halls: **GODS COME IN ALL SEXES. Don't join the oppressor! Meeting 8:00 tonight Classroom 201 to discuss opening our visions to encompass social change. Gay/Lesbian Dance, 10:00, Sager Lounge.**

Heavens, I hadn't seen one of those since my college days . . . and with good reason, I reminded myself. The era of innocence was over. Everybody was out of the pool and back in the closet. The prudent thing to do would be to ignore it, but I was charmed by its naïveté and curious about the fool who wrote it.

——— - ———

I took a look in classroom 201 at about 8:15; it was empty, much as I'd expected, except for a brown-haired woman in jeans sitting on the front desk. She looked up when the door opened. "Come on in," she said. "The party's jumpin'."

"Yeah, so I see." I closed the door behind me. The corridor had been empty, but there was no harm in being careful. If there were cameras, it was too late anyway. Goodbye, teaching career.

"I'm Branwen Selleck."

"Hello," I said. I did not volunteer my own name. There was no reason she needed to know it, and lots of places in the Fort were bugged.

"You coming all the way in?"

"Thanks, but I wasn't planning on staying. Just dropped by for a minute."

"Come on," she said, "be a mensch."

"Not likely," I said, and she grinned. I took a step further in. "Do you really think this is a good idea, my friend? Give out your name like that and it's only a matter of days till the Legion of Decency gets it."

"No worries. We're government property now, and I never met a government that cared what its weapons did in their spare time. I know. I got on the Legion's list twice since I made Oracle, and both times Uncle Sam wiped my name."

Maybe she wasn't so naïve. "How did you get on it twice in so short a time?"

"I got two weekend passes."

I had to laugh. "Didn't your mother ever tell you about discretion?"

"Oh, I was a good girl for years and years. But Apollo told me not to be such a pain in the ass."

Coming closer, I saw she was wearing Omega earrings. I hadn't seen them in years, either. Clearly she was taking Apollo's advice to heart.

"I didn't know he cared about stuff like that."

"He's much misunderstood."

I reached the desk. "What did you do before you were drafted?"

"Well, I was going to go for my MLS. But mostly I taught school in the Bronx."

"I give up," I said at that. I saw from here that her hair wasn't brown, it was redder than that; more mahogany-colored.

I could see trouble coming. Perhaps avoiding Mr. Sackville's Aphrodite hadn't been a wise thing to do.

We asked for the sweater department at Macy's front door information booth. A black-haired man in a leather jacket stood behind us, waiting patiently to get to the store maps. His hair was curly and his face was cheerful, and he gave me a flirty look as we passed, Middle-Aged Lesbian Schoolteachers From Hell or not. There is a special place in the Legions of the Blessed for Italian heterosexuals. Branny didn't see it; as usual, she was oblivious to these things.

I always noticed. It was the undersides and edges of things that I liked; details, eccentricities. It came out in our approach to the Oracle business. She was hooked on Apollo, light and healing and rationality. I liked the gods of the cold countries, who themselves suffered and bled occasionally — and I liked the wily and the wiry, the tricksters. Coyote. Loki. Hanuman. Being Norse and a trickster both, Loki was my favorite.

The shopping crowds swirled around us. "I guess we should decide where to go first," said Branwen.

" 'Better Dresses'," I read, looking at the store map. "What are the others, Worse Dresses?"

"There's an escalator," she said, and she pushed out into the sea of people.

I followed as best I could. We passed by a Chanel perfume counter and I thought about asking her to wait. Maybe I should take this opportunity to dive into the apparently bottomless credit card the Project issued me. But under the circumstances there didn't seem to be much point.

In the stream of shoppers I saw a fat kid in a blue t-shirt that read: **Things fall apart. The center cannot hold**. I blinked my eyes for a second and the message disappeared.

"You coming?" said Branny, turning back.

"Yeah, wait a minute." I caught up to her.

"See something you want?"

"No."

We went through handbags, hats, and accessories. As we were going up the escalator she said, "Sure you don't want a scarf? I never get to buy you anything."

"I just want to leave. I hate being in stores, Bran, I always feel as though the energy is being sucked out of my body and beamed into space."

She patted my arm. "We'll order pizza when we get back."

Up through lingerie, dresses, and trendy suits. "Here we are," she said cheerfully, and off we went through several miles of store.

When we reached the woolens she dug in like a

soldier, pulling sweater after sweater out of the shelves, checking them over, discarding and winnowing. Branwen *liked* to shop. "Almost perfection," she muttered at last. "Except for this dumb blue piping on the collar. I'll ask the sales guy where the ones without the piping are."

We approached a man of about fifty, in a shirt and tie with no jacket. He sat by the cash register in a state of apparent catatonia. Branny waited about thirty seconds and said, "Excuse me."

He continued to stare down at a piece of paper in his hand.

"Excuse me," she said again. "Can you tell me where the sweaters are without the piping on the collar?" She held up her sample.

Slowly his head rose. "What do you want?"

She pulled out the ad she'd clipped from the *Daily News* and placed it on the counter by the sweater. "These sweaters here," she said, pointing to the ad. "They're almost like this one, but this one has a blue stripe on the collar. I don't want a blue stripe. The picture on the wrapping doesn't have a blue stripe, either. Where are the ones without the blue stripe?"

For a second there I could place her in front of her grammar-school class, mining heaven and earth for signs of intelligence.

"That's it," he said.

"No," she said, "that is not it. This is a different sort of sweater. Where is the other kind?"

"That's it. That's what the package says. The package says what the ad says."

"But what's in the package doesn't match! Just look —"

"I don't want to look." There was a note of finality, and just a trace of viciousness in his voice. This did not surprise me. Of the ten rudest people I have met in my lifetime, seven of them worked at Macy's.

I withdrew a few yards from the scene, and started rooting through the shelves. After a minute I called, "Bran! Over here. This what you're looking for?"

It was the same wrapping, anyway, and no stripes. She looked at it, then at me. "You are a gift from heaven," she said.

As we stood there we heard a woman's voice raised in frustration. Someone else was trying to talk to Mr. Sunshine. "Think he's just nasty to women, or everybody?"

I said, "Do you suppose it's genetic?"

"It would make an interesting study. I don't believe anybody in social psych has ever profiled rudeness. It's worth looking into — think how the quality of life might be improved."

"Well, they've got a gold mine in this store."

Branny wanted to go to the Reebok sale upstairs. As we got on the escalator I looked back over the floor and imagined Pan stealing up behind that social pimple and — no, don't think about that. I felt that stirring off on the fringes that I thought of as "the Snake"; Jesus, I thought, not here. I started to

sweat, and took hold of the railing. We're only shopping, for Godsake. Leave me alone.

"You okay there?" asked Branwen.

"I'm okay. Just the normal energy-leech associated with shopping." Bran was a *Dr. Who* fan, so I forced a smile and said, "You know, if you die in a Macy's you don't regenerate."

"No wonder the place makes you nervous."

"**D**on't be nervous," the secretary had said. He was another in the line of nice, clean-cut young men I'd become acquainted with since I left New England. "Have you met the President before?"

My little cousin Eddie had asked me that once, too. "What's he like?" Eddie asked. This was before his mother asked me to leave.

I'd met the President. We'd all met the President. Big fucking deal, as one of my fourth-graders used to say. Once you've been wrung out by the gods, a man in a gray suit doesn't make as big an impression. He was shorter than they let you see on TV, and he had allergies. It was hay-fever season, and Fort Fear was in weed country; the poor man barely took the handkerchief away from his face the whole time he was there. He tried to be avuncular. You could see he thought it was a big treat for us, meeting him and him being just a regular guy. We tried to pretend it was.

I only saw him the once after that. "He's very nice," I told Eddie. "Very polite."

Things weren't going well. There was only one salesperson to handle the two dozen rabid Reebok fanciers in Sporting Goods. And he was busy doing paperwork. Branny decided to take me to the countertop restaurant on the eighth floor so I could sit for a little while and have a Coke. It was closing when we got there. They sent us to Le Petit Café on two. They didn't have Coke and were out of seats. They sent us to another café on three, but it was closed, so we sat on a display sofa on four and discussed, partly seriously, whether we'd offended the gods.

"I begin to think we should leave," she said.

"Hallelujah," I said.

The nearest down escalator was blocked off. We wandered through department after department looking for another. "Largest store in the world," muttered Branwen through gritted teeth.

"And we're seeing it all," I added.

I could have sworn I saw Coyote underneath that first escalator. I didn't say anything about it to Branny. She didn't like the company I kept, and anyway I ought to have better control over my invocations.

As we passed a cash register it began squirting out receipt-paper. The saleswoman banged on it angrily. "Stop it!" she yelled. Branny looked at me. I shrugged.

The next cash register we passed also began squirting paper. Branwen stopped and faced me, hands on her hips. "Loki," she said.

Far off, the Snake was stirring restlessly. "Look," I said quickly, "I'm the first to admit he's got an immature sense of humor. But you can't hold him responsible for everything that goes wrong, Bran."

She stared suspiciously for a second, then whirled and went on walking. "There's a working escalator somewhere," she said, much as Sir Edmund Hillary must have said, "There's a top to this damned mountain." We passed a third cash register and she glared at it, waiting. Nothing happened. We went on.

Behind us, we heard the paper start to eject.

"That's it," said Branwen.

"I swear," I said, "I haven't done anything consciously."

"That's what you said about Dr. Perlmutter's cap."

"It was true!"

She was looking behind me, and I saw her eyes widen. I turned. Goat-footed Pan was dancing down the aisle, hand in hand with a tall monkey. They were pushing over racks of clothing as they went. Bran said weakly, "Hanuman?"

I nodded.

I pulled myself together long enough to look around for witnesses, and there they were: at least half a dozen people staring at what to them would be racks turning over by themselves. And who knew, maybe not being Oracles brought them closer to the truth. Were these really gods and demons we were playing with, or were they self-generated? I thought about that question a lot lately.

But not now. I touched Branwen's shoulder. "You know what? I think the security staff will be here any minute."

She blinked, and said, "Let's get out of here."

Chaos followed us across the floor. I heard a joyous, bass-throated yell from somewhere behind, and the sound of a giant hammer hitting the wall. A minute later an arrow flew over our heads and buried itself in a bundle of London Fog raincoats.

Men in security uniforms and men with the white carnations of Macy's management were pouring onto the floor. Some of them looked at us strangely.

Another damned escalator closed for repair. How was this possible? The escalators were one of the *reliable* things about Macy's. We switched directions, and more security staff appeared. One man pointed to Branny and me.

Management was closing in on us, like the Indians on the wagon train. I hated to be outnumbered.

The Project administrative team surrounded me.

"I don't want to see the President," I said. "Why can't he talk to another Oracle?"

"You're the most consistent and controlled Oracle presently in the United States, and he wants to talk to one now."

"Consistent! Controlled!" I could feel tears coming, to my embarrassment. "I'm awful!"

"Nonsense," said the Chief, in that hearty, Let's-Buck-Up-the-Hysterical-Spinster voice of his. "Why, you even dream on cue."

"None of my dreams are good! Can't you understand that? None of my dreams are good!" I was shouting. And it was worse, because they didn't take it seriously when we were like this, they treated us like temperamental opera singers.

"You've said lots of good things," said the young one, the one I'd told was dying. "You said there would be no famine in Yemen, remember that?"

But by then I was really crying, and I couldn't answer them. *I* couldn't answer them.

"**T**here's nothing useful we can tell them," I said. "Let's run."

Branny threw down her sweater and started pumping after me.

"The elevator's opening!" I said, as we approached the banks.

"It's going up!"

"I don't give a damn," I said, and ducked in. She jumped after me.

We got off on the top floor. "Uh-oh," I said, surveying the fine crystal and china. I turned around, but the doors had closed.

We walked through as fast as we could, followed by the sound of crashing glassware. "This is very *strange,*" said Branwen. And I knew what she meant. She meant strange even for an Oracle. This was the most confusing, powerful, multiple invocation I'd ever heard of. And it was *involuntary.*

"Bran, I swear —"

"I know. I believe you, it's all right."

The Snake was waking up. The Snake was waking up, and I didn't even know His name.

We passed the book department. Hephaistos was reading there, curled under a table, but the books had changed to pornography. Doves fluttered by. His wife, Aphrodite, was there, but not Mr. Sackville's ideal. She was painted like a streetwalker. Branwen grabbed my hand with a desperate tug and we went out to look for the escalator again.

She stopped short suddenly. "We need help," she said. "This isn't funny anymore. Something bad is happening." She closed her eyes and looked toward heaven, an expression of calm coming over her face.

Apollo appeared, Branwen's Apollo, healer and protector of the rational. For once I was glad to see him, glad to turn to the more respectable gods. I was sorry that I'd ever felt uncomfortable around him.

He turned and went swiftly to a woman nearby, like an unnatural form of beauty — like a stalking deer — and pulled her down to the floor. She struggled.

"Oh, God," said Branwen, turning away. Her eyes were filled with tears, she looked like a child slapped by her mother. This wasn't Bran's Apollo, it was the Apollo I'd learned from Ovid, who specialized in making the gods look nasty.

Everything was tainted. It was my fault, it was the Snake's fault. It was one of our faults.

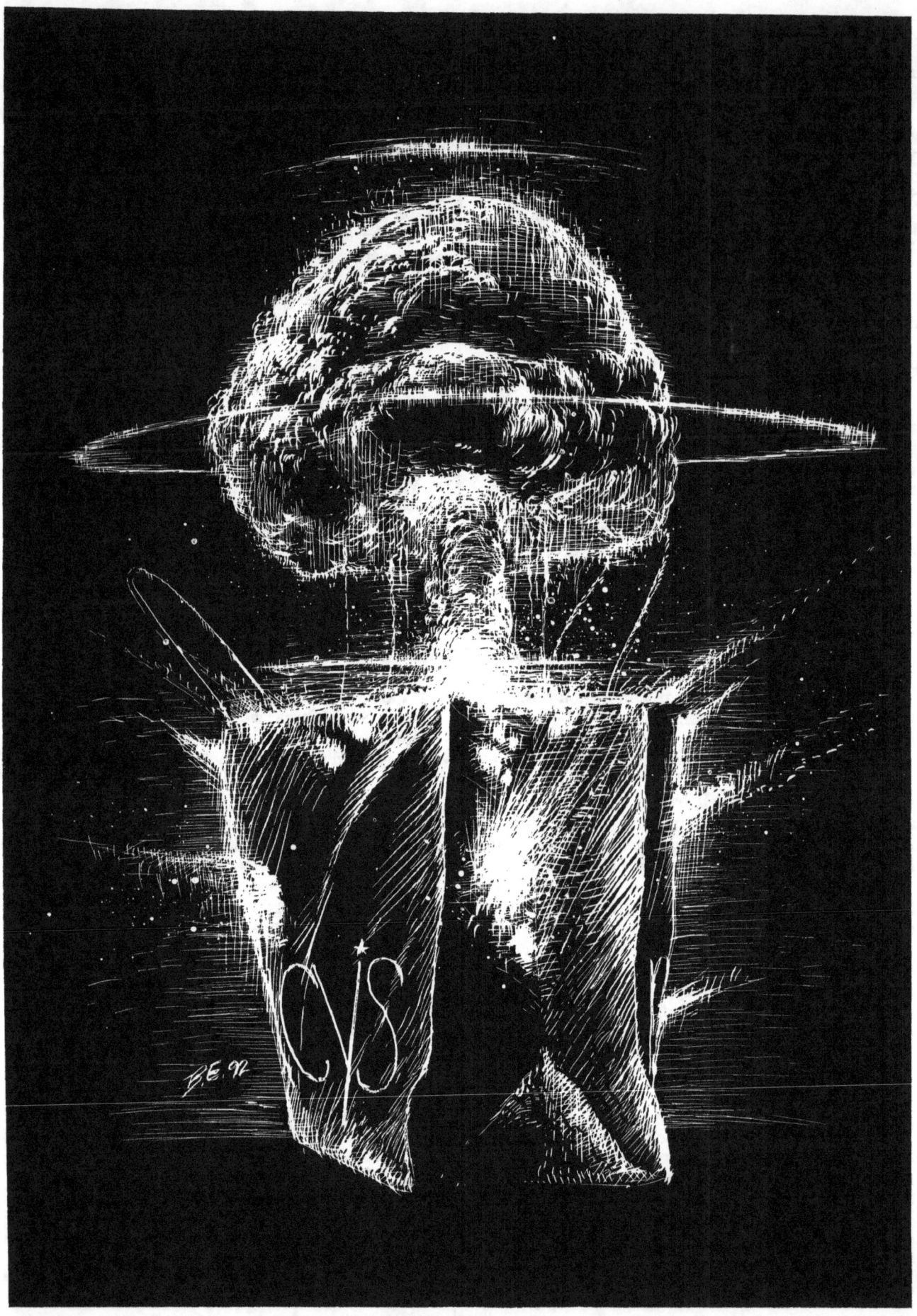

I heard hoofbeats from far away, getting louder. Not so soon! I yelled silently, miserably.

I saw Branwen turn to face Apollo again. I could sense a fierce Celtic blaze in that sturdy, plump little body, standing in the light of heroes, there by the cash register. You started to see things that way after you'd been on the Project for a while.

"Don't get hurt," I said to her. "It won't be long now." She didn't hear me. "I'll stop it," I said, and she didn't hear that either.

I looked around and saw the wolf padding quietly to the big wooden door over at the left wall. **EXIT**, it said. The wolf looked at me. Loki had a wolf for a son.

I hoped old friendships still had meaning. I followed the wolf to the door and pushed it open. An alarm sounded somewhere down the stairwell, but security had enough to deal with. I went up. One flight, two, past the employee floors to a steel door bolted on the inside. I was alone in this one, I thought. That's what I'd wanted, way back at the beginning.

Branny and I, we were two of the people who didn't go to Harvard or Wharton for our MBAs. Two of the women who didn't try to be good team players in American industry while raising healthy children and dressing above our budget. It was more than possible that there was something wrong with us. I'd known I would miss Branny terribly during the month off — that was why I'd wanted to be apart.

I opened the door.

President Kelliher was waiting for me when I got to the meeting place in Virginia. Point for him, I thought, he wasn't one of those pretentious types who made visitors sit outside to show them their place. He offered me tea from a silver tea service by his chair. My favorite blend, Russian Caravan, not the sort it was likely he would use by accident. Another point for him.

He congratulated me on my accurate record as an Oracle. I thanked him. We chatted a minute or two about this and that, then he said, "Tell me, do you already know what my question is?"

"No, Mr. President."

"Can't you find out?" He sounded genuinely interested.

"It seems that the question has to be asked," I said. "I think it's a matter of form."

"You know," he smiled charmingly, "there was another Oracle they offered me. But he said he got his answers directly from Allah, the all-merciful, and he wasn't *quite* what I had in mind."

"Mr. Korba," I said. "I know him."

"You don't get your answers from Allah, do you? They tell me you're more of a Norse persuasion."

I sipped my tea. This was an area I was a bit shaky on myself. "I do prefer the Norse gods, Mr. President. But it's rather like a hobby. I don't know who gives my answers, to tell you the truth. It could be the Greek gods. It could be my subconscious. It could be the Devil, for all I know."

He smiled. "But you have a fine record of accuracy, and that's what I need."

I made a motion like a shrug.

He leaned forward. "Things are happening right now that have some of us worried. We've gotten into some difficulties with a foreign power that we can't seem to get out of."

It sounded dull to me.

He said, "Tell me, what would be the result if we made a nuclear first strike?"

I sat up straight, eyes widened. I must have dropped the teacup. My stomach rolled nauseously, and I thought I was going to throw up then and there, but what came out was the room-filling voice I'd heard before: "A GREAT VICTORY WILL BE WON."

It took the breath out of me, and I fell back in the armchair. "Jesus!" I said, in my own voice. I stared at him.

He was totally unfazed. "I have more questions, if you don't mind."

"He's gone," I said.

Unlike the Project testers, he didn't ask for an explanation. "I suppose the answer can stand on its own," he said.

"Listen," I said to him, "that phrase — 'a great victory will be won.' That's from an old story."

He looked politely interested, personally uninterested. I spoke quickly. "An old king went to one of the Greek oracles — I don't remember which one — and he asked what would happen if he went to war on another king. And the oracle said, 'A great victory will be won.' So he went to war, lost, and was killed. A great victory was won, you see, but it was by the other side."

To my surprise he said, "Yes, I've heard the story."

I stared at him. "Then you won't take any action based on it."

He sat back in the chair, looking thoughtful. Not seriously thoughtful, just debating whether to share his thoughts with me. Finally he said, "You see — when it comes to a nuclear first strike, it's only possible for one side to have 'a great victory.' Logically, it would be too late for the nation fired upon. The only question that could arise is whether it would be one side or none."

"None!" I said, sitting back. I grasped my old purse firmly.

He said, gently, "But that's not what you said."

I opened the door.

The winds of early Ragnarok blew over the roof.

The Snake, whose name was Ouroboros, twisted and turned.

I looked across the Hudson to the factories, the highways, the palisades of the Jersey side; I imagined the empty motels further south. Pack up your cars, people; hard times are ahead for us all.

A great victory will be won, but not by us humans.

I'd given up the few days left with Branwen, but as I looked to the east and saw the sky turn orange I knew I hadn't punished myself nearly enough yet.

And so I jumped. I don't know if the Snake will die with me or not.   Ω

WEIRD TALES TALKS WITH IAN WATSON
by Darrell Schweitzer

Weird Tales: In a recent essay, you celebrated the mythic whole of science fiction — of the entire field as apart from individual works — and yet you seem to be writing more fantasy of late. "Stalin's Teardrops" in *Weird Tales*® #299 being a celebrated example. Why is this? Has your perspective changed, that now you find mythic power in fantasy instead?

Watson: What I'm basically trying to do is write across the whole spectrum, from hard science fiction to fantasy to horror. I did write three horror novels, one after another, within the last few years. People then started asking me, "Have you quit science fiction? Have you gone into the horror field?" That's not really true, because my most recent novel, published in England, *The Flies of Memory,* is a fairly hard science fiction novel, featuring aliens who are pursuing the Renaissance art of memory, which might not seem very hard as science. Nevertheless, the motivation and spirit of the book is realistic, hard SF: a journey to Mars, spacecraft, and so forth.

And I think that the novel I am going to be writing next, which I'm just beginning to visualize, is again going to be a science-fiction novel. It'll have mythic roots to it. I'm going to try and draw on the mythopoeic potential underlying science fiction, but it'll be science fiction. Strange impulses come over me from time to time. Short stories often emerge when I discover some bizarre quirk out of the corner of my eye and intensify it. I think this is best expressed in fantasy.

It's good that you mentioned "Stalin's Teardrops." It seems like fantasy, but again, I tend to approach things in a rational way. What might result is bizarrity, but there is heavy rationality and research in "Stalin's Teardrops." For example, the business about the cartography. This is hard SF, really. Cartography is a science. Then I just turn it upside down in that story. I look at how cartography is supposed to be pursued. You're supposed to do maps right. I visualize a situation where you are deliberately falsifying them and getting them wrong, exactly as the K.G.B. did. I also did a bit of research into what the inside of the K.G.B. headquarters is like. So this is realistic description.

Now, the stuff about eggs in Part Three, this too is based on my discovering something about the wonderful subworld of egg-crafting, which happened entirely by accident. I was driving home from a writing workshop held in Derbyshire, and we stopped in a hotel in the middle of nowhere. It turned out there was a craft fair going on. There were all these eggers holding their convention. They had their egg fanzines and all else. This got my

fantasy node ringing, and this joined up with the warped realism of the cartography, and the Russian fairy-tale aspect started welling up like oil welling up through sand or through shale. I agree the result is a fantasy story, with ectoplasm coming out of people's vaginas and people being swallowed up by giant eggs; but thereby I thought I was able to deal with something that was *of* the real world, the whole *glasnost* problem of how the old Stalinists are going to adjust to reality and the kind of sadness which a lot of them must feel. I was just watching on television this morning a story of the Russians and how there are still strong Marxist-Leninist tendencies residing in the Soviet bosom. Something has been lost in a sense, mythically. The whole spy-story milieu of Len Deighton and John Le Carré — how can you pursue this now that the Berlin Wall has fallen down? So I was dealing in "Stalin's Teardrops" with political realities, and I was starting from a realistic base, but the whole thing became twisted and strange, largely because the realities of the world had become so out of kilter with what our expectations were, say five years ago. The result is fantasy, but the initial impulse is savage realism, in a sense.

WT: We could see this as a form of satire. What you're basically saying is, "The world would make more sense if it were like *this.*"

Watson: Or I'm saying that the world actually is like this, just underneath the wallpaper, underneath the surface. It still maintains the pretense of being the familiar realistic, naturalistic world that we've been taught to perceive. Whereas, if you just pull off the wallpaper, underneath there are all these peculiar and essentially mythopoeic impulses. What is nationalism, which is welling up across eastern Europe, but a kind of mythopoeic nonsense? It's a romantic irrationality. This is going to overthrow the kind of neat, bureaucratic paradigms that have been operating for the last forty years. This might not necessarily be a good idea at all. It's going to lead to chaos and be an upwelling of the irrational and the anarchic. But this is what is going on in people's hearts. So perhaps, as it is irrational and anarchic, it is better to approach this in the fantasy spirit than mistakenly adopt realistic tools, which will not be quite true to the emotions that are possessing people among Hungarian minorities and Romanian nationalists, Croatians, Slovenes, and so on. There is a breakdown of what you might call consensus, bureaucratic realism across Europe. I think it is truer to look at this in a bizarre, fantastic, fairy-tale mode; because this will incarnate a truth which perhaps the newspaper stories and the realistic political analysis will not do justice to.

WT: Do you think that science fiction is primarily a form of realism?

Watson: The spirit of science fiction is primarily realistic. It's rationalistic in the sense that in science fiction we presuppose the rational structure of the universe according to the laws of physics as we understand them. These are the basic groundroots, that the universe has rules and that it is a rational construct, that underlying mathematical laws rule structures. Whereas, in fantasy, the rules of reality are magical.

I like to mix the two things up a little bit, mix the magic and the realism together. For example, in *Flies of Memory*, the aliens have a realistic biology. They come from a realistic star system. But the underlying philosophy of their lives is akin to Renaissance occultism.

I think that some of the most fertile things in science fiction, or the things that I can most fruitfully pursue, are where we have an intersection between the magic-impulse and the realism-impulse. The underlying roots of fantasy are magical. The underlying roots of science fiction are your basic, rational spirit. You can detect this, just as you can detect the difference between lemonade and beer, just by reading a sample paragraph from a fantasy novel and a science-fiction novel. It's difficult to describe, but there is the rational spirit, and the irrational spirit. I tend to be a kind of mystical rationalist.

At heart I am rational and skeptical, but I am extraordinarily interested in the whole gamut from shamanism to Renaissance occultism. I'm trying for a fusion of the two. I've been doing it for a long time, in a way. If you look at a novel of mine from 1979, *God's World*, there we have shamanism and space travel intersecting, with a journey to a realistically-envisaged alien planet which nevertheless represents metaphorically the thought-structures underlying shamanism. These are deep things in the human heart.

WT: Where does the author's own belief or disbelief figure in this? My own feeling is that skepticism is healthy for the fantasy author, because it enables you to make artistic rather than doctrinaire decisions about the content of the story.

Watson: I will auto-hallucinate myself into a belief-system if I'm writing a book involving Tibetan Buddhism or shamanism or Renaissance occultism. Then I take that for a while as my given belief-structure. But underneath I have the rational monitor surveying what is going on in my mind. Belief is always going to be subordinate to generating emotionally and intellectually meaningful narrative. So, I have impulses toward believing certain things, but I have a very strong reluctance to submit to belief. *God's World* has got a lot of Sufism in it. One of the main things in Sufism is that you've got to be willing to submit to a master, a guide. I could never do that myself. I would never give up my own independent

viewpoint. An artist has got to maintain the independent, high position, where he does not submit to a particular belief-structure, but rather employs that belief-structure as a way of illuminating human desires and fears, anxieties and hopes. I can't myself understand people who have a dominating point of view, which they will propagandistically employ in books.

WT: Like C.S. Lewis?

Watson: Yes. That's what goes wrong with the C.S. Lewis trilogy. I read it on two levels. The first volume, *Out of the Silent Planet*, is a good science-fiction novel, so it seems. Volume Two, *Perelandra*, is in fact very closely related to C.S. Lewis's *Preface to Paradise Lost*, which is a short book he wrote putting forth his own Christian view of *Paradise Lost*, and arguing against the William-Blake/Romantic notion that the Devil is the real hero of *Paradise Lost*. If you read these things, *Perelandra* and *Preface to Paradise Lost*, you'll see that one is the fictional version of the other. And fortunately, he's got that structure in the second book. There's a kind of literary-critical argument in the second book, although not many people have noticed this. But then Volume Three becomes Disneyland. It just bogs down and there we have the naked stupidity of the underlying beliefs revealed.

I could not talk to Lewis himself. If I had to talk to him, were he alive, I would have been thinking that he must have felt an underlying skepticism towards the belief-structures he was employing, whereas the whole tenor of his life was diametrically opposed to this.

I do have attitudes, beliefs, political ones myself, but I very much dislike fanaticism which goes with full, total acceptance of any creed. I find it hard, myself, to come to terms with artists who have a creed without skepticism, a creed without irony. Irony is extremely important. It is the sanity-governor.

WT: There are those who argue that rationalism is itself a creed, that you must accept on faith that your senses are reporting to you correctly.

Watson: I don't all the time. I distrust what I see, what I experience a lot of the time. Inevitably, you must interpret what you see, even if you're very familiar with the environment that you're in. I *like* to creatively misinterpret things, so that seventy-five percent of what I perceive of the world is true and twenty-five percent is imaginative hallucination. I'm aware of this and I use it.

WT: Have you any interest in or felt any attraction to the South American Magic Realist school of fantasy?

Watson: As somebody said, Magic Realism is the Spanish for fantasy. I've read very, very few of them. I've got some strange holes in my reading. Everybody is better read than I am. Though I did read a lot of Borges. I look at these magical-realist novels and think, yes, they will be fascinating and interesting, and I feel in a sense that I understand them without having read them. Now that sounds a bit arrogant. What I mean is that I've somehow missed out on them and perhaps I'd prefer to miss out on them because I might become drawn imitatively into their orbit if I did start reading them. Perhaps I am trying to invent my own form of magic realism. Sometimes it's better not to read things that might act as an influence on you.

WT: At the same time, isn't it often useful to read these things in order to learn from them? Not in the imitative sense, but to understand how the other writers achieve an effect. For instance, most of us have probably lifted something from Borges over the years. So, is it better for the writer to remain pristine from influences, or to wander around looking for gems other people have left unguarded on the floor?

Watson: I'd rather find a marginal gem, one that is on the floor unnoticed. Possibly too many people have noticed the magical-realist gang. Therefore I sort of sense that I wouldn't be making a discovery for myself. I'd be making somebody else's discovery. I do read science fiction, fantasy, whatever else, in order to see what the other people are doing, in a sense of examining the structures of books. I always think structurally when I'm reading a novel. I'm going through a kind of quality-control routine, which does feed back into my own books. I tend, when I'm reading, to observe balance and underlying structure and patterns.

I think in a kind of socio-anthropological way, the Lévi-Strauss kind of way. What I am seeing, usually, is the mapping of codes of behavior, dress-codes, food-codes, behavioral codes, the whole kind of mapping outward from a person's underlying belief structure into their ways of behavior. When I read any novel, I'm seeing it as a kind of network of structures. I examine that network of structures to see if it is a sound one that is internally consistent, if it is sound and beautiful like an equation. I tend to map books that I admire onto the books that I am doing, to see if I am producing something which is structurally beautiful — or reasonably beautiful — and coherent. It is in that sense that books act as an influence on me, rather than their particular content or literary techniques.

WT: Have you ever found something in a book which you felt was really good, but that the author botched it, to the extent that you felt like writing your own version to argue back and do it right?

Watson: Well, not botched, but didn't carry all the way. I did discover David Lindsay's *A Voyage to Arcturus* at a very early age, when I was a school kid. I've read it lots and lots of times. I did want to write a sequel to that particular book, to carry on the kind of argument in it and broaden it and expand it. This book had a great effect on me. Here have something which is superficially a science-fiction novel in which we've got an alien planet with lots of intersecting ecosystems. Yet it's also a metaphysical journey through different states of mind, in which you examine differing philosophies of life in each section, and embody these by growing special organs of

perception, and then abolish and eradicate these and decide these are wrong and sweep them away at the end of each chapter. It's a marvelously spendthrift book, throwing away whole philosophies of life every ten pages. Ultimately it comes down to a very harsh and bitter philosophy of pain, the acceptance and inducement of pain in order to prevent us from succumbing to sensual illusion and losing out on spiritual purity. I felt there was a vast amount more to this book. I wanted to write a sequel to it, taking the protagonist further and exploring the inter-relationships between pain and belief structures. I did float this notion with Gollancz, because they're the copyright-holders. I wrote a couple of chapters of *Arcturus*. These ended up being published in *Foundation,* or bits of them did. I wrote an article about how one should extend *A Voyage to Arcturus*. But Gollancz decided that I wasn't true to the spirit of Lindsay, which was, according to them, lush, sensual, pictorial, and that kind of thing. Their argument was that I was more philosophically-oriented. I think this is a load of garbage and a misunderstanding of the nature of *A Voyage to Arcturus*.

That was one book that I wanted to enter into dialogue with, and argue with the author, and take things further. I would act as the antithesis and the synthesis of David Lindsay's thesis. I've still got a hankering to do this in some decade or other.

WT: Did you also find yourself impatient with Lindsay as a stylist and sometimes want to rephrase what he said better?

Watson: No. I don't mind the fact that he was a bit clunky, because there was a kind of crude, harsh vigor throughout the book. This is part of the underlying philosophy, the stamping brutality of Krag mirrored almost in the style. It's lurid and clunky at times, but it's awfully effective and I think it ought to be lurid and clunky. It's not a clunk in the way that an ill-written pulp book is. It has a kind of pre-literate grandeur almost. It's the clunkiness of some medieval, pre-consciously-literary writing, but nevertheless produced in this century. So I would defend its style to the death.

WT: So what we have here is an example of naive art. The other example I can think of is William Hope Hodgson, with the exception of *The Night Land,* which I think is a gross blunder.

Watson: I know who Hodgson is, but I haven't read him. This is another yawning chasm in my reading.

WT: What do you make of the argument that Samuel R. Delany put forward some years ago that there is no such thing as content, that the style of a book *is* the book?

Watson: Well Chip is very unusual in that he is writing books that are simultaneously gloriously and rampantly fictional, and yet simultaneously they are academically critical within the same sentence. Now somebody was saying on one of the panels here [at Phrolicon, July 26–28, 1991] that you can't possibly write a book as fiction and operate as a critic simultaneously in regard to that book. But Delany *does.* He's working on a level where he is a structuralist sage and semiotician, while simultaneously he is pursuing a space-opera adventure or sword-and-sorcery adventure. These two things are totally interfused and operate to propel each other onward and develop each other. So you could expect Chip Delany to say that. He's almost unique in being able to pull this trick off, where the book is at once a story but is at the same time a semiotic construct, and he is aware of both impulses, and is writing with the left hand of action and the right hand of post-structuralism.

WT: Do you personally have any use for post-structuralism? I should think that it is the antithesis of most deliberate literature, since it holds that the author doesn't really write the text. This would seem to be sour grapes from academics who *can't* write fiction, and so they are trying to convince themselves that novelists don't either.

Watson: This is a marvelous trick, whereby the fruits of the author can be stolen from the author in such a way that the author cannot even complain. On the other hand, I am very interested in meta-fiction, in books which generate themselves. This is a tradition which goes back to *Tristram Shandy*, really, the auto-constructing book, as opposed to the innocent unrolling of narrative. The kind of books that the French *Nouveau Roman* were into, Robbe-Grillet and the like. They were operating in this mode also. I think it goes back to Flaubert, basically, because he was very concerned with writing a book which could support itself by style alone, that its own interior connections should be the motive force for the book. Ultimately, while post-structuralism has become very arid, I think it comes out of Romantic roots. Back in the Romantic period, artists were beginning to analyze the nature of their own creativity and trying to get at the wellsprings of creation within themselves and direct the channels, rather than writing innocently.

Now this failure of innocence has become arid in the post-structuralist debate, but it can be recuperated and turned into an engine of narrative power. I think the authors can grab this stuff back again from the *lecteur*. They can become *lecteur* at the same time they are *auteur*, in exactly the same way that Delany does. He operates as both of these creatures, fused together like a Siamese twin.

WT: First any author will have to dispense with most of the post-structuralist jargon, lest he become unreadable.

Watson: The whole thing is jargon-prone. Part of the problem there is that it is academically kosher because the more jargon that is involved, the more substantial this particular ghostly fabric appears to be. It's like fundamental particles. The more cloud chambers you look into, the more pions and mesons you are able to list, then seemingly the greater your understanding of the nature of reality. But ultimately this starts to collapse from sheer complexity, and you come back to old quark soup again.

I think you can fight your way through the structuralist stuff and get back to the basic quarks, the charm and strangeness of literature.

WT: Let's talk about your horror novels. Most American readers haven't read them, so could you describe them somewhat?

Watson: You haven't read them because none of them have been published in America, and the reason is, as I understand, the political content of these books. The first one, *The Power*, is about American nuclear bases in Great Britain, a nuclear war, ancient evil — or a new interpretation of evil.

The idea has been hanging around that it might be a good idea for evil to start a nuclear war and then just let the demons out of the closet. Basically, evil, if there is such a force, can only operate if there is a human race around to be unpleasant to. If you wipe out life on this planet, then evil gets wiped out as well. Unfortunately evil can only operate within the language of evil. So what happens in this novel is that there is a global nuclear war — whether by accident or design, this is not gone into — and evil retains a particular village in Britain in order to prevent all life from being wiped out, and to prevent evil from being extinguished too. It is preserving humankind, or a little bit of it, yet can only do so within the terms of evil. So it is fairly unpleasant for those who are the survivors.

The Power is a black comedy as well. The impulses to this book came partly because I moved out of the city and went to live in the British countryside among the sheep and cows. As soon as you do that, you begin to notice bits of World War Three hiding behind every bush and cow. I also got quite drawn into rural life. I became secretary of our local village hall and organized village fêtes and all sorts of absurd events. In a sense *The Power* is a way of compensating myself for the amount of work I had to put into our local community. I had some bizarre fun as a pay-back. The book has been published in Germany, but I had a letter from an American editor who said this was one of the very best horror novels of recent years and a book he wished he had written himself. Yet he just couldn't publish it because of its left-wing political content. Its heroes would be about as popular as Black Panthers. That was the reaction in general to it.

Apropos of this, Peter Lamborn Wilson lambasted me recently in *Science Fiction Eye* for rampant homophobia, particularly in my novel *The Fire Worm*, which we will get on to in a minute. Peter Wilson was raving that all horror is essentially counter-radical by definition. This peeved me because all three horror novels I did were definitely imbued with radical political spirit.

I followed *The Power* up with a novel about the Animal Liberation movement, again set in rural Britain, called *Meat*. This has been translated into Spanish, but again there is no U.S. edition. In retrospect, I think I was leading up in these two novels to what I think is my best horror novel, *The Fire Worm*, which is an intersection of science fiction and horror; the science in this particular case being largely medieval alchemy. (But I classify that as being within the ambit of science.) That novel is my *Roots,* really. It's the first time I have been able to write about the landscape of my childhood, which was to me at the time profoundly boring and depressing — northern England in the 1950s. Small wonder that I looked at the stars as an escape route and pursued the science-fiction path.

Speaking the language of horror, which turns a kind of searchlight upon the ordinary world and renders its banalities luminous and meaningful, albeit in a horrifying fashion, I was able to come to terms with the environment of my own upbringing. Not that I was particularly into buggery or was buggered myself, but that book acts as a kind of exorcism of my own deep past, as well as steering back towards science fiction by intersecting the traditional horror monster-in-the-cave with a medieval alchemical experiment which goes askew, a kind of medieval Chernobyl.

That's what the three horror novels are, and since then I have returned to the kind of thing I was writing at the beginning, in my earliest novels like *The Embedding,* towards an alien-world, but nevertheless philosophically-underpinned science-fiction adventure.

WT: So, you being a rationalist all the way through, what is the essential difference between your horror novels and your science fiction? Is it just a matter of tone?

Watson: Tone, yes, and also the particular conventions I was manipulating. A lot of my short stories have been horror stories. It depends on how you analyze them. They can be satires or fantasies or equally well be classed as horror. The novels have got an underlying web of ideas. In a science-fiction novel, this may be a web of ideas about linguistics and alien creatures. In a horror novel I'm dealing with, for example, a redefinition of evil, if evil should exist as a kind of entity, or examining the ethics of animal liberation and of meat eating, the motivations and beliefs of people who are into this. *The Fire Worm* involves the AIDS plague. This is what Peter Wilson was having a bash at me for, saying I was scare-mongering. I was really exploring *dread* there. I was writing about a contemporary phenomenon, yet I was also looking at the nature of dread, plus looking at the pre-science belief structures of alchemy.

I was also recreating, not just the landscape of my childhood, but also the 19th century prehistory of the same place.

There's a little constellation of ideas that belong in each book. In the horror ones the stars are a different color, but nevertheless they are stars. I see my books as part of a spectrum of continuous light. Horror is the black end — all good spectrums should have black at one end, beyond the ultraviolet — and from the black and ultraviolet of horror you pass through the pastoral shades of fantasy into the brighter actinic reality of realism and science fiction. They're part of a spectrum to me rather than being entirely separate modes.

WT: To backtrack a bit, how about something more about your background and what brought you into writing?

Watson: I wanted to be a writer from an early age. What would I write about? That was the problem. I had an impulse to be a scientist, a chemist; however I wasn't very good at the practical aspects of science. I also had romantic desires of being the Indiana Jones of the cactus world, off collecting cacti in the Arizona desert. What I ended up being pulled toward was literature. I read English Literature at Oxford.

Now, science fiction is pretty marginal in British cultural terms, so I tended schizophrenically to be reading van Vogt with one hand and the correct books with the other. Initially, I wanted to be a writer, though I was going to write Serious Literature, and I thought that science fiction was not the sort of thing that one ought to be writing.

I got propelled into science fiction out of necessity. After graduating from Oxford, I went to lecture in a university in East Africa, and there I discovered the politics of the Third World, global politics, plus alternative worldviews. This is enormously important as a stimulus toward writing science fiction, since if you're going to write about aliens on other planets it is as well to be aware of the alternative societies which still exist to some extent on our own world, and which existed much more strongly in the past. We tended to sneer and homogenize those. What actually forced me to write science fiction was the experience of working subsequently as a lecturer for three years in central Tokyo, which was the 21st century come true, all the techno-fun aspects of the 21st century and also all the ecological doom-horror. I started writing science fiction as a psychological survival mechanism.

WT: Did you start out by writing mainstream first?

Watson: I wrote three short novels. They were contemporary fantasy. That is, to say, they were set in the now-world, yet they did have very strong fantasy and bizarre streaks in them. But they were capricious in that there wasn't an underlying reason for writing them, other than the desire to construct a pretty artifact.

Basically, I need to have a motivation towards writing something. It's not just the act of writing itself, the Flaubertian art-for-art's-sake. I have to have art for the sake of opening the eyes of the reader, for the sake of opening my own eyes and reconstructing my mind and reconstructing the reader's mind.

I suppose I have a kind of didactic streak to me, plus a Protestant work ethic, which makes me write in a fairly disciplined way. I write every day, mornings only.

My particular writing methods are, in retrospect, absurd. I only went over to computers in the past fifteen months. Up until then I was typing. And I only type with one finger. I don't mean two fingers

— one on either hand — but *one* finger.

I realized how ridiculous this was when some guys visited to make a video of the writer at work. When I saw the video, I was horrified at the spectacle of this maniac sitting at the typewriter motionless apart from the one finger, which was racing from side to side of the keyboard. I can actually type faster than a professional typist, but all with one finger. You have no idea how crazy this looks.

So I crawled into the modern world of word-processing after a lot of Luddite obstructionism on my part. It's odd that a science-fiction writer and a rationalist could actually be a bit of an old-fashioned Luddite as regards word-processing. I'm overcoming this.

WT: But you wouldn't be willing to go back.

Watson: I would not be willing to go back. When I had to use a typewriter again, six months or so later, it was as if I was carving my words onto a stone wall with an axe. It was an incredibly clunky and violent experience. I wondered how I could have stood the vibrations for so many years.

WT: If you'd typed that way all your life, you'd have ended up with terrible arthritis in just that finger.

Watson: Or alternatively, a very short finger.

WT: Do you outline stories, write each one in a burst of inspiration, or what?

Watson: I've never outlined a story. Novels I did outline at the beginning, in a fair amount of detail, using card indexes and whatnot. The later novels I would tend to think about for a bit; then I would start writing them and just let the novel spontaneously and organically develop.

Stories themselves almost always develop spontaneously. I've never known when I started a story how it was going to end, or even what it was going to be like in the middle. I have the initial situation. The characters emerge fairly spontaneously and very soon, along with a particular cluster of concepts that I want to explore. I don't create characters to incarnate an idea, and I don't fish around for an idea to attach to a character. The two things come up in a kind of amorphous fusion and become gradually clearer as they interact. That's how stories work for me. Like a set of blobs that rise, as in a lava lamp, and gradually as they intersect through the course of the story they become clearer and reveal the necessary dynamic of that particular story to me.

WT: How much revision do you then do? Have you ever found that you've written yourself into a corner?

Watson: I've only written myself into a corner once. Well, it wasn't a corner. I had arrived at a precipice, really. That was in the story called "Cold Light," which is about a bishop who develops a halo. I got halfway through that and for the life of me I couldn't work out how to continue it. I had to leave that one aside for nine months. I talked to Mike Bishop about it and suggested that maybe we should collaborate on it as we did on *Under Heaven's Bridge*. We decided not to and nine months later I took the story out, and immediately it became transparently clear to me what should happen. I just continued the story through to the end. But that is unusual.

When I start a story, I'm going to finish it. I know that by now. I don't know how it's going to be possible to finish it, but I know that there will be a way, during the course of writing.

My first draft's a mess, badly-written and crazy and chaotic. Then I'll do a second draft, and the third draft is the finished one, usually.

WT: How market-oriented are you? Would you, for instance, continue to write a story which you thought a valid story, but which you really didn't think you would be able to sell?

Watson: I'd certainly continue it. I don't think that this particular story I'm writing is for *Weird Tales, Fantasy and Science Fiction, Interzone,* or whatever. I write the story and then I think which market it is best suited to. As I have so far sold all the stories that I have written, I therefore have this trusting faith that I'm going to sell the next one somewhere. It mightn't be the first market. It mightn't be the second, third, or fourth. But I'm going to sell it.

WT: Do you feel the impulse to switch between genres as the market fluctuates, writing horror when horror is hot, that sort of thing?

Watson: In market terms, my writing horror novels didn't benefit me particularly. There are flow-patterns in my consciousness. Those obey what is going on within myself, tectonic currents inside rather than the money-moon.

I'm conscious enough of the markets and I follow what is going on, but I don't think I would ever choose to write something just because it would fit into a niche, largely because it takes me a long time to write things. It might seem as though I write fairly fast, but that is not necessarily so. If I was pitching myself for what I thought was a particular golden slot that had opened, I'm pretty sure the slot would have closed by the time I had finished the book, let alone even submitted it. So, if we're talking about markets you've got to sense and produce the thing that does not yet exist. Then, if that particular thing coincides with a market need, that's beautiful.

WT: Thanks, Ian. Ω

THE COMING OF VERTUMNUS

by Ian Watson

illustrated by Stephen E. Fabian

for Hannah Shapero

Do you know the *Portrait of Jacopo Strada*, which Titian painted in 1567 or so?

Bathed in golden light, this painting shows us a rich connoisseur displaying a nude female statuette which is perhaps eighteen inches high. Oh yes, full-bearded Signor Strada is prosperous — in his black velvet doublet, his cerise satin shirt, and his ermine cloak. He holds that voluptuous little Venus well away from an unseen spectator. He gazes at that spectator almost shiftily. Strada is exposing his Venus to view, yet he's also withholding her proprietorially so as to whet the appetite.

With her feet supported on his open right hand, and her back resting across his left palm, the sculpted woman likewise leans away as if in complicity with Strada. How carefully his fingers wrap around her. One finger eclipses a breast. Another teases her neck. Not that her charms aren't on display. Her hands are held high, brushing her shoulders. Her big-navelled belly and mons veneris are on full show. A slight crossing of her knees hints at a helpless, lascivious reticence.

She arouses the desire to acquire and to handle her, a yearning that is at once an artistic and an erotic passion. Almost, she seems to be a homunculus — a tiny woman bred within an alchemist's vessel by the likes of a Paracelsus, who had died only some twenty-five years previously.

I chose this portrait of Jacopo Strada as the cover for my book, *Aesthetic Concupiscence*. My first chapter was devoted to an analysis of the implications of this particular painting. . . .

Jacopo Strada was an antiquary who spent many years in the employ of the Habsburg court, first at Vienna and then at Prague, as Keeper of Antiquities. He procured and catalogued gems and coins as well as classical statuary.

Coins were important to the Habsburg Holy Roman Emperors, because coins bore the portraits of monarchs. A collection of coins was a visible genealogy of God-anointed rulers. Back on Christmas Day in the year 800 the Pope had crowned Charlemagne as the first "Emperor of the Romans." The Church had decided it no longer quite had the clout to run Europe politically as well as spiritually. This imperial concoction — at times heroic, at other times hiccuping along — lasted until 1806. That was when the last Holy Roman Emperor, Francis II, abdicated without successor so as to thwart Napoleon from grabbing the title. By then, as they say, the Emperor presided over piecemeal acres which were neither an empire, nor Roman, nor holy. Of course, effectively the Habsburg dynasty had hijacked the title of Emperor, which was supposed to be elective.

History has tended to view the Habsburg court of Rudolph II at Prague in the late 1570s and '80s as wonky, wacky, and weird: an excellent watering hole for any passing nut-cases, such as alchemists, hermetic occultists, or astrologers — who of course, back then, were regarded as "scientists." Not that true science wasn't well represented, too! Revered astronomer Tycho Brahe burst his bladder with fatal result at Rudolph's court, due to that Emperor's eccentric insistence that no one might be excused from table till his Cæsarian Majesty had finished reveling.

Botanists were very busy classifying plants there, and naturalists were taxonomising exotic wildlife (of which many specimens graced Rudolph's zoo) — just as Strada himself tried to impose order and methodology upon ancient Venuses.

Strada resigned and quit Prague in 1579, perhaps in irritation that his aesthetic criteria held less sway over Rudolph than those of another adviser on the imperial art collection — namely *Giuseppe Arcimboldo*. . . .

My troubles began when I received a phone call at Central St Martin's School of Art in Charing Cross Road, where I lectured part-time in History of the Same. The caller was one John Lascelles. He introduced himself as the UK personal assistant to Thomas Rumbold Wright. Oil magnate and art collector, no less. Lascelles's voice had a youthfully engaging, though slightly prissy timbre.

Was I the Jill Donaldson who had written *Aesthetic Concupiscence*? I who had featured scintillatingly on *Art Debate at Eight* on Channel 4 TV? Mr Wright would very much like to meet me. He had a proposition to make. Might a car be sent for me, to whisk me the eighty-odd miles from London to the North Cotswolds?

What sort of proposition?

Across my mind there flashed a bizarre image of myself as a diminutive Venus sprawling in this oil billionaire's acquisitive, satin-shirted arms. For of course in my book I had cleverly put the stiletto-tipped boot into all such as he, who contributed to the obscene lunacy of art prices.

Maybe Thomas Rumbold Wright was seeking a peculiar form of recompense for my ego-puncturing stiletto stabs, since he — capricious bachelor — was certainly mentioned once in my book. . . .

"What sort of proposition?"

"I've no idea," said Lascelles, boyishly protesting innocence.

I waited. However, Lascelles was very good at silences, whereas I am not.

"Surely you must have *some* idea, Mr Lascelles?"

"Mr Wright will tell you, Ms Donaldson."

Why not? Why not indeed? I had always reveled in paradoxes, and it must be quite paradoxical — not to mention constituting a delicious piece of field work — for Jill Donaldson to accept an invitation from Thomas R. Wright, lavisher of untold millions upon old canvases.

One of my prime paradoxes — in my "Stratagems of Deceit" chapter — involved a comparison between the consumption of sensual fine art, and of visual pornography. I perpetrated an iconography of the latter based upon interviews I conducted with "glamour" photographers on the job. No, I *didn't* see it as my mission to deconstruct male-oriented sexism. Not a bit of it. That would be banal. I came to praise porn, not to bury it. Those sumptuous nudes in oils of yore were the buoyant, respectable porn of their day. What we needed nowadays, I enthused — tongue in cheek, several tongues in cheek indeed — were issues of *Penthouse* magazine entirely painted by latterday Masters, with tits by the Titians of today, vulvas by Veroneses, pubes by populist Poussins . . . Ha!

I was buying a little flat in upper Bloomsbury, with the assistance of Big Brother Robert who was a bank manager in Oxford. Plump sanctimonious Bob regarded this scrap of property as a good investment. Indeed, but for his support, I could hardly have coped. Crowded with books and prints, on which I squandered too much, Chez Donaldson was already distinctly cramped. I *could* hold a party in it — so long as I only invited a dozen people and we spilled on to the landing.

Even amidst slump and eco-puritanism, London property prices still bore a passing resemblance to Impressionist price-tags. Perhaps eco-puritanism actually *sustained* high prices, since it seemed that one ought to be penalised for wishing to live fairly centrally in a city, contributing to the sewage burden and resources and power demand of megalopolis, and whatnot.

Well, we were definitely into an era of radical repressiveness. The Eco bandwagon was rolling. Was one's lifestyle environmentally friendly, third-world friendly, future friendly? The no-smoking, no-car, no-red-meat, no-frilly-knickers, sackcloth-and-ashes straitjacket was tightening; and while I might have seemed to be on that side ethically as regards the conspicuous squandering of mega-millions on paintings, I simply did not buy the package. Perhaps the fact that I smoked cigarettes — oh penalised sin! — accounted in part for my antipathy to the Goody-Goodies. Hence my naughtiness in exalting (tongues in cheek) such a symptom of unreconstructed consciousness as porn. Paradox, paradox. I did like to *provoke*.

How many lovers had such a tearaway as myself had by the age of thirty-one? Just three, in fact; one of them another woman, a painting student.

Peter, Annie, and Phil. No one at the moment. I wasn't exactly outrageous in private life.

Peter had been the prankster, the mercurial one. For his "God of the Deep" exhibition he wired fish skeletons into the contours of bizarre Gothic cathedrals, which he displayed in tanks of water. Goldfish were the congregations — was this art, or a joke? Several less savoury anarchistic exploits finally disenchanted me with Peter — about the time I decided definitively that I really was an art historian and a critic (though of capricious spirit).

Sending a Mercedes, with darkened windows, to collect me could have wiped out my street cred. Personally, I regarded this as a *Happening*.

Mind you, I did experience a twinge of doubt — along the lines that maybe I ought to phone someone (Phil? Annie? Definitely not Peter . . .) to confide where I was being taken, just in case "something *happens* to me . . ." I didn't do so, yet the spice of supposed danger added a certain frisson.

When my doorbell rang, the radio was bemoaning the death of coral reefs, blanched leprous by the extinction of the symbiotic algae in them. This was sad, of course, *tragic*; yet I didn't intend to scourge myself personally, as the participants in the programme seemed to feel was appropriate.

The driver proved to be a Dutchman called Kees, pronounced Case, who "did things" for Rumby — as he referred to Thomas Rumbold Wright. Athletic-looking and bearded, courteous and affable, Case wore jeans, Reeboks, and an open-necked checked shirt. No uniform or peaked cap for this driver, who opened the front door of the Merc so that I should sit next to him companionably, not behind in splendid isolation. Case radiated the easy negligence of a cultured bodyguard-if-need-be. I was dressed in similar informal style, being determined not to doll myself up in awe for the grand encounter — though I refused to wear trainers with designer names on them.

Although Wright maintained a corporate headquarters in Texas, he personally favoured his European bastion, Bexford Hall. This had recently been extended by the addition of a mini-mock-Tudor castle wing to house his art in even higher security. The *Sunday Times* colour supplement had featured photos of this jail of art. (Did it come complete with a dungeon, I wondered?)

The mid-June weather was chilly and blustery — either typical British summer caprice or a Greenhouse spasm, depending on your ideology.

As we were heading out towards the motorway, we soon passed one of those hoardings featuring a giant poster of Arcimboldo's portrait of Rudolph II as an assembly of fruits, vegetables, and flowers. Ripe pear nose; flushed round cheeks of peach and apple; cherry and mulberry eyes; spiky chestnut husk of a chin; corn-ear brows, and so on, and so on.

The Emperor Rudolph as Vertumnus, Roman god of fruit trees, of growth and transformation. Who cared about that particular snippet of art historical info? Across the portrait's chest splashed the Eco message, *WE ARE ALL PART OF NATURE*. This was part of that massive and highly successful Green propaganda campaign exploiting Arcimboldo's "nature-heads" — a campaign which absolutely caught the eye in the most persuasive style.

These posters had been adorning Europe and America and wherever else for the best part of two years now. Indeed, they'd become such a radiant emblem of eco-consciousness, such a part of the mental landscape, that I doubted they would *ever* disappear from our streets. People even wore miniatures as badges — as though true humanity involved becoming a garlanded bundle of fruit and veg, with a cauliflower brain, perhaps.

Case slowed and stared at that hoarding.

"Rudolph the red-nosed," I commented.

Somewhat to my surprise, Case replied, "Ah, and

Rudolph loved Arcimboldo's jokes so much that he made him into a Count! Sense of humour's sadly missing these days, don't you think?"

My driver must have been boning up on his art history. The Green poster campaign was certainly accompanied by no background info about the artist whose images they were ripping off — or perhaps one ought to say "recuperating" for the present day . . . rather as an ad agency might exploit the Mona Lisa to promote tampons. (*Why is she smiling . . . ?*)

"Those paintings weren't *just* jokes," I demurred.

"No, and neither are those posters." Case seemed to loathe those, as though he would like to tear them all down. He speeded up, and soon we reached the motorway.

Under the driving mirror — where idiots used to hang woolly dice, and where nowadays people often hung plastic apples or pears, either sincerely or else in an attempt to immunise their vehicles against eco-vandals — there dangled a little model . . . of a rather complex-looking space station. The model was made of silver, or was at least silver-plated. It swung to and fro as we drove. At times, when I glanced that way, I confused rear-view mirror with model so that it appeared as if a gleaming futuristic craft was pursuing us up the M40, banking and yawing behind us.

Down where my left hand rested I found power-controls for the passenger seat. So I raised the leather throne — yes indeed, I was sitting on a dead animal's hide, and no wonder the windows were semi-opaque from outside. I lowered the seat and reclined it. I extruded and recessed the lumbar support. Now that I'd discovered this box of tricks, I just couldn't settle on the most restful position for myself. Supposing the seat had been inflexible, there'd have been no problem. Excessive tech, perhaps?

I felt fidgety. "Do you mind if I smoke?" I asked Case.

"Rumby smokes in this car," was his answer, which didn't quite confide his own personal feelings, unless the implication was that these were largely irrelevant amongst Wright's entourage.

Case ignored the 60-mile-an-hour fuel-efficiency speed limit, though he drove very safely in this cushioned tank of a car. He always kept an eye open well ahead and well behind as if conscious of possible interception, by a police patrol, or — who knows? — by Green vigilante kidnappers.

Bexford Hall was in the triangle between Stow-on-the-Wold, Broadway, and Winchcombe, set in a wooded river valley cutting through the rolling, breezy, sheep-grazed uplands.

The house was invisible from the leafy side road, being masked by the high, wire-tipped stone boundary wall in good repair, and then by trees. Case opened wrought iron gates electronically from the car — apparently the head gardener and family lived in the high-pitched gatehouse alongside — and we purred up a winding drive.

Lawns with topiary hedges fronted the mullion-windowed house. Built of soft golden limestone around a courtyard, Chez Wright somewhat resembled a civilian castle even before his addition of the bastioned, bastard-architectural art wing. A helicopter stood on a concrete apron. A Porsche, a Jaguar, and various lesser beasts were parked in a row on gravel. A satellite dish graced the rear slate-tiled roof, from which Tudor chimneys rose.

The sun blinked through, though clouds still scudded.

And so — catching a glimpse en route of several people at computer consoles, scrutinising what were probably oil prices — we passed through to John Lascelles's office, where the casual piles of glossy art books mainly caught my eye.

Having delivered me, Case left to "do things . . ."

Lascelles was tall, willowy, and melancholy. He favoured dark mauve corduroy trousers and a multi-pocketed purple shirt loaded with many pens, not to mention a clip-on walkie-talkie. On account of the ecclesiastical hues I imagined him as a sort of secular court chaplain to Wright. His smile was a pursed, wistful affair, though there was that boyish lilt to his voice which had misled me on the phone. His silences were the truer self.

He poured coffee for me from a percolator; then he radioed news of my arrival. It seemed that people communicated by personal radio in the house. In reply he received a crackly splutter of Texan which I hardly caught.

Lascelles sat and scrutinised me while I drank and smoked a cigarette; on his littered desk I'd noted an ashtray with a cheroot stub crushed in it.

Lascelles steepled his hands. He was cataloguing me: a new person collected — at least potentially — by his non-royal master, as he himself must once have been collected.

Woman. Thirty-one. Mesomorphic build; though not exactly chunky. Small high breasts. Tight curly brown hair cropped quite short. Violet vampiric lipstick. Passably callipygian ass.

Then in bustled *Rumby* — as I simply had to think of the man thereafter.

Rumby was a roly-poly fellow attired in crumpled bronze slacks and a floppy buff shirt with lots of pockets for pens, calculator, radio. He wore scruffy trainers, though I didn't suppose that he jogged around his estate. His white complexion said otherwise. His face was quizzically owlish, with large spectacles — frames of mottled amber — magnifying his eyes into brown orbs; and his thinning feathery hair was rebellious.

He beamed, almost tangibly projecting *energy*. He pressed my flesh quickly. He drew me along in his slipstream from Lascelles's office down a walnut-panelled corridor. We entered a marble-floored, domed hall which housed gleaming spotlit models. Some in perspex cases, others hanging. Not models of oil-rigs, oh no. Models of a Moon base, of spacecraft, of space stations.

Was Rumby a little boy at heart? Was this his den? Did he play with these toys?

"What do you think about space?" he asked me.

Mischief urged me to be contrary, yet I told him the truth.

"Personally," I assured him, "I think that if we cop out of space now, as looks highly likely, then we'll be locked up here on Mother Earth for ever after, eating a diet of beans and being repressively good with 'Keep off the Grass' signs everywhere. Oh dear, we mustn't mess up Mars by going there the way we messed up Earth! Mess up Mars, for Christ's sake? It's *dead* to start with — a desert of rust. I think if we can grab all those clean resources and free energy in space, we'd be crazy to hide in our shell instead. But there's neo-puritanism for you."

Rumby rubbed his hands. "And if Green propaganda loses us our launch window of the next fifty years or so, then we've lost forever because we'll have spent all our spunk. I knew you'd be *simpatico*, Jenny. I've read *Aesthetic Concubines* twice."

"*Concupiscence*, actually," I reminded him.

"Let's call it *Concubines*. That's easier to say."

Already my life and mind were being mutated by Rumby. . . .

"So how did you extrapolate my views on space from a book on the art market?" I asked.

He tapped his brow. "I picked up on your anti-repressive streak and the perverse way you think. Am I right?"

"Didn't you regard my book as a bit, well, rude?"

"I don't intend to take things personally when the future of the human race is at stake. It is, you know. It is. Green pressures are going to nix everyone's space budget. Do you know they're pressing to limit the number of rocket launches to a measly dozen per year *world-wide* because of the exhaust gases? And all those would have to be Earth-Resources-relevant. Loony-tune environmentalists! There's a *religious* fervour spreading like clap in a cathouse. It's screwing the world's brains." How colourfully he phrased things. Was he trying to throw me off balance? Maybe he was oblivious to other people's opinions. I gazed blandly at him.

"Jill," he confided, "I'm part of a pro-space pressure group of industrialists called The Star Club. We've commissioned surveys. Do you know, in one recent poll forty-five per cent of those questioned said that they'd happily give up quote all the benefits of 'science' if they could live in a more natural world without radioactivity? Can you believe such scuzzbrains? We *know* how fast this Eco gangrene is spreading. How do we disinfect it? Do we use rational scientific argument? You might as well reason with a hippo on heat."

"Actually, I don't see how this involves me. . . ."

"*We'll* need to use some tricks. So, come and view the Wright Collection."

He took me through a security-coded steel door into his climate-controlled sanctum of masterpieces.

Room after room. Rubens. Goya. Titian. And other lesser luminaries . . .

. . . till we came to the door of an inner sanctum.

I half expected to find the Mona Lisa herself within. But no . . .

On an easel sat . . . a totally pornographic, piscine portrait. A figure made of many fishes (along with a few crustaceans).

A female figure.

A spread-legged naked woman, red lobster dildo clutched in one octopus-hand, frigging herself. A slippery, slithery, lubricious Venus composed of eels and catfish and trout and a score of other species. Prawn labia, with legs and feelers as pubic hair . . . The long suckery fingers of her other octopus-hand teased a pearl nipple. . . .

The painting just had to be by Arcimboldo. It was very clever and, mm, persuasive. It also oozed lust and perversity.

"So how do you like her?" asked Rumby.

"That lobster's rather a nippy notion," I said.

"It isn't a lobster," he corrected me. "It's a cooked freshwater crayfish."

"She's, well, fairly destabilising if you happen to drool over all those 'We are part of Nature' posters."

"Right! And Arcimboldo painted a *dozen* such porn portraits for private consumption by crazy Emperor Rudolph."

"He *did?*" This was astonishing news.

"I've laid hands on them all, though they aren't all here."

Rumby directed me to a table where a portfolio lay. Opening this, I turned over a dozen large glossy colour reproductions — of masturbating men made of mushrooms and autumnal fruits, men with large hairy nuts and spurting seed; of licking lesbian ladies composed of marrows and lettuce leaves . . .

"You researched all the background bio on Strada, Jill. Nobody knows what sort of things our friend Archy might have been painting between 1576 and 1587 before he went back home to Milan, hmm?"

"I thought he was busy arranging festivals for Rudolph. Masques and tournaments and processions."

"That isn't *all* he was arranging. Rudy was fairly nutty."

"Oh, I don't know if that's quite fair to Rudolph . . ."

"What, to keep a chained lion in the hall? To sleep in a different bed every night? His mania for exotica! Esoterica! Erotica! A pushover for any passing magician. Bizarre foibles. Loopy as King Ludo of Bavaria — yet with *real* power. The power to indulge himself — secretly — in orgies and weird erotica, there in vast Ratzen Castle in Prague."

I wondered about the provenance of these hitherto unknown paintings.

To which, Rumby gave a very plausible answer.

When the Swedes under the command of von Wrangel sacked Prague in 1648 as their contribution to the Thirty Years War, they pillaged the imperial collections. Thus a sheaf of Arcimboldos ended up in Skoklosters Castle at Bålsta in Sweden.

"Skoklosters *Slott*. Kind of evocative name, huh?"

When Queen Christina converted to Catholicism in 1654 and abdicated the Swedish throne, she took many of those looted art treasures with her to Rome itself — with the exception of so-called *German* art, which she despised. In her eyes, Arcimboldo was part of German art.

However, in the view of her catechist (who was a subtle priest), those locked-away *porn* paintings were a different kettle of fish. The Vatican should take charge of those and keep them *sub rosa*. Painters were never fingered by the Inquisition, unlike authors of the written word. Bonfires of merely lewd material were never an issue in an era when clerics often liked a fuck. Nevertheless, such paintings might serve as a handy blackmail tool against Habsburg Emperors who felt tempted to act too leniently towards Protestants in their domains. A blot on the Habsburg scutcheon, suggesting a strain of lunacy.

The cardinal-diplomat to whom the paintings were consigned deposited them for safe keeping in the crypt at a certain enclosed convent of his patronage. There, as it happened, they remained until discovered by a private collector in the 1890s. By then the convent had fallen on hard times. Our collector relieved the holy mothers of the embarrassing secret heritage in return for a substantial donation. . . .

"It's a watertight story," concluded Rumby, blinking owlishly at me. "Of course it's also a complete lie. . . ."

The dirty dozen Arcimboldos were forgeries perpetrated in Holland within the past couple of years, to Rumby's specifications, by a would-be surrealist.

I stared at the fishy masturbatress, fascinated.

"They're fine forgeries," he enthused. "Painted on antique oak board precisely eleven millimetres thick. Two base layers of white lead, chalk, and charcoal slack . . ." He expatiated with the enthusiasm of a petrochemist conducting an assay of crude. The accuracy of the lipid and protein components. The pigments consisting of azurite, yellow lead, malachite . . . Mr Oil seemed to know rather a lot about such aspects of oil painting.

He waved his hand impatiently. "Point is, it'll stand up under X-ray, infra-red, most sorts of analysis. This is perfectionist forgery with serious money behind it. Oh yes, sponsored exhibition in Europe, book, prints, postcards, media scandal . . . ! These naughty Archeys are going to fuck all those Green Fascists in the eyeballs. Here's their patron saint with his pants down. Here's what red-nosed Rudy really got off on. Nobody'll be able to gaze dewy-eyed at those posters any more, drooling about the sanctity of nature. *This* is nature — red in dildo and labia. A fish-fuck. Their big image campaign will blow up in their faces — ludicrously, obscenely. Can you beat the power of an image? Why yes, you *can* — with an anti-image!

We'll have done something really positive to save the space budget. You'll write the intro to the art book, Jenny, in your inimitable style. Scholarly — but provocative."

"I will?"

"Yes, because I'll pay you three quarters of a million dollars."

A flea-bite to Rumby, really . . .

The budget for this whole escapade was probably ten times that. Or more. Would that represent the output of one single oil well for a year? A month . . . ? I really had no idea.

Aside from our crusade for space, smearing egg conspicuously on the face of the ecofreaks might materially assist Rumby's daily business and prove to be a sound investment, since he profited so handsomely by pumping out the planet's nonrenewable resources.

"*And* because you want to sock Green Fascism, Jill. And on account of how this is so splendidly, provocatively perverse."

Was he right, or was he right?

He was certainly different from the kind of man I'd expected to meet.

Obviously I mustn't spill the beans in the near future. *Consequently* the bulk of my fee would be held on deposit in my name in a Zurich bank, but would only become accessible to me five years after publication of *Arcimboldo Erotico*. . . .

Until then I would need to lead roughly the same life as usual — plus the need to defend my latest opus amongst my peers and on TV and in magazines and wherever else. Rumby — or Chaplain Lascelles — would certainly strive to ensure a media circus, if none such burgeoned of its own accord. I would be Rumby's front woman.

I liked the *three quarters* of a million aspect. This showed that Rumby had subtlety. One million would have been a blatant bribe.

I also liked Rumby himself.

I had indeed been collected.

And that 750K (as Brother Bob would count it) wasn't by any means the only consideration. *I approved.*

As to my fallback position, should the scheme be — ahem — rumbled . . . well, pranks question mundane reality in a revolutionary manner, don't they just?

That was a line from Peter, which I half believed — though not enough to stage a diversion in the National Gallery by stripping my blouse off, as he had wished, while Peter glued a distempery canine turd to Gainsborough's painting, *White Dogs*, so as to question "conventions." I'd balked at *that* proposed escapade of Peter's ten years previously.

This was a political prank — a blow against an insidious, powerful kind of repression; almost, even, a blow for art.

Thus, my defence.

I took a copy of the erotic portfolio back with me to Bloomsbury to gaze at for a few days; and to keep safely locked up when I wasn't looking at it.

Just as well that Phil wasn't involved in my immediate life these days, though we still saw each other casually. I'm sure Phil's antennae would have twitched if he had still been sleeping with a strangely furtive me. Being art critic for the *Sunday Times* had seemed to imbue him with the passions of an investigative journalist. Just as soon as *Arcimboldo Erotico* burst upon the scene, no doubt he would be in touch. . . . I would need to tell lies to a former lover and ensure that "in touch" remained a phrase without physical substance. Already I could envision his injured, acquisitive expression as he rebuked me for not leaking this great art scoop to him personally. ("But why not, Jill? Didn't we share a great deal? I must say I think it's damned queer that you didn't breathe a word about this! Very *peculiar*, in fact. It makes me positively *suspicious*. . . . This isn't some kind of *revenge* on your part, is it? But why, *why*?")

And what would Annie think? She was painting in Cornwall in a women's artistic commune, and her last letter had been friendly. . . . If I hadn't offended her with my porn paradoxes, then attaching my name to a glossy volume of fish-frigs and spurting phallic mushrooms oughtn't to make too much difference, unless she had become radically repressive of late. . . .

In other words, I was wondering to what extent this escapade would cause a hindwards reconstruction of my own life on account of the duplicity in which I'd be engaging.

And what about the *future* — in five years' time — when I passed **GO** and became three quarters of a dollar millionairess? What would I do with all that money? Decamp to Italy? Quit the London grime and buy a farmhouse near Florence?

In the meantime I wouldn't be able to confide the truth to any intimate friend. I wouldn't be able to afford intimacy. I might become some pursed-smile equivalent of Chaplain Lascelles, though on a longer leash.

Maybe Rumby had accurately calculated that he was getting a bargain.

To be sure, the shape of my immediate future all somewhat depended on the impact of the book, the exhibition, the extent of the hoo-ha . . . Personally, I'd give the book as much impact as I could. After all, I did like to provoke.

I returned to Bexford House a week later, to stay two nights and to sort through Rumby's stock of material about Arcimboldo, Rudolph, and the Prague Court. I have a good reading knowledge of German, French, and Italian, though I'm not conversationally fluent in those tongues. Any book I needed to take away with me was photocopied in its entirety by Lascelles on a high-speed, auto-page-turning machine. Pop in a book — within five

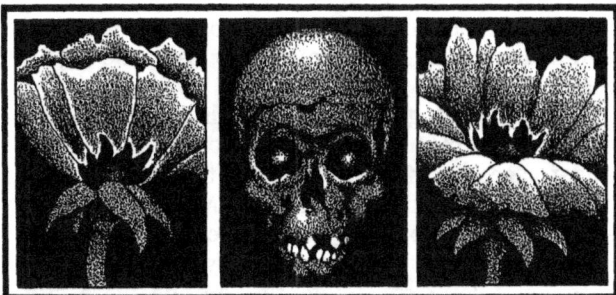

minutes out popped its twin, collated and bound. The machine cost twenty thousand dollars.

A week after that, Case drove me to the docklands airport for a rather lux commuter flight with him to Amsterdam, where I examined all the other Arcimboldo "originals"; although I didn't meet the forger himself, nor did I even learn his name. The paintings were stored in three locations: in the apartment of Rumby's chosen printer, Wim Van Ewyck, in that of the gallery owner who would host the show, Geert de Lugt, and in a locked room of the Galerij Bosch itself. In the event of premature catastrophe, the entire corpus of controversial work (minus the fishy masturbatress at Bexford House) wouldn't be wiped out en masse.

Presumably the printer didn't need to be in on the conspiracy. What about the gallery owner? Maybe; maybe not . . . *This*, as Case impressed on me, was a subject which shouldn't even be alluded to — nor did Mijnheer de Lugt so much as hint.

The other eleven Arcimboldos were even more stunning at full size in the frame than in colour reproduction. And also more . . . appalling?

I returned to Bloomsbury to write twenty large pages of introduction. Less would have been skimpy; more would have been excessive. Since I was being fastidiously attentive to every nuance of the text, the writing took me almost three weeks, with five or six drafts. ("Put some feeling into it," Rumby had counselled. "Smear some vaginal jelly on the words.")

The task done, I phoned Bexford Hall. Case drove the Merc to London the same evening to courier the pages personally. Next day, Rumby phoned to pronounce himself quite delighted. He only suggested a few micro-changes. We were rolling. Our exhibition would open in the Galerij Bosch on the first of September, coinciding with publication of the book.

And of course I must attend the private showing on the last day of August — the vernissage, as it were. (I did hope the varnish was totally dry!)

While in Amsterdam, our party — consisting of Rumby and Case and Lascelles and myself — stayed in the Grand Hotel Krasnopolsky because that hotel boasted a Japanese restaurant, and Rumby was a bit of a pig for raw fish. I wasn't complaining.

We arrived a day early in case Rumby had any last minute thoughts about the layout of the show, or Case about its security aspects. So the morning of the thirty-first saw us at the Galerij Bosch, which fronted a tree-lined canal not far from where dozens of antique shops clustered on the route to the big art museums.

The high neck gable of the building, ornamented with two bounteous sculpted classical maidens amidst cascades of fruits and vegetables — shades of Arcimboldo, indeed! — incorporated a hoisting beam, though I doubted that any crated paintings had entered the loft of the gallery by that particular route for a long time. Venetian blinds were currently blanking the three adjacent ground-floor windows — the uprights and transoms of which were backed by discreet steel bars, as Case pointed out; and already Mijnheer de Lugt, a tall blond man with a bulbous nose, had three muscular fellows lounging about in the large, spot-lit exhibition room. One in a demure blue security uniform — he was golden-skinned and moon-faced, obviously of Indonesian ancestry. The other chunky Germanic types wore light suits and trainers.

A high pile of copies of *Arcimboldo Erotico* stood in one corner for presentation that evening to the guests: the media people, museum directors, cultural mandarins and mavericks. Particularly the media people.

And my heart quailed.

Despite all the gloss, mightn't someone promptly denounce this exhibition? We were in liberal Holland, where the obscenity in itself would not offend. Yet wouldn't someone cry "Hoax!"?

Worse, mightn't some inspired avant-garde type perhaps enthusiastically *applaud* this exhibition as an ambitious jape?

de Lugt seemed a tad apprehensive beneath a suave exterior. He blew that snozzle of his a number of times without obvious reason, as though determined to be squeaky-clean.

"Ms Donaldson, would you sign a copy of the book for me as a souvenir?" he asked. When I had obliged, he scrutinised my signature as if the scrawly autograph might be a forgery.

Maybe I was simply being paranoid. But I was damn glad of this dry run amongst the exhibits.

Case conferred with the security trio quietly in Dutch. They smiled; they nodded.

The wet run that evening — lubricated by champagne to celebrate the resurrection of long-lost works of a bizarre master, and contemporary of Rabelais — went off quite as well as could be expected.

A young red-haired woman in a severe black cocktail dress walked out along with her escort in shock and rage. She had been wearing an Arcimboldo eco-badge as her only form of jewelry, with the word *Ark* printed upon it.

A fat bluff bearded fellow in a dinner jacket, with an enormous spotted cravat instead of bow tie, got drunk and began guffawing. Tears streamed down his hairy cheeks till Case discretely persuaded him to step outside for an airing.

Rumby was bombarded by questions, to which he would grin and reply, "It's all in the book. Take a copy!" One of the great art finds, yes. Casts quite a new light on Arcimboldo, that emotionally complex man.

So why had Mr Wright sprung this surprise on the art world by way of a private gallery? Rather than lending these paintings to some major public museum?

"Ah now, do you really suppose your big museum would have leapt at the chance of showing such *controversial* material, Ladies and Gentlemen? Some big city museum with its reputation to think about? Of course, I'll be perfectly delighted to loan this collection out in future. . . ."

I was quizzed too. Me, in my new purple velvet couturier pant-suit.

Geert de Lugt smiled and nodded approvingly, confidently. Naturally Rumby would have paid him handsomely for use of his gallery, yet I was becoming convinced that Mijnheer de Lugt himself was innocent of the deception. He had merely had stage nerves earlier.

We stayed in Amsterdam for another five days. Press and media duly obliged with publicity, and I appeared on Dutch and German TV, both with Rumby and without him. So many people flocked to the Galerij Bosch that our Security boys had to limit admittance to thirty people at any one time, while a couple of tolerant police hung about outside. Our book sold like hot cakes to the visitors; and by now it was in the bookshops too. ("At this rate," joked Rumby, "we'll be making a fucking *profit*.")

During spare hours, I wandered round town with Case. Rumby mainly stayed in his suite at the Krasnopolsky in phone and fax contact with Bexford and Texas, munching sushi. I nursed a fancy that Chaplain Lascelles might perhaps lugubriously be visiting the Red Light District to let his hair and his pants down, but he certainly wasn't getting high on any dope. Me, I preferred the flea-market on Waterlooplein, where I picked up a black lace shawl and a slightly frayed Khasmiri rug for the flat back in Bloomsbury.

I noticed a certain item of graffiti on numerous walls: *Onze Wereld is onze Ark*.

"Our world is our Ark," translated Case.

Sometimes there was only the word *Ark* on its own writ even larger in spray-paint. I couldn't but recall the badge worn by that pissed-off woman at the party in the gallery. Pissed-off? No . . . *mortally offended*. Obviously, Ark was a passionate, punning, mispronounced allusion to . . . who else but Emperor Rudolph's court jester?

When I mentioned this graffito to Rumby, he almost growled with glee.

"Ha! So what do you do in this fucking *ark* of theirs? You hide, anchored by gravity — till you've squandered all your major resources, then you can't get to anyplace else. Sucks to arks."

We all flew back to England on the Sunday. At

seven A.M. on the Monday morning the phone bullied me awake.

Lascelles was calling.

Late on the Sunday night, a van had mounted the pavement outside Galerij Bosch. The driver grabbed a waiting motorbike and sped off. Almost at once the van exploded devastating, demolishing the whole frontage of the building. As well as explosives, there'd been a hell of a lot of jellied petrol and phosphorus in that van. Fireworks, indeed! The gallery was engulfed in flames. So were part of the street and a couple of trees. Even the canal caught fire, and a nearby houseboat blazed, though the occupants had been called away by some ruse. The two security guards who were in the gallery on night shift died.

And of course all the Arcimboldos had been burnt, though that seemed a minor aspect to me right then. . . .

Case was coming pronto to pick me up. Rumby wanted us to talk face to face before the media swarmed.

Two hours later, I was at Bexford Hall.

Rumby, Lascelles, Case, and I met together in a book-lined upstairs study, furnished with buff leather armchairs upon a russet Persian carpet. The single large window, composed of stone mullions, seemed somewhat at odds with the Italianate plasterwork ceiling which featured scrolls and roses, with cherubs and putti supporting the boss of an electrified chandelier. Maybe Rumby had brought this ceiling in from some other house because it was the right size, and he liked it. The room smelled of cheroots, and soon of my Marlboro too.

"Let's dismiss the financial side right away," commenced Rumby. "The paintings weren't insured. So I'm not obliged to make any kind of claim. Hell, do I need to? The book will be the only record — and your fee stays secure, Jill. Now, is it to our disadvantage that the paintings themselves no longer exist? Might someone hint that we ourselves arranged the torching of the gallery before independent art experts could stick their fingers in the pie? I think two tragic deaths say no to that. Those poor guys had no chance. T. Rumbold Wright isn't known for assassinations. So, ghastly as this is, it could be to our advantage — especially if it smears the ecofreaks, the covenanters of the Ark."

What a slur on the ecofreaks that they might destroy newly discovered masterpieces of art for ideological reasons in a desperate effort to keep the artist pure for exploitation by themselves. When people saw any Arcimboldo badge or poster now, they might think, Ho-ho. . . . I was thinking about the two dead guards.

Lascelles had been liaising with Holland.

"The Dutch police are puzzled," he summarised. "Is this an outburst of art-terrorism? A few years ago some people revived a group called the SKG — so-called 'City Art Guerrillas' who caused street and gallery trouble. They never killed anyone. Even if

the couple on that houseboat were kept out of harm's way to make the attackers seem more benign, de Lugt's two guards were just slaughtered. . . .

"Then what about these Ark people? The loony fringe of the Dutch Eco movement have gone in for destructive industrial sabotage — but again, they haven't caused any deaths. This is more like the work of the German Red Column, though it seems they haven't operated in Holland recently. Why do so now? And why hit the gallery?"

"To hurt a noted Capitalist, in the only way they could think of?" asked Rumby. "No, I don't buy that. It's got to be the ecofreaks."

"The ecology movement is very respectable in Holland."

Rumby grinned wolfishly. "Mightn't be, soon."

"Ecology is government policy there."

How much more newsworthy the destruction made those naughty paintings! How convenient that they were now beyond the reach of skeptical specialists.

"I don't suppose," said I, "one of your allies in the Star Club might conceivably have arranged this attack?"

Drop a ton of lead into a pond.

"Future of the human race," I added weakly. "Big motivation."

Rumby wrestled a cheroot from his coat of many pockets and lit it. "You can forget that idea. Let's consider safety. Your safety, Jill."

I suppose he couldn't avoid making this sound like a threat, however benevolently intentioned — or making it seem as if he wished to keep my free spirit incommunicado during the crisis. . . .

"Someone has bombed and murdered ruthlessly," said Rumby. "I'm safe here."

"Yes, you are," Case assured him.

"But you, Jill, you live in some little scumbag flat in any old street in London. I'd like to invite you to stay here at Bexford for a week or two until things clarify."

"Actually, I can't," I told him, with silly stubbornness. "I have a couple of lectures to give at St Martin's on Thursday."

"Screw them. Cancel them."

"And it isn't exactly a scumbag flat."

"Sorry — you know what I mean."

"At least until there's a communiqué," Lascelles suggested to me. "Then we'll know what we're dealing with. It's only sensible."

"Don't be proud," said Rumby. He puffed. The cherubs above collected a tiny little bit more nicotine on their innocent hands. "Please."

And some more nicotine from me too.

"You don't need to feed some goddam cat, do you?" asked Rumby.

"No . . ." In fact I loathed cats — selfish, treacherous creatures — but Rumby probably wouldn't have cared one way or the other.

In the event, I stayed at Bexford. Until Wednesday afternoon. No news emerged from Holland of any communiqué.

Could the attackers not have *known* about those two guards inside the gallery? So now they were ashamed, and politically reluctant, to claim credit?

Unlikely. You don't assemble a vanload of explosives and napalm and phosphorus, make sure there's a getaway motorbike waiting, and bail out the occupants of a nearby houseboat, without checking everything else about the target too.

Lascelles was stone-walling queries from the media. ("Mr Wright is shocked. He grieves at the two deaths. He has no other comment at present. . . .") Stubbornly, I insisted on being driven back to Bloomsbury.

My little flat had been burgled. My CD player and my TV were missing.

Entry was by way of the fire escape door, which had been smashed off its none too sturdy hinges. Otherwise, there wasn't much damage or mess.

I hadn't wished Case to escort me upstairs; thus he had already driven away. Of course I *could* have reached him on the Merc's car phone. Yet this was so ordinary a burglary that I simply phoned the police. Then I thumbed the Yellow Pages for an emergency repair service which was willing to turn up within the next six hours.

The constable who visited me presently was a West Indian. A couple of other nearby flats had also been broken into the day before for electrical goods, so he said. Was I aware of this? He seemed to be pitching his questions towards eliciting whether I might perhaps have robbed myself so as to claim insurance.

"Fairly *neat* break-in, Miss, all things considered."

"Except for the door."

"You're lucky. Some people find excrement spread all over their homes."

"Did that happen in the other flats that were burgled?"

"Not on this occasion. So you reported this just as soon as you came back from — ?"

"From the Cotswolds."

"Nice part of the country, I hear. Were you there long?"

"Three days."

"Visiting friends?"

"My employer." Now why did I have to say *that*? Blurt, blurt.

"Oh, so you live here, but your boss is in the Cotswolds?"

"He isn't exactly my boss. He was consulting me."

The constable raised his eyebrow suggestively.

Obviously he believed in keeping the suspect off balance.

"You do have a lot of expensive books here, Miss," was his next tack.

Yes, rows of glossy art books. Why hadn't those been stolen — apart from the fact that they weighed a ton?

"I don't suppose the burglars were interested in art," I suggested.

He pulled out a *Botticelli* with library markings on the spine, from the shelf.

"This is from a college library," he observed.

"I teach there. I lecture about art."

"I thought you said you were a *consultant*. . . ."

By the time he left, he was half-convinced that I had burgled myself, that I habitually thieved from libraries, and that I was a call-girl who had been supplying sexual favours to Mr X out in the country. Would these suspicions be entered in the police computer? Did I have the energy to do anything about this? No, it was all so . . . tentative. Did I want to seem paranoid?

Bert the Builder finally turned up and fixed the door for a hundred and thirteen pounds . . . which of course the insurance would be covering. Otherwise the job would have cost just sixty, cash.

I did manage to look over my lecture notes — on Titian and Veronese. I microwaved a madras beef curry with pilau rice; and went to bed, fed up.

The phone rang.

It was Phil. He had been calling my number for days.

These weird long-lost Arcimboldos! Why hadn't I told him anything? And the terrorist attack! What had happened? Could he come round?

"Sorry, Phil, but I've just had my CD and TV nicked. And the helpful visiting constable thinks I'm a hooker."

I was glad of the excuse of the burglary.

Towards mid-morning my phone started ringing, and a couple of Press sleuths turned up in person, pursuing the art bombing story; but I stonewalled, and escaped in the direction of St Martin's where, fortunately, no reporters lurked.

At four in the afternoon I stepped out from the factory-like frontage of the art school into a Charing Cross Road aswarm with tourists. Beneath a grey overcast the fumy air was warm. A sallow Middle Eastern youth in checked shirt and jeans promptly handed me a leaflet advertising some English Language Academy.

"I already speak English," I informed the tout. He frowned momentarily as if he didn't understand. No points to the Academy.

"Then you learn *cheaper*," he suggested, pursuing me along the pavement.

"Do not bother that lady," interrupted a tall blond young man dressed in a lightweight off-white jacket and slacks.

"No, it's all right," I assured my would-be protector.

"It is not all right. Any trash is on our streets. They are not safe."

He waved, and a taxi pulled up almost immediately. The young man opened the door, plunged his hand inside his jacket, and showed me a small pistol hidden in his palm. Was he some urban vigilante crusader pledged to rescue damsels from offensive encounters? I just didn't understand what was happening.

"Get in quickly," he said, "or I will shoot you dead."

Help, I mouthed at the Arab, or whatever.

In vain.

I did as Prince Charming suggested. Did *anyone* notice me being abducted? Or only see a handsome young man hand me enthusiastically into that taxi?

The driver didn't look round.

"Keep quiet," said the young man. "Put these glasses on." He handed me glasses black as night equipped with side-blinkers, such as someone with a rare hypersensitive eye ailment might wear. Only, these were utterly dark; I couldn't see a thing through them.

We drove for what seemed like half an hour. Eventually we drew up — and waited, perhaps so that passers-by might have time to pass on by — before my abductor assisted me from the cab. Quickly he guided me arm in arm up some steps. A door closed behind us. Traffic noise grew mute.

We mounted a broad flight of stairs, and entered an echoing room — where I was pressured into a straight-backed armchair. Immediately one hand pressed under my nose, and another on my jaw, to force my mouth open.

"Drink!"

Liquid poured down my throat — some sweet concoction masking a bitter undertaste. I gagged and spluttered but had no choice except to swallow.

What had I drunk? What had I drunk?

"I need to see the eyes," said a sombre, if somewhat slobbery voice. "The truth is in the eyes." The accent was Germanic.

A hand removed my glasses.

I found myself in a drawing room with a dusty varnished floor and double oak doors. A small chandelier of dull lustre shone. Thick blue brocade curtains cloaked tall windows, which in any event appeared to be shuttered. A dustsheet covered what I took to be a baby grand piano. An oblong of less faded rose-and-lily wallpaper, over a marble fireplace, showed where some painting had hung.

On a chaise longue sat a slim elegant grizzle-haired man of perhaps sixty kitted out in a well-tailored grey suit. A walking cane was pressed between his knees. His hands opened and closed slowly to reveal the chased silver handle. A second middle-aged man stood near him: stouter, bald, wearing a long purple velvet robe with fur trimmings which at first I thought was some exotic dressing gown. This man's face was jowly and pouchy. He looked like Göring on a bad day. His eyes were eerie: bulgy, yet bright as if he was on cocaine.

My abductor had stationed himself directly behind me.

On a walnut table lay a copy of *Arcimboldo Erotico* open at my introduction.

Shit.

"My apologies," said the seated gent, "for the

God's, to give. God finally vested this title in the Habsburg family. Let us discuss *art* instead. And *sacred history*."

This, His Royal Heinrich proceeded to do, while the keeper of the keys contemplated me and my guard hovered behind me.

Rudolph and his father Maximilian before him had been astute, benevolent rulers, who aimed to heal discord in Christian Europe by uniting it under Habsburg rule. They lived noble and honourable lives, as did Count Giuseppe Arcimboldo. His supposed fantasias possessed a precise political and metaphysical significance in the context of the Holy Roman throne. The aesthetic harmony of natural elements in the *Vertumnus* and in the other portrait heads bespoke the harmony which would bless Europe under the beneficent leadership of the House of Austria. . . .

Jawohl, I thought.

Ever-present, like the elements themselves, the Habsburgs would rule both microcosm and macrocosm — both the political world, and nature too. Arcimboldo's cycle of the seasons, depicted as Habsburg heads wrought of Wintry, Vernal, Summery, and Autumnal ingredients, confided that Habsburg rule would extend eternally through time in one everlasting season. Under the secular and spiritual guidance of those descendants of Hercules, the House of Habsburg, the Golden Age would return to a united Europe.

Right on.

In due course of time, this happy culmination had almost come to pass. The "Great King," as predicted, nay, propagandised by Nostradamus, loomed on the horizon.

When the Habsburgs united with the House of Lorraine, and when Marie Antoinette became Queen of France, the House of Habsburg-Lorraine was within a generation of dominion over Europe — had the French Revolution not intervened.

What a pity.

Throughout the nineteenth century the House attempted to regroup. However, the upheavals attending the end of the First World War toppled the Habsburgs from power, ushering in chaos. . . .

Shame.

Now all Europe was revived and reuniting, and its citizens were ever more aware that the microcosm of Man and the macrocosm of Nature were a unity.

Yet lacking, as yet, a *head*.

A Holy Roman Imperial head.

Early restoration of the monarchy in Hungary was one possible ace card — though other cards were also tucked up the imperial sleeve. . . .

Arcimboldo's symbolic portraits were holy ikons of this golden dream, especially in view of their eco-injection into the European psyche. Those paintings were programming the people with a subconscious expectation, a hope, a longing, a secret sense of destiny, which a restored Habsburg Holy Roman Empire would fulfill.

"Now do you see why your obscenities are such a libelous blasphemy, Miss Donaldson?"

Good God.

"Do you mean to tell me that *you're* behind the Arcimboldo eco-campaign?" I asked His Imperial Heinrich.

"The power of symbols," remarked Voss, "is very great. Symbols are my speciality."

Apparently they weren't going to tell me whether they simply hoped to exploit an existing, serendipitous media campaign — or whether some loyal Habsburg mole had actively persuaded the ecofreaks to plaster what were effectively Habsburg heads — in fruit and veg, and flowers and leaves — all over Europe and America.

"You broke into my flat," I accused the man behind me. "Looking for some dirt that doesn't exist because the erotic paintings are genuine!"

Blondie slapped me sharply across the head.

"Martin! You know that is unnecessary!" H. von H. held up his hand prohibitively — for the moment, at least.

"You broke my door down," I muttered over my shoulder, thinking myself reprieved, "and you stole my CD and TV just to make the thing look plausible. I bet you burgled those other flats in the neighbourhood too as a deception."

Martin, on his *own*? Surely not . . . There must have been others involved. The taxi driver . . . and whoever else . . .

"Actually, we broke your door *after* the burglary," boasted Martin. "We *entered* with more circumspection."

Voss smiled in a predatory fashion. "With secret keys, as it were."

Others. Others . . .

They had blown up the Galerij Bosch! They had burned those two guards to death. . . .

I shrank.

"I see that the magnitude of this is beginning to dawn on your butterfly mind," said the Habsburg. "A united Europe must be saved from *pollution*. Ecological pollution, of course — a Holy Roman Emperor is as a force of nature. But moral pollution too."

"How about racial?" I queried.

"I'm an aristocrat, not a barbarian," remarked Heinrich. "The Nazis were contemptible. Yet plainly we cannot have Moslems — Turkish *heathens* — involved in the affairs of Holy Europe. We cannot have those who besieged our Vienna in 1683 succeeding now by the back door."

Oh, the grievances of centuries long past . . . Rumby and his science Star Club suddenly seemed like such Johnnies-Come-Lately indeed.

Science . . . versus imperial *magic* . . . with eco-mysticism in the middle . . .

"I just can't believe you're employing a frigging *magician* to gain the throne of Europe!"

"*Language*, Miss Donaldson!" snapped the Habsburg. "You are corrupt."

Voss smoothed his robe as though I had mussed it.

"You're a creature of your time, Miss Donaldson," said H. von H. "Whereas I am a creation of the centuries."

"Would that be *The Centuries of Nostradamus*?" Yes, that was the title of that volume of astrological rigmarole.

"I mustn't forget that you're educated, by the lights of today. Tell me, what do you suppose the *Centuries* of the title refer to?"

"Well, years. A long time, the future."

"Quite wrong. There simply happen to be a hundred quatrains — verses of four lines — in each section. You're only half educated. And thus you blunder. How much did your American art collector pay you for writing that introduction?"

Obviously Rumby would have paid me *something*. . . . I wouldn't have written those pages for nothing. . . .

"Three thousand dollars," I improvised.

"That doesn't sound very much, considering the evil intent. Is Mr Wright being hoaxed *too*?"

Again, he slammed the cane on to my book.

An astonishing flash of agony seared across my back. I squealed and twisted round — but Martin was holding no cane.

He was holding nothing at all. With a grin, Martin displayed his empty paws for me. Voss giggled, and when I looked at him he winked.

It was as though that open volume was some voodoo doll of myself which the Habsburg had just chastised.

The Habsburg lashed at my words again, and I cried out, for the sudden pain was intense — yet I knew there would be no mark on me.

Voss licked his lips. "Symbolic resonances, Miss Donaldson. The power of symbolic actions."

What drug had been in that liquid I swallowed? I didn't *feel* disoriented — save for nerves and dread — yet I must be in some very strange state of mind to account for my suggestibility to pain.

"We can continue thus for a while, Miss Donaldson." Heinrich raised his cane again.

"Wait."

Was three quarters of a million dollars enough to compensate for being given the third degree right now by crazy, ruthless *murderers* — who could torture me symbolically, but effectively?

I experienced an absurd vision of myself attempting to tell the West Indian detective-constable that actually my flat had been broken into by agents of a Holy Roman Emperor who hoped to take over Europe — and that I was seeking police protection because the Habsburgs could hurt me agonisingly by whipping my words. . . .

Was I mad, or was I mad?

The room seemed luminous, glowing with an inner light. Every detail of furniture or drapery was intensely *actual*. I thought that my sense of reality had never been stronger.

"Okay," I admitted, "the paintings were all forgeries. They were done in Holland, but I honestly don't know who by. I never met him. I never learned his name. Rumby — Mr Wright — hates the ecology lobby because they hate space exploration, and he thinks that's our only hope. I have a friend at the *Sunday Times*. I'll tell him everything — about how the paintings were a prank. They'll love to print that! Wright will have egg on his face."

"What a treacherous modern creature you are," the Habsburg said with casual contempt; and I squirmed with shame and fear.

"Just watch for next weekend's paper," I promised.

"At this moment," said Voss, "she believes she is going to do what she says — and of course she knows that our Martin can find her, if she breaks her word. . . ." He peered.

"Ah: she's relieved that *you* cannot reach her from a distance with the whipping cane.

"And she wonders whether Martin would really kill her, and thus lose us her testimony . . ."

No, he *wasn't* reading my mind. He wasn't! He was reading my face, my muscles. He could do so because everything was so real.

More peering.

"She feels a paradoxical affection for her friend . . . *Rumby*. Solidarity, as well as greed. Yes, a definite loyalty." If only I hadn't called him Rumby. If only I'd just called him Wright. It was all in the words. Voss wasn't reading my actual thoughts.

"So therefore," H. von H. said to Voss, "she must be retrained in her loyalties."

What did he mean? What did he mean?

"She must be conditioned by potent symbols, Voss."

"Just so, Excellency."

"Thus she will not wish to betray us. Enlighten her, Voss. Show her the real depth of history, from where we come. Your juice will be deep in her now."

Numbness crept over me, as Voss loomed closer. The sheer pressure of his approach was paralysing me.

"Wait," I managed to squeak.

"Wait?" echoed H. von H. "Oh, I have waited long enough already. My family has waited long enough. Through the French Revolution, through the Communist intermezzo . . . The Holy Roman Empire *will* revive at this present cusp of history — for it has always remained in being, at least as a state of mind. And *mind* is what matters, Miss Donaldson — as Rudolph knew, contrary to your pornographic lies! Ah yes, my ancestor avidly sought the symbolic key to the ideal world. Practitioners of the symbolic, hermetic arts visited him in Prague Castle — though he lacked the loyal services of a Voss . . ."

The Habsburg slid his cane under the dustsheet of the piano, and whisked the cloth off. Seating himself on the stool, he threw open the lid of the baby grand with a crash. His slim, manicured fingers started to play plangent, mournful Debussyish chords in which I could almost feel myself begin to drown.

Voss crooned to me — or sang — in some dialect of German . . . and I couldn't move a muscle. Surely I was shrinking — or else the drawing room was expanding. Or both. Voss was becoming vast.

I was a little child again — yet not a child, but rather a miniature of myself. When I was on the brink of puberty, lying in bed just prior to drifting off to sleep, this same distortion of the senses used to happen to me.

The music lamented.

And Voss crooned my lullaby.

A bearded man in black velvet and cerise satin held my nude paralysed body in his hands. He held the whole of me in his hands — for I was tiny now, the height of his forearm.

Draped over his shoulders was a lavish ermine cloak.

I was stiff, unmoving.

He placed me in a niche, ran his fingertip down my belly, and traced the cleft between my thighs.

He stepped back.

Then he left.

I was in a great gloomy vaulted chamber housing massive cupboards and strongboxes. The slit windows in the thick stone wall were grated so as to deter any slim cat burglars. Stacked several deep around a broad shelf, and likewise below, were mythological and Biblical oil paintings: Tintorettos, Titians, by the look of them. . . . Neither the lighting nor the decor were at all in the spirit of any latterday museum. Here was art as treasure — well and truly locked up.

Days and nights passed.

Weeks of static solitude until I was going crazy. I would have welcomed any change whatever, any newcomer. My thoughts looped around a circuit of Strada, death in Amsterdam, Habsburgs, with the latter assuming ever more significance — and necessity — with each mental swing.

Eventually the door opened, and in walked a figure who made the room shine. For his face and hair were made of a hundred springtime flowers, his collar of white daisies, and his clothes of a hundred lush leaves.

He stood and gazed at me through floral eyes, and with his rosebud lips he smiled faintly.

He simply went away.

A season passed, appalling in its sheer duration. I saw daisies like stars before my eyes, in an unending afterimage.

Then in walked glowing Summer. His eyes were ripe cherries. His teeth were little peas. Plums and berries tangled in his harvest-hair; and his garment was of woven straw.

And he too smiled, and went away in turn.

And another season passed . . .

. . . till rubicund Autumn made his appearance. He was a more elderly fellow with an oaten beard, a fat pear of a nose, mushroom ears, clusters of grapes instead of locks of hair. His chin was a pomegranate. He wore an overripe burst fig as an ear-ring. He winked lecherously, and departed even as I tried to cry out to him through rigid lips, to stay.

For next came Winter, old and gnarled, scabbed and scarred, his nose a stump of rotted branch, his skin of fissured bark, his lips of jutting bracket-fungus.

Winter stayed for a longer grumbly time, though he no more reached to touch me than had his predecessors. His departure — the apparent end of this cycle of seasons — plunged me into despair. I was as cold as marble.

Until one day the door opened yet again, and golden light bathed my prison chamber.

Vertumnus himself advanced — the fruitful God, his cheeks of ripe apple and peach, head crowned with fruit and grain, his chest a mighty pumpkin. His cherry and blackberry eyes glinted.

Rudolph!

He reached for me. Oh to be embraced by him! To be warmed.

He lifted my paralysed naked body from its dusty niche.

The crash which propelled me back into the drawing room might almost have been caused by his dropping me and letting me shatter.

For a moment I thought that this was indeed so.

Yet it was my trance which had been shattered.

A policeman was in the room. An armed policeman, crouching. He panned his gun around. Plainly I was the only other person present.

The crash must have been that of those double oak doors flying open as he burst in.

Footsteps thumped, elsewhere in the house.

Voices called.

"Empty!"

"Empty!"

Several other officers spilled into the room.

"You all right, Miss?"

I could move my limbs — which were clothed exactly as earlier on, in jeans and maroon paisley sweater. I wasn't tiny and naked, after all. I stared around. No sign of von Habsburg or Voss or Martin.

"You all right, Miss? Do you understand me?"

I nodded slowly. I still felt feeble.

"She was just sitting here all on her own," commented the officer, putting his pistol away. "So what's happening?" he demanded of me.

How did they know I was here?

"I was . . . forced into a taxi," I said. "I was brought here, then given some drug."

"What sort of drug? *Why?*"

"It made me . . . dream."

"Who brought you here?"

"A man called Martin . . ."

He's the Habsburg Emperor's hit-man. . . . The drug was concocted by a magician. . . .

How could I tell them such things? How could I explain about Rudolph Vertumnus . . . ? (And how could I *deny* Vertumnus, who had almost rekindled me . . . ?)

"They were trying to get me to deny things I wrote about the painter Arcimboldo. . . ."

"About a *painter*?"

I tried to explain about the pictures, the bombing in Amsterdam, and how my flat had been burgled. My explanation slid away of its own accord — for the sake of sheer plausibility, and out of logical necessity! — from any Habsburg connexion, and into the ecofreak channel.

The officer frowned. "You're suggesting that the Greens who bombed that gallery also kidnapped you? There's no one here now."

"They must have seen you coming and run away. I'm quite confused."

"Hmm," said the officer. "Come in, Sir," he called.

In walked Phil: chunky, dapper Phil, velvet jacketed and suede-shoed, his rich glossy brown hair brushed back in elegant waves, as ever.

It was Phil who had seen me pushed into the taxi; he who had noticed the gleam of gun from right across the street where he had been loitering with intent outside a bookshop, waiting for me to emerge from St Martin's so that he could bump into me. He'd managed to grab another taxi and follow. He'd seen me hustled into that house in North London, wearing those black "goggles." It took about an hour for him to stir up the armed posse — an hour, during which four seasons had passed before my eyes.

The fact that Phil and I were long-term "friends" and that he turned out to be a "journalist" — of sorts — irked the police. The abduction — by persons unknown, to a vacant house, where I simply sat waiting patiently — began to seem distinctly stage-managed . . . for the sake of publicity. Nor — given the Amsterdam connexion — did my mention of drugs help matters. Calling out armed police was a serious matter.

We were both obliged to answer questions until late in the evening before we could leave the police station; and even then it seemed as if we ourselves might still be charged with some offence. However, those deaths in Amsterdam lent a greater credence to what I said. Maybe there was something serious behind this incident. . . .

I, of course, was "confused." Thus, early on, I was given a blood test, about which the police made no further comment; there couldn't have been any evidence of hash or acid in my system.

I needed to stay "confused" until I could get to talk to Rumby.

Peeved Phil, of course, insisted on talking to me over late dinner in a pizzaria — we were both starving by then.

I lied quite a lot; and refrained from any mention of Habsburgs or the Star Club. The Arcimboldo paintings had all been genuine. Rumby was an up-front person. Euro ecofreaks must have bombed the gallery. Must have abducted me. Blondie Martin; elderly man, name unknown; stout man, name of Voss, who wore a strange costume. German speakers. Just the same as I'd told the police, five or six times over. The kidnappers had tried to persuade me to denounce what I had written because my words were

an insult to Arcimboldo, emblem of the Greens. They had drugged me into a stupor — from which I recovered with surprising swiftness. Rescue had come too soon for much else to transpire. . . .

Phil and I were sharing a tuna, anchovy, and prawn ensemble on a crispy base, and drinking red wine.

"It's quite some story, Jill. Almost front-page stuff."

"I doubt it."

"The Eco connexion! Bombing, abduction . . . I'd like to run this by Freddy on the news desk."

"You're an art critic, Phil — and so am I. I don't want some cockeyed blather in the papers."

"Jill," he reproached me, "I've just spent *all evening* in a police station on account of you."

"I'm grateful you did what you did, Phil. Let's stop it there."

"For Christ's sake, you could still be in danger! Or . . . *aren't you*, after all? Was this a publicity stunt? Was it staged by *Wright*? You're in deep, but you want out now? Why would he stage such a stunt? If he did . . . what really happened in Amsterdam?"

Dear God, how his antennae were twitching. "No, no, no. It couldn't be a stunt because the only witness to it was *you*, and that was quite by chance!"

"By chance," he mused . . . as though maybe I might have spied him from an upper window in St Martin's and promptly phoned for a kidnapper. "Look, Phil, I'm confused. I'm tired. I need *sleep*."

Into the pizzaria stepped a stout, bald man wearing a dark blue suit. He flourished a silver-tipped walking stick. Göring on a night out. His bulgy eyes fixed on mine. He swished the stick, and I screamed with pain, jerking against the table, spilling both our wines.

"Jill!"

Phil managed to divert the red tide with his paper napkin at the same time as he reached out towards me. Other customers stared agog, and the manager hastened in our direction. Were we engaged in some vicious quarrel? Wine dripped on to the floor tiles.

Voss had vanished. I slumped back.

"Sorry," I said to the manager. "I had a bad cramp."

The manager waved a waiter to minister to the mess. Other diners resumed munching their pizzas.

"Whatever happened?" whispered Phil.

"A cramp. Just a cramp."

Could one of those Habsburgers have trailed us to the police station and hung around outside for hours, keeping watch till we emerged?

Had I truly seen Voss, or only someone who resembled him? Someone whose appearance, and whose action triggered that pain reflex? That agonising hallucination . . .

Phil took me back to the flat in a taxi. I had no choice but to let him come up with me — in case the place was infested.

It wasn't. Then it took half an hour to get rid of my friend, no matter how much tiredness I claimed.

By the time I phoned Rumby's private number it was after eleven.

Him, I did start to tell about the Habsburgs.

He was brevity itself. "Say no more," my rich protector cut in. *My Rumby Daddy*. "Stay there. I'm sending Case now. He'll phone from the car just as soon as he's outside your place. Make quite sure you see it's him before you open your door."

I dozed off soundly in the Merc. When I arrived at Bexford, Rumby had waited up to quiz me and pump me — attended by Case, and a somewhat weary Lascelles.

I got to bed around four . . .

. . . leaving Rumby aiming to do some serious phoning.

Had Big Daddy been breaking out the benzedrine? Not exactly. Rumby always enjoyed a few hours' advantage over us local mortals. So as to stay more in synch with American time-zones he habitually rose very late of a morning. A night shift duo always manned the computer consoles and transatlantic satellite link. In that sense, Bexford never really closed down.

I'd already gathered that *crisis* was somewhat of a staff of life around Rumby — who seemed to cook up his own personal supply of benzedrine internally. During my previous two-day sojourn, there'd been the incident of the microlite aircraft. Thanks to a Cotswold Air Carnival, microlites were overflying Bexford at a few hundred feet now and then. Rumby took exception and had Lascelles trying to take out a legal injunction against the organisers.

Simultaneously, there'd been the business of the starlings. Affronted by those microlite pterodactyls, and seeking a new air-base for their sorties, a horde of the quarrelsome birds took up residence on the satellite dish. Their weight or their shit might distort bits of information worth millions. What to do? After taking counsel from an avian welfare organisation, Rumby dispatched his helicopter to collect a heap of French *pétard* firecrackers from Heathrow to string underneath the gutters. So my stay had been punctuated by random explosive farts. . . .

I woke at noon, and Rumby joined me for breakfast in the big old kitchen — antiquity retrofitted with stainless steel and ceramic hobs. A large TV set was tuned to CNN, and an ecologist was inveighing about rocket exhausts and the ozone holes.

"Each single shuttle launch releases a hundred and sixty-three *thousand* kilograms of hydrogen chloride that converts into an atmospheric mist of hydrochloric acid! So now they're kindly promising to change the oxidizer of the fuel — the ammonium perchlorate that produces this vast cloud of pollution — to ammonium *nitrate* instead — "

As soon as I finished my croissant, Rumby scuttled the cooks — a couple of local women — out to pick herbs and vegetables. He blinked at me a few times.

"Any more sightings of flowerpot men? Or Habsburgs?" he enquired.

"That isn't funny, Rumby. It happened."

He nodded. "I'm afraid you've been given a ring-binder, Jill."

"Come again?"

"I've been talking to one of my best chemists over in Texas. Sally has a busy mind. Knows a lot about pharmaceuticals." He consulted scribbles in a notebook. "The ring in question's a molecular structure called an indole ring. . . . These rings *bind* to synapses in the brain. Hence, ring-binder. They're psychotomimetic — they mimic psychoses. Your little pets will probably stay in place a long time instead of breaking down. Seems there's a lot of covert designer drug work going on right now, aimed at cooking up chemicals to manipulate people's beliefs. Sally has heard rumours of one drug code-named *Confusion* — and another one called *Persuasion*, which seems to fit the bill here. It's the only explanation for the hallucination — which came from within you, of course, once you were given the appropriate prod."

"I do realize I was hallucinating the . . . flowerpot men. You mean this can continue . . . indefinitely?"

"You flashed on for a full encore in that pizza parlour, right? Whiplash! Any fraught scenes in future involving old Archey could do the same. Media interviews, that sort of thing — if you disobey the Habsburg view of Archey. Though I guess you mustn't spill the beans about them publicly."

"They told me so. How did I get away with telling *you* last night?"

"They were interrupted before they'd finished influencing you." He grinned. "I guess I might be high enough in the hierarchy of your loyalties to outrank their partial hold on you. Media or Press people wouldn't be, so you'd be advised to follow the Habsburg party line with them. Maybe you could resist at a cost."

"Of what?"

"Pain, inflicted by your own mind. Distortions of reality. That's what Sally says. That's the word on these new ring-binders. They bind you."

The more I thought about this, the less I liked it.

"How many people know about these persuader drugs?" I asked him carefully.

"They haven't exactly featured in *Newsweek*. I gather they're a bit experimental. Sally has an ear for rumours. She's part of my research division. Runs a search-team scanning the chemistry journals. Whatever catches the eye. Any tips of future icebergs. New petrochemical applications, mainly." He spoke as if icebergs started out fully submerged, then gradually revealed themselves. "She helped dig up data on the correct paint chemistry for the Archeys."

How frank he was being.

Apparently. And how glib.

"So how would a Habsburg *magician* get his paws on prototype persuader drugs?" I demanded.

Rumby looked rueful. "Hell, maybe he *is* a

magician! Alchemy precedes chemistry, don't they say?"

"In the same sense that Icarus precedes a jumbo jet?"

One of the cooks returned bearing an obese marrow.

Impulse took me to the kitchen garden, to brood on my own. The sun had finally burned through persistent haze to brighten the rows of cabbages, majestic cauliflowers, and artichokes, the rhubarb, the leeks. An ancient brick wall backed this domain, trusses of tomatoes ranged along it. Rooks cawed in the elms beyond, prancing about those raggedy stick-nests that seemed like diseases of the branches.

Had the old gent whom I'd met really been Heinrich von Habsburg? A Holy Roman Emperor waiting in the wings to step on the world stage? Merely because he told me so, in *persuasive* circumstances?

What if that trio in the drawing room had really been *ecofreaks* masquerading as Habsburgs, pulling the wool over my eyes, trying to bamboozle me into confession?

Did puritanical ecofreaks have the wit to stage such a show?

How much more likely that the Star Club, with its presumed access to cutting-edge psychochemistry — and a penchant for dirty tricks? — was responsible for the charade, and for my drugging!

Whether Rumby himself knew so, or not.

Wipe me out as a reliable witness to my own part in the prank? Eliminate me, by giving me an ongoing nervous breakdown?

Would that invalidate what I'd written?

Ah no. The slur would be upon ecologists. . . .

And maybe, at the same time, *test* that persuader drug? Give it a field-trial on a highly suitable test subject, namely myself? The Club's subsequent aim might be try similar persuasion on influential ecofreaks to alter their opinions or to make them seem crazy. . . .

In my case, of course, they wouldn't wish to turn me into an eco-groupie. . . . Thus the Habsburg connexion could have seemed like a fertile ploy.

Was there a genuine, elderly Heinrich von Habsburg somewhere in Germany or Austria? Oh, doubtless there would be. . . .

The vegetable garden began slithering, pulsing, throbbing. Ripe striped marrows thumped upon the ground, great green gonads. Tomatoes tumesced. Leeks were waxy white candles with green flames writhing high. Celery burst from earth, spraying feathery leaves. Sprouts jangled. Cauliflowers were naked brains.

The garden was trying to transform itself, to assemble itself into some giant sprawled potent body — of cauli brain, leek fingers, marrow organs, green leaf flesh. . . .

I squealed and fled back towards the kitchen itself.

Then halted, like a hunted animal.

I couldn't go inside — where Rumby and Case and Lascelles plotted . . . the downfall of Nature, the rape of the planets, the bleeding of oil from Earth's veins to burn into choking smoke.

Behind me, the vegetable jungle had stilled. Its metamorphosis had halted, reversed.

If I thought harmoniously, not perversely, I was safe.

Yet my mind was churning, and reality was unstuck.

In my perception one conspiracy overlaid another. One scheming plot, another scheming plot. Therefore one reality overlaid another reality with hideous persuasiveness. Where had I just been, but in a *vegetable plot*?

I couldn't go into that house, to which I had fled for safety only the night before. For from inside Bexford Hall invisible tendrils arched out across the sky, bouncing up and down out of space, linking Rumby to star crusaders who were playing with my mind — and to whom he might be reporting my condition even now, guilefully or innocently.

On the screen of the sky I spied a future world of Confusion and Persuasion, where devoted fanatics manipulated moods chemically so that Nature became a multifold *creature* evoking horror — since it might absorb one into itself, mind-meltingly, one's keen consciousness dimming into pulsing, orgasmic dreams; and from which one could only flee in silver ships, out to the empty serenity of space where no universally linked weeds infested the floating rocks, no bulging tomato hæmorrhoids the asteroids . . .

Or else conjuring up a positive lust for vital vegetative unity!

I slapped myself, trying to summon a Habsburger whiplash of pain to jerk me out of this bizarre dual vision.

I *must* go indoors. To sanity. And beyond.

The ring-binder was clamping more and more of me; and my mind was at war. I was scripting my own hallucinations from the impetus of ecofreak ideology, exaggerated absurdly, and from the myth of the Holy Roman Empire . . . I was dreaming, wide awake.

And Case stood, watching me.

"You okay, Jill?"

I nodded. I shouldn't tell him the truth. There was no truth any more; there was only potent imagery, subject to interpretation.

Certain bedrock facts existed: the bombing, the deaths in Amsterdam, my abduction . . . Event-*images*: that's what those were. The interpretation was another matter, dependent upon what one believed — just as art was forever being reinterpreted in the context of a new epoch; and even history too.

Persuasion — and Confusion too? — had torn me loose from my moorings, so that interpretations cascaded about me simultaneously, synchronously. I had become a battlefield between world-views, which different parts of my mind were animating.

With dread, I sensed something stirring which

perhaps had lain dormant ever since humanity split from Nature — ever since true consciousness of self had dawned as a sport, a freak, a biological accident. . . .

"You sure, Jill?"

You. I. Myself. *Me.*

The independent thinking entity, named Jill Donaldson.

I wasn't thinking quite so independently any longer. An illusion of Self — that productive illusion upon which civilization itself had been founded — was floundering.

"Quite sure," said I.

I, I, I. Ich. Io. Ego.

And Jilldonaldson hastened past him into the kitchen, where one of the cooks was hollowing out the marrow. The big TV set, tuned to CNN, scooping signals bounced from space, shimmered. The colours bled and reformed. The pixel pixies danced a new jig.

The countenance of Vertumnus gazed forth from that screen, he of the laughing lips, the ripe rubicund cheeks of peach and apple, the pear-nose, the golden ears of corn that were his brows. Oh the flashing hilarity of his berry-eyes. Oh those laughing lips.

With several nods of his head he gestured Jill elsewhere.

Jill adopted a pan-face.

She walked through the corridors of the house, to the front porch. She stepped out on to the gravel drive.

Ignition keys were in the red Porsche.

Jill ought to be safe with Annie in a colony of women. Rudolph Vertumnus was a male, wasn't he?

A hop through Cheltenham, then whoosh by motorway to Exeter and on down into Cornwall. She would burn fuel but keep an eye out for police patrols. Be at Polmerrin by dusk. . . .

The Porsche wasn't even approaching Cheltenham when the car phone burbled, inevitably.

She had been counting on a call.

A stolen bright red Porsche would be a little obvious on the motorway. So she had her excuse lined up. She was going to visit her brother — in Oxford, in roughly the opposite direction. She'd be back at Bexford that evening. Brother Bob was a banker. Let Rumby worry that she was going to blab to him to protect her 750K investment, about which she no longer cared a hoot. Let Case and some co-driver hare after her fruitlessly towards Oxford in the Merc.

The voice wasn't Case's. Or Lascelles's. Or even Rumby's.

She nearly jerked the Porsche off the road.

The voice was that of Voss.

"Can you hear me, Fräulein Donaldson?"

Hands shaking, legs trembling, she guided the car into a gateway opening on to a huge field of close-cut golden stubble girt by a hawthorn hedge. A Volvo hooted in protest as it swung by. A rabbit fled.

"How did you find me, Voss — ?" she gasped. Horrid perspectives loomed. "They told you! They know you!"

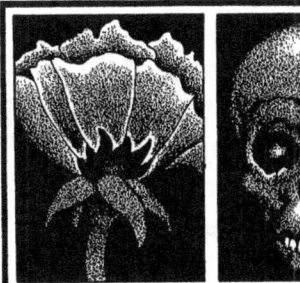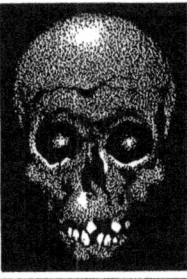

The caller chuckled.

"I'm merely the voice of *Vertumnus*, Fräulein. My image is everywhere these days, so why shouldn't I be everywhere too? Are you perhaps worried about the collapse of your precious Ego, Fräulein?"

How persuasive his voice was. "This has all happened before, you know. The God of the Bible ruled the medieval world, but when He went into eclipse *Humanity* seized His sceptre. Ah, that exalted Renaissance Ego! How puffed up it was! By the time of Rudolph, that same Ego was already collapsing. Its confidence had failed. A new unity was needed — a bio-cosmic social unity. The Holy Roman Emperor Rudolph sought to be the head of society — hence the painting of so many regal heads by the artist you have libeled. Those biological, botanical heads."

"I already know this," she said.

"He would be the head — and the people, the limbs, the organs. Of one body! In the new world now a-dawning life will be a unity again. The Emperor will be the head — but not a separate, egotistic head. Nor will the limbs and organs be separate individualists."

"You're telling me what I know!" Aye, and what she most feared — namely the loss of Self. Its extinction. And what she most feared might well win: for what is feared is potent.

"Who are you? What are you?" she cried into the phone — already suspecting that Voss's voice, the voice of Vertumnus, might well be in her own wayward head, either ring-bound or else planted there by alchemical potion.

She slammed the hand-set down on to its cradle by the gear shift lever, thumbed the windows fully open, and lit a cigarette to calm herself. Whispers of smoke drifted out towards the shorn field.

A mat of golden stubble cloaked the broad shoulders of the land. A ghostly pattern emerged across the great network of dry stalks: a coat of arms. The hedge was merely green braiding. Her car was a shiny red bug parked on the shoulder of a giant sprawling being.

Angrily she pitched her cigarette through the passenger window towards the field, wishing that it might start a fire, though really the straw was far too short to combust.

She drove on; and when the phone seemed to burble again, she ignored it.

She smoked. She threw out half-burned cigarettes

till the pack was empty, but no smoke ever plumed upwards far behind her.

Half way through Cheltenham, in slow-moving traffic, she passed a great billboard flaunting Rudolph Vertumnus. *WE ARE ALL PART OF NATURE,* proclaimed the all-too-familiar text.

Evidently unseen by other drivers and pedestrians, the fruity Emperor shouldered his way out of the poster. A pumpkin-belly that she had never seen before reared into view. And marrow-legs, from between which aubergine testicles and a carrot cock dangled. Vertumnus towered over the other cars and vans behind her, bestriding the roadway. His carrot swelled enormously.

Raphanidosis: ancient Greek word. To be fucked by a giant radish. To be radished, ravished.

Vertumnus was coming.

A red light changed to green, and she was able to slip onward before the giant could advance to unpeel the roof of the Porsche and lift her out, homunculus-like, from her container.

Even in the heart of the city, a chthonic entity was coming to life. A liberated, incarnated deity was being born.

No one else but Jill saw it as yet.

Yet everyone knew it from ten thousand posters and badges — wearing its varied seasonal faces.

Everyone knew Vertumnus by now, deity of change and transformation; for change was in the air, as ripe Autumn matured.

The death of Self was on the horizon.

When she reached the motorway, those triple lanes cutting far ahead through the landscape opened up yawning perspectives of time rather than of space.

Deep time, in which there'd been no conscious mind present at all, only vegetable and animal existence. Hence, the blankness of the road . . .

Soon, a new psychic era might dawn in which the sovereign virtue of the conscious Self faded as humanity re-entered Nature once again — willing the demise of dissective, alienating logics and sciences, altering the mind-set, hypnotising itself into a communal empathy with the world, whose potent figurehead wasn't any vague, cloudy Gæa, but rather her son Vertumnus. Every eating of his body — of fruits and nuts and vegetables and fishes — would be a vividly persuasive communion. His royal representative would reign in Budapest, or in Prague, or Vienna. His figurehead.

The phone burbled, and this time Jill did answer as she swung along the endless tongue of tarmac, and through time.

"Jill, don't hang up." *Rumby.* "I know why you've skipped out. And you must believe it ain't my fault."

What was he talking about?

"I've been the well-meaning patsy in this business. I've been the Gorby."

"Who was *he*?" she asked mischievously. Here was a message from a different era.

"I'm fairly sure by now that my Goddam Star Club *was* behind the bombing and the ring-binder. Didn't trust me to be *thorough* enough. The whole Archey situation was really a lot more serious than even I saw. Those damn posters were really imprinting people on some deep-down level — not just surface propaganda. These are power-images. Fucking servo-symbols —"

"You're only *fairly* sure?" she asked.

"What tipped you off? Was it something *Case* said? Or Johnny Lascelles? Something Johnny let slip? I mean, why did you skip?"

Something Case or Lascelles had let slip . . . ? So Rumby was becoming a tad paranoid about his own staff in case they were serving two masters — Rumby himself and some other rich gent in that secret Star Club of theirs . . . a gent whom she had perhaps met in that drawing room in North London; who had caned her at a distance. . . .

"Come back, Jill, and tell me all you know. I'm serious! I need to know."

Oh yes, she could recognize the authentic tones of paranoia. . . .

"Sorry about taking the Porsche," she said.

"Never mind the fucking car. Where are you, Jill?"

She remembered.

"I'm going to Oxford to see my brother. He's a bank manager."

She hung up, and ignored repeated calls.

Polmerrin lay in a wooded little valley within a couple of miles of the rocky, wind-whipped North Cornwall coastline. Sheltered by the steep plunge of land and by oak wood, the once-derelict hamlet of cottages now housed studios and craft workshops, accompanied by a dozen satellite caravans. Pottery, jewelry, painting, sculpting, candle-making . . .

Kids played. Women worked. A few male companions lent an enlightened hand. Someone was tootling a flute, and a buzzard circled high overhead. A kingfisher flashed to and fro along a stream, one soggy bank of which was edged by alder buckthorn. Some brimstone butterflies still fluttered, reluctant to succumb to worn-out wings and cooling nights. The sunset was brimstone too: sulphur and orange peel. A few arty tourists were departing.

Immediately Jill realized that she had come to the wrong place entirely. She ought to have fled to some high-tech airport hotel with gleaming glass elevators — an inorganic, air-conditioned, sealed machine resembling a space station in the void.

She was too tired to reverse her route.

Red-haired Annie embraced Jill, in surprise and joy. She kissed Jill, hugged her.

Freckled Annie was wearing one of those Indian cotton dresses — in green hues — with tiny mirrors sewn into it; and she'd put some extra flesh upon her once-lithe frame, though not to the extent of positive plumpness. She had also put on slim, scrutinising glasses. Pewter rings adorned several fingers, with scarab and spider motifs.

One former barn was now a refectory, to which she led a dazed Jill to drink lemonade.

"How long has it been, Jilly? Four years? You'll stay with me, of course. So what's *happening*?" She frowned. "I did hear about your book — and that awful bombing. I still listen to the radio all day long while I'm painting — "

"Jill's drugged," said Jill. "Vertumnus is reborn. And the Holy Roman Empire is returning."

Annie scrutinised her with concern. "Holy shit." She considered. "You'd better not tell any of the others. There are kids here. Folks might worry."

They whispered, as once they had whispered confidences.

"Do you know the *Portrait of Jacopo Strada*?" Jill began. She found she could still speak about herself in the first person, historically.

Presently there were indeed kids and mothers and a medley of other women, and a few men in the refectory too, sharing an early supper of spiced beans and rice and salad and textured vegetable protein, Madras style, while Vivaldi played from a tape-deck. The beams of the barn were painted black, and murals of fabulous creatures relieved the whiteness of the plaster: a phoenix, a unicorn, a minotaur, each within a maze-like Celtic surround, so that it seemed as if so many heraldic shields were poised around the walls. Tourists would enjoy cream teas in here of an afternoon.

Sulphur and copper had cleared from a sky that was now deeply leaden-blue, fast darkening. Venus and Jupiter both shone. A shooting star streaked across the vault of void; or was that a failed satellite burning up?

Annie shared a studio with Rosy and Meg, who would be playing chess that evening in the recreation barn beside the refectory. The whole ground floor of the reconditioned cottage was a studio. Meg's work was meticulous neo-medieval miniatures featuring eerie freaks rather than anyone comely. Rosy specialised in acrylic studies of transparent hourglass buildings set within forests, or in crystalline deserts, and crowded with disembodied heads instead of sand.

Annie *used* to paint swirling, luminous abstracts. Now she specialised in large acrylic canvases of bloom within bloom within bloom, vortexes that sucked the gaze down into a central focus from which an eye always gazed out: a cat's, a bird's, a person's. Her pictures were like strange, exploded, organic cameras.

Jill looked; Jill admired. The paintings looked at her. Obviously there was a thematic empathy between the three women who used this studio.

"The conscious mind is going into eclipse," Jill remarked, and Annie smiled hesitantly.

"That's a great title. I might use it."

A polished wooden stairway led up to a landing with three bedrooms.

Annie's wide bed was of brass, with a floral duvet. Marguerites, daisies, buttercups.

In the morning when Jill awoke, the flowers had migrated from the duvet.

Annie's face, her neck, her shoulders were petals and stalks. Her skin was of white and pink blossoms. Her ear was a tulip, her nose was the bud of a lily, and her hair a fountain of red nasturtiums.

Jill reached to peel off some of the petals, but the flowers were flesh, and Annie awoke with a squeak of protest. Her open eyes were black nightshades with white blossom pupils.

And Jilldonaldson, whose name was dissolving, was the first to see such a transformation as would soon possess many men and women who regarded one another in a suitable light as part of Nature.

Jilldona stepped from the brass bed, towards the window, and pulled the curtains aside.

The valley was thick with mist. Yet a red light strobed the blur of vision. Spinning, this flashed from the roof of a police car parked beside the Porsche. Shapeless wraiths danced in its dipped headlight beams. One officer was scanning the vague, evasive cottages. A second walked around the Porsche, peered into it, then opened the passenger door.

"Hey," said Annie, "why did you tweak me?"

Annie's flesh was much as the night before, except that Jill continued to see a faint veil of flowers, an imprint of petals.

"Jill just wanted a cigarette," said Jill.

"I quit a couple of years ago," Annie reminded her. "Tobacco costs too much. Anyway, *you* didn't smoke last night."

"Jill forgot to. Fuzz are down there. Fuzz make Jill want a fag."

"That braggartly car — we ought to have driven it miles away! Miles and miles." Yet Annie didn't sound totally convinced that sheltering this visitor might be the best idea.

Jilldona pulled on her paisley sweater and jeans, and descended. Annie's paintings eyed her brightly as she passed by, recording her within their petal-ringed pupils.

She walked over to the police, one of whom asked:

"You wouldn't be a Miss Jill Donaldson, by any chance?" The burr of his Cornish accent . . .

"Names melt," she told her questioner. "The mind submerges in a unity of being. Have the Habsburgs sent you?" she asked. "Or was it the Star Club?"

One officer removed the ignition key from the Porsche and locked the car.

The other steered her by the arm into the back of the strobing vehicle. She could see no flowers on these policemen. However, a pair of wax strawberries dangled discreetly from the driving mirror like blood-bright testicles. Ω

Weird Tales

THE UNIQUE MAGAZINE   ISSN 0898-5073

Spring 1994 (Previous issue was Summer 1993)   Artwork by Phil Parks

Weird Tales® is published 4 times a year by Terminus Publishing Co., Inc., 123
Crooked Lane, King of Prussia PA 19406–2570. Postmaster: please send address
changes to this address. Application to mail at 2nd Class Postage rates pending at
King of Prussia PA & additional mailing offices. Single copies, $4.95. Subscriptions:
4 issues (one year) $16.00 in U.S.A. & possessions; $22.00 elsewhere, in U.S. funds.
Copyright © 1993 by Terminus Publishing Co., Inc.; all rights reserved; reproduction
prohibited without prior permission. Typeset, printed, & bound in the United States
of America. *Weird Tales*® is a registered trademark owned by Weird Tales, Limited.

THE EYRIE

We mourn the passing of Avram Davidson, who died recently after a short hospitalization. Although he had been in ill health for several years, he continued to write; he left material for a collection of Jack Limekiller stories, a horror novel, and another Virgil Magnus novel, all of which may see print. Alas, the last volume of our own favorite, the the Peregrine series, set in the Middle Roman Empire, though planned, was never begun.

The Convention Scene

We find that quite a bit of a writer's (or a magazine's) professional life revolves around conventions. Somewhere, almost any weekend of the year, there is a science-fiction, fantasy, or horror convention going on. They are, by and large, friendly affairs, a combination of enormous weekend party, trade-show, business meeting, and public relations event. For writers and editors, they are seriously important, a place to meet both colleagues and one's readers, to publicize new works, give readings, and generally maintain a credible presence in the field. Conventions are places to make contacts, talk shop, pick up hot, inside information, and — as a business expense — they're tax deductible for the working professional.

For readers — fans — they are a lot of fun, and that is the heart of the matter. What we particularly like about good conventions is that they are *friendly* affairs, at which writers, editors, and readers of the literature mix freely.

Not all conventions are equally valuable or successful. About the recent World Science Fiction Convention in San Francisco, we think, the less said the better, save that the committee's mass exclusion of many professional writers and editors from the program and artists from the art show is hardly a way to build bridges between the pro and fan communities. Hopefully, sanity will prevail in the future. We're looking forward to Glasgow in '95.

Meanwhile, let's list and describe a few of our favorites:

The World Fantasy Convention. The Terminus incarnation of *Weird Tales*® was born at the World Fantasy Convention in Nashville in 1987. (We had a memorable moment coming home on the plane. We had a large zippered bag stuffed into the Editorial Coatpocket in such a way that a thief would have to rip off the whole side of the jacket to get it. "What's in there?" the airport security person wanted to know. "Money," we said in a hushed, conspiratorial voice. "Rather a lot." Fan and dealer response to our first issue had been enthusiastic.) Many new books and magazines make their debuts every Halloween at WFC. It is the place to be *seen* by the pro community, and by leading book dealers. If you attend a World Fantasy Con, bring an extra, empty suitcase for the goodies you may pick up, or make arrangements for the hotel to ship your books back.

A typical World Fantasy Convention is limited to 750 attendees, among whom may be as many as 200 professionals, writers, artists, editors, publishers, agents, and so on. But — for the price — *anyone can attend*. It's not exclusionary. There is usually a reception Thursday night. Regular programming begins Friday morning, with panels, readings, single-author speeches, and the like. The dealers' room and artshow also open Friday morning. Friday night comes the grand autographing session, in which virtually every writer present is available for signing books. The convention proceeds through Sunday evening with programming, parties, guest-of-honor presentations, and the banquet at which the World Fantasy Awards are presented. (Your editor and publisher, Darrell Schweitzer and George Scithers, shared one in the Special Professional category in 1992, for our work on *Weird Tales*®.)

What we particularly like about World Fantasy Cons is the intelligent tone of the proceedings, and the fact that everybody there seems genuinely enthusiastic about the literature. We hope to see a lot of you at this year's convention in Minneapolis, but since, alas, this issue won't be out until then, it's useless to give further information on the 1993 event. (Next year in New Orleans. Write to World Fantasy Convention 1994, PO Box 791302, New Orleans LA 70179–1302.)

We also recommend the World Horror Convention, which is rather like World Fantasy, if a little more narrowly focussed. Last year's affair in Stamford, Connecticut, was pleasant, featuring the usual, plus such unlikely extras as a "dead guest of honor," Mr. Edgar Allan Poe himself, ably impersonated by Paul Clemmons, and an ear-blasting concert by a heavy-metal band consisting of splatterpunks John Skip, Craig Spector, and others. The 1994 World Horror Convention will be in Phoenix, Arizona. Announced author guests include Charles L. Grant and Dan Simmons. Edward Bryant will be toastmaster. Gahan Wilson will be Artist Guest. (1994 World Horror Convention, PO Box 60008, Phoenix AZ 85082–0008.)

And we are particularly fond of Northeast Regional Fantasy Convention, NECon for short, often jokingly called "Camp NECon" by the regulars. (Camp NECon T-shirts exist; they have little bats on them.) This one is far less formal than most, held every July on a college campus in Rhode Island, so that everyone not only parties together, they have their meals together, then head off to "class," which may be a panel, the guest-of-honor presentation (one of last year's guests, Gahan Wilson, showed slides, then drew cartoons based on ideas from the audience) or even the hilarious "Game Show," presided over by Craig Shaw Gardner and Douglas Winter, which may bear a superficial resemblance to *Wheel of Fortune,* but the answer is more likely to be "Zontar, the Thing from Venus." A certain amount of serious business goes on at NECons (ye Ed has conducted author interviews there, often for *Weird Tales*®), but it definitely has a "summer camp" atmosphere. We drive a long way for this one. (Write to Steve Schleifer, NECon, PO Box 528, East Greenwich CT 02818.)

We also had a lovely time at Necronomicon, the Lovecraftian* convention in Danvers, Connecticut (formerly Salem Village, the actual scene of the witchcraft panic of 1692), which was an odd mixture of serious Lovecraftian scholars and *Call of Cthulhu* rôle-playing gamers, a co-mingling of two worlds on the common topic of the Old Gent of Providence. Guests of Honor were Robert Bloch and Gahan Wilson. Unfortunately, the next Necronomicon will not be until 1995.

Finally, personal bias makes it impossible to avoid mentioning Philcon, the Philadelphia Science Fic-

---

* One of us insists the adjective should be "Lovecrafty," but the rest of us manage to keep him quiet.

Publisher: George H. Scithers.
Editor: Darrell Schweitzer.
Managing Editor: Carol Adams
Art Director: Michael W. Betancourt.
Assistant Editors:
Leslie Smith, Dainis Bisenieks,
Diane Weinstein, Don Keller, & Nicholas Beauchamp
Computer Consultant: David J. Williams III.
Of Counsel: Matthew Wolfe
Typesetters: Owlswick Press
& Campus Copy Center

Manuscript Submissions:

Yes; we read unsolicited submissions — but **only** if they are in standard manuscript format. To survive, all editors insist on a few Rules: each submission must be in proper format and must include a return envelope addressed to you with enough postage affixed to bring the manuscript back to you. If you want us to discard the manuscript if not bought, tell us so, but include a business-letter-size envelope with postage affixed, addressed to you, so we can send you our comments. No loose stamps, please!

If want a copy of our guidelines, send us a business-letter-size envelope, with postage affixed, addressed to you, and ask for those guidelines.

Proper manuscript format is also discussed in many reference works. Some of us have even written one: *On Writing Science Fiction: the Editors Strike Back!* by Scithers, Schweitzer, & John M.Ford; $19.50 in hardcovers, from Owlswick Press, 123 Crooked Lane, King of Prussia PA 19406-2570. Another excellent work from the same publisher is Barry B. Longyear's *Science-Fiction Writer's Workshop*: $9.50 in trade paperback. These prices include shipping and handling; in Pennsylvania, please include 6% sales tax.

We are not responsible for manuscripts in our hands or in transit. You **must** keep a copy of every manuscript you send out. You **must** put your name and address on the first page of every manuscript. Please: **no** binders, folders, or padded envelopes; and especially: **no** registered or certified mail for which we would have to stand in line at the post office!

tion Conference, which is one of several regional science-fiction conventions held every year. Your editor just happens to be co-chairman of programming for Philcon. This is more of a science-fiction convention than a horror/fantasy one, but we can tell you that we have invited well over a hundred professionals of all sorts, in addition to the Principal Speaker, Fred Saberhagen; special guests Ian Watson, Emma Bull, and Will Shetterly; and Guest Artist, David Cherry. Philcon features the widest range of programming and events, and we hope there will be something there for everyone. It takes place at the Adam's Mark Hotel in Philadelphia, November 12–14, 1993. We hope to see some of you there. (Philcon, PO Box 8303, Philadelphia PA 19101–8303.)

At a convention in Boston in the early 1980s, we met the charming **Tanith Lee** for the first time and conducted the interview (over lunch, as her soup grew cold, as we recall) which you saw slightly updated in our first Special Tanith Lee issue, WT 291 (Summer 1988). (And will be seeing again, about the time this issue appears, in an interview collection, *Speaking of Horror* by Darrell Schweitzer, from Borgo Press.)

Now we present our *second* Tanith Lee special. She is the first — and for the foreseeable future, only — writer to be honored by being featured this way twice.

Why? We can only say it's inevitable. If *Weird Tales®* were a monthly, we would happily publish a Tanith Lee story in virtually every issue. Since we are quarterly, her stories tend to pile up in inventory — so many we absolutely *cannot* turn down — that necessity brought us to this happy conclusion: It was time for another Tanith Lee issue.

We can only say that the lady is one of the literary dynamos of our time, enormously prolific in the novel, the short story, and all lengths in between (look for her recent *Dark Dance* from Dell/Abyss, and the four-volume *Books of Paradys* sequence from Overlook Press); but, quite unlike most hyperprolific writers of the past, she has maintained an astonishingly high level of quality throughout her career.

At the rate she is going, there will be many more shelves of first-rate Tanith Lee fiction before she is through. We hope to continue publishing as much of it as we can in *Weird Tales®*.

Reprints

We have recently bought rights to three more rare, previously unknown and unreprinted stories by **Lord Dunsany**, the author of *The King of Elfland's Daughter*, and one of the greatest fantasy writers of all time. The first of these, "The House of the Idol Carvers," we managed to squeeze into this issue.

The story first appeared in *Vanity Fair* in November of 1917 and is copyright 1917 by Lord Dunsany and reprinted by arrangement with Curtis Brown

Literary Agency, agents for the Dunsany Will Trust. One of the others, with the unlikely title of "The Dwarf Holobolos and the Sword Hogbiter," originally appeared in 1950 but approximates the masterpieces of Dunsany's *The Book of Wonder* period (pre-World War I) better than any other unreprinted stories yet discovered.

Andrea B.M. Wood writes:
. . . my vote for best story this issue (#307) goes to "Taking Her Time." I was also rather partial to "An Examination Paper"; it reminds me of an assignment I once handed in for an English composition class. However, I would like to say that of all the issues of Weird Tales® *I have read yet — and I have every one in this incarnation — this issue was my least favorite. It seems to me that, too often in this issue, politics interfered with storytelling. "King Weasel" struck me as one long aside, and "The Wrath of the Gods at Macy's" simply went too far to establish a politically-correct (sort of) rather than a believable character. I am not too discouraged —* Weird Tales® *is a terrific journal and I have faith in the editors — but I really hope we won't be seeing the politicization of literature similar to what is going on in the rock-and-roll world these days.*

But on to more fun things . . . Personal biography, for me, plays little to no part in my appreciation of an author's work, but I truly enjoy the Weird Tales® *interviews with authors included in the magazine. It is always interesting to hear an artist speak on his own work, even if one disagrees with the conclusions drawn. And do I have a disagreement with Ian Watson! Adherence to a belief system, the "full, total acceptance of any creed," to quote Mr. Watson directly, does not at all necessarily make one a fanatic, and "[submission] to a particular belief-structure" does not necessarily require one to surrender independent or rational thinking. There is no particular reason why an author of fantasy need be a skeptic. While it is certainly true that Lewis's* That Hideous Strength, *to keep with the example employed in the interview, has its problems, Lewis's Christianity should not be a stumbling block to non-believers where most of his fiction is concerned. It is pretty obvious that Lewis was employing a Christian world-view in his* Chronicles of Narnia, *but it is quite possible for the non-believer to read and enjoy those books and never once be distracted by Lewis's indirectly demonstrated Christianity. The same is true for J.R.R. Tolkien, to use a related example, a devout Catholic much read and appreciated in the Wiccan Neopagan community. As a Catholic (convert, thanks, in part, to Tolkien's influence), I can readily point out the Catholicity in any one of Tolkien's works of fiction, but obviously belief in or acceptance of a Catholic cosmology is not required for an appreciation of Tolkien.*

For many hundreds of years stable religious beliefs of one variety or another have contributed to, not constrained, great literature. If Mr. Watson finds

it more conducive to his creativity to remain a skeptic, then by all means he should do so. However, that Mr. Watson "find[s] it hard . . . to come to terms with artists who have creed without skepticism" strikes me as a rather unyielding posture. It is more than possible to be both rational and religious if one chooses one's religion with care and reason.

We can't speak for Ian Watson, but considering that we once authored an essay entitled "The Necessity of Skepticism" for the late, lamented *Science Fiction Review*, we tend to be somewhat sympathetic to his point of view. Certainly Tolkien's faith *limited* his ability to make up additional "pagan" gods, the way Dunsany did by the dozens, if the story needed them. An author who holds that one set of supernatural beliefs is *true* and therefore to be adhered to as part of the story's *realistic background* cannot possibly be as versatile as one to whom all supernatural material is freely manipulated for the purposes of the story. At the same time, we wouldn't deny that the works of a Lewis or a Tolkien might carry greater conviction than those of a more playful writer.

On a similar topic, and recalling the exchange we had over Devil Worship in these pages, **Lelia Loban Lee** informs us:

I lived in Berkeley, California in the late 1960s, when I was an undergraduate at the University of California. During that period, Anton Szandor LaVey actively promoted his Church of Satan. In those days, at least, it wasn't a one-man show, although I'm sure you're right that it existed mainly as a promotional school for his Satanic Bible. I went to one of his Satanic masses out of curiosity. It struck me as awfully silly, but not particularly horrific. There was a lot of talk about acts that, if they'd actually been performed, would have been illegal, then as now; but apparently these were reserved for special ceremonies by invitation only. Whether anybody ever really got invited, I doubt. The masses were in San Francisco. I had the strong impression that most of the 15 or so people who attended were there to gawk, and had trouble, as I did, keeping their faces straight; but there were a handful of people there who took the whole business seriously. LaVey was pushing the Christian version of Satanism, quite different from today's Wiccan and other pagan cults. Most of the attendees acted stoned out of their gourds.

. . . And probably were, we suspect.

Otto Bumberger writes:

. . . D'ya wanna know what would really be an interesting read? Picture the world in the very far future sometime after the Great Old Ones have finally risen to power after breaking their shackles.

Cthulhu would have finally come into His own; and R'lyeh brought to the ocean's surface again. The Wendigo is not as elusive as he was and stalks through the northern latitudes demanding sacri-fices; night-gaunts are as common as crows near certain marshy areas; Dagon's hordes have made inroads through virtually every seaside town. Man's civilization is in ruins. Horrors of every sort lurk and skulk through mutated forests.

This would be a Grave New World indeed. How would one view such a world through the eyes of the few scattered remnants of humanity? Humanity, under the yoke of the Old Ones, and always at the mercy of the lesser, minor horrors, living the life of scavenging rats or fatted like cattle in certain blasphemous prisons?

Using the bits and fragments of HPL's idea of what such a terrifying future would be (including huge, intelligent spiders — Colin Wilson did a real good job in his Spider World *series), intelligent beetles, our own Sun in the beginnings of its red giant stage, and what not else, it would be a literal hell on Earth.*

But I think a couple of tales of this sort would be interesting reading!

Actually there's a story in Fred Chappell's *More Shapes Than One* written from the perspective of such a future in which the Old Ones have won, but it's very subtle, and he comments in a recent interview we did (for a future Chappell issue of *Weird Tales®*) that we seem to have been the only reader to notice. Otherwise, aside from Robert Bloch's *Strange Eons*, and Darrell Schweitzer's "The Last Horror Out of Arkham," both of which are semi-parodic or overtly parodic attempts (Bloch's by

far the more artful) at "mercy-killing" the Cthulhu Mythos, writers have tended to avoid the endgame scenario. There's no reason it has to be set in the remote future. The Old Ones could dispossess mankind tomorrow. But then, even if they do not simply "clear off the Earth" the way Wilbur Whateley said they would in "The Dunwich Horror," there is still the problem that the all-powerful Things could not be convincingly restrained or defeated in any way, which allows few possibilities for fiction. Still, we think this is one of the very few areas of the Mythos left to be fruitfully explored.

On a similar note, a reader who signs himself **Loki**, but is not, as far as we can tell, a Norse god, wonders why we were not represented at the recent Necronomicon in Danvers. But we were. Had he attended the panel, "Is the Cthulhu Mythos Funny?" he might have understood the answer to his second question, which is why there isn't more Mythos material in *Weird Tales*®, since this is, after all, the magazine where it all began.

The answer is that we would be happy to run Mythos stories, if we could get any that were good. Easily 99% of all post-Lovecraftian Cthulhuvian tales, *at best* merely remind us of Lovecraft, or make us smile at the reacquaintance with old favorites. They are in-jokes and exercises in nostalgia. Surely the test of a contemporary Mythos story is that it must be effective, *as horror*, to an audience which has never even heard of Lovecraft. Such a story must be serious, original, and completely self-standing. There aren't a lot of those in the post-Lovecraft Mythos. Fred Chappell has written perhaps three, T.E.D. Klein three or four more, Fritz Leiber a couple, and beyond that we find ourselves grasping for a single example. If we get a genuinely good one, we'll use it.

Writer **Matthew St. Armand** seems mightily frustrated at the numerous rejections he's gotten from *Weird Tales*®, and offers to go to great lengths to specifically tailor a story to our specific needs. While we appreciate his willingness to make the effort, this is not, alas, the way to go about it. If you "slant" a story to what you imagine the editor's requirements to be, chances are all you'll get is an insincere story. If we've got a "formula," we don't know what it is; and as soon as we find out, we'll stop using stories like that. We want to be surprised and delighted by something we haven't seen before. Beyond that, we have only the broadest parameters: fantastic fiction of all sorts, with a tendency toward horror and the imaginary-scene fantasy and away from most (particularly the more technical) science fiction. The only market research we can suggest is reading the magazine, and even with that, we don't want a repetition of what we've already published. Few editors do.

Karen Blicker would like to nominate John Ordover's "All Flesh Is Clay" for an award (" . . . so innovative yet creepy that it should not be overlooked") and asks how to go about it. Alas, there is no popular-vote award for horror. The Bram Stoker Awards are given by professionals, the Horror Writers of America. The World Fantasy Award is given by a panel of judges. However, popular nominations may add two items to the ballot in each category for the World Fantasy Award, so the best thing to do, then, would be to join the World Fantasy Convention and nominate the story.

An Editorial Book Review:

When a book review columnist illustrates a book, he's not in a position to review that book — no matter how deserving — in his own column. Instead, your editors present here our own opinions on *A Night in the Lonesome October*, written by Roger Zelazny, and illustrated by Gahan Wilson. The publisher is AvoNova/Morrow (an imprint of Avon Books); the price, $18.00 in hard covers.

The story is told in 31 chapters, one for each day of an October in the late 1880s, an October with a full moon on the 31st:

"I am a watchdog. My name is Snuff. I live with my master Jack outside of London now. I like Soho very much at night with its smelly fogs and dark streets. It is silent then and we go for long walks. Jack is under a curse from long ago and must do much of his work at night to keep worse things from happening. I keep watch when he is about it. If someone comes, I howl.

"We are the keepers of several curses and our work is very important. I have to keep watch on the Thing in the Circle, the Thing in the Wardrobe, and the Thing in the Steamer Trunk — not to mention the Things in the Mirror. . . ."

Snuff and his master are trying to prevent the Elder Gods — "Nyarlathotep, Chthulu, and all the rest of the unpronounceables" — from invading our world again. Other characters include the Count who sleeps by day; the Great Detective and his companion; the Good Doctor and his Experiment Man, whom he assembled from bits and pieces; a witch; a Druid; a friendly werewolf; and their assorted familiars — some want to summon the Elder Gods, some want to keep them out — and it's not entirely clear who is on which side.

Zelazny tells a thoroughly entertaining story. Wilson's interior illustrations — 31 of them, one for each day of that October — marvelously complement Zelazny's tale of Snuff, and Jack (yes, *that* Jack) and the rest of these weird yet familiar characters.

The Most Popular Story

Voting was again light for *Weird Tales*® #307, but most voters seem to have agreed with Ms. Blicker, because John Ordover's "All Flesh Is Clay" won by a substantial margin, easily outdistancing the second-place winner, John Brunner's "Taking Her Time," and the (closely following) third-place contender, Ian Watson's "The Coming of Vertumnus."

Best-of-the-year anthologists please note. Ω

THE DEN

by Gahan Wilson

It was clear from the start, has been obvious all along, and is confirmed more and more by each new book, that Peter Straub is one of the best writers of horror fiction living today.

If, by some sad chance, you have not yet read his books, you should certainly do so as soon as possible. Unlike many worthy authors whose works go permanently out of print after one or two runs, the publishers do keep Straub's books in print, not from any altruistically lofty motives, but because his writing sells as well as it deserves to, so you can assemble a basic library of his writings with a minimum of difficulty.

The earlier books which established his wide and highly deserved fame were solidly in the genre of the fantastic.

I always think of the first three as a kind of trilogy: *Julia* is a marvelous haunted mind/house story, which explores the profound potential for horror that lurks in the parent-and-child relationship mishandled; *If You Could See Me Now* concerns a spectacular revenant resulting from sexual young love botched, and *Ghost Story* is an astonishingly rich work involving a series of truly marvelous hauntings which are put to peace at last by the heroes, for there are more than one, finally coming to terms with the guilty errors which started the spectral doings off in the first place.

There are two more fantastic novels: *Shadowland,* a delightfully sly examination of "reality" and "unreality," which involves, among many other riches, a portrait of Aleister Crowley which is both witty and scary; and *Floating Dragon,* a kind of political Lovecraftian tale in which the all-too-familiar immoral and ofttimes fatal misuse of modern technology by greedy — and astoundingly stupid — corporate types is tellingly interrelated with the doings of a nasty old sorcerer of the Joseph Curwen stripe. My personal favorite moment in it involves something pink and gelatinous in a tub.

But then Straub wrote *Koko,* a mystery story, which concerns itself with the attempt to track down a wonderfully sinister killer spawned by the Vietnam war; and with that novel his work essentially departed from fantastic horror — though by no means entirely, for with Straub there is always a genial sprinkling of good, old-timey spooky bits — and plunged into a series of very dark mystery novels, still ongoing, of which the latest — and the best of them yet — is *The Throat.*

The fundamental horror underlying *The Throat* is, as with the rest of this new cycle of books, the Vietman war. The action of the book commences with a bone-chilling and simultaneously hilarious account of the narrator's adventures as a member of a motley group of misfit soldiers, who have been shunted into the "body squad," and whose more official title is "graves registration," and whose thoroughly gruesome duty is to open body bags as they're helicoptered in from the battlefields and to fumble through what's left of the variously-mangled dead in a search for the bagees' name tags. Vietnam is the ominous background to all these books; and Straub presents the war, I think very correctly, as enormously basic to just about everything we have become, here in America.

I have begun to suspect with the passage of years that it is probably impossible, at this short range, to understand how thoroughly Vietnam changed this country and absolutely everybody in it, unless you were/are around to see the place before and after the thing happened. Later on, as it recedes into history, I think its full implications will probably become clearer to those who arrived after the event, in the same way that the impact of the Civil War has become clearer with the passage of six score and twelve years. We were one way before the Vietnam war; we are very much another way after it. It has been, I have absolutely no doubt of it, a genuine quantum change.

One interesting aspect of the change which Straub

selects and stresses in these books is the increasing emergence and dramatic growth of the unnerving phenomenon of serial killers, those weirdly impartial beings who slay total strangers because of cracked notions the murderers carry around in their heads and not for reasons which have anything soever to do with the victims themselves, except that those victims are unfortunate enough to fit into some human category which offends or attracts their slayers. They are slaughtered because they are women, say, or because they are young men who arouse their murderers, or because the victims have long hair which they part in the middle.

All the purely classic-detective-story elements of *The Throat* are highly entertaining and well handled, and Straub constantly pushes the form's envelope. The cast not only features a wide range of convincing sleuths from hard-bitten professional cops all the way to the most dandified of Holmesian amateurs (which are all in active competion with one another); but also, now and then, one turns out to be a victim and it looks as if another might be drifting over to the other side.

They all prowl through a grand variety of remarkably scary places such as the mysterious St. Alwyn Hotel, which may or may not be the lurking place of one or two murderers, and the positively sinister Green Woman Taproom of ancient ill repute, which figures prominently in the plot and has a history as ambiguous as anything in Le Fanu, and a dank, dark cellar as creepy as your heart could desire.

As a special treat, Straub gives us a marvelous example of what has now become the classic tabloid version of a serial killer in his portrait of the person of the "Meat Man," Walter Dragonette.

"Whoever goes into my house," says Walter, smothering a giggle with his hand over his mouth, "is in for a little surprise." And in a way, of course, it isn't a surprise at all because we've come to know all too well what to expect these days: the refrigerator full of human fragments wrapped in clingfilm next to withering carrots and Branola; the well-stocked freezers; the larger items preserved in metal drums; boiled and decorated bones; and, positively *de rigueur,* Polaroids meticulously preserving the various stages involved in producing all these wonders lest any moment fade from memory.

And of course Straub goes on to describe the local television's All Action News Team's efforts to "stay with events as they broke in the Walter Dragonette case . . . giving us advice and commentary by experts . . . counseling us how to discuss these events with our children, and trying in every way to serve a grieving community through good reportage by caring reporters."

Highly recommended in all respects   Ω

THE PERSECUTION MACHINE

by Tanith Lee
Dedicated to the Matchless Edward Gorey

I: Uncle

My father galloped into the library with a look of terror.

"Your uncle is coming!"

"My — uncle? Who do you mean?"

"Constant."

"But I thought —"

"No," said my father, running to the window and glaring out nervously. "He isn't dead. Only mad."

"I see."

"Of course you don't." My father spared a look of distaste for me. As his son, I had had certain duties never properly explained, one of which had been to become a perfect replica of himself in the city of business. Instead I had metamorphosed into a fashionable writer, and it was not in him to forgive me. "Well," he said now, "since you're so clever, I'll leave you to entertain him. Try telling him who you are."

"We've discussed this previously. I'm not clever, only a genius. As for Uncle Constant, if he's calling here, presumably he wishes to see *you*. After all, does he even know of my existence? I'm sure I didn't know of his."

"It was kept from you. I expect *he* will have learned. Twenty years since I saw him. Horrible."

"Is he deformed?" I inquired with pleasant anticipation.

"No. Only his mind. Stall the wretch. Get him to leave if possible."

I shrugged. "Does mother share your aversion?"

"Your mother will faint," said my father, "if he so much as touches the panels of her parlour door."

My mother tended to faint continually when confronted by annoyance. She had already fainted once at my arrival. My father had had the grace only to offer to throw me out. A recent short novel of mine, dealing with forbidden love, very, I may say, tastefully, had caused their latest dislike of me. I, meanwhile, came to visit them from a sense of responsibility, since they were always in want of money.

But what was the motive for mad Constant's arrival?

The doorbell rang below. My father shrieked and rushed from the room.

When Steppings appeared presently in the library door, I accordingly asked him to show the visitor up.

A moment later, my Uncle Constant was revealed to me.

He was a man of about fifty-eight or sixty, corpulent but pale, with a mane of grey hair and disordered clothes. He seemed out of breath, as if he had been running, and he darted a wild look about the room.

"Are we alone?" he demanded.

"I believe so."

"Who are you?"

"Your nephew, Charles."

"Who? Oh, never mind it. Only let me sit down. I'm exhausted. They've pursued me all day. Not a second's peace." He fell noisily into a large chair.

Steppings reappeared, mostly from nosiness, but I sent him off to bring some of my father's Madeira. I had no qualms in this, since I had supplied the wine myself.

"Well, uncle. How may I help you?"

"Help? Impossible. No one can help. I ask only a minute's respite." His breathing quieted a little and he blew his nose into a gigantic handkerchief. "It's no use my explaining. Only I understand what I suffer."

"This may be said of each of us."

"I see you're a philosopher, sir. Did you say we are related? My God, I've run into my brother's house, haven't I?"

"Didn't you know?"

"I will run in anywhere I am able when they are after me."

"Who? Do you mean the police?"

My Uncle Constant was racked with melodramatic laughter.

Steppings came in with the wine and a tray of biscuits.

Constant struck the tray and the biscuits flew in all directions. Steppings did not flinch, merely put on the expression — of a surprised chicken — which has seen such good service over the years. I rescued the Madeira and poured two glasses, waving the chicken away as I did so.

"Drink this."

"Is it poison?"

"I don't think so."

"Nothing short of poison is any use to me. I pant to be released from my suffering. But suicide is a sin." He reminded me of my father. Uncle Constant drank the Madeira at a gulp and I refilled his glass. "They're after me, worse than ever. Their weapons — If only you knew."

He, as my father had done, bustled to the window. He stared out, I assumed, at the peaceful street.

"Not yet," he muttered. "But soon."

"And you have no matters to consult my father upon?" I asked.

"Who? Who is your father?"

"Your brother."

"I have no brother, "said Uncle Constant. "I am cast out into the wilderness." Then his face contorted. It grew red, then blue. "I hear it!" he cried. And flinging the goblet on the ground, or rather the carpet, he sprang away and was gone. I heard his cascade down the stair and the crash of the street door.

I stood by the window and presently saw him emerge and scuttle fatly down the street. He disappeared from view.

2: Uncle's Story

Although I questioned my father and mother about my Uncle Constant, neither told me anything. My father ranted and my mother fainted. Steppings looked like a chicken, and when I tried to enlist his help, only importuned me to persuade my parents to use a new sort of cheese in the mouse-traps. I told him that I disapproved of mouse-traps. Steppings confided that he himself ate the cheese. It was a harmless perversion, during which he sometimes emitted small squeaks.

I was touched by his trust, but it did not help me to discover my uncle.

However, a month later, endless searching led me to a tall gaunt house in the south of the Capital. Here a gentleman bearing my uncle's name resided. The instant I beheld the house, I knew it must be he.

Large bars were on all the windows, and a sort of portcullis was let down outside the door.

On my ringing the door bell, through the portcullis, no one came.

It was a sunny day, and I sat down across the street on a low wall, to watch and wait.

Presently a maid came out of the house with the low wall.

She attempted some ineffectual dusting of the privet hedge, and then bent to my ear.

"He's a madman, that one. You after him for a debt?"

"Not at all. I am a long lost lover of his, come to call on him."

"You're one of them preeverts," said the maid, and ran in.

Half an hour later, two somberly-clad women, with the figures but not the charm of pigeons, came down the street, mounted my uncle's steps, and banged on the portcullis.

I could tell at a glance they were religious persons, and that a lack of response would not put them off. It did not. Getting no reply, they banged the louder. And the larger lady began to cry: "Open the doors of your hearts, O ye lost children of the Lord. Hear the word of the Master!"

I expected a window to be raised and some missile inserted through the bars and thrown.

Instead, to my surprise and delight, sounds of vast unlockings eventually echoed over the street, the portcullis lifted, and my uncle appeared in the doorway.

He wore a yellow dressing-gown and a look of fear and loathing.

"Be off," he yelled at the two ladies, "I know your tricks. Where is it? Is it near? I won't be decoyed."

"Repent," said the large lady. "Here is a tract —"

But Uncle Constant swept the article from her gloved hand.

"Away!" howled uncle, and thrust her down the steps.

The lady fell upon the other one and both toppled to the ground. There was the hideous noise of bursting corsets.

Before my uncle could shut the door and the portcullis I leapt across the street, over the wallowing ladies, and up the steps. I seized Uncle Constant's hand.

"Uncle Constant!"

"Aah! Villain! Unhand me."

"I am your nephew, Charles," I intimated, as he tried to run me through with his sword-stick.

"Who?"

"Your nephew. We met a month ago."

"You're not one of their spies?" He peered at me. "No. Your hair's too long and you have no moustache. Come in then. Quickly. Let me lock the house. I am in deadly peril. If they should once gain a foothold — There! Do you hear it? No. No, you would never hear it."

He slammed the door against the world and we were in a dark hall papered with a design of large red bats, or perhaps prehistoric birds.

"But I did hear —" I began. My uncle took no notice.

Once he had let down the portcullis by means of a switch, locked the door three times and bolted it twice, my uncle led me up a carpeted stair and into a small dim room. The bat wall-paper persisted, but otherwise there were chairs and a sofa and some brandy on a stand. Through the bars of the windows and heavy dusty lace, little was visible, and I imagined that he preferred this to be so.

"Sit down," said my uncle, "whoever you are."

"Uncle Constant, I did hear a noise. Perhaps a train?"

My uncle looked at me strangely. He frowned. Then, going to the stand, he poured out two generous brandies.

He did not, though, give either one to me, or take one himself, he left them where they were as a decoration.

"I will tell you my terrible tale," said my uncle.

"Thank you."

"You must not interrupt."

I nodded mutely.

Assuaged, perhaps, my uncle seated himself in a vast armchair that rather resembled a pig.

"In my youth," he began, "I had no cares. I did very much as I wanted. I had been thought too clever for school, and so a number of tutors had taught me at home. I had no friends and wished for none. My only interest, as I grew older, was collecting young actresses. Then one evening, on my way home from the theatre, I was met by a messenger in the street. My parents had perished in a fire at the house of an ice-cream manufacturer, and I had now inherited the family fortune."

Although I knew that my grandparents were not dead, and that there had never been a family fortune, I did not argue with Uncle Constant at this point. I felt that probably he was instinctually lying in order to give some framework to what might follow.

"I fell," he continued, as if gratified by my sensitive abstention, "into a melancholy. I stayed indoors and only wandered from room to room of the house, recalling the unhappy hours I had spent there with my parents, who were both obtuse and ugly. The prettiness of my actress collection came to repel me, and I saw these girls no more. After some months, I ventured out at night, and walked the nastiest thoroughfares of the city, until it was almost dawn. Gradually, as I was returning to the house, I became aware that I was being, and had indeed been for some while, followed, by a number of mysterious shadowy figures. At length, a peculiar noise resounded distantly behind the smoking chimneys and smouldering refuse pits of the alleys."

My uncle looked at me expectantly, but, true to his wish, I did not interrupt. Consoled, he went on.

"I can only describe this noise as that of some curious engine, which also whistled, rather like a factory hooter. **Chug chug**, it went, and then **Whoop! Whoop!** Alarmed, I hastened home, but after I was indoors I heard something move down the street and a shadow was cast up on my windows."

My uncle got up, and going to the brandy glasses, he poured their contents into an aspidistra, then refilled them carefully from the decanter. He left them on the stand, and resumed his chair and his tale.

"Soon after this, when I had gone out once more on some necessary business, I was again followed, and after a time I heard repeated the ominous chugging and whooping of the sinister engine. I hurried at once on to a busy thoroughfare, and there the din of the crowd somewhat mitigated the sound of the pursuit. After a few minutes, however, a frightful shooting pain began in my right knee. And then another, worse, in my right arm. I fell against a lamppost, and an old gentleman came up and smote me in the face, accusing me of being drunk. As I partly lay there, I saw, through the ranks of the oblivious and jeering crowd, a fearful thing rolling slowly and mightily down from the end of the street. It was a sort of carriage, yet it had no horses, and from it protruded all manner of pipes and coils, wheels that whirred and the nozzles of what could only be guns. Suddenly one of these flashed with a cold green fire, and a new pain lanced through my belly. Atop the device was a crew of men clad like explorers in long coats, goggles, and unlikely hats. They had moustaches and their lips were thin and cruel. From the midst of them a funnel glowed and steamed and out came the noise. **Chug, chug**. And then **Whoop, whoop**. No one in the street but I could see this evil equipage. I turned; and, as best I could for my hurts, I ran. The more distance I could put between myself and the engine of torment, the more relief I gained, and finally I shut myself into the house and knew an end to my pain. Its four walls, imbued as they were with boring memories of my parents, protected me. But as I crouched behind the door, the machine passed down the street. Its shadow fell again inside the house. From that day, I have not been free of it."

My uncle rose once more and paced to an empty parrot cage. He stared into it and shook his head.

"So far, they have not gained access to my home. Now and then their spies seek me. The machine never lies in wait for me outside the house . . . a sporting chance is allowed me — although they are not really fair. If ever the machine can by stealth enter these premises, I am lost."

A vague rumbling sounded in the street. A faint shadow crossed the window and next the ceiling. I got up and went to look out. The street was empty but for another maid dusting a hedge, and two porters carrying a stuffed bear. The religious ladies had picked themselves up and gone away.

"You may speak now," said my uncle.

"Have you," I asked, "approached no one for help?"

"In the beginning, ceaselessly. I went to the police, and then to private companies. But all laughed me to scorn. An eminent doctor has certified that I am harmlessly mad."

"The engine or machine is invisible to all others but yourself?"

My uncle returned to the brandy stand and drank both glasses of brandy. "I am doomed." He then showed me out of the house.

3: Uncle Pursued

After that second meeting, I took to following my Uncle Constant.

He went out, as can be imagined from his fears, very seldom, and so my vigils were frequently long, dull and unrewarded — except by the emergence of the privet-dusting maid, who seemed to think, despite my 'preeversion,' that I fancied her person. This was rather trying. However.

Finally, my uncle began to slip cautiously out of the house on hobbled rapid errands.

He would first of all open the door a crack, having of course noisily unlocked and unbolted it, and raised the portcullis. He would then gaze fixedly at each side of the street in turn. He never noticed me, even when I had not taken the trouble of obscuring myself behind the hedge. And I noted presently that, even if he looked at me on the street, he never recalled who I was or that I was anyone but a complete stranger.

Having perused both directions, Uncle Constant would leap forth and bolt one way or the other. Being portly, his quickness soon flagged, but he kept up what pace he could, his arms clutched to his chest,

rather in the manner of a squirrel. Now and then he would break into a run. And frequently, he would glare behind him. In doing this, he often saw me, but paid, as I have said, no heed.

I, on the other hand, listened as intently and turned round as often as he.

It seemed to me that I heard a familiar noise in the distance, but I could not be sure how near we might be to some bizarre railway line or extraordinary factory, which might produce such sounds. Then, too, it sometimes seemed to me that shadows appeared at the ends of streets which bisected those pavements along which Uncle Constant rattled. Yet too I was never certain ordinary objects might not somehow have cast these shadows, and besides they were always fleeting.

Meanwhile other people and things moved all round us in the normal manner. My uncle occasionally barged into them, so oblivious was he of anything but the persecuting pursuit.

He never returned from his expeditions by the same route he had set out on, but always via a roundabout circuit. For presumably he was afraid, if the machine of torment was somewhere behind him, he might otherwise meet it head-on.

Uncle's outings were mundane and sketchy. Sorties upon shops of food and chemists' emporiums, and once a journey to a well known and reputable bank. On this last foray, he emerged from the august portals amid cries and clangs, and squirreled down the steps, clutching at his left leg and muttering: "They're near." He was obviously in pain, and intercepting his terrified glance, I too looked back along the street.

The vista was thronged with people, and on the road were several carriages. It was apparent that no vehicle could pass unseen, if it were really there. As I gazed, it seemed to me that there was indeed something moving slowly and ponderously under the archway that opened the street. A faint greenish beam was struck from the place that might only be the morning sun upon some harness or other metallic item. My uncle distracted me with a hoarse scream. I turned and saw he had dropped to his knees. A bank-note fell from his hand, and I ran over, stopping the money before someone should snatch it, and next trying to assist him.

"Uncle —"

"Let me go, wretch!" screeched Uncle Constant, hitting me so violently in the chest that I too was flung on the ground. Before I could right myself, he was up and hobbling and moaning away.

I then decided that, rather than rush after him in the usual fashion, I would wait at the roadside to see if any unusual carriage came past. I was encouraged in this idea by a repetition of the unlikely noise I had heard before — the **chug** and **whoop** of a mad engine, whistle or hooter. Then again, the street was noisy itself and I could not quite be sure.

I waited at the kerb for twenty minutes, by which time all the approaching traffic had gone by and my uncle was completely out of sight.

Irritated, I then stalked back up the road, and found an intersection. Staring down one of the opposing boulevards, I had the impression that something was trundling away there. Before I could go after it, a band of religious choristers enveloped me, and I was forced to give them cash before I could escape. By then, naturally, any hint of what might have been a strange vehicle, or only an optical illusion generated by sympathy and hope for the unnatural, had vanished.

I returned to my uncle's house in a bad mood, and he was already indoors, the portcullis down and all signs of life concealed.

After this jaunt he did not venture out again, though I waited for many weeks.

Unfortunately my own life was becoming complicated. I was supposed to be at work upon a new volume of tasteful obliqueness, and had neglected it sadly. Various creditors were restless, and I was already receiving fewer social invitations. My publisher advised me that, unless I took up my employment, the public would forget me, and I feared I would therefore no longer have the money to support my feckless parents, who were just then in the process of buying whole suites of unsuitable furniture, busts of Roman generals, and a black parrot.

Regretfully, I left my post at the low wall opposite to my uncle's house. It was a fine evening, the west still flushed with dusk, and a lone light burned in an upper window. And far off without a doubt at this moment, I heard it in the stillness, **chug chug chug** and then its **whoop** on a high weird note. It was circling at a distance, like a beast of prey, the campfire of that solitary lamp.

But I could no longer stay.

I went to my home, and my novel; so much more real than uncle's predicament.

4: The Machine

It was on the afternoon that I delivered the finished manuscript of *The Fateful Kiss of Night* to my publishers that the last act of Uncle Constant's tragedy was played before me, and I was pulled irresistibly into it.

A beautiful afternoon of early summer, it had drawn the idle and the pleasure-seekers into the park. As I walked along beside the river the swans glided past like pillows with white necks, and the nurse-maids wheeled their bonneted toy babies up and down in perambulators. Young men pensively reflected in the glassy water, maidens sat reading under the statues, hoping the young men were secretly watching them, which, usually, they were not.

About two hundred yards off, over the wall of the park and its line of tall trees, an ominous sound came and went, and I had glanced that way in a consternation I did not at first fathom. But although

an apparatus was out there, it was only a steam engine, resurfacing the roadway with pitch. With a sense of relief or disappointment, I returned my eyes to the picture-postcard scene of the park.

Across the flower-beds lay a lawn, at the centre of which was a coloured bandstand. Here the bandsmen were going at full blast, and on the lawn couples bumpily danced a polka.

The warm day lay limpid on the park with all its safe and proper comings and goings, a postcard view, as I say, into which an unsuitable figure abruptly burst: Uncle Constant.

Of those assembled, I was not the least startled.

How he had come there was beyond ascertaining, he seemed merely to erupt into being. And my premonition of the steam-roller was appropriate. Uncle was as usual in headlong flight. Indeed, he was in the most abject condition I had yet beheld, and through his wheezing, he faintly screamed.

As people hastened from his way, a few turned their heads anxiously to see what it was he fled from, what it was he saw as his head craned at a painful angle over one shoulder. But having turned, they shrugged and one or two made good-mannered gestures relating to insanity, while three pompous gentlemen began to shout for the police.

I also turned, more from habit than from the hope of finding anything.

And so I saw, at last, coming across the wholesome green grass on which little children played and young ladies walked with their parasols, the moving engine of my uncle's terror.

It was unmistakable. It was tall as the second storey of a fashionable house, and it glided smoothly forward on great black runners. Its look was of a monstrous bathchair, but one which bristled like a porcupine. Pipes and nozzles protruded from it, ornamental and deadly: One glance assured me that each must be a variety of gun. And even as I stared one indeed gave off a puff of dull viridian smoke followed by a quick white flash. And over the merry noise of the park I heard my uncle howl with pain. I did not look to see if he had fallen. My eyes were fastened to the machine of his persecution.

Aloft, on a sort of balcony above the horseless, rolling carriage-front, were packed about ten persons. Perhaps they were men, they appeared to be, and yet . . . and yet there was something palpably wrong about them which my study unpleasingly revealed. Their dark overcoats were moulded to their bodies in the same manner that wings mould to the back of a black beetle. Their black moustaches quivered and seemed to move of their own will. And their eyes had been goggled over with curious dark green glasses that were faceted in many tiny winking panes.

Above them, and behind, a funnel rose from the top of the machine. Even as I glared at it, one of the riders touched its side with a gloved hand on which, perhaps, there were two or three extra fingers. The funnel responded with a dim glow and a gout of steam burst from the crown. Over the horrible thundering rattle and chug of the vehicle's progress shrieked a deafening **Whoop! Whoop!**

Frantically, I at last gazed about, to see if the bystanders were forced to put their hands over their ears.

But, just as they did not appear to see the machine, so they apparently could not hear it.

Even so, even so. As it trundled its inexorable and menacing way forward over the emerald grass, the children gambolled from its path, the girls increased their pace and swept aside. As if at a whim. Yes, as it advanced, the crowd parted before it, but not one of them paid it the slightest overt attention. Not one — save I. And my Uncle Constant.

He had certainly collapsed, but soon struggled up again. And now he limped and tottered on, striving to escape across the park. How desperate he looked. His face was white and blind with fear. He did not think, it was evident, he could on this occasion get to safety.

The machine went by me. It passed within three feet. I too must have taken some instinctive steps aside.

A furnace heat came from the thing, and the terrible chugging was accompanied by showers of cold green sparks from its runners.

Uncle limped over the flower-beds and rambled out on to the dancing sward. Couples bumped into him and waved him aside. He skirted the bandstand and went painfully on towards the wall.

The machine did not, or could not, improve its speed. Yet its unavoidable quality was somehow augmented by its very slowness, as in a dream.

It ploughed in among the dancers, who bounced and swung from its way, not looking at it, not hearing or seeing it. Unlike my uncle, seeming to have to move in a straight line, it came directly at the bandstand, and there, peculiar protuberances, like the rubbery legs of some enormous fly, poured out and raised the runners, and so walked the whole contraption up into the midst of the band, the top of the machine only narrowly missing knocking off the roof.

The musicians were forced to scramble to the perimeters, juggling their instruments.

And yet — even in this extremity — not one man regarded the invader, and not *one* lost the beat of their foolish dance.

And then the horror had marched on, and over, and was down on the lawn again, and all the band resettled, banging and tooting the jolly tune without a break.

A fierce ray flashed.

I saw my uncle sprawl headfirst.

Instantly he had pushed himself up, but now he could not rise from his knees. He began to crawl towards the wall of the park.

For a moment I stood at a loss. And then some primal spirit took hold of me.

I raced.

I sprinted over the lawn, scattering and possibly felling the polkists left and right. I tore past the machine itself, and felt again its awful heat, and

smelled its metals and its odour of a chemical swamp, and of some location inexplicable.

Even past my Uncle Constant I sprang, and reaching the wall, I bolted through the gate.

Outside, the steam-roller majestically moved, and its motion was very like that other one, that wallow of the machine. I flung myself upon the steam engine and wasted no time in hauling myself up its side. The driver was startled as I barged in beside him. I thrust some coins into his palm and cast him out, and he plummeted angrily on to the pitchy road, shouting.

I turned the steam engine with difficulty but with determination, and drove it back through the gates.

My uncle was crawling steadfastly on, but thank God he had the sense to pull himself from my road. I cranked my colossus onward, until I beheld the persecution machine exactly in my path.

It did not veer, perhaps it could not. No expression crossed the faces — if such they were — of its malefic crew. Only the moustaches wrinkled and the goggles glittered, and from the stack of the funnel went up another gout of white and another fiendish whistle.

I sent the steam-roller headlong. With a grinding of gears and a furious hissing, it pounded forward into battle.

Until I could see every beaded decoration on the nozzles of the ray guns, I held to my post. Then I jumped away. I landed in a rhododendron bush. And at that moment the two leviathans came together.

There was an explosion like the Trump of Doom. And then a tumult only like that of some apocalyptic train crash.

A light like an incendiary burst, and out of it huge pieces of things were hurled into the air and dashed all about, boiling and gushing, and black metal rods, wheels, plates, cogs, screws, all types of mechanical and peculiar debris smashed down over the park.

Not a single cry or scream attended this.

But looking up from my bush, I saw the monstrous crew of the machine also hurtling through space, and they were broken in a way human creatures do not break. Black blood or slime rained all around. It smelled medicinal and acid.

Presently the hurricane ceased, and a great stillness should have settled, but did not, for the park had gone on at its music and its chat uninterrupted.

I stared. Swans swam peacefully among black irregular objects in the river. Young ladies, blood-splattered, danced brightly with their bloodied gentlemen between rivets and black smoking shafts stuck down in the earth like flaming bones. Craters had appeared. And these the dancers carelessly circled. While the band played on, despite the green-goggled heads which had fallen on the bandstand roof, the instruments streaked with blood and coiled with what were, conceivably, alien entrails.

Of the machine nothing but a sort of heaving slag remained. There was little either of the noble steam-roller.

I went to my uncle and helped him up.

"It is over," I said.

"Who are you?" he demanded.

Outside the wall, the driver of the steam engine had left off his complaints. He sat smoking at the roadside, as if that was his only purpose, and touched his cap to me.

I assisted my uncle to his house.   Ω

HE UNWRAPS HIMSELF

He unwraps himself, like a Christmas package,
the ribboned clothing, the greeting-card hair,
nose and ears, nipples, penis, cast aside,
off —

He unfolds himself, with silent grace;
the face is next, a delicate mask,
lifted away to reveal
the skull beneath the skin;

Stealing phrases from John Webster —
Or was it Marlowe? One of
those leotarded guys — he unlocks himself,
declaiming "Come Sirrah! Gut me like a fish,
and give these groundlings
their sup of gore!"

Frenzied and fierce, he unbinds himself,
bloody sinews, lungs and heart,
the deeper flesh all steaming
at his feet, the gray-white skeleton
chattering in the dark, "But wait, my Love! There's
    more!"

At the very last, he reveals himself,
bones crinkled, heaped like newspaper,
the flickering candle's flame of his genuine self,
soul's truth, there, unadorned.
"Dearest, what you see is what you get."

But she hastily escapes through
shattered French windows,
and the night breeze
blows the candle out.

— Darrell Schweitzer

VOICES OF THE DAMNED
by Lois Tilton

The stableboy heard the sound as he started to lead the Carthene merchant's horses from their stalls. In the market square, a vendor of cooking oil looked up from her booth. A gang of boys ran shouting toward the town's western gate. The Carthene merchant, rings gleaming on his well-manicured hands, paused in the doorway of the inn.

The sound was a low, dull moaning, as if a herd of cattle were being driven to market. A crowd began to gather in the square, drawing back as the barbarian prisoners came into sight, shackled together at the ankles and neck, a wretched, limping procession of misery and defeat. The clank of chains and the crack of the lash were a counterpoint to their groans. The odor of them filled the square: sweat, filth, blood, and the putrid smell of infected wounds.

To Eral Dhar Tann, the watching, jeering crowd was a blur of color and noise. He was past anger, past even shame. A Djieddin soldier crowded his horse into them, and Pall, chained next to Dhar Tann, stumbled. Dhar caught his brother, staggering under his weight.

Suddenly there was a cry: *water!* The captives were pushing forward, all of them crazed with thirst. One man ahead of Dhar was down, half-dragged, half-trampled in the rush. Cursing, the Djieddin guards flailed down at them with their whips. Dhar struggled to keep his grip on Pall, to keep both of them on their feet. He could hear the sound of splashing just ahead of him, where men were tearing each other away, trying to get at the water. Would there be enough? Would the water be gone by the time he reached it? Dhar shoved forward in sudden panic, as maddened as the rest.

They were senseless of what they had been reduced to. Altall warriors — the defeated survivors of a once-proud tribe, now on their knees in the dust of some Djieddin town, fighting each other to reach the edge of a cattle-trough.

Savagely lashing out at their captives, the Djieddin soldiers forced them back into their lines. A fresh whip-cut smarted across Dhar's cheekbone. He was still supporting Pall's half-inert weight.

Slowly he grew conscious of the jeers of the Djieddin townspeople. He could make out a little of what they were shouting: *Filthy barbarians! The Lords will spit out your souls!*

Shame crept back into his soul, the shreds of a defeated warrior's honor and pride. The Altall had thought they could defeat Djied's soldiers, take their pasturelands for their own herds. Instead —

Pity in a pair of black eyes met his for an instant, and Dhar felt a spark of irrational hope quicken into life, then die again as the immaculately-robed stranger turned his face abruptly away.

There was no hope, not for any of them. At the end of this road they would end up in chains on some Djieddin slave-block. Or worse. There were rumors of worse. The power of the Djieddin Sorcerer-Lords was real, horribly real, as the Altall survivors had learned to their sorrow and grief. The women and children . . .

Pall swayed, and Dhar moved quickly to catch him again. The guard shoved them forward, another few steps closer to the water. It might be the last they would get before they came to the walls of Djied. One more day on the road? Two? How many more men would die before the end, their clansmen too weak to drag them any farther?

After Dhar's turn at the water, he noticed that two of the soldiers were coming out of a wine shop with straw-wrapped pottery jugs under their arms. They would rest, then, for a while in this place. Next to him, Pall sank down onto the ground and dropped his head down onto his knees. The cut on his scalp had broken open again.

Dhar knelt down beside him. There was the well-groomed stranger again, striding impatiently up to the Djieddin captain in charge of the captives. The two spoke a few words, and there was a quick gleam of gold changing hands. The stranger — not Djieddin, not with that lean, hawk-nosed face — glanced over the wretched throng of captives, then pointed in Dhar's direction.

The captain nodded. Dhar shrank inside as he strode over and addressed him with a kick. "You, up! You know any Carthene?" he asked in the language of the Empire.

With an effort, Dhar got himself to his feet. "Some . . . a little," he whispered. Carthene was the universal language of trade on the steppes.

"He'll do," the hawk-faced stranger said quickly, without directly meeting Dhar's eyes again. "These barbarians all grow up on horseback. Send him directly over to the innyard as soon as you get rid of that iron. I've already been delayed too long in this place."

Numbly, Dhar heard the captain bellow orders for someone to take the shackles off the barbarian and get him over to the inn, double-quick. Before he could collect his wits, his chains were struck off, and a Djieddin soldier was shoving him through the gate of the innyard. "This one's yours," he said to the Carthene, who was standing next to a wagon loaded with rugs.

19

Dhar was suddenly conscious of his own filth, his torn and bloodstained clothes, the raw shackle galls on his neck and ankles. Another Carthene stood nearby, more plainly dressed, with a bandage around his wrist. This one's expression spoke his distaste clearly: *filthy barbarian.*

"Your name?" he asked aloud.

"Eral Dhar Tann."

"You can handle this wagon, can't you?"

Dhar glanced blankly at the rig, nodded.

"All right. From now on, you belong to the Carthene merchant Carrimene Aliotimes. I'm his steward, Hammad. I'd be driving the wagon myself, except . . ." He made a gesture of his injured arm in explanation. "We leave right away. Master Carrimene doesn't want any more delays."

His mind whirling with exhaustion and confusion, Dhar grabbed hold of the wagon seat to pull himself up, but weakness made him fall back. Hammad had to reach out with his good arm to help him. Dhar set his teeth and gathered up the reins while the Carthene merchant swung into the saddle of the sleek black gelding just led out of the stable.

Dizzy and hollow from exhaustion, Dhar managed nevertheless to maneuver the wagon with its load of rugs out the gate of the yard and into the square, where the Djieddin soldiers were starting to lash their captives back up to their feet. Pall! Dhar half-stood, nearly dropping the reins, but Hammad caught hold of his arm. "Keep driving!" he hissed, low-voiced. "Don't turn around!"

Dhar was torn. He could not recognize his brother among the mass of beaten tribesmen. Hammad jerked him back down to the wagon seat with a whispered curse, and the Carthene merchant turned the gelding's head back in an impatient demand to know what the delay was this time.

Dhar whipped the horses into a trot.

A few leagues down the road, the market town out of sight behind them, Hammad took over the reins and handed Dhar a chunk of bread from a basket under the wagon's seat. He seized it, tearing off chunks and bolting them down, aware that he looked like some starving animal. Hammad gave him more, making no move to hand him back the reins. The Carthene was having no trouble handling them, despite the bandage on his wrist. Dhar was confused, but he was too weary to wonder about it. In the end, he spent most of the rest of the journey to Djiedd collapsed on the carpets in the back of the wagon, falling in and out of a fitful sleep.

It was while he was half-awake, too weary to stir or open his eyes, that he heard Hammad's voice speaking.

"Sir, are you sure this is a good idea? Taking him with us to Djied? "

"He was in the battle. He can tell us what happened. He looks intelligent enough under all that yellow hair. And we need the information."

"But afterwards? An ignorant barbarian — if he talks . . ."

"What would you do? Leave him on the road? Sell him back to the Sorcerer Lords?"

"I'm thinking about the risk."

"The Empire expects us to take risks."

That reply silenced Hammad for a few moments. Then he said, "There's another alternative, you know."

There was a pause.

Then, "No, I don't think that will be necessary. I hope not."

The horses stamped restlessly, jingling their harness. The Altall warriors were drawn up along a low ridge. The scent of crushed grass beneath their hooves was freshly pungent. Dhar Tann wiped his sweating palms on his trousers and nervously shifted his grip on his spear. Beside him, Pall reached over to give him a reassuring touch on the elbow, but the feeling of wrongness persisted.

On the plain below the Djieddin waited in ordered ranks. The sunlight glinted off their polished bronze armor, but there were no more than two hundred of them, and their backs were to the river. The Altall were almost a thousand warriors. They would sweep down, annihilate the enemy, and claim this land for their own. Except . . .

Dhar Tann wanted to cry out a warning, but someone had already signaled the attack, and the charge thundered down from the ridge. He was swept along, crouched down on his horse's neck, spear in his hand, but his unease had grown into dread.

Suddenly — but somehow he had known this — the steppe erupted into whirlwinds of flame. The Altall horses bolted in panic, screaming. He saw his brother thrown and disappear behind a wave of driving hooves, but his own horse was out of control and he could not turn back to save Pall.

Ahead of him, the warleader Faren Hal Barr stood up in his stirrups, shouting to rally the warriors. A few of the Altall had managed to master their mounts and were starting to regroup, shouting that the flamespouts were illusion only, harmless.

Dhar moaned, tried to will himself not to see what he knew would happen next, but the vision proceeded inexorably. One moment Hal Barr was shouting out his warcry, and in the next he burst screaming into flames. This was no illusion! The Altall host broke, pursued now by the enemy, who slaughtered them as they fled.

Dhar Tann watched, helpless, voiceless, while a Djieddin spear transfixed his brother, and Pall screamed out in anguish — *Dhar, help me!*

Drenched in sweat, he woke and lay for a few moments in the straw of the stable. It seemed that he could still smell the burning flesh, hear the screams. At last he rose unsteadily and went to the well, plunged his face into the bucket of chill water.

The dreams were getting worse, night after night. He dreaded sleep, knowing he would be forced to relive the battle again, to hear the voices of Pall and the others crying out for help. Were the voices their ghosts, haunting him? Was Pall dead, not in the fighting, but in chains on the road to Djied?

Grief and guilt washed over him. He did not belong in this place. He was grateful to Carrimene, who had struck off his shackles, fed him, healed his wounds. Bondage was the fate of battle-captives, and a slave of the Altall would not have been treated so well. But he had deserted Pall. Left his brother, his whole tribe, behind him on that road.

The restless stamping of hooves came from one of the stalls. Dhar went into the black gelding's stall, and its grace struck him again — a horse made for the gods to ride! He stroked its neck, then lowered his head to inhale the scent. Daily, he brushed the sleek coat until it gleamed like the silk in Carrimene's warehouse.

Dhar frowned. He had encountered merchants in scores of towns, greedy and grasping every one of them, thinking of nothing but how to cheat an ignorant barbarian tribesman. Carrimene was like no merchant he had ever known. It was true, carpets and silks came into the warehouse, were shipped out again on vessels sailing to the Empire and other distant places. But why should any merchant have been so eager to know about the massacre of his tribe?

Carrimene had questioned him for hours about the battle, asking him over and over again to describe the sorcery that had defeated the Altall.

"These flames. They were not just illusion? You're sure?"

"Yes, I'm sure. We thought, at first, it might just be some kind of sight-trick, like our shaman could do. But it was . . . it was more than that. I saw men burning, men of my own clan. Burning alive, their horses too. We couldn't hear anything but the screaming."

"They just burst into flame? Or did the fire come out of the ground, for example?"

"No, I don't know. I don't think so."

"That's all right, Eral. Just try to remember what you saw. Now, the Djieddin soldiers — how closely could you see them? Do you know for sure that they were all human men? Were there any you might describe as demons, for example?"

Dhar had not protested when Carrimene called him by his clan name. A slave had no clan, or no name of his own. He had answered the questions as well as he could, though most of what he remembered about the battle had been confusion, men and horses screaming in terror of the flames, the Djieddin cavalry with their sabres in pursuit of the maddened survivors.

In his dreams, though, he remembered it all, the horror of every moment.

It was the dreams he was fleeing. The more he stayed in this place, the worse they grew. He felt a slight pang of regret for what he was about to do now, for he had an honor-debt to Carrimene — not as his slave, a slave had no honor, but for that moment on the road. This was a poor way to repay him.

Summoning his resolve, he quickly saddled the black. The lock on the stable yard's gate was easy enough to break. Outside, the sky to the east was a light, rose-tinged gray. The dreams always were worst just before dawn. Silently, Dhar took the horse through and out onto the street. The sound of hooves was alarmingly loud on the cobbles. He fought the temptation to kick the horse into a run. This was not the open steppe, and he did not know his way through Djied's maze of narrow streets.

Everywhere he turned there were buildings and walls, whitewashed houses of fired brick and stone, trapping him in this place. Was there no way out? The sky's gray was shading into blue by now, and Djieddin citizens were venturing out into the streets. How long before he was stopped and questioned? His fair barbarian hair was too conspicuous, and he barely could speak the language.

Desperation mounting, he turned a corner and suddenly found himself facing the massive blocks of the Djieddin city wall. The fortifications loomed above his head, six times a man's height. No way over, no way through. He was trapped!

No, there had to be a gate. But what of the guards, when they saw a barbarian slave trying to ride through on a horse worth a hundred Imperials?

Dhar dismounted, staring up to the top of the wall. It looked only half-completed. On the ground were piles of stone and sand. Ropes hung down from pulleys fixed to massive beams. It shouldn't be too hard to climb. It hurt, to think of abandoning the horse, but he could steal another once he was outside this place.

Then in the distance he saw approaching a line of ragged, starveling figures harnessed to a sledge loaded with blocks of roughly-cut stone. He stared. There was something about them, the way they strained against their rope harness in utter silence. Slaves, certainly, but where were the guards and their whips? What drove them?

Dhar shrank back behind a block of stone. As the line came closer he could see their blond hair and the light skin of their faces. His heartbeat surged. Here were the men of his tribe!

Then elation died, turned slowly to horror. Their movements were unnatural, the way they hauled the sledge forward with stiff, jerky steps. *Like the dead,* came his unwilling thought.

He ran forward to a man he recognized, a clansman, calling out to him, "Dann!" But even at the sound of his name the man made no response. He kept moving, never turning his head. Dhar grasped his shoulders, turned him around. And looked into a pair of empty, soulless eyes.

He backed away, crying out aloud in shock. One after the other he stared into the vacant faces of the walking dead, searching for Pall. Where was he? Dhar could hear the echo of his dreams mocking him. *This* was the fate he had abandoned his brother to. This was what he had escaped!

A hand seized his arm from behind, pulled him around, and he found himself facing the suspicious dark face of one of the Djieddin municipal guard. "You! Wait, you're not — Just what in the sixty hells are you doing around here? Who are you, anyway?"

Dhar tried to summon up some excuse, that he was out early exercising his master's horse and had gotten lost, but the sight of his tribesmen had robbed him of the power of coherent speech.

Carrimene, along with a grim-faced Hammad, came to fetch him from the prison. Dhar looked up once, briefly, to meet his master's eyes. He had found mercy there, once, but he saw none now. Nor, did he suppose, was any deserved. He looked down again at the floor.

"This is your slave?" the Djieddin guard captain asked.

Carrimene nodded. "My steward here reported him and the horse missing this morning."

The captain glared at Dhar. "He was picked up at the wall. Interfering with the Lords' slaves. I suppose you know the penalty."

Carrimene was conciliatory. "I'm sure he had no idea what he was doing. He's a barbarian, new to the city. He probably got lost, trying to escape."

Dhar opened his mouth to protest, but there was a tone in his master's voice that made him hesitate. Under the guard captain's stare, he kept silent.

"A good flogging will teach him," Carrimene added.

The captain was still staring suspiciously at Dhar. "We could make sure he learns his lesson, right here."

But Carrimene quickly protested, "No, that won't be necessary. He's my slave, after all. My responsibility."

"The next time," the Djieddin warned, glaring at Dhar, but Carrimene was quick to reassure him.

"There won't be a next time, Captain. I'll make sure of that!"

They released Dhar into Hammad's custody. The Carthene steward said nothing until they were back in the compound. Overwhelmed by the horror what he had seen, the soulless beings that had once been his tribesmen, Dhar had forgotten about the flogging until Hammad led him into the stable, where two of the other Carthene slaves were waiting. Their faces were set and expressionless.

They stripped off his clothes and tied his wrists up to an iron harness ring on the wall. Hammad took a horse whip and stood for a moment running its length through his fingers. He looked uneasy, reluctant. Dhar braced himself and held his breath. Then there was the whistle of leather cutting through the air and the searing impact of it across his back.

Dhar endured the blows gripping the harness ring until he thought the iron must be twisted out of shape. By the time it ended there were droplets of his blood spattered on the stable wall. Finally Hammad let the whip drop to the floor of the stable, and they cut Dhar's wrists free. His knees buckled, refusing to support his weight. The other slaves caught him, dragged him over to his bed in the straw. As they left the stable, Hammad turned back for a moment. The blood had drained from the steward's face, and he whispered a single word: *Fool!*

Bitterly, Dhar could not deny it. The flogging was nothing. A slave of the Altall would have had his leg tendons severed for what he had done, and counted himself still lucky to be alive.

No, he had been a fool to think he could escape his dreams.

The Altall host was arrayed along the ridge. Soon would come the charge, then the flames. Dhar was powerless to stop it. There was Pall on the ground, transfixed by the enemy's spear. As Dhar watched helplessly, the spear was transformed into a spike of flame, and soon all the Altall were burning, pleading with him for release.

Chains weighed him down. He strained to crawl to Pall's aid, but the weight of the iron held him fast.

Awake, sweat-soaked and shivering, Dhar still felt the chains, the leg-irons he had worn since his escape. It was no more — less, in fact — than he had expected. The Carthenes were not unnecessarily cruel. Dhar understood now what Carrimene had saved him from, and the sense that he had betrayed that debt gnawed at him still.

But Pall! His clan, his tribe — their voices . . .

He buried his face in the gelding's sleek neck, close to tears in his despair. The nightly torment of his dreams was worse than any flogging. It would have been better if he and all his tribe had died on the road to Djiedd.

The stable door opened, and Dhar straightened himself when he saw Carrimene come inside. His master ordered him to saddle the black. Then Carrimene looked at him for a moment. "I want you to know, Eral," he said slowly, "that I regret this. But it's necessary. I can't explain why, not now. Someday . . ." He seemed to struggle with himself for a moment, then added, "You know, you came very close to ending up like . . . the men you saw by the wall."

The words burst out of Dhar. "They were my tribe! My brother!"

Carrimene shook his head. "I'm sorry for that. But your tribesmen — it's as if they were dead. You understand, they don't feel anything, no pain . . ."

Dhar bit down his protest: *But they do! I can hear their voices! They're in torment!* Aloud, he pleaded, "Sir, I have to know. What did they do to them? Is it sorcery? Are they possessed?"

Carrimene sighed. "We don't know, not for certain. The Sorcerer Lords are jealous of their secrets. There's nothing to be done, no way to help them, Eral. Only death can release your tribesmen now."

Dhar nodded and began the task of saddling the horse, but the words seethed in his mind while he pulled on the straps: *only death. Only death can release your tribesmen.*

He had once seen the Altall shaman revive the body of a dead clan leader to try to learn his murderer's name. Dhar had never forgotten the sight of the corpse's ruined face. The mouth had opened, but only a groan had issued forth. The shaman had lain like the dead himself for ten days afterward. But he had felt the touch, he claimed, of the dead man's soul.

And now Dhar felt them again, the souls of his tribe clutching at him. Sorcery possessed their flesh. Their voices whispered inside his mind, crying out in agony, pleading for release. Dhar closed his eyes and pressed his hands to his head as if he could shut them out, but instead he saw the image of Pall, his hands clutching the spear transfixing his chest, begging him to pull it free.

Each day it grew worse. The tortured voices of his tribe haunted even his waking hours, until he would have pounded his head open against a wall to silence them. But there would be no silence. They would give him no peace as long as they remained as they were. And Carrimene himself had said it, only death would release them.

For days Dhar had sharpened a scrap of metal and probed at the lock of his shackles. This morning the lock had yielded. Now, in the darkness of the stable, he pulled out the lockpick from the straw and went to work. Within minutes his chains lay on the ground. Quietly, free of iron's weight, he slipped into the house and stole a knife from the kitchen.

The streets of Djied looked different by moonlight, like the canyons of the far-distant desert his tribe had crossed when he was a boy, losing one out of four beasts to thirst. This time he went on foot, hooded in one of his master's cloaks. If he could have done one thing more, it would have been to somehow explain to Carrimene what it was he had to do, and why.

At last he came to the building site at the wall and hid himself, waiting for the procession of the undead and damned to come into sight. His hand was sweaty on the knife's handle and he felt sick with dread, recalling the moments before the battle. If he were discovered again, he doubted that Carrimene could save him this time.

The silence of the city night was unlike the steppe, where packs of wolves howled, and the nighthawk cried out as it struck. But finally Dhar could hear the distant scrape of a loaded sledge over the cobbled pavement, and he looked out from his hiding place to see it approaching, drawn by the slaves of sorcery. Somewhere, their souls lingered in agony, trapped between life and death. He gripped the stolen knife, whispering to himself as if the words had power. *Only death can release them. Death.*

Pall was in this line, near the end where the weight of the sledge bore most heavily, and Dhar wanted to weep at the sight of him. His face was an empty-eyed skull, skin drawn taut, and raw, ulcerated sores showed where the rope harness had dug into the flesh. In one place Dhar could see the white gleam of bone, and then he knew for certain that Carrimene was right, that life could never return to this decayed thing that had been his brother. It had

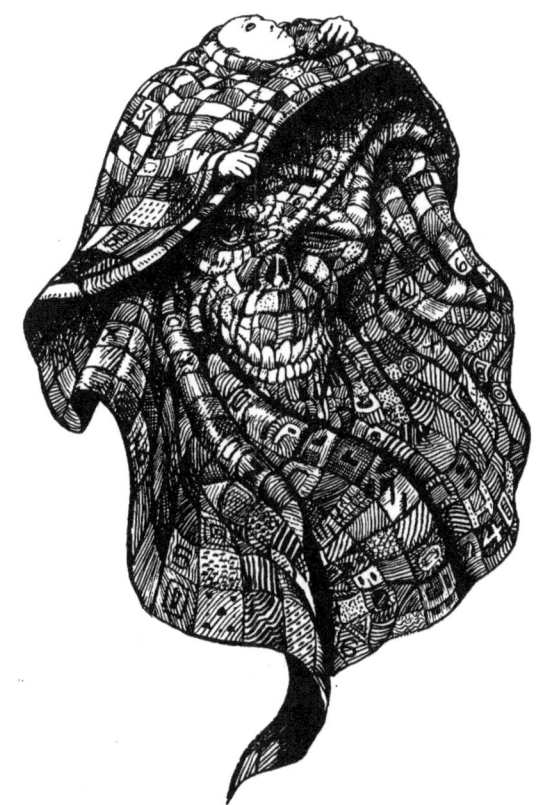

to die, to free his soul from the evil that possessed it.

Dhar took a breath, summoned all his resolve, and drove his knife into the heart.

The undead body reeled backward, then seemed to recover its balance. Driven by some unseen purpose, it continued to strain to move the sledge forward. Dhar stared in shock, then struck again, again, but his blows had no effect. Blood welled out slowly from the wounds, dark and clotted, but otherwise . . .

They would not die! Dhar sobbed aloud. For all that he had risked, they couldn't be killed!

The wall loomed beyond him, massive and dark in the moonlight, with freedom beyond it, out of reach for him now. No matter where he went, the dreams would follow. He could never escape.

Dhar could not bear to look into the contempt in Carrimene's eyes. Hammad stood behind him, angry and fearful, and Dhar recalled the words overheard on their way to Djied. Hammad had not wanted to take the risk of leaving him alive, had spoken of alternatives . . .

"What's all this about?" Carrimene demanded. Carrimene, who had rejected those alternatives.

Dhar took a breath. "You told me, death was the only thing that could save them. I had to try. But it was no use . . ."

Carrimene shut his eyes and whispered a curse — *Tannit's blood!* His hands shot out and took Dhar's shoulders in a hard grip. Not a merchant's hands.

"*What have you done?* Did anyone see you? Were you followed?"

"No . . . no, I don't think so. Sir, I'm sorry, I never wanted to cause you more trouble. Believe me, I wouldn't have told them —"

Carrimene's fingers dug into his arms. "You wouldn't have told them *what?*"

Dhar swallowed, suddenly unsure. He had assumed — what? That Carrimene was no ordinary merchant, certainly. What merchant would have questioned him for so long about the Djieddin battle-sorcery? What merchant would keep a slave he had no real use for? "You serve Carthia," he said finally. "The Empire."

Carrimene's eyes bored into his. "Eral, do you have any idea what happens to people who are questioned by the Sorcerer Lords? Everything you know, every thought you ever had, would be theirs. *You* would be theirs. Do you know what you risked?"

"Sir, I know what I owe you — more than my life. It was just . . . my brother . . ." Dhar clutched his head. "I hear him, day and night. All of them, screaming, begging me to save them. I couldn't go on . . ."

Carrimene sighed. He looked very weary. "You should have told me. But I don't suppose I gave you much reason."

Dhar started to protest, but Carrimene waved him silent. "Well, you're right, of course. I'm a Carthene agent, here to gather information about Djied, how much risk the Sorcerer Lords pose to the Empire." He paused. "It isn't just a question of burning men alive on the battlefield — though the gods know that's bad enough. But can you imagine a whole *army* of those things? The Empire can't counter that kind of sorcery. If they can't be killed . . . Eral, just what exactly did you do?"

"I took a knife." He pulled it out of his shirt, and Carrimene, seeing the engraved crest, shut his eyes briefly. "It was my brother. I stabbed him in the heart. I hit one, two more times, but he just kept moving."

"All three times in the heart?"

"I think so, yes. But nothing happened."

Carrimene frowned. "There might be one other way. Listen to me, Eral. Eventually, the Empire is going to bring down the Lords of Djied, and this evil will end. But in the meanwhile your brother and the men of your tribe are suffering. Is that so?"

Dhar held his head. "If you could hear them . . ."

"Eral, I have no right to ask you this. You owe the Empire nothing."

"I'd do anything," Dhar insisted. "Even if it cost me my life."

"You have until the third watch," Carrimene had told him. "It won't begin to take effect until then. After that, I understand it works quickly, without too much pain." He had added, "As far as we know, there's no antidote."

Dhar had stroked the black gelding's sleek neck one last time before swallowing the capsule Carrimene held out to him. He understood now what would happen if he were questioned by the Sorcerer Lords of Djied. But he would be beyond that by the time this was over and Carrimene had reported to the authorities that his troublesome barbarian slave was missing again.

If only this worked. "You're a brave man, Eral Dhar Tann," Carrimene had told him. Dhar had shaken his head. The damning voices had left him no choice. Now he had only to wait.

Carrimene had arranged all the details. The jar of volatile lamp oil, as tall as Dhar, stood in the entrance of an alley near the building site. Day and night the undead processions passed by this place, laboring to build up the defenses of the Sorcerer Lords. Sooner or later, Pall would come. Dhar had until the third watch.

The watch had passed, and Dhar was just beginning to feel the first twinges of pain in his gut, when he finally saw Pall, still roped to the heavy sledge full of stone. Gritting his teeth, he waited until the line of the possessed was half-way past the alley, and then he gave the jar a hard shove, overturning it, breaking it open.

Oil spilled out in a wave, flowing across the cobbled pavement beneath the feet of the walking dead. Several of them fell. Others stumbled unseeing over the bodies, tangling the ropes. The line halted, anchored there by the weight of the loaded sledge.

Dhar lit a torch and threw it directly into the spreading pool of oil.

This time the burning figures did not scream.

One by one, the tormented voices fell into silence.

Ω

PRINCESS OF SHADES

. . . . . for Tanith Lee

She worships moonlight, abhors the sunlight,
Is never to be seen abroad by day;
Black-shuttered windows hiding her away
Until the restoration of sweet night.
Her skin forever pale, translucent, white,
Her hair as black as ravens' wings; the sway
Of her dreamy pose; sleepy eyes that say
"In my embrace find dark love sable-bright."

To believe such promises unspoken
Is the sorrowful fate of bravos who
Soon enough must weep, illusion broken
On bleak shores of despair survived by few.
Whosoever loves the Princess of Shades
Shuns light thereafter and like a dream fades.

—Jessica Amanda Salmonson

MIRROR, MIRROR

by Tanith Lee

In the early winter a vampire began to call at our house. What made it so terrible was that my mother, who was wise and lovely and perfect, was infatuated with her. Inside a week she was calling the vampire 'Miriam', and they would sit overcast afternoons face to face, on the long backless couch, which caused them to lean together like two dark tulips in a vase.

Both wore black, my mother because she was still in mourning for my father, though he had died five years before. The vampire because, presumably, she favoured sombreness, just as she liked the night and the winter days when the sun was hidden in a cloud. Miriam the vampire's dresses were long, with tight boned waists and flounces. She wore black hats with veils fixed to her hair with an enormous ruby pin. When she came in the house she would draw out the pin and take off the hat. She would then play with the pin as if with a red berry or a drop of frozen blood. She was eccentric, and did not put up her hair as my mother did. Miriam's hair hung to her waist like the black cloud that kept the sun in. She was extremely beautiful, in an awful way, her face so white and smooth without a single line, so it was like the face of a child turned to marble. Her eyes were black and rather dull but large enough they must be called beautiful too. Her lips were the pale pink of a faded sugared almond kept in the dark.

All the children on the block knew that Miriam was a vampire. The moment we saw her we knew. The way she came from nowhere as soon as the sun was obscured, and vanished again if it chanced to escape. The way she walked in her black clothes and now and then looked at us with soft hatred, as if we were flowers she would uproot. Adults passed Miriam often with a second look, but without an inkling of what she was. We were aware, sadly, we too would move eventually into that realm, where we would be half-blind and half-deaf. It was the fee that must be paid for losing our half-dumbness. So soon as we had learned to speak fully, to control language, our other senses would be mutilated.

But for now, we saw the vampire and we recognized her. We understood it was only a question of time. And then, as in a horrible game, it was my gate she approached, and our narrow patterned steps she ascended. On my mother's door she knocked, and my mother fell in love with her at once and let her in.

I have no idea what excuse Miriam made for coming to the house. Perhaps that she was looking for some lost relative. It did not matter really. Within minutes, seconds, she had won. And I, returning from play, found her there on the long couch, her hat beside her, the pin twirling in her fingers, and her other hand uplifting a smoking cigarette in a long holder of bone.

My mother introduced her by some foreign name I could not assimilate and have forgotten. In any case soon it was 'Miriam.'

Soon, too, I came to know the particular grey afternoons, like dusks, when I would enter the house and find my lovely mother in the thrall of the vampire, on the long couch, with the long windows and long ruched blinds behind them.

"Look, here's Miriam."

And the table would be piled with dainty cakes and jugs of homemade lemonade, and the mat lacquer teapot, none of which Miriam, of course, could ever be persuaded to sample, although my mother would beg her: "You're so slight, Miriam. And with the winter coming . . . I must try to fatten you up a little, darling."

When Miriam's leaden eyes would go over me, there would come the soft flicker of hatred once again. How easy I would be to pluck. When Miriam gazed at my mother her look was quite unreadable and dense. Yet in it my mother seemed to find irresistible magic. My mother had once stared into my eyes like that, but no more.

There was another reason too why the vampire had come to our house, beyond my mother's loving and marvellous nature.

Just as she must avoid the sun, and all holy things, sacred wine and bread, the cross, Miriam must avoid a looking-glass. And in our house there were none. The night my father had died of pneumonia, my mother had veiled all the mirrors, and later she had sent them away like wicked servants who had stood by and coldly watched her husband's final struggle and defeat. In rather the same way, maybe, she had locked up a drawer in the bureau which contained all his treasures, things I did not know about, as if no one must be permitted to look.

For Miriam, naturally, a house without mirrors, which would refuse to reflect her and so would give her away, was a wonderful piece of luck. How had she known? But then, everything about her was mysterious and foul. Where for example did she come from and return to out of the twilight? Probably a graveyard, but none of us had dared to follow. The very swish of her skirt warned us we must not.

"Oh, Miriam," said my mother adoringly, "do try a little of this raspberry cake. I baked it just this morning."

But Miriam did not touch the cake, only smoking her pale cigarettes in the ivory holder, and fiddling with the strange fruit of the ruby pin.

How long would it be before she could delay no more, before the exquisite foreplay could no longer be drawn out, and she pulled my mother into her rustling embrace and pierced my mother's human neck, and drank her blood?

Every night, when I kissed my mother good-bye before the journey into sleep, I examined her throat closely. Once she had scratched herself with a little brooch she sometimes wore, and my heart stopped. But it was not the mark of teeth.

I had never tried to *tell* her the truth, for I knew infallibly that despite her wisdom, because of the blindness and deafness of her adult state, she either would not hear or could not grasp what I would say. And if she found that I was Miriam's enemy, she might keep us apart. Probably my presence in the room, or the possibility of my arrival there, were part of the reason Miriam had held off from her deadly kiss.

In the monosyllables of our dumbness and lack of language, I conferred with other children. What could I do?

"If only there were a mirror," said Dorothy.

Then Dorothy hung her head and made her confession. "The vampire came to our house once. I saw her in the hall. There's granny's old green mirror there like a pond. And my mother saw in it. I couldn't see in the mirror, only my mother did, but she blinked, two or three times, as if something had got into her eyes. And then she said to the vampire, 'No, I can't help you.' And she shut the door."

Dorothy and I realized that Dorothy's mother, being partly blind, did not comprehend what she had glimpsed — Miriam's invisibility in a reflecting surface. But nevertheless some preserving instinct had been activated.

It seemed to me that, since my mother was special, she, seeing or not seeing Miriam in a mirror, would know the truth fully. For my mother had beheld a fairy woman once in the park when she was all of seventeen. She had told me, solemnly, about the tinsel antennae and the tiny wings. So she had more sight left than most adults. It was only that Miriam had put a spell on her.

How then to bring Miriam to a mirror and to let my mother see?

In a way it might be easy, for when Miriam was in the house, my mother paid me scarcely any attention. I could have eaten all the cakes on the table. Then again, Miriam was subtly conscious of me, as one would be of an animal one did not like prowling in the room.

Dorothy ran up to me in her big old garden. It was a sunny wintry morning, but by two o'clock the cloud in the east would have swallowed up the sun, turning it from gold to smothered silver.

In Dorothy's hand, a misty foretaste of that silver sun.

"My shell mirror," said Dorothy. "It's all I've got."

We considered the mirror, staring down into each of our faces, puzzled to see ourselves so different from what we knew we were.

"There's a little loop," I said.

"Yes, I hang it on the wall. Then when I sit my doll on the chest, she can watch her face."

Dorothy and her doll were making a sacrifice for my sake, and I took the mirror carefully. It was the size of a small pumpkin, and the shells which decorated its edge hardly hid any of the surface. Yet it was light too, and would hang from the loop.

I took it home quickly. My mother was busy in the kitchen, sifting flour and stoning summer damsons, sensing of course that darkness was coming, and so, Miriam.

I wandered about the room where Miriam would sit, looking for a spot to set the mirror. Normally Miriam would surely detect such a thing at once, but I sensed that she was by now so involved with my mother, the clean scent of her, cologne and brushed hair, my mother's delicate skin with the tiny fairy antennae lines about the mouth and eyes, that Miriam's vampire cleverness was slightly dimmed. If I could only find a place that she avoided, perhaps she would not realize.

Ultimately it was simple. The area of the room which Miriam intuitively did not care for was, not unnaturally, the two long windows. She would seat herself on the backless couch, turned away from them, and would not look in that direction even if my mother went through this part of the room. My mother also had taken to pampering Miriam's aversion. When she guessed that Miriam would be coming, my mother let down the ruched yellow blinds, and today, already, they were in place.

Going upstairs I took a large safety pin from my mother's pottery bowl. Returning with it below, I stood on a chair and attached the loop of the mirror to the yellow ruched blind of the second window. Something useful occurred. The reflected yellow folds of the blind shone into the mirror, like a buttery sun into a pond. It was not easy to see. I got down, crossed the room and stood in my usual position, just beyond the table where the cakes and tea were laid. It seemed to me that Miriam, sitting on the right of the couch as she always did, would now be reflected from the back into the mirror. Except there would be nothing to show.

As the sun moved low over the sky and the cloud rose after it like a bank of fog, the light died from the windows and the mirror too turned dull.

A glorious smell of baking drifted from the kitchen. But I felt sick with hope and rage.

At two o'clock, as the cakes were lifted from the oven, cloud absorbed the sun and all down the block grey dusk breathed out into the day. The sun was pale at first as a lemon, and then it melted entirely. And as I glared out from my bedroom window, I saw the black figure of the vampire walking up the street. About her slender ankles her black skirts bounded like little dogs, and in her hat the red pin smouldered like a coal.

I ran downstairs, and as I stationed myself behind the table, our front door was knocked upon.

My mother came, washed and powdered and sweet, with combs in her hair.

"Oh, Miriam," she sighed, "oh, Miriam. How good to see you."

The vampire glided into the room as she had so often done, and as so often over me her dead eyes glimmered, and with her colourless tongue she licked her lip, thinking, I suppose, of when she could pull me up and throw me on the compost. How aggravating for her that I was always here, always about. How she would have liked to cut off my head and be done with me. Her hatred was so vast, so cushiony, she could not catch sight of mine, nor of my excitement.

She drew out the ruby pin and let fall her ghastly hat. She lit a cigarette in the bone holder. But she did not sit down.

I would not let my eyes go to the blind. Not yet. She must not have a hint. I squinted instead at her black buckled shoes and her nasty flounced yipping dog of a skirt.

My mother entered with golden cakes and the steaming teapot. Putting them on the table, she added the frosted decanter of sherry.

"Something to warm you, Miriam?"

But Miriam gently shook her head. What could warm her after all, but one thing only?

"It seems so long since I saw you, darling," said my mother, and she sat down on the long couch, to the left. I would not glance at the mirror on the blind. I stared at Miriam's ruby pin spinning in one set of her fingers, and the other set with the smoking bone of the cigarette holder.

She gazed at my mother, and seduced, Miriam also sat.

Then I looked straight up into the mirror.

What I saw was so ludicrous, so terrifying, that it produced a spontaneous and unforeseen reaction.

I had forgotten, or never thought, that while Miriam would not be caught in any reflective surface, her clothes were still corporeal.

And so I beheld a corsetted black dress sitting upright on the couch, straight as a rod, and in the air there flashed a turning jewel, and then, floating some four inches free of the black cuff, an ivory holder and a cigarette, which was borne higher up into the headless space where the collar of the dress ended, sparkled with sudden life, and out of nothing came a gush of smoke like a cloud.

Never before or since have I known the sensation, but at that instant my blood ran cold. Cold as liquid ice beneath a river at midnight.

And I screamed.

From the corner of vision I noticed my mother's head jerk up. What Miriam did I could not see, but in the looking-glass her clothing did not shift.

My mother spoke to me sharply, but I was beyond response. My eyes were wide and fixed, glued to the image in the mirror, the headless dress of the invisible smoking woman.

And then my mother was beside me. I felt her kneeling, staring into my face. I wanted to shriek that she must turn round, look there, *there* — but no further noise would come out of me and I could not seem to move.

My mother stood up abruptly.

"How foolish children are," she said, quietly.

These terrible words loosened all my limbs, and I flopped down on the floor. I was able to look about now, and saw my mother go over to the bureau. She was unlocking the drawer with my father's treasures in it.

"But then," said my mother, slipping in her hand and taking something out, "here's a thing I'd like to show you, darling."

From my mother's hand depended a golden crucifix which shone and burned brighter than either the coal of the ruby or the cigarette.

The vampire started up. She snatched on her hat and drove the pin into it, as it seemed right through her skull.

"Oh, must you be going? What a shame."

My mother saw Miriam to the door. Miriam opened and slipped round it like a puff of smoke, already perhaps vanishing.

My mother shut the door. She held the crucifix in her hand, and slowly her gaze settled on me.

"Silly child, not to have told me. Did you think I wouldn't believe you?"

I stammered something.

"Or did you only suddenly see?" asked my mother.

"The mirror!" I cried.

"What mirror?" inquired my mother.

I babbled that surely she must understand, she must have seen into the mirror on the blind — though how? — for why else had she fathomed what Miriam was?

"Oh, yes," said my mother calmly, "of course I saw. Her dress without anyone in it. But not in a mirror." I gaped at her miraculousness. She smiled, and said, her voice trembling slightly, "I saw the reflection in your eyes." Ω

THE DEAD ORCHARDS

by Ian MacLeod

I used to live in a house made from the bones of the City. Stones plundered from the dreams of palaces peered from every wall. It was too big for me alone, yet I rarely sought any company other than that of my servants. Forgotten rooms reached into tunnels, doorways opened on rotting boards. But there was still a core where a tarnished kind of luxury flourished. This was my home, and the living was as easy as it could be in this City, which is to say that my suffering was less than that of many others.

Sometimes when my solitude became a burden I used to wander the streets searching for some female from whom the City had yet to drain the last dregs of grace. A difficult quest, but I had my successes. I would draw my guest back to my house with the necessary threats or promises, filling it with the silvered clash of china, the fragile aromas of good food. And when the feast had ended and contentment played on the air, when my guest sat on her golden chair and all past life was an ugly dream, I would offer her one last luxury: a glass of the clearest water drawn from a well deep in the foundations of my house. Pure water in this City where the sewers foul the river and the river feeds the wells. Crystalline water in a crystal glass.

The goblet would rise in hands I had scented and cleansed, the water would tremble on the bevelled rim. And after it had touched those delicate lips, after the shapely throat had moved to swallow, the hand would fall, the glass would shatter, the eyes would blink once, then widen forever. For the clear water was invisibly polluted by the mutterings of some ancient spell. It caused a living paralysis for which, in all my experiments, I could discover no release, least of all death.

Once, I used to take endless pleasure in seeing my guest sitting motionless, clothed in whatever fairness youth had granted her, with every muscle down to heart and lungs magically stilled, yet her mind alert, her senses singing. After weeks of slow study, I would take a knife to her flesh, blowing the dust from her unblinking eyes that she might better see the riches she contained. Each organ within was a gleaming jewel, strung like a wet necklace on the bones beneath. Once, towards the end of my explorations, I found another life enclosed within the first. A child. I cut the burden from its ropes of flesh and lifted it into the candlelight. But the eyes of the half-finished thing seemed to stare at me, and I replaced it hurriedly in its mother's belly.

Inevitably — and as with life itself — my guests didn't keep their freshness forever. The spell allowed them to retain thoughts, sensation and life, but putrescence is an unavoidable fact even amongst the truly living in this city. Maggots eventually began to burrow the warm flesh. Gazing into the sockets of eyes that had run like tears, I used to wonder if death ever came to my guests. Did they sense every moment of decay? Was there ever an end to their pain? But I could find no answer from those rotting lips, and eventually I would call my servants to take the stinking burden from my sight and carry it to the dead orchards, there to dispose of it in the traditional way.

Eventually, such diversions began to bore me. I found that although the human body is a rich and ornate vessel, its variety is far from infinite. I came to treasure only the moment when the lips moistened and moved. When the delicate throat swallowed. When the glass fell. When the eyes widened with that last moment of knowledge. That was all: when the shadow passed, and when certainty began.

There came a time when I had not left my home in months. But boredom brought restlessness, and the horrors of the City beyond my door sometimes seemed less than the atrocity of my own company. One day, in the bland depths of my discontent, I went out. I had been long away from this City. I was surprised that life still passed so busily in these streets filled with mud. My senses clogged with the smell of it, with the separate ugliness of every face. I shook my head when the beggars offered me their blood in bowls. I kicked and stamped at the little creatures that crawled towards me from the gutters.

I took a path that led by the fringes of the dead orchards, passing many on the way who pulled, dragged or carried burdens in that same direction. I went that way without thinking, but as the hovels gave way to grey-green grass and the little hill reared up before my steps, I wandered on amid the stained and sapless boughs. They were sharp as spears, and similarly blackened with the blood of their victims. The trees were a deathly army, proffering trophies for the delectation of whatever Gods gaped down from the dismal sky. Some of the corpses were still fresh enough from their impaling to have kept a trace of character in their sunken eyes, or at least to make their sex and age discernible. But the majority had shrivelled to leathery anonymity, preserved by the parasitic tendrils of the trees as withered sketches of humanity. The branches pierced rags of flesh. Arms lifted and waved in the stinking breeze. Here, somewhere amid the leafless avenues, were the remains of my guests, doubtless roughly pinioned by my servants with their usual lack of care . . . perhaps dead, perhaps dreaming, perhaps still screaming voicelessly with pain.

I found a corpse that somehow still retained a shabby parody of young femininity. Several tumescences were thriving on it, green, apple-like parasitic growths of the tree itself, one a grey parody of a breast, another swelling on the shrivelled remains of the tongue, forcing apart the jaw. The wind struck up a keener note, dipping the branches all around, setting limbs clicking and bobbing, heads nodding. The woman-corpse tilted up, her mossy backbone curving as though still tormented by whatever agonies had brought her to this place. I turned and quickly made my back through the trees, towards the life of the market.

The market awnings flapped their damp wings. Those who lived and needed jostled with those who had forgotten all but the fears and habits of life. The smell of rotting meat and vegetables was heavy. That day, in what passed, I think, for the season where there is more cold and less rain, I had already eaten and the food had lodged in my stomach, an unwelcome but tolerated guest. Everywhere there were shouts and squabbles. I was swept along and almost off my feet as a fresh basket appeared, dripping mud and the offal of white-eyed fish from the river. The crowds were almost as sickening as what was on offer. I felt glad of my wealth, my gold, my servants. I smiled at the thought, remembering why I had come. And as I smiled my eyes settled on a face that was part of the crowd, yet separate from everything. My shock was immediate and intense. Even under the grime and rags, I could hardly believe that chance had brought me this close to beauty.

She had a basket wrapped around her filthy arm. In it, as I drew close, tumbling rickety stalls and people aside, I saw the remnants of a loaf of bread, grey-green with mould. She turned with slow and perfect wonder towards me. Heart-shaped face, eyes of tremulous green. She could almost have been a child, had the city not forgotten true childhood in the age before it remembered death.

Determined that she would be my guest that night, I stopped her and offered money, grasping an oily sleeve that went slick though my fingers, grasping tighter and again. Her delicate arms scrabbled in fear, weak claws reaching for my face. I drew out coins and pushed them towards her fluttering palms, not caring how they fell. They fountained from my hands. Those around us began to scramble in the mud, raking the gold from the ooze. At last she caught a coin in her palm and drew it to her lips, touching it to her perfect teeth. I offer this, I said, and more. Her eyes widened and blinked, clear pools in a world of mud. She nodded. She understood. I kept my hand on her in case she should run, but in truth I sensed within her that fatalism that is part of this City. I never bothered to enquire about her background. No doubt others knew her but were too blind or ignorant to see her beauty. So be it; this City has withered everything down to a single moment of need, endlessly repeating itself. I took her hand and

she let me lead her away under the leaning walls. Through the tunnel of a toppled tower where dark things whispered to the echo of our breath. To the place that was my home.

My servants pointed and shivered excitedly as they gathered for a sight of my prize. I chased them away with curses and threats and led her quickly up the wide stairs past rotting tapestries and green statues, along corridors streaked with decay. Some emotion caused her to cry. The tears washed bands down her face. I asked her name and she sobbed it through the bars of clear skin: it was a thing that fell uselessly between us. I changed it to Caitlin.

Caitlin. I drew water from the purest butts of rainwater, straining the soup of spiders and leaves. I warmed it with magics to fill a rusted marble tub. I stripped her of her rags and bathed her. As the water clouded, she grew glistening white. Touching the wonder of her flesh with my own ragged claws, I could hardly believe that we shared humanity. As I dried her, I saw that Caitlin was like none of my guests who had gone before. She was perfection. I anointed her with scents and oils. I seated her before the brightest, warmest fire and combed the knots and lice from her wet hair, working through and through until it sparked and glowed to the touch. And I dressed her in the best fabric I could muster. Velvet that still retained its colour in patches, seams of lace that the damp hadn't yet unraveled. I stood her before a mirror, and once again she cried. And as I gazed upon her my own eyes stung as though with the touch of flames.

My Caitlin smelled of apples and sunlight. She made me weep with a long-interred memory of a happy interval in my otherwise cheerless youth. Of lying on sap-scented grass to drown in snow flurries of blossom, of the broken certainty of waiting for the one-who-loved, the one who never returned.

Amid the unavoidable pathos of decay, I tried to give our feast solemnity. My efforts exceeded everything that had gone before, just as Caitlin herself outshone all the past. In the great hall, I sat her down on the gilt chair raised on a stone above the moss-carpeted floor. I cleaned silver and china with my own hands, ransacked ancient chests to find a ragged tablecloth that was almost white. I polished a glass until its facets were like knives and drew on the whispering darkness of my secret well until I was sure that the poisoned water would match Caitlin's purity. I even discovered an old machine from the time beyond the City's memory that wove melodies in sounds that were neither voices nor drum.

The preparation of the food, pampered idiot that I am, was beyond me. I set my servants to work with terrible threats. What emerged on platters from the steaming dungeons was an insult to Caitlin's loveliness. I took a skewer from the filthy meat and showed the leading servant my disgust, stopping before fatality only to avoid the inevitable distraction that dragging another body to the dead orchards would cause. Their second offering was many times better. When I put the sauce to my lips, I could only wonder at the contrast with the foul stuff I was normally forced to tolerate. But still, it failed to match Caitlin's perfection. As, inevitably, did the third offering. But nevertheless I carried the abject dishes up to her myself, rare fruits and savories, sweetmeats that the City had long forgotten, riches on the palate beyond dream.

I watched as she ate, seated on that gilded chair. Her movements were swift with hunger, yet delicate, fluttering like leaves in sunlight. I poured wine from a bottle furred with the centuries of dust into her silver goblet. The light of the candelabrum formed a heart within the hall, intimate and yellow. I moved the plates and dishes with my ugly, clumsy hands, drawing her attention to this or that culinary treasure. Music played from my newly discovered box, trembling the shadows around us. She looked at me and smiled, her fingers twisting the frayed edge of the cloth. With each flicker of movement another facet of her beauty stung my eyes.

Finally, she sat back, and I asked her if there was anything else she wanted.

She shook her head, and I asked her if she was happy.

A shadow crossed her face for a moment. Then her clear eyes fixed on mine, that green that seemed to flicker with more than flamelight.

She told me that she had lost her mother when she was still a child. How she heard the rumours that she had been taken away while she was at the market, just as I had taken her. Someone with riches, it was said, someone such as I. Eventually, she had

found her mother's body in the dead orchards, dangling upside down, her guts hanging out over her face, not living, but somehow not yet dead.

I nodded. But of course, I had no way of telling whether Caitlin's mother had once been my guest. In truth, my memories of my many guests had flooded together like the blood-scent of their hidden jewels. And Caitlin outshone any from the past. But still, I was pleased with the symmetry that should bring my guests here, generation on generation.

Certain in the knowledge than I could not be lying, I told Caitlin that she was infinitely more beautiful than her mother.

She nodded gravely. She had seen herself in the mirror; she knew that there was no point in arguing. I watched her eyes travel across the dishes and condiments, the glowing candelabrum, the crystal glass filled with crystal water.

I asked if she was thirsty.

Slowly, she shook her head. To my astonishment, I felt a rush of well-being, almost equal to that which I had felt as I watched the throats of my previous guests move to swallow. My heart raced at the thought that here, at last, I had found something new. A guest who survived the feast! Weeks and months stretched before me in my delirious excitement. Caitlin and I together, her beauty and my power, King and Queen of this City.

Then what, she asked, what shall we do?

My face must have betrayed my sudden confusion. I wanted us to become lovers, I wanted to drown in her blossom-honeyed scent. After I had stammered out some inadequate expression of this, Caitlin put her head back and began to laugh.

Laughter. The sound rebounded from the wet walls. Laughter. Unheard in centuries. Laughter. Thick, ugly laughter. I gazed at Caitlin in disappointment as her lips twisted back with the cackle and bray, as knotted roots of tendon formed in her neck, as her face distorted beyond recall. She sniffed and gave a last bark.

I was sickened, but I forced myself to shrug. So quickly, the possibilities had faded.

Her face was smoothly solemn now, but it was only a sick parody of my memory of her beauty. Love is impossible in this City, she said. So what would you have me do?

Knowing it was true, I lifted the glass. The words were easy now. I suggested that we could share the crystal water together. Her, and then me.

Caitlin nodded. Unhesitatingly, she took the glass in both her slender hands and lifted it to her lips. The facets danced light on her cheeks. I felt coolness and calm wash through my agitation as I witnessed the movement, that familiar part of the ritual. She tipped the glass up. Inch by inch. Degree by degree. Her eyes were momentarily closed like the child she almost was. In the last moment, as the water broke into her mouth, I even saw her beauty return.

The glass tumbled and broke. She slumped from the gilded chair, down into the filth below the table. It drew a black streak across her flaccid face, as though nature was reasserting itself. Gazing at her strewn there, eyes open again and staring wide at me, I pondered for a moment my old pleasures, the way the inner jewels of a body could be drawn out gleaming for display. But I shook my head, knowing that to do that would only sour further an already bitter memory. I called for my servants. I bade them carry her to the orchard, fresh and as she was, with her skin unmarred. And recalling Caitlin's grim story of her roughly pinioned mother, I decided to accompany them.

The moon was howling in the sky, the light of madness breaking over blind chimneys, shattered towers, seed husks of broken rooftops. The City was still seethingly alive. The night people, gory rags of flesh and fabric, scuttled their trails in the solemn wake of our procession. My servants bore Caitlin on a stretcher of silk, albeit blackened with the stains of its previous occupants. Although motionless, her eyes stared unrelentingly at me as I walked beside her along ways where firelight bloodied the darkness, beyond the deep pools of sickness where the nightbirds fluttered, through the empty market itself ransacked by the day. Now that she was stilled by the water, I could see her in abstraction, the planes of flesh, the intersections of beauty and imperfection.

We reached the dead orchards, grey boughs weaving the grey light. The wind was faint, but everywhere there was the scratchy sound of movement. We passed along the avenues of withered flesh and stopped at a tree that was tenanted only by chattering ancient bones. My servants put Caitlin down and hovered fretfully, awaiting their instructions. I waved them away and crouched down close to Caitlin, over her face. My shadow blocked the wild moon. Her eyes glittered. As I had done many times before, I wondered how it must feel to be trapped in a body that possesses every faculty but movement, that sensed my foul breath and the ripe smell of decay. That felt pain. I moved a fraction closer still and bit a piece from her nose. Just a small piece: I had already disciplined myself not to spoil this moment with petty disfigurement. I chewed it slowly. My Caitlin was bitter-sweet, unlike any human flesh I had tasted before, yet still resonant with memory. I closed my eyes momentarily, glimpsed dappled light, the moist white flesh of a golden-green fruit offered to me in the hand of the one-who-loved, a smiling child, the one who never returned. I blinked, and gazed lovingly down at Caitlin, at the sweetness she contained. When I took another small bite of her nose, a bead of moisture broke from her eye and ran down her cheek. A pretty cheek, yes I could see that now. Still imperfect, but possibly less so than any other I had known.

You should never have laughed, I said. Never.

The eyes poured back at me, wet stones in the stillness of her face.

I lifted her from the stretcher alone. My servants shivered around the distant trees, whinnying and muttering in pitiful excitement. Her flesh was warm and living, youthful and elastic. Pushing it onto the spears of the branches was difficult, messy work. My hands grew slickly black in the moonlight. Her sweet-apple smell grew stronger. I licked my glistening fingers, expecting the salt taste of blood, but discovering instead a stronger, sappy sweetness. My Caitlin, I thought, you are so, so beautiful, so unlike the rest. The limbs of the tree skittered and creaked. Although there was little wind, the surrounding orchard grew agitated in sympathy. I felt a cold rising of fear, but forced myself through it. And soon, almost too soon, the job was done.

I stood back. My Caitlin, hanging there in the moonlight. In the orchard, the living amid the dead. She now possessed a different kind of beauty — something dark and impossible to explain. I shivered in anticipation, knowing that it would give me pleasure to visit this spot in the grey months and years to come.

My Caitlin. As my servants gathered closer to see, I stretched up to her. Wetly stained branches projected through both of her arms. It was an inexpert job, but far better than my foolish servants could ever have managed. The sweetly scented blood was still flowing from the wounds, splattering the earth, betraying life: somehow, it spoiled the effect, but I didn't doubt that she and the tree would gain equilibrium as she began to wither and rot.

I leaned forward to kiss her, and the howling moonlight softened to a glow around her, spinning green rainbow webs, filling my heart to the choking. Caitlin. My Caitlin. I touched her lips, breathed the

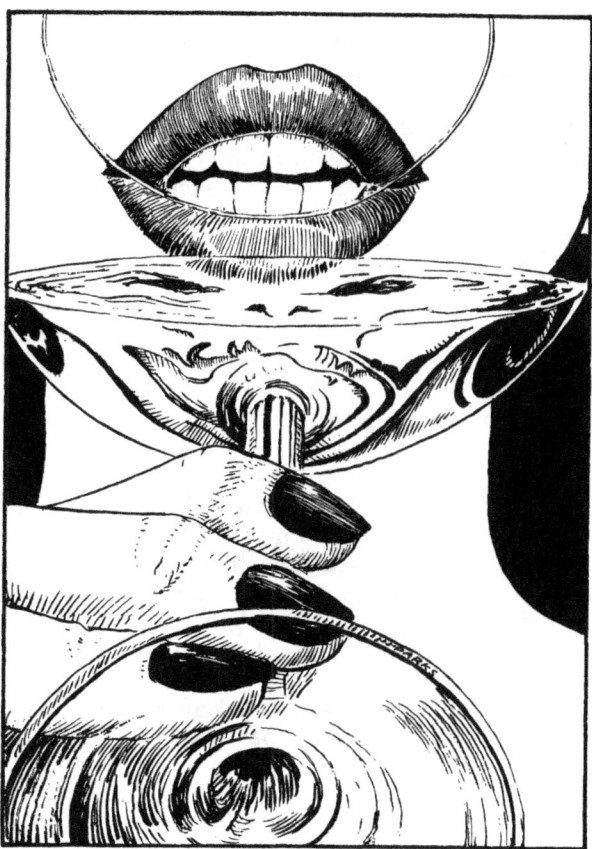

apple scent of love and memory and childhood.

But something was wrong. The tree shuddered movement and her arm shook on the branches, breaking loose and spraying sappy petals of blood. She circled me with it and drew me in, her lips seeking mine, pressing, her tongue a strong root, inexorably parting my lips.

Holding me like ivy, she spat the contents of her mouth out into mine. A flood of crystal soaked my lips and tongue. My throat contracted. I held the poison tight in my mouth, wanting to vomit it out with all the contents of my stomach, but held back by the knotted pressure of her lips. Then her other arm curved out from the tree and drew me deeper into the embrace. I felt the leafy fire of her beauty. I felt living branches clawing at my flesh. I felt my throat weaken and dissolve, the cool crystal flood of magic through my body.

The sky spun up.

The earth thudded my back.

Lying motionless, I heard the rasping scream of fresh wood on old bark as Caitlin pulled herself fully away from the barbed branches. I smelled her greenly resinous tang. She stood over me, the sap still dripping from the gleaming white rents in her limbs, revealing the knotted intricacies of grain within.

She leaned over me with her leafy-apple scent. I heard her voice like the whisper of spring, quiet and strong.

"My Lord," she said, "the story that I told you at our banquet is true. You did kill my mother, or at least bring her to hang in that frozen place which is worse than death. Yet when I said that I was a child, I revealed less than all of the truth." I gazed up at her, suddenly conscious of the huge silence of my heart and lungs.

She said, "My Lord, you lifted me from my mother's womb. And doubtless you toyed with me a while before eventually you grew disgusted or bored, and pushed me back in with the other entrails, bidding your servants take my mother to these dead orchards.

"But *I* was living too. And I did not drink your magic potion — for magic is not like poison or dreamsmoke or alcohol, it does not pass through the blood. I was not caught in your spell.

"So the boughs of the dead orchards received my poor mother — hanging upside down in much the way I described — and the trees found within her something untainted by that dreadful paralysis, a life that still lay on the brink of living. It was a life that the tubers and roots revived and nourished, tended, caused to grow and be brought out as a new fruit, half human, and yet half of the wood."

She blinked slowly, as though at a happy memory. But her beauty was terrible, and her hair was drifting like a forest in a storm. "My Lord," she whispered, "do you understand what I am saying?"

Yes, I understood, and although I had no way of showing, she knew that I did. My thoughts now were quick, freed from all the normal distractions of living. My senses were heightened too — every nerve receptive and glowing — which made me realise the delicious, searing torment that my guests must have experienced.

Caitlin unbowed into the moonlight. She turned away from me and towards my servants. I could not see them, but I knew from the sounds I heard that they were bowing and muttering in fear of this new and terrible wood-God.

Caitlin said one word. She said, "Now."

My servants' clumsy hands were on me, around me. They lifted me up. My feet were in air, and I then felt the pressure of the tree. Splintered boughs breaking through my clothing, on into the flesh. For once, they did a good job. They skewered me deep on the branches through belly and limbs.

And I tried to scream, as I have been trying ever since.

Caitlin visits me often, brushing the dead things from my yawning mouth, lovingly smoothing each new tendril as it works its way through my spine. She talks to me about life in this unchanging City, about the discoveries she has made in my house since she became its tenant. Sometimes her face crinkles with disgust, like old bark. But after all these years, she still retains her beauty. And when the pain is no more than bitter agony and a small corner of my thoughts remains my own, I find time to wonder if the fresh wood in her heart and the timber of her bones will ever die.

Yes, Caitlin visits me often. She smiles like sunlight and brings the memory of snow-flurried blossom, of waiting for the one-who-loved, the one who never returned.

I pray to the Gods that my Caitlin will never desert me.   Ω

AESTHETICS OF EVIL

He said, that's a sign of **SATAN, SATAN**.
Talking about my skateboard graphics.

But he wore a T-shirt
showing a skeleton with a long blade
riding a real mean horse.

So I asked him,
how can you tell
what's a sign of Satan?

He said,
the pastel colors are okay.
The little china kids with triangular blue eyes
dripping cute tears
they're okay.

But when you get into the bright colors,
you know
RED, ORANGE, GREEN — blue's okay, bright
    blue
except not **DAY-GLO BLUE**. Or **BLACK**.
And pictures of teenagers with knowing grins
those are satanic.
Hm, I said,
Let's talk speaking in tongues.
How do you tell that
from demon possession?

He said, easy.
Listen: eulalia ukelele alleluja cecilia alabaster
    alfredo
alleluja alleluja liquidity mahi mahi a la carte.
That's speaking in tongues. But:

**GARBANZO JAPAN ALGEBRA GARBAGE
    GORGONZOLA! ALGEBRA! GORGONZOLA
JAPAN ZUCCHINI! ALGEBRA! ALGEBRA!
    ALGEBRA!**
Any fool can tell that's heavy metal
and backward it says "Come get me, Satan, you
    sexy monster."

The pentacles, I asked.
What about the pentacles?
Like, if I make a shopping list, and I draw a five
    point star
then circle it, that's a sign of Satan?

Definitely, he said. A pentacle.
But only if the point is up.
Point down, it's just a grocery list star.

Heh heh heh. Little does he know.
He got the part about the star
dead wrong.
                                    — Mary A. Turzillo

LISTENING AT GRAVES

by J. J. Russ

That crazy Boll.

I shouldn't have let him listen to the graves, no, not in the first place. But I didn't think so clearly with all that wine I'd been drinking. It was good to have someone to talk to besides a bottle. It was so good to have a friend.

The first time I saw him I thought he was praying. He knelt on the grave of *Elvira Jonson, 1868–1891,* a neglected plot in the old section of Greenhaven, overgrown with weeds and creepers. He moaned, then sort of rocked from side to side. The leaves under his legs made soft rustling noises.

I never disturbed mourners at graveside before; in fact, I was forbidden to do it. But there was something peculiar about the way this one crouched over the grave, so I moved closer, approaching from behind. He had tire-soles on his sandals, a narrow hunched back, and long brown hair drooping forward to the ground.

I cleared my throat and spat loudly to one side.

He jumped up, shaking. His grey eyes, scared and watery, were a head above mine. Skin well-tanned except where it was peeling over the nose, T-shirt hanging straight as one of the tombstones from his thin and sharp-edged shoulders — he couldn't have been more than twenty.

"What the *Hell* are you doing?" I said in my best caretaker's voice.

His eyes focussed vaguely on my face.

"Better answer. I'm in charge here, sonny, and I don't take no crap."

"She only wants to see her baby." His voice was thin, with the tone of an owl at night. He began to cry. "That's all she wants, for Christ's sake." Something long, like a cord, swung from his neck.

"Who?"

"She died just when it was born, and didn't even find out the sex." He wiped tears from his cheek, and I recognized what he had around his neck.

"Hey — you a paramedic?"

He laughed in a way that was half a sob. "This? It's my instrument. It lets me hear." He looked back at the grave. "Poor Elvy." He took off the stethoscope and curled it in his palms as if to warm it. When I reached for it, he jerked back. "Nobody's supposed to touch it but me. Just let me show you."

He turned it over in his fingers, showing all the parts. At one end was a sculpted ear, silver, the size of a walnut shell. Its details were blurred, smudged, as if from too much handling, crevices shadowed with a dense and ancient grime. Tubes of cracked rubber ran from the silver ear to twin curved pipes tipped with earpieces made of a dark brown wood.

"Wasn't I lucky?" he said. "Got it for just three bucks last year. It called to me."

"Called?"

"In a way. Something I can't explain. Even the pawnbroker didn't know where it came from. But it called. And reminded me how I thought I'd be a doctor before I learned I was stupid. I wanted to listen to people's insides so I could know how they really felt. Nobody tells you, not really."

I nodded. I should have chased him off right then, but there was something special, something that made him easy to talk to. "So. Does the thing work?"

"It helps." He knelt down, scooped a bit of dirt in one hand, then let it sift through his fingers. "You know, most people wouldn't like it here."

"*You* like it?"

He nodded.

"Well, I got no choice. It's the only job I can get." Surprising, how I was talking to a stranger, and a crazy one at that. But maybe that was the only kind I trusted any more. I thought of the bottle waiting in my shack and my tongue felt dry. I never did like to drink alone.

"You're lucky." He stood and turned around slowly, gazing at the weathered slabs. "I'd love to stay here." He fingered the stethoscope and stroked it against his chest. "Do I have to leave?"

"We'll see." I knew what I should have done, but Greenhaven was so damn lonely. Nothing but graves, trees, sometimes people in dark coats . . . "But first tell me more about *her*."

He grinned and held out a hand colored by dirt. "Everybody calls me Boll."

"Like . . . Super Bowl?"

"Boll, like boll weevil. You know, that insect. The name just stuck."

"Jake Norden," I said, and licked my lips. "Come on, we can talk at my place."

"Be back, Elvy," he said to the ground.

It was the first afternoon I ever enjoyed at Greenhaven. His talk was insane, impossible, but I didn't care. I drank, and offered some wine to Boll.

"Critelli. Nothing fancy, but the best damn port you can get for three bucks. Sherry too, for that matter."

"No thanks, mister Norden. It might keep me from hearing. But I was telling about my brother's dog, it got run down and we buried it. That was the first time I tried my instrument, something just made me try." He began to cry again — seemed like he was always crying or laughing.

At first I didn't believe his stories, but the time

went fast for a change. I agreed to let him listen to the graves if he told me what he heard. After a few days I began to go with him, watch him kneel, first listen and whisper back at the ground, later wail or guffaw. I told myself I was keeping watch for mourners, protecting my job.

And he shared it all.

"Con artist!" He laughed, hoarse and wheezing, gasping to catch his breath, talking about *Jason Crane, 1870–1943,* according to a small coarsely-chiseled headstone.

"What about him?" I'd never thought about Crane before, never thought much about any of them.

"Was a bigamist, had wives in two nearby towns, three kids to each wife. There was the time they ran into each other at the Solano County Fair . . ." Boll sputtered, slapped at the ground with a dusty palm. Times like this, he couldn't hold his laughter, couldn't talk except in gasps, his narrow shoulders heaving: "Jase . . . you . . . bastard!"

"Let *me.*" I held out my hand for the stethoscope. I don't think I believed him yet, not really. I just wanted to humor him. And I wanted to try for myself.

"I'm sorry, mister Norden. It's only mine."

"We could take turns. You won't have to do so much."

"I can't. But I'll share with you. Don't I always?"

Yes, Boll shared. He told me how Crane snuck from one bedroom to the other at three A.M. most nights. And he talked about others: outlaws, spinsters, prospectors. And every one made him cry or laugh in his weird, night-bird voice.

There would have been no problem if he'd stayed in old Greenhaven. No one came to visit those graves, and the shrubs were so overgrown that Boll could hide while he listened. But sometimes when I wasn't with him he moved to fresh graves, the ones just buried. On a Sunday, I surprised him talking to the grave of an eight-year-old girl, just days in the ground after a hit-and-run.

"Beat it. Her mother comes every day, regular. She'll see you for sure. I'll get the goddam sack."

"Appomattox," Boll murmured, his face close to the earth.

"I told you, keep far from the new ones. Dammit, how'll I get another job?"

"Xenia, Ohio? Xenia! God," he told me, "this Risa's good at Geography."

My job was crummy, but it put a roof over my head, paid cash enough for food and all the wine I needed. And nobody cared if my breath smelled a little or I stumbled over the weeds. I began to tug Boll away.

"No. I have to, mister Norden. The new ones need to talk. They make sense. Old ones just repeat, talking so long with nobody to hear them. They don't listen when I answer, just repeat, faded and rustly as straw. Risa needs me. She's not used to being alone."

"Maybe. But I got my job."

I persuaded him to try an old one instead, a woman left widow by her husband, deserted by her sons. Boll winced, then whispered near her headstone. After a minute he took off the stethoscope and covered both ears with his hands.

"No good. Her screams keep coming, they feel like spikes. Nothing I say will stop her." Tears rolled freely down his face.

That made me think. After my last drink that night I figured screaming should be easy to hear, even with no instrument. Next day, before Boll returned, I traced my way back to the grave and pressed my ear against the weeds. I didn't hear screams. I didn't hear nothing.

Then, at Risa's grave, I heard only the noise of dirt against my ear.

I looked around to be sure no one was looking. Then I whispered, "Yugoslavia . . . ? Afghanistan . . . ?"

Nothing.

That crazy Boll.

Slowly, Greenhaven seemed to change. It used to remind me of a ruined city, especially when I leaned on a tree and saw it against the sunset, the shape of tombstones squared up to different heights like bombed-out buildings. Since Boll, it looked the same, I guess, but it began to feel like there were people. Quiet people, sure. Silent, alone and separate. But now I felt like I had company even when Boll wasn't there. Sometimes a bottle lasted half a week.

That was before Loni.

I never did find out why she came. Celebrities mostly went to Verdant Hills, up north on the mountain. Here, we had no reflecting pools or view of the city. Maybe Loni wasn't quite famous till the day she was buried. Anyway, she had a Hell of a funeral. Black Mercedes and Rolls-Royces jammed the dirt roads, along with men with cameras on their shoulders. The place crawled with security guards.

"Watch where you're going," I said under my breath. "Sacrilegious bastards."

Loni Harte had appeared in only one second-rate movie. But she'd died in just the right way, overdosed on sleeping pills and gin the night she appeared on a national talk-show. It was rumored she had AIDS. Whatever, the TV and newspaper jerks made her a big deal. Right at the funeral one of them, a gal in a long cashmere coat, followed by a cameraman, motioned me over.

"How old is this cemetery?"

"Greenhaven? I don't know. Eighty, ninety years, maybe. Why?"

"Are you sure? Older would be good for juxtaposition. A young thing barely out of her teens, dies. She's significant, almost a human sacrifice, like Marilyn Monroe. And she has her curtain call on this spot . . . Tell me, is anyone important buried near here?"

Ready to puke, I started for my shack and Critelli. Then I saw *him* at the corner of Loni's fresh plot, acting in a way I'd never seen. On his knees, he swayed and grinned and snapped the tube of the stethoscope like a bass fiddle.

I called in a hoarse whisper, "Boll, no!"

He jerked up and down, giggling between times he put the silver ear against the ground.

"Hey you," a guard yelled, "get that geek out of the way. What is he, some kind of *fan?*"

Boll kept moving, listening, laughing. "Marvelous," he said. "Oh that's right, you're so right!"

Then the cashmere lady spotted him and began to move in his direction. I could see what would happen next. They'd find out what he did — what I *let* him do — and I'd be back on the streets. After years with a roof over my head, I couldn't face that again.

"It's okay!" I yelled, thinking fast. "He's not dangerous if you're careful."

"Dangerous?" She stopped.

"Just watch what you say. He's stronger than he looks. It's from digging graves since he left the hospital."

"My God, get him *out* of here."

Boll looked up. "Mister Norden, no. Please!"

But all the same he got up and came with me to the shack.

"You can't listen now," I told him. "Not with those people around."

"But this is special." There was a new look in his eyes, a wet and shining look different from tears.

"You have to wait. Why not let me listen for you? I'm supposed to be around the grave. You can go back in a few weeks."

"Please, I'll be careful. I'll wait until night. That's it. I'll listen at night all the time. No one will see me any more, I promise."

I knew by then he couldn't be trusted. "Not till next month, if then. Just lend me your . . . instrument."

"No. It has to be *me*."

"What did she tell you, anyway?"

He blushed. "I can't say."

"You always said before." I admit it, I was pissed. Partly that he'd tricked me near believing his listening crap, partly because he wouldn't let me do it. I grabbed for the stethoscope and yanked one of its tubes.

Boll began to snivel.

"You," I said. "Get the Hell off this property."

He pulled back on the stethoscope. "But she needs me.

"What the Hell for?"

"She *needs* me!"

I pulled harder, and a flat spring linking the earpieces snapped, the tube I was holding came loose. Boll ran outside with the rest of the instrument — including the silver ear — crying, hooting as he went.

As for me, I felt like drinking, and began just after I hid the single tube and earpiece underneath my mattress.

It didn't surprise me that Boll came back. I'd chase him from Loni's grave almost every day when I'd catch him kneeling, rocking, listening with one earpiece of the stethoscope held in his fingers. He laughed, his breath going out in high-pitched gasps.

He was getting stubborn. So this time, instead of just shouts, I threw a pebble in his direction. "Get the Hell out!"

Still, he acted like I wasn't there, kept grinning, listening. I picked up a handful of stones, took more careful aim, and finally connected behind his ear with a piece of granite the size of a plum. For an instant I felt frightened, but then a glow of satisfaction took over as I saw Boll get to his feet and run away, shaking his head. His knees left two dents in the sod.

On my next day off I saw Loni's film, *They Never Wait to Knock*. It became a box-office smash since her death, and even in the afternoon the theater was jammed. She was a lousy actress. But her breasts defied the law of gravity, and she had a voice halfway between the purr of a cat and a mother's lullaby that put shivers down my spine. I saw her film two more times before leaving, four times again the next week. Pretty soon I knew all her moves, each smile of her lips, every blink of her lashes. There was more to that girl than just sex.

Late one afternoon I stole a flat of Gladwin Irises from the gardener's truck and planted them in the shape of a heart near the head of Loni's grave. When I squinted, the flowers seemed to beat in waves of blue and yellow-green.

And Boll came back. Not once, but many times each week I had to threaten him, toss stones, frighten him away. Each time he looked thinner, as if the hard bones at his shoulders would poke through the skin. It was his own fault. He shouldn't have messed with me.

After a few months, Loni's grave was as deserted as most of Greenhaven, private enough for me to try. Punching a hole in the side of a tin cup using a can opener, I pressed my single length of tubing into the opening. Then I listened for Loni's voice beside the irises. I listened with my right ear and then my left, at dawn and noon and after the sun went down. I couldn't hear a God-damned thing.

The place got that bombed-out feeling again: two hundred acres of holes in the dirt, holes full of silence. I kept seeing Loni's film, sometimes travelling to the suburbs where it was still running. I knew her movements, her husky sound. I imagined what she'd say to me. Above my bed I pinned a yellowing copy of the *National Confider* with the headline:

LONI —
DID SHE DIE FOR LOVE?

In the picture she wore a shred of short black lace. Her tongue was pushed out against her upper lip and she was looking right at me. I wanted her so much it hurt. Drinking twice the port didn't change the feeling, so I drank even more. At night it was hard to sleep, and I was shaky half the mornings.

Again, Boll came back. This time I found him

lying flat against Loni's grass, his arms spread wide, hugging the curve of the mound. His lips were pressed against the ground near the headstone and his hands grabbed the irises as if they were her hair. There was the sickening smell of bruised flowers.

"Enough!" Something bitter welled in my throat, stronger than the stench of old wine. I threw a few rocks, but my aim had gone bad, so I moved closer, almost on top of him, reached down for one of the bricks that line Greenhaven's paths. Then I thought of the first time I saw him, his smile, all his stories, his breathless laugh. I wanted to be friends again, forget all the anger and stones.

But he had to spoil it. "Oh Loni, yes, isn't he a fool?" Boll laughed, high-pitched, almost a giggle, stopping with gasps to catch his breath. "Oh, Loni, Loni —" They were laughing at me.

It was the wine that did it — I didn't mean to hit him so hard. Even so, the sound was kind of muffled and there wasn't any blood.

But he stopped. Boll did stop laughing.

His body was so light it seemed hollow and was easy to carry into the bushes. I put my ear near Boll's mouth but didn't hear a breath; he'd stay quiet enough. I hid all parts of the stethoscope under my mattress and then drank to quiet my trembling as I waited for the night.

After dusk, I dragged him all the way to a grave they would close the next morning. With pick and shovel I dug it deeper, fighting the tough clay of the soil. It was nearly midnight when I was ready, sweating, my face and arms caked with dirt. I pushed Boll into the pit, covered him with no more than a foot of soil, then stamped it firmly down. "Asshole, you just couldn't leave her be, could you?"

I kept my mind on Loni as I smoothed the new bottom of the grave. A double, false-bottom grave. We'd see who was a fool.

As I expected, no one messed with that grave before the casket went in. Why should they? I don't know, but it struck me funny that Boll was stuck under a banker's walnut and brass coffin, of all things. Afterwards, I tried to forget about him and think only of Loni. When I closed my eyes I saw her lips. Some mornings I thought I heard her calling. It was hard to wait, but I admit it, I was afraid. Of being caught. Or something.

I waited a month before assembling the stethoscope. The earpieces fit me well, the rich wood warm and smooth against my skin. A few rubber bands made up for the broken spring.

It was a Monday, overcast with clouds, Greenhaven more deserted than ever. A perfect day to be with Loni.

I decided to practice first by listening to an old one, *Hannah Damson, 1803–1870, beloved wife of Benjamin and mother of Joshua, Paul and Agatha.* At first I didn't notice anything but the rush of blood surging in my ears. And then I heard faintly, almost lost in other sounds, the question, "Ben, where are

you? Ben, where are you?"

"Hello!" I shouted.

"Ben . . . Ben."

"Hello, Hannah Damson!" The sod was damp under my palms.

". . . where are you, Ben?"

Then I remembered. *The old ones don't listen.* Of course, that was the reason.

I waited till night to try again, drinking a fifth of wine to get up my courage, bringing another with me to Loni's grave. By then the clouds were dissolving into fine rain, almost a mist.

The stethoscope seemed less comfortable somehow, the earpieces damp, slimy. I knelt over the mound, leaned forward, pressed the silver ear cup against the grass.

"Loni?" I whispered. Listened.

At first, nothing. I pulled the instrument apart, yanked the tubes from the earpieces, blew through the channels. Clear. But the earpieces were half-blocked with wax, so I cleaned them with a spruce needle. Assembling the stethoscope was difficult in the rain, the pieces no longer seeming to fit. I was shaking, trembling, not just from the rain and wine. Loni, only Loni mattered. I listened and held my breath.

I heard her then, very clear and loud, her voice that husky sob that made me ache. "Boll, please, you promised! When are you coming back?"

"I'm here," I said. "Jake. You can talk to me."

"Boll, when?" That voice. Through the wet sod I could almost feel her skin.

"He's gone. Listen to me. I love you, too."

"Boll . . ." Her cries welled up from the earth. I shouted and beat my fists against the ground but she couldn't hear me at all.

I stumbled to the place of the double grave,

slipping on wet grass and bricks, accidentally smashing my bottle against a tombstone. "You bastard!" I shouted at the night.

The grave wasn't hard to find, marked as it was with an imposing new stone and fresh flower wreaths. I knelt on a dirt surface that was melting in the rain.

"Boll, please, how do I get through?" I roared the question down, shaking so hard I could barely set the stethoscope in my ears. Then, almost against my will, I pressed the silver ear beside the stone.

First I heard a mumbling in a tight, senile voice, talk of rates and assets and reserves. . . . Then, piercing through like a slash of lightning — Boll's laugh. Guffaws. Sound so close I almost jumped.

"How did they hear *you?* Damn you!"

Familiar laughter, high-pitched, like an owl. Only now different.

A laugh without end, without pauses. Laugh without need for breath or gasping. Ω

AT TEA IN THE MORTUARY

Of all the corpses around the table,
None had suffered more than Mabel.
We could see from her cheek, where the fat worm
    fed,
Though she chattered away, she was plainly dead.

Then Rose spoke up with a strident voice,
"I suffered too, for I died by choice,"
And showed us the bruises from the noose
On her twisted neck, where the flesh hung loose.

"That's nothing!" snorted Aunt Floss in derision.
"Just let me show you my incision."
So, with a flourish, our cries unheeding,
She showed us the stitches, black from bleeding.

And poor old Willie, not to be outshone,
Displayed a piece of splintered bone
Where his chest had crushed under heavy wheels.
"Now, how the Hell do you think that feels?"

The sorriest sight was old Leprous Lil,
Whose life was snuffed by a cyanide pill.
While she spoke to us, one eye came free
And slid from its socket right into her tea.

With nothing to show and nothing to tell,
I squirmed with shame when a silence fell
And they turned to me. I felt so cheap
To confess I had simply died in my sleep.

—Stanley McNail

THE TOWER

The walls are there no longer: the thirsty walls
That like roots of evil vines
Drank their arterial blood, suddenly set free
By axe and cleaver in that monstrous tower.

These forty years demolished, the tower is gone
With just a crumbling ring of stones
To mark its circumference, the merest trace
Remaining on the shore of that lucid lake
That once bore its landmark image, stark as bone.

Yet on moonless nights, on stairs not there they
    climb,
Carrying festive lanterns as they go, laughing in
    innocence,
Spiraling upward to that other time
When axe and cleaver, whistling, found their flesh,
And walls no longer there, the porous walls,
Thirsty as sinister vines, imbibed the copious flow.

Upward in darkness, once again they mount
The unseen stairs of that vanished tower,
And laughter turns to screaming as the gleaming
    blades
Drip red. The echoes die among the willows
And a terrifying silence, like a shroud, descends.

— Stanley McNail

THE HOUSE OF THE IDOL-CARVERS

by Lord Dunsany

Showing That an Artist is Never a Prophet in His Own Family

There was a family living beyond the Pale Jade Mountains, living in Li Lang Ho, whose wont it was to carve from soft rock, small images, no larger than leaves of laurel. These they used to set in hollows of the wall scooped out above the fire.

When the fire was bright, of an evening, it shone on the further wall, and the further wall shone back on the little carven faces, so that many expressions flitted across them, between the firelight and dusk — sometimes smiles, sometimes frowns.

A man in this family would carve perhaps six in his lifetime. For ten years he would study in the workshops under the priests, and then he would carve the figures.

And some of the figures so carved would be given to brides that wedded away from the house, or perhaps to holy men that passed that way from the mountain, or they would be set up in jungles far away to keep the tiger at home, or on far-off headlands looking out over the Hlo-Hlang Sea, to guard those coasts from enemies while the watchmen slept. So the old images passed from the house, but the chief of the house would carve new ones so that the places were filled in the hollows over the fire.

One day a young man — the latest chief of the house — set out and travelled away from his home till he came to the Pale Jade Mountains. It is he that cut Hi Long, a lesser one of the Pale Jade Mountains, into the likeness of a god. For more than a year he quarried, and carved, and lo, head, body and shoulders! The Pale Jade Mountain was a colossal god.

At sunset the light and the shadows would flicker over the god's face. Men came forth from their huts and wondered.

And the young man went home. There spake to him, then, the elders of his house, he coming back to Li Lang Ho from out of the Pale Jade Mountains. It was ever the custom, of those that warmed at their fire, to carve certain little figures that should stand in the scooped out hollows; five or six they

carved. And lo! the hollows over the fire were empty.

And the young man answered and said he had carved a god before whom men worshipped and wondered in far lands. And they said that the number of gods in the scooped-out hollows should be five or six.

Then the young man took his staff and went back to the Pale Jade Mountains. And he labored for many years and he made a hundred gods; wonderful shapes he made them out of the mountains, for he had the skill of his fathers to give things shape, but he shaped the dreams of his mother. Men came to see them who knew not Li Lang Ho, they came on dromedaries by desert ways, they came in curious barques down holy rivers out of the Inner Mountains, they came frm cities of which the young man had not dreamed.

At sunset most curious shadows passed over the wonderful faces of the hundred gods. The multitude looked at them and sang.

And, one day, the young man returned again to the hearth of his fathers' house. And the small, scooped hollows were empty. And the elders of his house had speech with him again and bade him remember the ancient ways of the carvers, saying, "Lo, the hollows are empty."

And the young man answered and said, "I have seen the gods in a dream and have carved them all these years, yea, I have carved all the hundred gods out of the Pale Jade Mountains. Men came in to see them from Zial and Djeel and Dzol, the cities so far inland that they have not known Hlo-Hlang. There are those who say that the gods all smile at sunset, yet others say that they frown. They are very strange and awful, and they perceive the truth with their eyes. I am often afraid to see them. Men worship them and wonder."

But the elders only answered and said: "It was not the wont of the old folk."

And they wagged their heads and said: "Behold, the hollows are empty." Ω

REPAIRS

by Steve Schlich

Works had existed for some time before he realized it. *I think, therefore I must be.* He called himself *Works* because it had once been emblazoned on his canister, and because it represented the greatest milestone in his life. The chrome frame that connected his canister to his runners proclaimed *Electrolux* in indestructible cut-out lettering, but that name belonged to his maker, not him.

A man at St. Vincent De Paul had named Works in wax pencil long ago, following repairs and a spiff-up in the back room. The destructible lettering was quickly lost, but the impressions left by that gentle being stayed with him. The man loved his job and marked almost all his mechanical patients *Works*. It seemed appropriate to preserve his memory by taking the label as a name.

The blooming of Works's consciousness did not occur all at once, of course. It was slow and deliberate, like the progress a flower makes from seedhood to blossom. Age — specifically, exposure to living things — granted him depth. With each contact, his awareness of things around him grew. But the sense of it all remained shrouded and mysterious. He perceived people and events but he didn't understand them.

Works was a total product of Nurture. He retained traces of electromagnetic residue — ethereal souvenirs — from every living thing that ever touched him. And his final step to consciousness came through nurture, at the hands of the St. Vincent De Paul repairman. This man was different from other living things: he carried metal in his body. A lot of it, and not all concentrated in one place. When the repairman's metal-strewn body came into proximity with Works, something clicked.

Both felt it, though neither could interpret the experience at the time. The vague waves of natural radiation that emanate from all metals may have intersected. Perhaps the man's metal parts interacted with the electromagnetic fields generated by Works's running motor in a unique and special way.

Why didn't matter. When he was switched on, Works reached self-awareness. Before, he never felt more than the basic moods of the people who touched him. Suddenly he was completely in focus with this being. He drank deeply of human hopes and fears, joys and pains. Subsequent human contacts would be stronger and more clear, but none as pure. With this man Works felt communion. The man left and did not come back again, but Works would never be the same. He had been touched.

After St. Vincent De Paul, Works did hard time in a run-down apartment building. What a horrible

contrast after his awakening! Other people were not like the repairman. They had no metal in their bodies, for one thing. And they functioned more smoothly. They did not seem as worn as his repairman had been. Works knew well what happened when you wore out completely. That time came sooner for some than for others, it seemed.

The worst part, though, was the neglect. His various owners did not care for him. They banged him around, skipped his maintenance and abused him. He was a classic, a real workhorse, but even champions wear down. With mistreatment they lose their spirit. One dark day, Works was shut off for the last time and deposited into a dumpster. Soon after he found himself in a shopping cart, wobbling down a sidewalk in the rain. It felt like the end. After the apartment house, that held more relief than dread.

Sammy Spade pushed his cart off the sidewalk and down a long, gentle embankment to his culvert, where he spread out his stuff. The culvert ran under the street and was tall enough to walk through. It provided excellent cover except when really needed: during heavy rains it was full of running water. There was a flat plateau near the bottom of the embankment, bordered by bushes and protected from the cool November rain by a sprawling bay tree. Almost private.

Emptying the cart was work. A bulky army jacket rendered Sammy clumsier than he already was. His gimp arm and leg and stiff, rebuilt neck were burden enough. But the metal in his body cooled quickly in weather like this and the jacket kept him warm. It might have belonged to him in his previous life; he couldn't remember.

Sammy lost his last name in Vietnam. A fragmentation grenade (he was later told) filled his entire left side with shrapnel. Doctors spent most of a day extracting one bloody fragment after another, along with pieces of brain, arm, side, and leg. Almost twenty years later, the occasional tiny chunk still escaped his system like a droplet of jagged steel sweat.

Old Sammy was pinned and bolted and alloy-plated together like some walking Erector set. He lacked one finger and two toes — and his last name. He knew what it was; he saw it each time he cashed his Veterans' Administration check, but he felt no connection to it. He liked *Spade* because the name was cool and Truth in Advertising. Let's call a pot a kettle, now. So. Sammy to his friends, Spade to everyone else.

Sammy looked over his newest acquisition, an old

Electrolux. Probably didn't run, coming from a dumpster, but you never knew. It was the kind you got for $25 at St. Vinnie's with the announcement *Works* scrawled on its side in wax pencil. Usually it was true. He ought to know; he'd written that word on vacuums just like this one when he worked there.

He'd take it to the pawn shop. The old sucker looked pretty good. No big dents. The hose didn't have any holes. The man at the shop would plug it in and, if it ran, Sammy might walk away with a few dollars. You could always use a few dollars when your career in redeeming discarded aluminum cans was on the skids.

Sammy cleaned the Electrolux with his T-shirt and water from the culvert. It was worn but not rusted. It brightened where he polished it. Polishing felt good in a way he couldn't quite describe, just as fixing vacuums felt good in the hazy past before his worsening ailments cost him his job. Sammy mused that the old vacuum appreciated his efforts. He found a dry section of his T-shirt and polished some more, smiling on the side of his mouth that worked.

Works was glad to be out of the shopping cart. That contact had been disappointing. The shopping cart perceived nothing at all. It had few moving parts and no variance in materials. No changing magnetic fields, no juxtaposition of different metals, no fluid relationships between components. The cart was a poor excuse for a machine and had an awareness to match.

The man polishing him was a different story entirely. The fluids coursing through him produced electromagnetic fields and negative ion streams that touched Works, the way all organic life did. But there was more in this man. One whole side was littered with metal: an alloy steel plate at the top, two pure steel pins at the middle and bottom, and constellations of tiny fragments scattered throughout.

Works was not running and therefore not as receptive as he could be, but the contact had richness and depth. He had experienced that only once before. Could this be the St. Vincent De Paul man who had awakened him? Not likely. That man had been worn, but this one was much, much more so. The metal in him made their contact cleaner than most, but it was far from pure.

With longer contact came increasing sadness. Works sensed the pain that pulsed through this man like power fluctuations. Works had forgotten that there were two kinds of pain. One kind resided in the body and the other in . . . well, this other pain was everywhere and nowhere.

The man served needs easily grasped. Works would be exchanged for money — and in turn, the money exchanged for food. A true shame that people couldn't simply plug into a socket the way Works did, drawing sustenance from an unlimited source. But people were connected to a portable power source. Always hungry. They ran around feeding it, performing their inscrutable tasks, never simply *off*.

Works appreciated being dried and polished.

Water rusted his moving parts slowly when he was unplugged and triggered instant disaster when he wasn't. Treatment meant that his value would increase. Groomed and shiny, he'd be traded a few more times, maybe repaired again. He needed a new motor. Then he could go back to vacuuming floors. It was his life's work. With luck, he'd draw an owner who would care for him.

He was wrapped gingerly in a ragged blanket, placed back into the cart and pushed along the stream bank until they reached a road. The cart, acting as a crutch as much as a mobile home for his temporary owner, rattled along the sidewalk toward downtown.

Works searched his memory and tried to decide if this man was indeed the one from his past. What had he called himself?

Sammy fretted about the vacuum as he got closer to the pawn shop. Was it worth anything at all? There were no attachments. At least it had a hose and a cord. He wished he knew where there was a socket so he could see if the thing ran. He used to repair that stuff.

Maybe he could fix it if he had tools and a place to work. Maybe the pawn shop had attachments in the back room. Maybe the man would find the vacuum useful and want to buy it. Maybe, maybe, maybe . . . Maybe he wouldn't be going through this kind of bullshit if he had a job.

Yeah, maybe. His life was a fragile daisy chain of if's and maybe's. *If* the vacuum ran, *maybe* he would get money. *Maybe* he could get a few hours of decent sleep tonight *if* it didn't rain hard. *Maybe* he'd be someone useful, someone employable, *if* he hadn't taken that damned frag back in the Nam. . . .

He almost stopped at a dumpster and dropped the old vacuum into it. Everything put together falls apart. Maybe he should climb in there with it. Sooner or later, he too would fall apart. Why prolong the wait?

No, his conscience answered. *Don't quit. Try. See it through.* The shopping cart of his psyche held enough if's and maybe's without adding opportunities squandered to the clutter.

The pawn shop entrance was set back from the street, walled by displays of useless desirable junk such as old stereos and power tools and simulated gold watches. The entryway ramped up from street level. The window-walls slanted in and narrowed the corridor as you approached the door. With Sammy's infirmities, it was like pushing his cart up a spillway to the top of a dam.

Sammy felt mildly victorious: the shop door was cracked open. He wouldn't have to hobble around and turn the knob, careful not to let go of his cart lest it roll back down the entryway into the sidewalk and the street. He unwrapped the Electrolux and stood it on its end inside the cart, balancing it upright against his chest for the best presentation. Then he nudged the door with the front of his cart and pushed.

Sammy was over the threshold and trying to close the door behind him when he finally saw the man with the gun.

They locked eyes. Funny how you notice little details in the midst of a crisis. The gunman's eyebrow was parted in the middle by the hairless slit of a scar. The man — no, he was young, too young, just a kid — the kid was trying to grow a mustache without much success.

But the kid had a stack of wrinkled dollars in one hand, a gun in the other, and terror in his eyes. On the far side of the counter, the shopkeeper holding up his hands wore the same look. The gun barrel bobbing in front of him swung around suddenly and pointed at Sammy. It was going to blow his head off.

"Get out!" the kid screamed. "Get outa here!"

From a shrouded somewhere in his past, Sammy dredged up the will to survive. He lunged toward the kid, leading with the cart. The kid panicked and fired. At the gunshot Sammy went down gripping the cart handle. The front of the cart flew up in the air and caught the kid squarely under the chin. He went down flailing. Bills fluttered to the floor like dead leaves. The gun went flying through a display case window. The Electrolux and the toppled cart pinned Sammy to the floor.

When the smoke cleared, the shopkeeper dialed the police. Then he loaded a shotgun from the display case and held it on the groggy kid until they arrived.

The pellet of hot lead lodged inside Works's motor throbbed with heat and radiation. The electromagnetic interplay of the metals inside of him was altered and energized by the intruder. Even though he was unplugged and turned off, he became fully aware. Works reached out with his consciousness to feel the damaged parts of his body.

His tired old motor was ruined. His canister had been punctured, probably beyond repair. Much of him would have to be replaced. Works had to retreat from the pulsing lead in his motor. It emitted painful waves of energy. The effect drove him further away from the center of his own body.

He touched . . . new territory, new metal that had not been part of him up to now.

Sammy! He was perceiving through the metal inside the man who held him, and that man was Sammy. Sammy, his repairman at St. Vincent De Paul. Sammy, the man who fixed him up and named him *Works* in wax pencil. Sammy!

It was like the last time he was in Sammy's hands. Even more intense. Sammy's thoughts, his feelings, his memories were an open book to Works. And this time, Works could understand them.

Sammy had not fared well since they last had contact. Sammy was in poor, poor shape. He walked around in a fog that grew thicker each day. Sammy had not been entirely well when Works knew him last, but he was so much hazier now. He had little in common with that gentle repairman.

Works understood things that he had only won-

dered about ago. He followed the path of Sammy's life and absorbed the man's experiences with eagerness.

That path did not go back to Sammy's birth, only to the time when the metal fragments were added to his body. But it was enough. Works followed Sammy's progress from sickness to health, and then oh-so-slowly back to sickness again. He felt the shame and frustration that grew as Sammy's ability to cope with the world diminished. He felt Sammy's pride drift into the mental fog that grew inexorably thicker.

Electromagnetic interference permeated all of Sammy's system. A non-physical dust coated the man's insides and blocked the connections between his parts. No wonder he didn't operate as well as he had before. No wonder it got worse every day. However insubstantial, the fog had its effect.

In understanding Sammy's illness, Works realized something about himself. He didn't need power to operate. This was a special case. He didn't need to be plugged in or turned on because what he wanted to clean had no physical substance. He was a vacuum, perhaps the best ever made, and he could perform his task without electricity or attachments.

He could return the favor that Sammy had done him so long ago.

Works vacuumed. His motor wasn't on and he didn't make noise or suck up any real dirt. But the fog inside Sammy's mind began to thin out. Works drew it from him and deposited it deep in his own belly. The process didn't take long; after all, the fog had no sense of its own existence and no way to prevent itself from being moved. It might not have cared anyway. Having no substance, it would have no preference as to where it resided.

As he drew out the fog, Works traveled through Sammy's history as a repairman. It was of special interest to Works. Questions came to him. If he could flee from the radiating lead pellet lodged in his motor, if the motor itself could be replaced, then where exactly was *he*, Works? Was he in his hose or his canister?

If Sammy replaced every part of him one at a time, would he still be Works? Yes, he would. Because he was not his body. He could leave it. His consciousness already included the steel plate and pins and fragments that inhabited Sammy. Yesterday it hadn't. What if tomorrow it *didn't* include the canister or the hose?

Leaving that "body" behind was not unthinkable. His canister was ravaged. His motor was dead. And if he inhabited the metal inside Sammy, he would never be separated from his friend again. With a mixture of sorrow and joy only recently remembered, Works withdrew from his Electrolux body and left it to the fog he had drawn from Sammy.

When Sammy opened his eyes, Works looked through them and saw his own former body — a battered Electrolux wiped clean of impressions, fresh and blank and ready to begin anew.

Sammy woke to the question, "Are you all right?" and wasn't sure he knew the answer. He felt . . . different, as if he were seeing the world through new eyes. Everything seemed so clear. Not his vision, but his mind — the haziness that had permeated his thoughts was simply gone.

He felt like a drunkard who had finally dried out. He was thinking and reasoning and wondering, and he wasn't confused. Well, he felt some confusion. He didn't know how long he'd been out, but it seemed like a lifetime. He had this dream. It lay past the edge of his consciousness and defied recall.

"He's coming around. Mister, are you all right?"

Sammy sat up. The shopkeeper and a cop were bent over him. The Electrolux sat on the floor next to him. Inside was a bullet with his name on it.

"What happened? How long was I out?"

"Ten, fifteen minutes," the shopkeeper told him. "Hey, buddy, thanks! You saved me!"

Sammy remembered. He looked around and saw the kid being taken away. His shopping cart was pushed over to a corner of the store. Some of his stuff was in it and some was on the floor. He stood up, woozy. The cop and shopkeeper supported him while he got his balance. Pain! His head might be clear, but his body was still stapled and wired together. Things hurt.

The cop took down his statement about the foiled robbery, which consisted of the shopkeeper reminding him what had happened with Sammy agreeing and adding a few details. He convinced the cop that he didn't need to go to a hospital, and finally the officer left.

The shopkeeper seemed embarrassed that he hadn't introduced himself before now. "My name's Josh Green."

"I'm Sammy, uh, Sammy . . . Works." It sounded right. He didn't know why.

Green looked embarrassed. "I didn't think . . . I mean, you don't look like you could do what you did."

Sammy hadn't thought so, either. "I spent some time in Nam," he explained. "Guess that's where I learned how to defend myself. Same place I got messed up."

"I'm sorry," said Green. "I want to thank you for what you did." He opened his cash register. "Were you going to sell that vacuum? The one that took the bullet? I'll give you forty bucks for it."

Sammy chuckled. "I don't think it runs any more. Besides, I changed my mind. Can't get rid of a thing this lucky!"

Green pushed two twenties into Sammy's hand. "That's okay. I don't need it anyway. Got a half dozen in the back and none of 'em run. I just want to thank you."

Sammy stood there for a moment, staring at the money.

"I'd rather have some work," he said.

The shopkeeper stared at him.

"I can fix that stuff in your back room. I used to do it for a living. I do need money, but . . . Look, Mr. Green, I need to be doing something, you know? I can work. That's my name," he remembered with a grin, "Sammy Works!"

Green nodded his head. "I guess I owe you that much. I might not be standing here if it weren't for you. Listen, keep the forty. You earned it. And I'll give you ten bucks for every vacuum you can fix. How's that sound?"

That sounded pretty good. Sammy got his stuff together and shuffled into the back room. It was warm and dry. There were tools, not many, but enough to get the job done with a little ingenuity.

The first vacuum he fixed was the Electrolux that saved his life. The bullet had done its damage, but with spare parts he found, Sammy fixed the machine. He welded a scrap metal patch onto the canister with a hand torch from Green's display window. He replaced the motor with one from another vacuum and cleaned all moving parts. He performed these repairs lovingly. When he was done, he took a wax pencil and proudly wrote his new last name on the patched canister. *Works.*

Not everything put together falls apart.   Ω

HOLLOWS

by Kim Antieau

Faith opened up the house when she first arrived on the West Coast. She wanted light, fresh air, sound. She could smell the ocean just below the bluff and hear waves pounding shale. Occasionally someone in a car, usually a tourist, drove down the twisted dirt road to look at the lighthouse that sat almost in Faith's backyard. Sometimes Faith stood outside and waved to the cars, trying to step back into life.

It didn't work. She missed her husband, Jack. She heard him in every sigh of the house he had never been in. She saw him in every shadow in the woods east of her house. And at night, she felt the emptiness against her breasts, stomach, and thighs where she used to spoon up against him.

So she closed her windows and curtains and tried to forget the world. Tried to forget her husband was dead.

When she went for her mail at the post office, Mr. Winters, the postmaster, talked to her about the latest local death, birth, marriage, or divorce. Faith listened politely as she threw away her junk mail. She never knew who the people were he spoke about, and she didn't care.

"You okay way out there by yourself?" he would often ask. "You're awfully young to be so alone."

"I'm fine," she would tell him. Smiling. Trying to be polite. She wasn't that young: old enough to have a dead husband.

Later, when she got home from the post office, she usually threw away the rest of the mail, especially those letters from her family back home in the East. She didn't want to hear about anyone else's happiness or unhappiness. The bills she paid. Once in a while, she wondered what she'd do when she ran out of money.

One night she awakened from a dream to darkness and thought she was not alone. The thought comforted her until she remembered her dream. Jack was alive, and they lay together on the couch in their home in Michigan, giggling as they took off each other's clothes. He was close to her. Their hearts beating together.

Then she opened her eyes to the darkness. She put her hands between her legs, curled into a ball, and cried until she fell to sleep again.

The next morning, the rabbit ran by her window. It looked half-dead, its coat matted with blood. Faith stepped out the kitchen door into the misty rain. The rabbit stopped when the door opened. Faith knelt down on the wet earth, and the rabbit hopped over to her. She laid her hand gently on its back and tried to smooth down the fur. The rabbit stared at her. It was so still. Not like any rabbit she had ever seen.

A car came down the dirt road. Startled, the rabbit ran away.

When Faith went to get the mail that day, Mr. Winters told her about Betsy Cramer's divorce and poor Mary Downer's boy Kevin killing himself. Faith smiled, took her mail, and went home again. Outside her back door, a gray gelding stood looking toward the ocean. Faith went to him and petted his back. He remained in the backyard all afternoon. Faith brought a book and chair outside and stayed with the horse until he wandered away toward dusk. She wondered if he was sick. She hadn't seen it graze all day.

That night, she had empty dreams, nightmares about the hollow places in her life.

She awakened to a knock on the kitchen door. She quickly pulled on jeans and a shirt and went to the door and opened it.

A young man stood in the rain. His face, hands, and bright red hair were dirty.

"Are you all right?" she asked. He looked as though he had been in a car accident. She thought of Jack lost in all that twisted metal. She opened the screen door. "Are you all right?" she asked again. "You look like you're in shock. Come in. Sit down. Can I call someone?"

He came into the house and sat in a chair at the table. He shook his head. "No, I think I'm all right." He spoke haltingly. Faith wondered if she should try and find some identification on him and call someone. She went to the door and looked out. No car. She looked back at the table. The man stared at her.

"May I stay here?" he asked.

Faith looked around the dark house and thought of her empty dreams and said, "Yes."

She made tea and gave him a cup. It seemed to revive him a bit. She took him to the bathroom and gave him a towel. He stared at her, so she showed him how the old shower worked.

"It's tricky," she said. He began unbuttoning his clothes. She quickly left the room. She pulled a box of Jack's clothes down from the closet. She took out jeans and a shirt and hung them on the outside of the bathroom door.

She made breakfast and wondered why she had let a stranger into her house. She knew why: she wasn't afraid of him or anything else. What could he do to her? Nothing could make her hurt anymore than she already did.

He came to the kitchen in Jack's clothes. She wanted to cry, but she gave him food instead.

"My name is Faith," she told him.

The man looked around the room, unsure of himself, it seemed. "Tom. My name is Tom. Is this what you wanted?"

"Pardon me?" she asked.

He stared at her. She smiled. He smiled and reached across the table to touch her hand. Startled, she put her hands in her lap.

"Can I call someone for you?" she asked.

"I just want to stay here for a while," he said. "If that's all right."

She nodded.

He sat with her all day, flipping slowly through magazines while she read. It was strange having another body in the house. When she looked over at him, he smiled at her. At lunch, she talked to him about people he didn't know. She enjoyed the talking anyway. At dinner, she read him letters Jack had written to her before they were married. She brought him a blanket and pillow when it got dark and told him he could sleep on the couch.

He reached for her hand again and said, "Is this what you want?"

She shook her head. She thought of her empty bed, of Jack pressing against her, and she wanted to scream.

She sat on the couch next to Tom. He unbuttoned her blouse as she reached to turn off the lamp. Then she stood and took off her jeans. She saw his hands move toward his shirt in the semi-darkness. "No, leave it on," she whispered. She wanted to smell Jack in his shirt, feel a part of him in the cloth.

She opened herself to him, and he gently pushed into her. Her heart raced. She unbuttoned his shirt, grasped it tightly, and pressed her breasts against his. She started to cry as he moved faster, against her, in her, she wanted him to go deeper, reach inside her, touch her heart and bring her back to life again. He kissed her neck and she shivered. "I love you," he said as he moved in her, as she climaxed, Jack's body against hers in her mind's eye.

Then he lay gently on top of her, for just a moment, and all the hollow places disappeared.

In the morning, Faith awakened with Tom next to her. He smiled and leaned over and kissed her stomach.

"Good morning," she said.

"Is this what you want?" he asked.

"I don't know what you mean by that," she said, "but I guess this is what I want." She suddenly had an urge to open the curtains, let in the light. She got off the couch and stretched. "I haven't gotten the mail in two days. The postmaster is liable to send out a posse. I better go. You want to come?"

He shook his head.

She slipped on her clothes. "Will you be here when I come back?" she asked.

"Yes."

She smiled and leaned down to kiss him. He took her hand in his. The sleeve of Jack's shirt fell away from his arm, revealing a long thick red line down his arm.

"Does that hurt?" she asked.

"No," he answered.

"A man of few words," she said. She went to the door, grabbed her purse from the counter, and waved good-bye to him. "I'll be back."

Mr. Winters told her he had missed her. Betsy Cramer was having second thoughts about her divorce and, funny thing, Old Man Cooper's horse disappeared from the barn hours after it had died and the body of Mary Downer's carrot-haired son Kevin, the one who had killed himself, disappeared from the funeral parlor. A grave robber on the loose?

Faith thought of the horse she had seen day before yesterday. Staring at her. Like the rabbit. Asking her with those big brown eyes if this was what she needed to make her happy.

"He was a good kid, Kevin was," Mr. Winters said. "Kind of lost though. Slit his arms open."

Faith remembered Tom pressed against her, inside of her, her heart pounding alone.

She drove home and found Tom sitting at the kitchen table. A patch of skin had fallen away from his face.

"I scratched it on mistake," he said.

"Who are you?" she asked. Thinking of him inside her. Dead.

"I don't know," he said. "Part of this house. The land. You weren't at rest. I had to find some form that would comfort you."

"But you're dead," she said.

He looked at her. "I thought you were, too."

She stared at him. "I suppose I was," she finally said.

She went to the table and sat next to him. Maybe she could take him — whatever he was — back home to Jack's decaying body and make him come alive again. Tom blinked and another patch of skin fell from his face. No. That would not work.

She leaned over and kissed his cheek. "Thank you. You can go now. I'm all right."

He nodded, touched her hand lightly, and walked out of the house and into the day. Faith stood and watched him disappear into the woods.

Then she opened all the curtains and windows in the house. As she packed her bags, she wondered if Mr. Winters would soon be talking about her, the nice lady who used to live on Lighthouse Road. She hoped he found someone else to talk to.

She took her bags out to the car, put them inside, and then turned to look at the house. She pressed her hands against her breasts, hugging herself. She smiled. The hollow places didn't seem as empty as they had been.

She got into the car and drove away from the house, east, toward home. Ω

TROY: THE MOVIE

The wind still blows from Hisarlik
Shaking the great white sign, four letters
In painted plywooden proclamation
That this is the City of Dreams:
The Place of the Epic, Where Heroes Lived
And sometimes Died. If you will cut
As Schliemann cut, guided by the tale,
Through the hill, the cities,
Ordering the setups and scenes into continuity,
What runs through the many-gated light
Of the fabulous Moviola
Will be not Homer not Virgil not Truth
But in its own way real
As anything in the darkness:
Popcorn and figs in the lobby,
Ladies remove your hats,
The lights go down —

————— - —————

You know from the first Cinemascope frame
An endless expanse of Monument Valley
Elmer Bernstein score thundering, soaring,
That Achilles and Hector cannot both walk into the
    sunset alive;
The whole 70mm screen isn't big enough for the two
    of them.
It's over a woman. It's over range rights.
It's tons of gold in a fortress beyond the border.
It's about men burnt hard in civil wars
Banded together for whatever it is a man's gotta
    do
Or what he's afraid of not doing —

They shoulda been saddle pals, you know that,
But the gold of Troy and the face of Helen do funny
    things.
And even then Hector, the best bronco-buster
Man or god ever saw, mighta shoulda said
"She ain't rightly yours, Paris, give her back,"
But along comes Patroclus the Kid
All dressed up in his pal Achilles' fancy suit,
Callin' Hector out:
The Kid's fast, but we all know Hector's faster,
Bang you're dead.
Nothing will do then. Achilles howls
Like a wild coyote at the sky
And the Destiny Makers send him down a gunbelt
Cut from the hides of Apollo's oxen,
Hanging a pure white silver Hephaestus .45.
He straps on the gun
And the lucky spurs his ma gave him
(One of 'em busted back at Chancellorsville)
For the last walkdown under the Trojan walls.
Hector goes out game, but he sees the loco glint
Off Achilles' eye and sixgun and like any sane
    varmint
Aims for gettin' the Hell out of Dodge;
But then he stops. He won't die yellow,
Maybe, or maybe there's a mirage in Apollo's sun,
Or the ole Injun hoodoo's on him. Whatever,
He stops and he turns and the two of 'em draw down.
Bang.
The screen, the music, spin.
Last roundup, Hector breaker of horses.
Achilles ain't done. Two more shots,
So the dead warrior's spirit
Will wander between the winds forever.
Priam's turn to howl.
The fastest gun alive blows smoke off the muzzle,
Whistles up his horses,
Turns and shows that busted spur.
Bang.

————— - —————

We now take leave of the Western
Electric Noiseless Recording System
For tinted orthochrome black and white,
Rupert Julian at the mighty Wurlitzer,
Title card:

> THE GREEKS AND TROJANS DECIDE
> PARIS SHOULD FIGHT MENELAUS
> FOR HELEN'S HAND
> (AND THE REST OF HER)

by John M. Ford

Cut to Helen's bedroom, where
Priam's son, in crested helm
And baggy boxers, looks for a hiding place.
Title:

NOBODY ASKED PARIS . . .

He tries on one of Helen's gowns
Comes up a bit thin, but
All the fruit in the bowl is different sizes.
Two big lugs pound pound on the muslin door:

"TIME TO SEE MENELAUS AND DIE!"

Paris frantic holds his head, notices the helmet,
Chucks it out the window.
It crowns a passing Trojan delivery boy
(Hornrims, toga, hightop sneakers)
Before he half knows what to do
The big guys grab the schlep and hustle him off.
Music higher tootlier now.
The little guy gets armed, sort of, everything's too
  big,
The spear (he turns and bops two people)
The breastplate, the sandals (he bunches his socks)
The greaves, the belt (pants around ankles)
He scratches his head over the brazen jockstrap.
Then in a flash and puff of smoke there's a lady
  present:

APHRODITE
GODDESS OF LOVE
(IT'S ALL HER FAULT)

The helmet's over the little guy's head
So she thinks he's Paris
(Hey it's comedy)
She tells him the fix is in
(The motion for the Trojan's
From the goddess with the bodice,
The Greek who's got the grief
Is in the stew from the blue,
As they'll say in the talkie remake)
Big hug. Smackeroo. Vanish. **Thud.**
Field of battle: Menelaus is big as a Mack
Sennett truck, black beard, black mustache, black
  derby hat.
Hector and Odysseus, in striped shirts, whistles,
  caps,
Toss for first spear

IT'S IN HOMER, FOLKS
BOOK THREE
NO KIDDING!

Paris (our boy, that is) wins the flip. Spear's
Bigger than he is, but he gives it the old college try
(Music: Freddie the Freshman)
And Aphrodite transparently double exposed
(No pun really) helps the thing along whizz**bang**.
Menelaus catches it, picks his teeth. His throw
Punches through Paris' toga between his kneecaps
Trojan ladies faint away thump thump thump
  leaving
The real Paris standing there in drag
The little guy steps clear, tidying his skirt.
The goddess points an invisible finger
Closeup: bolts on big M's sword untwist:
He draws. **Clunk.**
Big man chases little man all over the map
Undercranked, sped up, always good for a laugh
They grapple, Menelaus twists Paris' helmet round
  and round
Till **poink** it comes off empty
Pan down: our hapless hatless hero grins and
  shrugs.
More charley chase until the second reel's nearly
  gone
The schlep's cornered, Mooselaus closing in
Organist plays train whistles and we crosscut
Little guy big guy
Little guy *big guy*

47

Little guy BIG GUY
Cut to
Mount Olympus, the Gods at Home
(Zeus zapping dartboard, Poseidon walking fish,
Hebe shaking martinis)
Mrs. Hera Cleaver leans out the door:

"APHRO*DI*TEE! DINNER'S READY!"

Love goddess grabs erstwhile love object by scruff
Zoooooom into sky
Menelaus knocks down cardboard wall, staggers off
    hat over eyes.
The real Paris (still dressed to kill)
Gets yanked out of frame:

FOR SOME,
THERE'S HELEN TO PAY . . .

Back on Olympus, the shrimp is in Love's lap
    literally:

FOR OTHERS,
A LITTLE BIT OF HEAVEN . . .

Our hero pulls down a cloud like a shade;
Silhouette smooch;
Iris out.

―――― · ――――

The lights on the city walls cast rippling pools of
    light
That hide more than they show.
Down these mean streets walks Ajax,
Stronger than anyone,
A man who doesn't seem to care whether
Gods or heroes or anydamnbody's on his side;
Has he got a side, the dumb ox, the moose
Unalloyed, the Front-de-Boeuf among knights,
Deaf to the laughter of Greek and Trojan both?
You load him up,
Point him at the Trojans, and he kills, Iron Mike
Hammering the many-gated city.
Just now as there is no one to kill
As there is never anyone to talk to
Ajax stands in the Trojan torchlight, feeling the
    Trojan wind.
He knows the Hisarlik wind is a crazy wind;
It blows the dust of ages past the tired walls
To scour the shining helmets of dead heroes
And when men listen to it for too long
They hear gods talking.
Where are the gods now? Ajax doesn't hear them.
The day he did has gone. Zeus the old lecher
Is boss of bosses now, practically half legit;
White-robed, nobody touches him now.
Apollo owns a theatre where the performers use the
    rear door.
Athena drives by with the dark windows rolled up
    tight.
Aphrodite? She dresses nicer than she did.
The little heroes tossed around below by the crazy
    wind

Still do the Destiny Makers' fighting,
Take the long fall for them like always,
Suckered by the crazy wind's promise of the Olym-
    pian move,
The shot at making their own destiny.
It's all lies, Ajax knows, but he stays under the walls,
It's all lies but he takes the punches,
It's all lies but he defends the hollow ships.
In his tent, the light from Troy flickering on, off, on,
    off,
He holds the weapon a dead hero gave him
And plots the insoluble mystery.

―――― · ――――

COMING SOON TO THIS THEATRE:
From the producers of *Quo Vadis, Quo Vadis We
    Vadis II,*
And *The Son of Hercules vs. Some Pro Wrestlers,*
Gimme Tax Shelter Films presents
The Aeneid
All Roads Lead to Rome. . . .
Starring a Large Number of Extremely
Pulchritudinous Italian Ladies
And Some Guy from a TV Show
As Aeneas

ALSO AVAILABLE AT THE REFRESHMENT
    COUNTER:
The Odyssey* Soundtrack Album
Featuring the hit singles
"Sirens on the Rocks"
"Nobody Calypsos Like Calypso Do"
"Well, Telemachus (What Did You Do in the War,
    Dad?)"
"Ways of Knowing Each Other" (Love Theme from
    The Odyssey)
Available on LP, Cassette, and CD (CD contains two
    bonus tracks we didn't really use in the movie)

NOW BACK TO OUR FEATURE
PRESENTATION
BUT FIRST A NEWSREEL
SO YOU HAVE TIME TO BUY SOME MORE
POPCORN

Black and white a little longer,
And documentarily grainy:
When the cinema wants to be real it shakes the
    camera.
Cassandra ties a scarf around her head
Picks up a rush broom, goes to sweep
Streets clear of the bits of topless towers.
A tramcar rattles by, a little car two-ended
As her memory. She knew in 1938
When her relative — uncle? said
"See who I have brought home with me,
See with whom I have divided mine own,"
And now they are sealed within the city,
Shaken by the Achaian guns that chew the stones
As those within chew books for their binding glue

―――――――――
*   Not to be confused with that Stanley Kubrick movie
    with all the boring classical stuff on the soundtrack.

Eating the paper words are written upon.
Once in each year, when Persephone
Tosses in uneasy bliss, and her mother
Withdraws softness and color from the world, then
  the chariots
Walk on water, and the morsels that make more war
  possible
Trickle in from the uncles far away, the desolation
Wrought by an abduction easing the desolation
Likewise made. War they say is like that.
For Cassandra life is like that;
The inevitable bending its back to bite itself.
She is not beautiful, Priam's fairest. We know that
Historical beauty was invented by von Sternberg;
Only Helen and Dietrich will be spared this curse.
Cassandra knows her own death like her own body
And she knows too the last joke of all, that in 1951
The studio will recut all extant prints
To defocus Trojan heroism
And escape the wrath of the committees.
Her fragments will lie waiting for a Schliemann of
  the negatives.
This is the destiny made for her:
The endless tramride between life and the grave.

—— - ——

Odysseus shoves the clip home in his Walther PPK
Diomedes his companion opens Channel D
Their mission
Which being heroes they naturally accept
Is to enter Troy itself and steal
The only operational prototype
Intermediate range solid state laser guided Pallas
  Module
Latest in the McGuffin series.
The Achaian agents' last operation,
The Arrows of Hercules Affair,
(You remember the great aerial stuntwork over
  Lemnos)
Was a cakewalk compared to this.
They are dressed in leather and Kevlar and the teeth
  of boars
And armed with the weapons of terror:
The silenced bow, the jet greaves,
The bronze sword of innumerable deadly functions.
The Destiny Makers themselves have sent a heron
(High Efficiency Reconnaissance Observation Node)
As spotter and close air support.
The agents disappear into the ethical darkness.
The Other Side plays the game as well, of course
Though not so well; Dolon of the Committee for
  Trojan Security
Is out there too. His bad luck.
Diomedes puts a quiet round past his head,
  phunt,
While Odysseus, master of deception, dons a latex
  mask
And asks the telling questions. Poor Dolan,
He's the patsy; you know what happens to him.
The Achaians pierce the enemy stronghold and raise
  Hades,
Dispose of countless Thracian extras
And Rhesos the criminal mastermind

In a fury of explosions, collapsing sets, and wise-
  cracks,
Escaping at last in Rhesos' personal armed super-
  chariot.
Congratulations from M
-enelaus. A thought for Moneypen
-elope back home. The war is far from over, though;
Double O
-dysseus will return in
From Calypso with Love.

—— - ——

A pre-title map of Troy city and nation
Dissolves through some splendid high-tech anima-
  tion
Into a crane shot of the swell population
Cue overture, Dolby with full orchestration
Now swoop on Troy's walls, and its grand ocean view
So what it's a model, they win Oscars too
Cue the lights and dancing waters,
Cue King Priam and his daughters
Gals in fishnets, guys in tailcoats
Shiny floors and woodwind wailnotes
Scored for jazz and fingersnap
Priam's court knows how to tap

—— - ——

Hey King Priam
Give us a moment now
Hey King Priam
Lend us your ear
You may have noticed Menelaus
Has an army here to slay us
And we think it's time your Paris
Reconsidered his dear

—— - ——

Now we need young lovers, a pair is what's expected
He's Troilus and she's Cressida, the scenarist's
  directed
No one in any major market will have read the play
And some young comic Pandarus can walk his scenes
  away
The kids are shot through colored filters indicating
  joy
Song video in embryo, the Lovers' Theme from Troy:

This didn't begin as something exceptional
Sometimes it's hard to see
The castle for all the stone
We just walked into something exceptional
No way that one could be
This wonderful all alone

The complications complicate, as complications do
As Boy Meets Girl and Loses Her while there's a war
  on too;
Enough of that. To raise suspense we redirect the
  action;
A song with both contesting sides would be a cute
  distraction.
Now Trojans largely stay in Troy, the Greeks down
  on the seaside,
But movies can do anything. Besides, we need a
  B-side.

So Priam, Paris, Agamemnon, Menelaus jilted
In parallel sing barbershop (we use a split screen,
    tilted)
About how fickle femalefolk have bollixed up their
    lives,
A light misogynistic tune, we call it simply "Wives."
But to return to real romance (before we all get
    lynched)
We turn to bold Odysseus, whose love is firmly
    clinched
He wants to see his lady wife, who's leagues and
    leagues away,
He's in good with Athena, though, so simply has to
    pray
And Pallas on Olympus, smartest goddess of 'em all
Is switchboard operator for a telepathic call:

Odysseus: *Hello Olympus, hello Athena*
Won't you put me through to where the grass grows
    greener
Hello Penelope, wish I was gonna be home
Penelope: *Yes, this is Ithaca, surely we'll take it*
We've got a connection and we sure won't break it
Hello Odysseus, miss you so much you don't know

——— - ———

We now turn our attentions to Achilles, mighty man
Who's got a little grievance that's about to hit the
    fan
He had a gal, Briseis, he was given as a gift
But Agamemnon swiped her, and is bold Achilles
    miffed
He figures if the other heroes feel that way about
    him
Then they can simply go ahead and win the war
    without him
He steps out of the action with a dancing girl or
    three
(Briseis gets some really stormin' choreography)

——— - ———

I'm mad (he's mad)
Does it matter at who
So mad (he's mad)
Tell you just what I'll do
I'll take off my armor, this bronze-plated bulk
I'll put up my sword and I'll sit here and sulk
I'm mad (he's mad)
So I hardly can speak
So mad (you bet)
Gonna quit bein' Greek
My momma's a sea nymph, my buddies are gods
I think all you heroes are stinky old sods
You wanna fight Trojans, I'll even the odds
'Cause Achilles is just plain mad
(Ain't gonna take it)
Achilles is just plain mad

——— - ———

Let's quickly return to the plot we left floating,
To Troilus and Cressida, lovers emoting,
(You haven't forgotten them? Okay, just checking)
They're up on a tower, PG-rated necking
And just when you're sick of their starcrossed
    affection
The enemy fleet scoots the seaward direction
The ships silhouette as the sun is declinin'
Leaving only this horse and a fella named Sinon
A silvertongued Greek
And an absolute sneak
Who lies into sometime the end of next week
Laocoon sneers, says the horse is a fake
Exits left (just pursued, keep it light) by a snake
So they bring the horse in. Cue the fog and the dark
A trap door goes slam, armored guys disembark

——— - ———

Ranks of bronze and black and blue
What is a soldier boy to do
Pull up your greaves and run some Trojan through
Ranks of bronze and aches and pains
Here for a soldier's ill-got gains
Pull down your helmet, bash some Trojan's brains

——— - ———

And they set Troy alight and they bust the gates in
All in grand Technicolor like *Gone With the Wind*
We bring Troi-boy and Whatsername back to reprise
We've got the whole audience down on their knees
They'll weep and wring hands till their popcorn goes
    soggy
When here comes Odysseus armed to the noggy
And just when you think that true love's on the skids
Odysseus smiles and says, "That way out, kids."
Troilus gulps and grabs Cressida. They're both home
    free
(Telepathic approval from Penelope)
Comes another bold Greek in his burnished bronze
    suit
It's Diomedes, arms full of vittles and loot:
"Hey Odysseus! What are you standing there for?"
He replies, "I'm just watching the end of the
    war. . . ."
The camera cranes up. Fires in darkness diminish,
The music crescendos. We got a sock finish.
Fade to black. Credits roll. House lights up. Play the
    theme.
Hey, it's only a movie. A celluloid dream.

——— - ———

The wind still blows from Hisarlik
Down through and over the stones of the Troys of
    the tales;
Fluttering the pages of the mind,
Flickering in the strong white beam of the eye,
Rustling the draperies of the great movie palace of
    the heart
The tales and Troy endure
As long as there is film to show the light
And corn to pop in the lobby.   Ω

GROON

What is the Groon?
My young dog said.
What is the Groon;
Is it live, is it dead?
Did it fall from the Moon,
Has it arms, legs, or head?
Does it walk,
Or shamble and amble or stalk?
Does it grumble or mumble or whisper like snow?
Is it dust, is it fluff?
Is it snuff
For a ghost that will sneeze itself inside-out,
Then, outside, in, turnabout?

Can it walk on the wall?
Will it rise, stay, or fall?
Does it moan, groan, and grieve?
What tracks does it leave
When it walks in the dust
And makes prints by the light,
By the moldy old light of the Moon?

What's the Groon?
Is it he, she, or it?
Does it sprawl, crawl, or sit?
Is it shaped like a craw or a claw or a hoof?
Does it tread like a toad in the road
Or mingle on the shingle-high path
Of our roof?
There, aloof, does it tap in the night
And go down out of sight in the rain-funnel spout?
Is it strange going in,
But even more strange coming out?

Has it shadows to spare?
Is it rare?
Does it croon for a loved one, oh,
Much like itself
Put away on a shelf
In a grave or a tomb
Where it shuttles a loom,
Spins new shapes for itself
Made of moon-moss and lint,
Sparked with Indian flint
Struck from Indian graves
Where old Indian braves
Put their bones up on stilts
Where their mummy-dust silts
Join the corn-stalks in dance;

And the wind off the hills
Chills wild smokes torn from rooves
And the dust churned from hooves
Of ghost horses stormed by
In the middle of night —
What a sight! what a sight!
Is *this,* then, the Groon?

Is it old as the Sphinx?
Is it dreadful, methinks?
Is it Dire, is it Awe?
Does it stick in your craw?
Is it smoke or mere chaff?
Do you whimper or laugh
At this skin of a snake left to blow on the road?
Is it cool-iced hoptoad or deep midnight frog
That goes *Splash!* if you jump?
Does it . . . bump . . . 'neath your bed
Near the head or the toe?
When it's there, *is* it there?
When it's gone, where's it go?

What's the Groon?
Tell me soon . . .
For the Moon's growing older,
And the wind's growing colder,
And the Groon? It grows larger and bolder!
And darker and stranger!
My *soul* is in danger!
For there creep its hands
Twitched from shadowy lands,
Reaching out now to touch
And to hold and to . . . clutch!

Quick, sunlight, bring Noon!
Fight shadows, fight Moon!
Give me morning, bright sun!
Then my battle is won.
For the Groon cannot fight
What is Sun, what is Light!
It will wither away
With the dawn, with the day!
But . . . !
. . . come back . . . next midnight . . .
With its scare . . . and its fright . . .
Once again we will croon:
What's the Groon!

What's . . . the . . . Groon . . . ?

— **Ray Bradbury**

A HONEYMOON TO REMEMBER

by Hugh B. Cave

Right up to the day of their wedding, Roger Holley had been certain he would find the courage to tell Melinda Markham the truth about himself.

He didn't, though. He was too afraid of losing her.

So they were married without her knowing about his mother, and what his mother had done to his father. And immediately after the reception they took off for a honeymoon villa on the north coast of the West Indian island of Jamaica. "Come to Jamaica!" the TV travel ads were crooning at the time, against a backdrop of swaying palms, snow-white beaches, emerald-green waters, and happily smiling, brown-skinned girls in skimpy bikinis.

Roger had his first inkling of impending trouble soon after the plane left New York for Montego Bay. He sat in the middle seat of three. On his right, by the window, an older man read a paperback novel. On his left, his lovely Melinda appeared to sleep. He was holding her small white hand and thinking how very much he adored her when a stewardess came along the aisle pushing a cart.

The cart was filled with little bottles of Scotch, bourbon, gin, vodka, and such, and the lady asked Roger and the man with the book if they cared for drinks. The reader shook his head without even lifting his gaze from the page. Roger said, "Well, yes, please, a Scotch and soda."

Glancing at the sleeping Melinda, the stewardess said, "And the young lady?"

"Well — I don't think so," Roger replied, because his bride had consumed more than a few at the reception and been a bit woozy in the car when a friend drove them to the airport.

So the stewardess handed Roger his drink and continued along the aisle with her cart. Everything quite normal — up to here.

But Melinda suddenly awoke. "Hey," she said. "What's that you've got?"

"Scotch," said Roger, who seldom drank anything alcoholic.

"And you didn't get me one?" Completely awake now and sitting straight up, Melinda gazed at the attendant's back, now some four rows farther up the aisle. "Miss! Wait!" she called sharply. "I'd like a drink, too!"

It was a tone of voice Roger hadn't expected to hear today. To be sure, he'd heard it a few times before. His brand-new wife did have a temper that belied the tenderness of her smile and the promise of eternal love in her beautiful brown eyes. But he had expected this day to pass without her finding an excuse to display it.

The stewardess looked back, and without ac-

knowledging Melinda's request continued to propel her cart up the aisle. Perhaps there was some rule against her doing otherwise, lest she create a traffic jam.

Melinda sat even straighter then, and Roger was just a bit startled to see her fingers, so delicate and white, dig into the knees of her pale blue designer slacks exactly as the claws of an angry cat might have done.

Five aisles away now, the stewardess suddenly stumbled and clutched at the cart to keep herself from falling. But she fell to her knees in spite of desperately trying not to, and somehow managed to pull the cart over on top of her.

An ice bucket, assorted glasses, and many little bottles of booze rolled in the aisle, with passengers scrambling to help her retrieve them while a second attendant came running from the rear. In a moment everything was right again, except that Roger was staring wide-eyed at his wife and wondering if he had seen what he thought he had.

She turned to him and smiled. "Now wasn't that a coincidence?" she murmured in the purring voice that always made him think of her as just a little girl. (She was the same age as he, to the day, and he was twenty-four, which still made him rather young to be a successful TV meteorologist.) "But you'll share your drink with me, won't you, lover," his wife added.

He handed her his glass and she returned it nearly empty. Then she leaned over to touch her lovely lips to his cheek and said, "Now I think I'll really take a little nap, dear."

She was asleep as soon as she closed her eyes.

Roger sipped what was left in the glass and thought of his mother.

He had never known his mother. Less than an hour after bringing him into the world she had died of injuries suffered in a car accident on the way to the hospital, with his father at the wheel. Miraculously his father had suffered only bruises and lived another fourteen years before passing away of —

Well, of what? Something more than pneumonia, Roger was certain, despite the findings of the doctor who had signed the death certificate.

No, Roger had never known his mother. But during the fourteen years he had lived with his father and a succession of housekeepers he had come to learn rather a lot about her. How, for instance, she and Father had so furiously argued about such esoteric subjects as life after death, the transmigration of souls, and reincarnation. She believed in such

things with a passion while Father just as fiercely denounced and denied them.

"My boy," Father had said once, "the two of us fought like a cat and dog at times. Never having known your mother — only seen pictures of her that made her look angelic — you can't possibly understand what I'm telling you."

Well, maybe so. Maybe he hadn't understood then, because Father had not yet told all.

But he understood now.

Oh, yes, indeed!

The Jamaican villa was everything the travel agency had promised. It had a luxurious living room, two nicely furnished bedrooms, a kitchen, a servant's quarters, and a freshwater swimming pool. It was so close to the sea that the gentle slurping of waves on the white-sand beach was plainly audible in every room.

The one drawback was the servant.

She came with the villa, and her name was Darleen Something-or-other. (She told them, but Roger promptly forgot it, having other things on his mind at the time.)

She was, of course, Jamaican. Most attractively Jamaican, too, with smooth skin the golden brown of that island's tasty naseberry fruit, and cocoa-brown eyes every bit as expressive as Melinda's.

About forty — Roger was aware that his guess might be off in either direction by as much as ten years — she stood a little under six feet tall and was, in his opinion, both competent and cheerful.

But from the moment the woman introduced herself as the housekeeper-cook who came with the villa, and her black cat Obi as her inseparable companion, Melinda did not like her. In fact, positively and intensely *dis*liked her.

For one thing, Melinda was not a cat lover and never would be. "I'm not allergic to them, darling; I just don't like the little monsters." And Darleen's cat, Obi, was no ordinary feline. Though full grown, she was the size of a young kitten. Though otherwise totally black, she had a white ring around her left eye as though she'd been peering through a spyglass dipped in flour. And her eyes, both of them, were the same mystic green as the villa's private sea in which Roger and Melinda were dying to cavort.

"Hey, now *why* don't you like her?" Roger asked when after a joyous hour on the beach on their first day in residence they walked hand in hand back to the house. He meant Darleen, not the cat.

"I don't like her attitude," said Melinda with a quick scowl. "I don't like the way she looks at me, as though I were — well — a *rival.*"

"A rival for what, for heaven's sake? You can't mean for me!" The notion was so ridiculous, Roger nearly laughed. But of course, his new wife would not have appreciated hilarity at such a moment.

"I can't explain." Withdrawing her hand from his, she turned to face him. "But I can tell you this, sweetheart: I don't like her and I don't like the cat.

And if we don't get someone else at once, this won't be the honeymoon you planned on having."

"I'll call on our landlord this very evening," Roger promised.

The villa had no phone, but fortunately its owner lived but a few miles away and Roger had rented a car on their arrival. After a delicious dinner that evening — of roast pork, local vegetables, papaya, and Blue Mountain coffee — he obtained precise directions from Darleen and departed.

The owner and his wife were well-to-do people in their sixties who occupied a handsome house in the hills. They listened in amazement as, seated in their living room, Roger explained the reason for his visit.

"Darleen doesn't please you?" The wife shook her head in disbelief. "But she's one of the best cooks in Jamaica!"

"I'm sure it isn't the cooking my wife objects to," Roger said uncomfortably. "The dinner this evening was wonderful."

"But she's an excellent housekeeper, too!"

"I don't think it's that, either." By this time Roger was really squirming.

"Then what *is* it, Mr. Holley?" the husband asked with a touch of impatience.

"I — you'd have to call it a personality clash, I suppose. And the cat."

The woman actually laughed. "The *cat*? You mean that little bit of nothing Darleen calls her 'Obi'?"

"My wife just doesn't like cats," Roger sighed.

Husband and wife looked at each other, and after a few seconds of silence both moved their shoulders in shrugs of apparent resignation.

"Very well, sir," the man said in dismissal, obviously not feeling cordial toward a tenant who so quickly had found fault. "I shall endeavor to find someone to replace Darleen during your brief stay. But this is the height of the season, and it will not be easy. Good cooks and housekeepers — cats or no — just don't grow on coconut trees."

Mumbling apologies for having caused so much trouble, Roger was glad to get out of there. As a TV weatherman, he knew a storm cloud when he saw one.

It must have been true that replacing Darleen would be difficult. At the end of the third day of their stay she and her cat were still on the premises, and Roger's bride was really angry.

It was not merely a "personality difference" that was causing her anger, she took pains to explain to Roger word by word, in slow motion. "Do you know how many callers that woman had today?" she demanded after dinner that evening, when they sat together on the sofa in the living room watching a reggae group on television.

"Callers, darling?"

"Have you been paying any attention to her at *all*?"

Roger really hadn't been, and supposed he ought to feel guilty about it. When not enjoying the delicious meals Darleen placed on the table, or swimming in the emerald-green sea just beyond their veranda, he'd been content to stroll down to the village and talk to Jamaicans in the shops there, or to sit around the house browsing through books from the beautiful mahoe bookcase in the living room.

These were about Jamaica, and ranged from tales of early buccaneers at Port Royal to some rather frightening but seemingly authentic accounts of present-day obeah.

Obeah. Why was it, whenever he picked up a book on that fascinating subject and settled down with it, the little black cat named Obi almost always appeared at his feet and jumped up on his lap as if to help him read? Did the creature know something he didn't?

As an offshoot of African voodoo, obeah was outlawed by the Jamaican government, he learned. It was, however, practiced secretly by certain country folk and could be exceedingly nasty. "Be alert," one book warned. "Don't dismiss it as mere folklore, lest you pay a terrible price for your ignorance."

On the subject of callers, Roger's wife angrily informed him that their housekeeper had entertained no fewer than four of them that day. "And all of them in our kitchen, where they had no right to be. Roger, I want it stopped!"

"All right, dear." He sighed in surrender. "I'll talk to her right now."

It was almost eight o'clock, and on opening the kitchen door and walking in, he was surprised to find Darleen had a caller even then. A man at the kitchen table looked up in apparent alarm, as though startled by the intrusion. Well dressed, even wearing a jacket and tie, he could easily have been the proprietor of one of the better village shops, or perhaps a politician. Darleen sat facing him.

Between them on the table lay a small drawstring pouch of some leathery material that reminded Roger of one he had carried marbles in when a child. Beside it sat the little black cat with the one white-ringed eye.

The housekeeper turned her head. "Yes, Mr. Holley?"

"I'm sorry," said Roger. "I thought you were alone."

"I was just leaving," the man said, and thrust the pouch into a jacket pocket as he stood up. Taking out a billfold, he handed Darleen a number of colored bills. "Thank you," he said. "And you, little one," he added, reaching out to stroke the cat. Then, with a nod to Roger, he departed.

Now what was that about? Roger wondered, but of course did not ask. What he did ask, because he knew Melinda would not be happy if he failed to, was why Darleen was having so many callers.

Still seated, she gazed at him in silence for a moment. Then he discovered a side of the Jamaican personality for which he was quite unprepared.

"Mr. Holley," she said almost haughtily, "are you saying I may *not* have callers while employed here?"

"Well, really, I don't know what arrangement —"

"When the owners are in residence, I am never told I may not have callers, Mr. Holley. If any such rule is to be established now, I shall have to quit."

What, dear God, was he to say to Melinda? He had no idea. But he knew what he must say to this woman who had just accepted a rather large sum of Jamaican money for some service rendered.

He said it.

"Darleen, please — there's no need for you to quit. I just didn't understand. Everything is all right."

Back he went to the living room to confess to his bride that he had failed. She, of course, was furious.

"You mean to say you let that woman tell *you* what to do?"

"Now, dear, it wasn't like that. She's always been allowed to have callers, she said, and just can't understand what —" The look on her lovely face silenced him, and she did nothing to end the stillness. Then he said helplessly, "What else could I do?"

"You could at least have told her to get that cat out of here! You know I detest cats!" Melinda got up from the divan. "I'm going to bed."

Telling himself he shouldn't let such an outburst go altogether unpunished, Roger tried to watch television for a while. But the reggae group was nothing very special. (Some in Jamaica were, some weren't.) And he had, after all, been married only — what was it? — three days. Deciding he had shamefully let his bride down when she was counting on him to be manly and protective, he trudged head-down to the bedroom.

The light was already out. Nothing was said as he undressed in the dark. Then on getting into bed he discovered to his astonishment that Melinda was not in it.

He sat up, turned a bedside lamp on, and looked around — naked, of course, for in this tropical paradise who would wear pajamas? The two bedrooms in the villa were exactly alike: same size, shape, wall-and-woodwork color, even identical curtains. Had he, distraught by his failure with the housekeeper, walked into the wrong room by error?

With a feeling he ought to be grinning at his stupidity, he went to the door and grasped the knob. It wouldn't turn. It simply would not turn.

Should he call out to Melinda? No, he decided. She was annoyed with him and might not choose to respond. Maybe she was even responsible somehow for his having chosen the wrong room, and had secured the door to demonstrate her displeasure.

Back in bed after moments of struggle and frustration, he lay there thinking. There was something oddly familiar about all this. What was it?

Ah, yes. His father!

"Let me tell you about a thing that used to happen before you were born, son. Many a night when your mother and I had argued about all those esoteric beliefs of hers, we would go to bed and I would find myself not in our bedroom but in the guest room. Alone in the guest room, wondering how I'd got there, and unable to open the door."

There was something else Father had told him either then or later. Something that might be significant now if he could recall it. But his mind was not working well tonight. After a while he gave up the struggle and fell asleep.

At breakfast Roger apologized to his bride for having quarreled with her. She merely smiled at him and shrugged her pretty shoulders. When he apologized further for having gone into the wrong bedroom, she smiled again.

"I don't think I *meant* to sleep there," Roger said. "I mean, you know, it wasn't deliberate. It just sort of happened."

"As though you'd been drinking?" she said.

"Well, yes. But I never take more than one drink. You know that."

"Let's not talk about it," she said, and her smile now was somehow enigmatic, even mysterious. "We never promised each other perfection, did we?

Roger was glad to let the matter drop.

After breakfast, their housekeeper-cook announced she had to go to market. Her duties, she explained, included shopping whenever supplies were low. Within ten minutes after her departure, Melinda was in her room — the door had not been locked — methodically going through the contents of her bureau.

Obi, the little green-eyed cat, sat on the bed and watched her, but did nothing to interfere. When Melinda paused to hiss at him on her way out with a cardboard shoe box from a bureau drawer, however, he bared his tiny teeth at her.

"Monster!" she said. "I ought to drown you!" Then, marching into the kitchen, she placed the box on the table, removed its cover, and triumphantly summoned Roger from the living room. "Look at this!" she cried.

Roger did not feel quite right about it, and shook his head at her. "Should you have done this, do you think?"

"*Look* at these things! Don't you know what they *are?*"

After having seen the man pay their housekeeper for the drawstring pouch and guessing the payment was for something the pouch contained or was meant to accomplish, Roger had re-read parts of a volume from the bookcase. He thought he knew what the assorted objects in the box were for.

Not that he could identify all of them, of course. But some that resembled dried peas might be the desiccated eyes of small animals, and bundles of twigs that might be herbs for seasoning food probably were not. There was no question, however, that what looked like a dried toad *was* a dried toad, or that the tiny white animal skull was that of an unborn goat.

"It would seem your precious Darleen is an obeah woman," said Roger's wife. "In other words, she's a witch. And I'll bet you anything you like, that damned cat is her familiar."

"What do you mean, her familiar?"

"A familiar, stupid, is a spirit that guards and serves a witch. Your precious Darleen —"

"Now wait a minute," Roger protested. "She's not 'my precious Darleen'! Just because I didn't know how to deal with her —"

"All right. But she *is* into obeah. And now we know why she has so many callers. They're clients."

"I suppose you're right," Roger had to admit. "So what are we to do now? Fire her, even if we can't get anyone to take her place?"

"You leave her to me," his wife retorted. And after returning the obeah box to its owner's room, she departed for the village.

She had gone, Roger surmised, to enquire for a cook-housekeeper at some of the local shops, expecting to be referred to some woman, competent or not, who would agree to take Darleen's place. A shortage of such help there might well be, but Melinda would solve that problem by offering a temptingly better-than-standard wage and not looking too closely into a candidate's qualifications.

But her lovely face was a thundercloud when she returned.

"Such stupidity!" she all but shouted while pacing the livingroom floor. "Such ignorance! I'm beginning to hate this island!"

"Please," Roger said. "What happened?"

"What happened? Nothing happened! Four different women agreed to come and do the cooking here until I told them *where* they were to come! Then they backed off like a blind person touching a hot stove. Oh, no, they really didn't know how to cook for foreigners. They could never keep a house like this one tidy. They couldn't leave their children. Excuses, excuses!"

"Meaning, I suppose, they wouldn't risk offending an obeah woman. But can you blame them, really? They believe in obeah, you know, even if we don't."

His wife eyed him strangely. "You don't believe in such things, Roger?"

"In what such things?" Were they about to fall into the kind of argument his parents used to have?

"In obeah, voodoo, the occult? Are such things merely superstitions to you, Roger?" The challenge in her voice made him feel as though *he* had touched a hot stove.

"Well, I —"

"You don't know what to believe. Is that it?"

"You could say so, I guess."

"Well, then, as I told you before, I'll attend to our obeah woman myself," Melinda said. "I wasn't counting on much help from you in any case."

Roger was beginning to feel cornered and frightened. "What will you do?" he heard himself saying against his better judgment.

Would she have told him? Knowing he couldn't stop her from doing it even if he wanted to, she just might have, he thought later. But at that moment the subject of their discussion returned from market, and the conversation abruptly ended.

Roger slept with his bride that night, though it

was a close thing when just before bedtime she brought up the subject of his beliefs again. Did he, she wanted to know, believe in life after death? In the transmigration of souls? In reincarnation?

She did. Did he?

It was no doubt the familiarity of the terms she used that caused a warning bell to jangle in his mind. Thinking of what his father had told him, and fiercely wishing he could remember what else he had been told, he knew he must not be drawn into an argument. His wife might punish him the way his mother had punished Father.

"Well, I don't really understand such things," he hedged. "But I'm sure I have an open mind. Someday you'll have to instruct me."

The reply seemed to satisfy her, though when he sought to make love to her a bit later, she claimed to be overtired and urged him to go to sleep instead.

Roger just might have done that — he really wanted to — had not his mind persisted in remaining wide awake. For some reason it kept struggling to exhume that old, half-dead memory of what his father had told him about his mother. The one about her being . . . but what it was she had been was what he couldn't recall. The effort made sleep impossible and he became aware presently that his wife, too, was not sleeping. Or if she was, she was talking in her sleep. She had never done that before. Not to his knowledge, at least.

Motionless on his back, he listened with great care, but her mumblings were not actual words. They sounded more like a ritual of some sort — an invocation, say — in some alien tongue. On and on it went for some ten minutes, in a performance that both baffled and scared him.

He heard a door being opened then — that of the housekeeper's room, was it? — and this was followed by a sound of footfalls in the kitchen. Slow, deliberate footfalls, as though their maker were sleep-walking.

A second door was opened, this the one to the yard, and with a glance at his wife, who was still mumbling but did seem to be asleep, Roger carefully sat up in bed to look out an open window beside him. The window provided an unobstructed view of the yard and the swimming pool, both now awash in mother-of-pearl moonglow.

Into view came a figure in a white nightgown, taking one slow step after another as though in a trance. In her outthrust hands she held the little black cat with the white ring around one eye.

Apparently the pool was her destination. Did she mean to throw the cat into it? Was she being *commanded* to do that by the woman at Roger's side?

But on reaching the pool Darleen did not stop. It was a pear-shaped body of water, and from its wide shallow end she continued around its tiled edge to the narrow deep end. Perhaps she had no intention of stopping at the pool, Roger speculated. Perhaps she was on some nocturnal mission having to do with her calling as a purveyor of magic, and would continue on across the yard to some destination outside the property.

But no. At the deep end of the pool her trance journey ceased and she stood there gazing down at the water. Then, still holding the cat out in front of her, she took one more deliberate step and was *in* the water, feet first, plunging down out of sight.

Roger waited for her to reappear. When after a reasonable time she did not, he knew something had to be wrong and flung himself naked out of bed. Yelling at his bride to assist him, he raced from the bedroom into the kitchen, where he found the door to the back yard open. Crossing the yard to the pool took but a moment. There in the moonglow he saw, on or near the bottom, a dark shadow enveloped in its undulating cloud of nightgown.

Without hesitation he plunged in after it.

He was a fair swimmer. It really was no great feat for him to thrust his hands under the woman's arms and bring her to the surface. At the edge of the pool he held her aloft with one hand while scrambling out, then pulled her out after him.

At this point his troubles began.

Though alive, the housekeeper was unconscious, and Roger knew very little about how to bring an almost-drowned person back from death's door. Yet obviously he must do something and do it quickly.

Recalling a life-saving technique he had probably seen demonstrated on TV — and just as probably had paid little attention to at the time — he turned the woman onto her back, leaned over her, and tried to breathe air into her lungs.

While he was doing this, his bride came leisurely from the house and with her hands on her hips stood over the two of them as though in judgment. She wore pink pajamas she had not been wearing before, and her lovely face was taut with displeasure. Roger, however, did not look up to see it but continued his ministrations.

His hands were now under the housekeeper's waist and arching her dark body upward. That was the way to do it, he seemed to remember. His mouth maintained its pressure on hers as he sought to invoke a response. And at last — thank God for miracles! — she did respond, weakly shuddering at first, then opening her eyes wide to look into his, then finally gasping hugely for a breath.

Roger struggled to his feet. "Help me get her into the house," he said to his wife.

"You're naked!" she flung back.

But this was a Roger his bride had not known before. "Damn it, so what?" he shouted with controlled fury. "Shut up and help me!"

Melinda gazed at him in total astonishment for a few seconds, then obeyed without further comment. Together they carried the woman to her bedroom and laid her on the bed.

"You'd better get this wet nightgown off her," Roger said then.

"If you say so," his wife replied with a controlled fury of her own.

But the woman on the bed, shaking her head, said

quickly, "No, no! Please, Mr. Holley — save Obi! In the pool! My cat! I had him in my hands!"

The cat, Roger thought. Her precious little cat. Dear God, he'd forgotten it. Still naked, he rushed back out to the pool and peered into the water.

There it was — just a small dark blur on the bottom.

He dived and brought it up. Sat on the edge of the pool and held the tiny thing cupped in his hands and stared at it. Those marvelous green eyes were closed — did that mean anything? He had no idea whether the eyes of a dead cat ought to be closed or open. When it still did not move, he lifted it to his ear to listen for a heartbeat.

There was no sound.

With the cat still cupped in both hands, he walked slowly back to the housekeeper's bedroom. "I'm sorry, Darleen," he said, and handed it to her.

Seated there on the bed, still in her wet night-gown, Darleen too held the creature in both hands and looked at it, just as he had done. Then she put it down on the bed, where it looked like a small puddle of spilled black ink, and she transferred her gaze to the face of Roger's wife.

In total silence she stared at Melinda until Melinda took a backward step and turned away. Then the housekeeper said to Roger, "Please, Mr. Holley, will you take me home?"

"Home?" Roger was puzzled. "Now?"

"Yes."

Roger glanced at his wife, hoping for a look that might tell him how to handle this. For once her face told him nothing. "All right," he decided. "What do you want to wear?"

"I can go as I am."

"Whatever you say. Can you walk to the car?"

"With your help."

"Just let me get some clothes on, then." Roger hurried from the room. Returning dressed, he looked at the small dead cat on the bed. "What about him? Do you want to take him with you?"

"No," Darlene said.

"I can bury him, then?"

"Yes. Thank you. You are kind."

To his wife Roger said, "I'll be back as soon as I can." Then with no help from her he managed to get the housekeeper to his rented car and asked where she lived.

"In the village. When we get there, I'll direct you."

She did so — to a small, zinc-roofed house on an unpaved lane. When she knocked on her door it was opened after a brief delay — the time, after all was nearly one A.M. — by a handsome lad of about thirteen whom she introduced as her son. Then after gra-ciously thanking Roger for saving her life, and vowing she would repay him, she bade him goodnight.

Roger drove home deep in thought and found his wife sitting on their bed with a look of fury on her face that said she was not likely ever to forgive him. Hoping for the best, he said, "You're angry with me, aren't you?"

"Why should I be?" Her voice was ice.

"Well, I don't know. But you obviously are. Did you have anything to do with Darleen's nearly drowning herself?"

"How could I have had anything to do with it?" she flung back. "If the woman was stupid enough to —"

"You were mumbling some weird stuff in your sleep. If you actually *were* asleep. I'm not sure you were."

"Mumbling *what?*"

"Some kind of incantation, it sounded like. I know a little about such things, you see. My mother —" He hesitated.

"Yes? Your mother?"

He could not say it. Walking out of the bedroom, into the living room, he sat on the sofa and remembered another of those times when his father had talked to him at length about his mother.

"She was a witch, you know, son. I mean that literally — not 'witch' as in 'bitch' but the real, ungodly thing, full blown. She belonged to a coven that met secretly, once a month, in an old farmhouse. Of course she never admitted it, but I found out by doing some detective work. On the nights the coven met she always insisted she was visiting her sister. The sister covered up for her."

All right, his mother had been a witch. Roger bit his lip as his frustration returned to plague him. Why, damn it, couldn't he remember the rest of it?

He *had* to remember. His very life might depend on it.

He spent the rest of that night in the second bedroom, fully convinced that if he did not do so voluntarily he would end up there anyway. In the morning, while shaving, he recalled still another conversation with his father.

"Once, after we quarreled, I cut myself shaving," Father had said. "I was using a straight razor then — always liked them better — and gave myself a nasty slash below the chin. I believe I was trying to cut my throat, though of course there's no way I can be sure of that. All I know is that my hand did something I didn't direct it to do. *She* must have given the order. The slash required eight stitches."

Roger decided he had nothing to be apprehensive about on that score. He was an electric-razor man.

But after wrapping the little dead cat in plastic and burying it under a hibiscus bush in the yard, he found he had another problem.

With Darleen gone, there was no servant on the premises to prepare breakfast, and he was sure Melinda in her present mood would never conde-scend to do so. Opening the fridge to see what was available, he decided to concoct, for the two of them, a Mexican-style omelet.

And while peeling an onion for it, he slashed the heel of his hand so deeply that blood turned the sink crimson as he tried in vain to stop the flow with paper towels.

In the end he had to beg Melinda to help him get

to a doctor. The name and address of one in the village appeared on a list headed "In Case of Emergency" that was posted on the kitchen wall.

"I suppose I'll have to," his bride said peevishly. "But after the way you behaved last night, I ought not to."

"I'm sorry about last night," Roger said.

"Well, that's something."

"And are *you* sorry about *this?*" He held out his hand, now wrapped in a towel that was already red.

His wife's lips parted barely enough to let her answer. "And just what is *that* supposed to mean?"

"Oh, forget it." He wanted a doctor, not another argument. But he should not have challenged her. On the way to the medic's she spoke only once, and that was to ask a policeman for directions.

Other patients awaited their turn in the doctor's outer office, but after a glance at Roger's wound the man attended to him at once. It was a bad one, he said as he stitched it. "I suppose you spend a good deal of time at the beach, eh?"

"Well, yes," said Roger.

"Fair enough, but stay out of the water for a few days. And don't be alarmed if this is painful for a while. It will throb a lot."

Roger winced. "Believe me, doctor, it's throbbing now."

The pain worsened. Roger's wife went to the beach without him while he retired to the second bedroom and stayed there. On finding her still absent when he emerged, he did a strangely out-of-character thing. Propelled by an urge totally foreign to him, he went straight to a kitchen cupboard in which the landlord in a gesture of good will had left two bottles of the island's Appleton Rum.

With his bandaged hand still throbbing, it was no easy task for him to open a bottle. He managed it, though, and having poured a good six ounces into a water glass, gulped it down neat.

During the next half hour, in the process of getting very drunk, he had a few lucid moments during which his mind struggled with certain questions. Their housekeeper, for instance. Had she really been walking in a trance, and if so, why to the pool? Why with the cat? And Melinda. *Had* she played a part in the near tragedy? *Had* she caused him to cut his hand? *Had* she — to go all the way back to the beginning of this strange honeymoon — caused the stewardess on the plane to stumble and fall?

Finally — and this now seemed important — would Darleen return to work here when she felt better? To "repay" him as she had promised? And if she did, what *else* might happen?

There were, of course, no answers to these questions, and presently Roger was too smashed to care. Having finished nearly an entire bottle of Appleton, he reeled into the living room and collapsed on the sofa.

Still, he was not quite out of it when Melinda returned. Through an alcoholic haze as thick as gungo-pea soup he was aware that his wife came into the room and stood beside the sofa gazing down at him. And that she said at last, in a voice that surely purred with triumph, "I see you found the rum." And he was still conscious enough to realize he hadn't known there *was* any rum in the house before going straight to it.

How had he known where to find it?

With that final question tormenting him, he passed out.

When he awoke the next morning, Roger was still pretty much out of it. Stumbling into one of the villa's two bathrooms, he strove to revive himself by splashing cold water on his face with his good hand, remembering he was not supposed to get the bandaged one wet.

About those questions he had asked himself — they were still valid, he decided. Indeed they were. And now he remembered something else.

His father, a genuine teetotaler, had become violently drunk one night after a quarrel with his mother. "First time in my life," Father had said when telling him about it. "Absolutely the first, and, my God, was I drunk. As I told you before, your mother was a practicing sorceress and could make me do just about anything."

He must be careful. No more arguments.

He slept most of the morning. If Melinda ate any breakfast, she must have prepared it herself. The same for lunch, which she did indeed prepare — he heard her in the kitchen — and which he passed up, knowing his stomach would refuse it. The day was not one of the kind Jamaica promised its visitors. A leaden sky made the villa's windows look as though they were covered with gray plastic. Melinda had turned the lights on.

Still, when his bride had finished lunch she put on a swim suit and said, "I'm going to the beach. Do you want to come?"

"The doctor told me not to go swimming."

"All right, if you want to lie here all day doing nothing."

Another quarrel would ensue if he refused, he guessed. And what would she do then to make him regret having crossed her? "I'll come. But I really can't go in the water unless you want to drive me back to the doctor to have my hand dressed again."

"Just come as you are," she said.

On the way down to the sea she walked ahead of him, lovelier than ever in the revealing swim suit she had bought for their honeymoon. Very few women were as lovely as she anyway, he thought.

Suddenly he recalled still another remark his father had once made. "Your mother, son, was a damned beautiful woman. I'd have forgiven her for anything."

Trudging along behind his bride over white sand that now looked as gray as wood-ash, Roger heard himself sighing. Why couldn't life be a little less complicated, for God's sake? Another unanswerable question. There were so many now.

Why was he so sure there would be more?

Except for a few small birds running along the water's edge, the beach today was deserted. Turning to look both ways, Roger saw not a single soul on the sand itself, only a shadowy human figure moving in slow motion behind a screen of sea-grape bushes some sixty yards distant. The shadow was tall, and he had a feeling he recognized it.

But why should their housekeeper have come here today? She had never done so when working for them at the villa.

As he trailed his wife to her favorite spot just short of the sea grapes, he saw the figure again. Yes, it had to be Darleen. Very few of the Jamaican women he had encountered were as tall as she. But now there were two shapes. At the housekeeper's feet a small, four-legged creature kept pace with her.

A cat? Yes, and a black one, too. In fact, it looked *exactly* like the one he had buried under the hibiscus bush, even to the white ring around one eye! But could there be *two* black cats that small, with the same unusual marking?

He nearly called out to the woman, but Melinda interrupted the impulse. "You can sit here, Roger," she said. "Even the doctor would approve of that."

She had brought along a beach towel, and with something of a flourish she spread it out for him. Roger lowered himself onto it, careful to keep his bandaged hand out of the sand. With an indifferent wave, his bride ran down to the water's edge and splashed on into the sea.

He watched her, sadly wishing he could do the same to rid himself of his hangover. He couldn't, of course. He was so hung over that even if he hadn't cut his hand, any attempt to enjoy a swim would probably end in disaster. He would just stumble around, fall down, swallow a lot of the sea, and be violently sick.

Why, he wondered again, had the Jamaican woman, Darleen, come here on a day when the beach was so gray and deserted? And was she still here? Carefully turning his aching head, he looked for her again among the sea grapes.

She was there, yes. Motionless now, she was just a dim, dark statue among the greenery, but she was there and seemed to be gazing fixedly at the sea.

And that second, smaller shape, that so resembled the tiny, four-legged creature he had buried in the garden — it was there, too, at her feet.

What was the woman staring at?

And the cat, too, unless he was mistaken. Perhaps at Melinda?

Roger turned back to watch his wife and suddenly realized she was not behaving as she usually did. Not a very good swimmer, she normally just cavorted around in waist-deep water like a happy puppy, splashing a lot. But now she was stroking her way straight out to sea and must already be well beyond her depth!

He struggled to his feet in a panic, forgetting his bandaged hand and getting it layered with sand. "Hey!" he yelled. "Hey! Come back!"

She didn't hear him — or, if she did, was not about to pay any attention. As if her very life depended on her reaching the distant horizon in the shortest possible time, she thrashed on out to sea.

Still shouting, Roger went lurching to the water's edge and stumbled on in, losing his balance and falling forward when the water reached his knees. Unhappily the warm tropical sea did not clear his senses as the colder water back home might have. It merely made him feel drunk again, and though he flailed away wildly with his arms, he was in no condition to swim or even stay afloat.

Swallowing huge quantities of water, he staggered to his feet and retreated in surrender to the beach, where the swallowed water came back up for the next several minutes. When he had recovered enough to look for his wife again, she was far out and still swimming toward the horizon, though with less energy.

He saw her head go under and reappear once, twice, thrice. Knowing what had to happen, he frantically looked for someone to help him. There was no one in sight.

Well . . . no one but the tall, shadowy figure in the sea-grape bushes, with the equally misty cat at her feet. Why did he have a feeling that if he called to *her* for help, she would simply vanish?

"Melinda . . . oh, God, darling, why did you make me cut my hand?" Was he sobbing the words aloud or only thinking them? "Why did you get me drunk, Melinda? I could have saved you if you hadn't!"

He could have, too.

He began to cry. And his tears, it seemed, washed up from some deep chamber of his mind the one remark of his father's that had so long eluded him. Father had made it while dying, with Roger at his bedside.

"Don't grieve for me, lad. I may come back, you know. Your mother always insisted *she* would come back. Her soul would go into a child who was being born about the time she died, she always said. And she was convinced of it. She truly was."

About the time she died.

And she had died, of course, just after giving birth to Roger.

And in that very same hospital, that very same morning, the woman who would one day become Roger's wife had come into the world.

My mother, my wife. Roger's tortured mind presented the words in a blaze of fireworks. *My mother, my wife!*

His wife had gone under for the last time. The sea was mockingly empty. Turning, he looked toward the sea-grape bushes.

The Jamaican woman and her cat had disappeared.

Darleen. An obeah woman. What was it she had said to him when he took her home after the incident at the pool?

"Thank you for saving my life, Mr. Holley. Never doubt that I will repay you." Ω

As I watched — choked by a sudden rise in the fishy odour after a short abatement — I saw a band of uncouth, crouching shapes loping and shambling in the same direction . . . and one wore a peaked diadem which glistened whitely in the moonlight. The gait of this figure was so odd that it sent a chill through me — for it seemed to me the creature was almost hopping.   "The Shadow over Innsmouth" by H.P. Lovecraft

LIFE PARTNER

by David J. Schow

The dirty gray light told JJ the sun was still waking up. Next to her, Walter continued the cadenced respiration of his own sleep. She hated him for the sleep he could achieve when she had to fight for every Z.

JJ was on her back, only her right calf brushing Walter, who was also on his back. He did not snore. Walter never snored. Snoring was for less cultured beings. He told her that she, in fact, did snore — lightly, delicately, "daintily" was how he put it. The telling did its insidious damage and became just one more thing to push her awake when she most sought sleep's oblivion.

What had jolted her back early to the real world this morning was a weird dream about Walter. Sort of.

In the dream, JJ was ten years older, and Walter was there, which meant they were still together. It was less a commitment or a sentence than simple inertia; after a while you compensate for your private losses by taking petty agonies out on your mate of record. She stood before a mirror in the dream, having lost a decade. Her eyes looked lost and haunted. Walter appeared behind her. They were both naked. He embraced her, reaching around to cup and collect her. He told her they both still had each other. She could feel his erection prodding her butt. They still had each other. His palms brushed her nipples and brought them up; he knew her body too well. And she was warming . . . the old reliable process, and soon Walter would be inside of her, and they still had each other . . .

. . . but JJ no longer had herself.

Bang — awake. So to speak.

JJ awoke feeling so lost that her reach to Walter was on the instinctual level, flesh seeking the comfort of flesh. She ran her hand from his navel to his nipples, then all the way down.

Pause. One more breath. She did not hear a husky inhalation; that sleepy-warm pre-coital sound that certifies and bonds what follows. Walter slept on, limp as a juvenile offender's alibi, as unconcerned as a snake's prey in mid-swallow. He breathed onward, regularly, and slept.

Maybe his dream was better than hers.

The moment ebbed. JJ gave up. A little reciprocity, for cryin out loud. A touch of tactile reassurance. Did she ask too much? Had she taken so much from him?

She released a long breath as a sigh. No way she'd get back to sleep now.

To hell with Walter. She could do herself, and if he finally decided to wake up, so much the better. Maybe the rigorous wiggle of the bed would do it.

It took time, but JJ lost herself for a few moments of the new day, inside another kind of dream.

JJ dozed. It was a thin, greasy kind of sleep, like passing out with gas heat clogging the room. When she awoke, she found semen drying on the bottom sheet of the queensize and silently cursed Walter as a deep-sleeping son of a bitch.

Awake, he'd never admit to her that he preferred the dream.

He lay exactly as before, respirating exactly as before.

JJ stared blankly at the ceiling. She survived that horrible moment when your body enables the getting-up process.

She sat up, her sinuses cracking and shifting. Coffee.

"Walter?"

Nothing. No change. No acknowledgement of her. He usually rose way ahead of her.

She wondered perversely if he were feigning sleep, monitoring her through slitted eyes when she was not looking. Cataloging the moves she made while she thought herself unobserved. You could learn things about people by watching them when they believed they were alone and unaccountable.

"Walter." She nudged him. Firmly enough. She counted off five more of his regularly-spaced, undisturbed breaths. Intake. Outflow. The neutral expression on his sleeping face was so serene she wanted to rearrange it with a razor, make the look garish and unhappy, like a mutilated clown face.

"Fine," she said to herself, as closure.

She kicked out of bed, gearing up to do the bathroom thing. As she passed the hall mirror she avoided the sight of herself.

Two hours later Walter had not stirred, nor shifted position. JJ had to lean close to ascertain he was breathing at all, and for the first time that day she felt ill and frightened. This was not funny. This was like being told your best friend is considering suicide.

She shook him. Cajoled and demanded. Walter did not move, except as she moved him.

"Fine. *Fine*. I give! I don't have time for this crap. I don't *care* what I did. You're being an asshole, and I have a real walloper of a headache, *thank you*, and I have a full day to deal with, so I am out of here. Goodbye."

She stalked out. He did not react. He gave her no satisfaction.

"Fine." She closed the bedroom door and got on with her errands.

—— : ——

By dinner time Walter still had not budged.

Bags in hand, JJ had pushed open her front door and discovered the living room *smelled* the same as it had when she'd locked up, hours earlier. It was an actual scent of sameness, the olfactory presence of air undisturbed since her last passage through it.

That had struck her as odd, until she remembered Walter. And there he slept on. She didn't try too hard to wake him up this time.

Spitefully, she prepared dinner — for one — and pounded down three goblets of very good Beaujolais while cooking. She left most of the food untouched, but by the time the alcohol was in mid-metabolic burn she felt quite randy and forgiving.

It had become an amusing little game, a divertissement.

Topless, stockings and skirt still on, nipples stroking his shins, she went down on him. He stayed erect until she finished him off. The meter of his breathing did not alter. She got mad, a match head flaring aflame, and spat his own semen onto his bare chest. Then she stomped off to pour another glass of wine, to rinse her mouth, and watch TV, to rinse her mind.

She fell asleep on the sofa, always a refuge of comfort for her. She forgot about Walter until morning.

One of the things that separated them, these days, was talk. Not communication — yammering. It was Walter's habit to begin deluging her the moment she opened her eyes, and Walter did not converse so much as lecture.

Twelve topics, all waiting in ambush for her, JJ, before she even got the sleepy seeds out of her eyes, while the coffeepot was still yards distant.

No, not communication. JJ had learned there was safety in pretend sleep. Perhaps if *she* was the one who faked it, she might observe some truth about Walter otherwise obscured.

JJ woke up with this thought hot in her mind. Her semiconscious occasionally provided tidbits of insight just like this. She made an effort to hold the thought in focus, to transport this intellectual cargo from the fuzzworld of half-sleep to the stuffy comfort of the sofa, in the real, the right now.

No yammering.

JJ had been able to hold her thought because, upon waking, Walter had not been there, unloading as usual.

It was pleasant, this silence.

She sat up on the sofa, her clothing wretched from the night's twists and turns and the humidity of her own body. Alone. On the sofa.

She padded to the bedroom to see if Walter was . . .

JJ had thought that if bogus sleep might provide a fly-on-the-wall insight regarding Walter, then perhaps Walter had figured this out himself and was making her pay, bigtime. Walter forever needed to prove how he could go harder, longer, faster, better. If Walter thought JJ was playing him, he'd play

back, double force, and show her good. If Walter was . . .

. . . yeah. He was.

But he had not twitched a muscle, flicked a finger, blinked or changed position for more than twenty-four hours. No bathroom runs. No food. No prints on his water glass. A quarter-inch of water had evaporated since yesterday.

Yesterday, thought JJ, a knuckle between her teeth. He's still breathing, but he hasn't moved since yesterday.

If he was still breathing. She checked. In. Out. Slow.

She knew she should hurry to the living room, phone an ambulance, help him *out* of whatever he was in. He did not seem to be in any sort of distress, and this stayed her. If she *did* summon paramedics and EMTs, they might revive Walter on the spot, and god, would he be pissed when she told her story.

Her really *lame* story.

JJ caught a breath. She had thought of phoning an ambulance from the living room when there was a telephone less than two feet away, on the night stand, on Walter's side of the bed. If she had called from the living room, there was less risk of waking Walter up.

Less risk. Her mind's ear hated the sound of that.

"Walter . . . ?" She spoke loudly, defiantly. Walter remained still, unstirring.

There. No risk at all.

JJ pulled the bedroom door shut for the rest of the day.

Danielle Dax thundered, singing of ashes and betrayal. The TV was on, sound off. Pots steamed in the kitchen. It was five o'clock and all the activity was JJ's. For her.

If Walter had been up and at 'em, he would have killed the TV to save power — an exhaustible resource, he'd remind her — and asked JJ *can we please turn this down* in a tone engineered to convey several tracks of information, to wit:

Walter does not rock and roll.

Walter only listens to compositionally superior music.

Walter did not sanction this performance.

Walter plays music at a reasonable and consistent volume.

All of which messed together to make JJ seem either frivolous, silly, or insane. The *real* reason Walter disliked music playing when there was more than one person in the room was because it drowned him out, and he resented being upstaged.

JJ had once made a game of timing Walter, to see how fast he'd make for the volume knob on the TV or stereo once she'd powered it up. It was not a game from which she could derive any pleasure or lesson, let alone a win.

She did not have that problem this evening. Her problem was trying to recall what she and Walter had been up to the last time Walter had been upright.

Oh, god. Memory wasn't that bad. The night of the party at Burke's.

After a silent ride home, Walter had chugged a lot of aspirin and seltzer, then bumped around the house with a vaguely pinched look on his face indicating that the fount of his evening's irritation was most likely named *JJ*. She retreated to a hot bath and bedded down first. When he slid in next to her — she was still wide awake, hoping he would nudge her — he was fully pajamaed. He turned his back on her.

JJ knew how it felt to lose an erection.

She also knew that Walter was no monster. Did he deserve the pain she returned him? Wasn't she being just a tot *harsh?*

She surveyed his form, still but for the breathing, steadily in and out. What if he was suffering right now, deep in the hell of some coma? Some interior agony lacking external symptoms? She fiddles, he burns, and who was to know?

She merely felt — irrationally, maybe; so sue — that Walter *judged* everything she did. Disapproval was his life. And now that that onus was gone, or, at least, suspended, she felt a peculiar freedom, a sense of her own life regained.

That night, she began by confession. She gave voice to the inner words. All things bothersome about their relationship, especially his obsession with commitment and obligation. To Walter, life was one big contract to be dragged and flayed from one litigious lawyer's desk to another. Death by nitpicking. JJ found herself saying things that would never have come up, had Walter been half of the exchange. Things like:

"Goddamit, Walter if you want a *guarantee,* buy a *stereo* and sign a limited *warranty!*"

After an hour or so of cleansing talk, with tears, she got physical — shaking, cajoling, scooting him around on their bed. She edged him nearer to the right side so she would have more room when she lay down next to him.

JJ gradually tired of the silent treatment.

It had gone from an amusing little game, yesterday, to absurd, tonight, to violent, five minutes ago. She had become emboldened, rather than afraid.

First she slapped his face, the Imp of the Perverse flooding her with strength and aiming her swing. The first blow to fall was no accident.

Accident, Jesus Christ, wasn't she being forgiving to herself?

She hit him once for each transgression, real, imagined or feared. She balanced the scales of pain given and pain received. But had Walter hurt her this badly, to the point where the only response was the extreme of violence?

JJ was not a violent woman.

She saw she had split his lip and raised dots of blood. The sight of it made her feel like a Nazi torturer, and she wept as she told him over and over that she was sorry. For the first time, she suffered the queasy inkling that he was lost to her forever,

beyond apology or forgiveness. She needed him to understand that she wasn't *like* this, a vengeful and shrieking harpy, flailing and hateful. For the first time in a long while, she suffered the need to tell Walter that she loved him.

She did not need a reciprocal sentiment. The words of love were fragile and transient. She did require, however, evidence that Walter knew she loved him. No words — a nod, an embrace, a quiet *mmmm* from him would have done the deed.

Walter lay in state, exactly as before, but for the dots of blood.

JJ cleaned him. She changed the bed clothing around him gingerly, as though tending a terminal invalid. This was one night where the tears would just not cease.

And if she called outsiders, they'd ask her why she waited so long. *Love* was not an acceptable answer.

"Come back to me," she begged his unmoving form.

His form kept on not moving.

It was as though his spirit and soul had been thieved, leaving the shell. The part of him that loved her was gone, departed. The body that had loved her was still there on the bed, so she tried again.

She successfully coaxed him erect with what she knew of hydraulics. She slid him snugly home with judicious use of almond oil. As she guided him inside her she lied to herself that he was sleeping, that this would be just like doing him sneaky before wake-up call. She worked at it, her pelvis mustering motion enough for both of them. She fell easily into rhythm.

Neither of them orgasmed this time, and JJ fell asleep crying, desperately holding onto the man she loved.

At Burke's party, both of them drank too much. Him, Mudslides; her, Long Island iced teas — heavy on the "long." They both got trapped in one of those edgy conversations about love, marriage and nomenclature.

"POOSSLQ," said a doughboy. He was soft and pudgy, with chipmunk cheeks and a beard of anus bristle. A Buttface. "Person Of Opposite Sex, Same Living Quarters."

"Thank god the Seventies are history," said Walter. His drink was turbid and sludgy. It reminded JJ of an alcohol milkshake.

"How about "Significant Other," said the Blonde with Too Many Degrees. "Of course, that presumes one could be an *insignificant* other."

"Or a not-so-significant only," said JJ.

"Here, here," said Walter, raising a toast. "I prefer *sperm bitch,* myself."

JJ saw he was in one of his moods, teasing, shocking solely for effect. She showed him her middle finger. "And I prefer *sex chimp.* Cheers."

"That's kind of sexist," said the Blonde with Too Many Degrees, unnecessarily. She could be counted on to answer rhetorical questions, too. She was so darned smart that she rarely maintained a liaison for more than a month . . . and breakup was always the guy's fault . . . and the guy was *always* a lunatic.

"Life partner," said JJ. "That does it for me better than cohabitant, or lover, or boyfriend, or beau."

"Sounds like a life sentence," chimed in Buttface, who hadn't been laid for over a decade. Laid for real, with a woman, that is.

JJ never liked the sour expression Walter pulled whenever she said "life partner." She had said it, just now, to test him. It was a party; there was a chance his defenses were lax. Walter failed the test again.

JJ finished her Long Island iced tea. Walter could be such a pisser.

All eyes had turned to Walter. "Our friends understand the arrangement JJ and I share," he said, all grown up.

"And what sort of arrangement might that be?" said the Blonde with Too Many Degrees. She *always* talked like that. Buttface was staring at her tits as though he wanted to frame them. In peanut butter.

"None of your business, dear."

It was Walter's standard trap-them-and-kill-them reply. When JJ had first witnessed this tactic, she admired his combat smarts. Right now, it was just a mean party trick. The Blonde looked to JJ to be the sort of chick who thought tossing a drink in an aggressor's face was some sort of elegant social riposte. Walter had timed her coolly — she was down to a shard of ice in her glass. She steamed and pawed around inside her skull for a comeback. Another future victim of staircase wit. JJ did not pity her.

But sometimes, she acknowledged, Walter could be so infuriating. Sometimes, it was easy to wish he'd drop to sleep and just never wake up.

JJ jolted awake with the image of Buttface's wormy-lipped Clutch Cargo mouth flash-fading in her memory. Close enough to nightmare, that.

Walter's status was quo.

JJ's jaw ached from crying. The corners of her eyes felt violated, torn. Tear streaks petrified both cheeks. A muscle tension headache had nested at the base of her skull and squeezed the back of her head like a killer's hand.

Goddamn Walter.

She threw up, and took some aspirin with milk. She added an allergy tablet, a brand name she knew would knock her out after fifteen minutes on the sofa.

How long would Walter stay this way? Uncontentious. Not attentive, yet ever there for her. She could see him whenever she pleased. She never had to ask where he was going, what he was up to, what time he'd be home. It was more than most of her friends had.

Odds on, Buttface and the Blonde were sleeping alone, these days.

"Walter. I know things haven't been okay between us, that we settled into kind of a rut. And if this is a coma or something, and you can hear me, then you know about the last couple of days . . ."

It had actually been four days. More than half a whole week.

" . . . and I only did it because I still love you, and I'm sorry if I hurt you, or caused this to happen in any way. And if it's just an accident, I'm here for you. I just need to know how to help . . . okay?"

She had planned on making this little speech just in case Walter was cognizant. Then her plan was to call Cecily for a meal and a movie, a good girls' night out, well-earned. Walter, she could deal with later, because she accepted that he would be waiting for her in the bedroom.

JJ completed her speech successfully. Took a deep breath. Job done.

Then she noticed Walter was no longer breathing.

Cecily understood about JJ's rain check. So fortuitous, Cecily had said, since that guy Cleve Madison had called to ask if she was busy even though it was late. Cecily had met Cleve — of all places — at the airport. He'd come on strong and Cecily had been flattered by the scent of musk.

JJ had told Cecily she understood, surrre, no prob. What she had thought was: *Cleve is calling you late because some other sperm bitch canceled on him. He'll listen to you yammer on for as long as it takes to get into your pants. He'll use your toothbrush, drink the last diet beer in your 'fridge, and leave wet towels on your bathroom floor. He'll take up too much of the bed. You'll hate waking up next to him. If he stays the whole night.*

JJ hung up the phone. And what if manly, musky Cleve didn't bother to wake up, like Walter? What if he laid in state until he finally . . .

Finally. Finally what?

JJ's father would have said *departed.* Her mother, *called by the good Lord.* JJ could never say — you know — and so she settled on the word *lost.*

She had just lost Walter.

As if Walter had not shuffled off the coil but caught a cab; not been deprived of life so much as misplaced. Lost.

Dead, thought JJ, is what Walter is as of today.

Walter is dead. Eternal, not-breathing-ever, doornail dead.

She kept lifting the phone, then cradling it. Who should she call now? They'd ask, he stopped moving *when?* He stopped breathing *when?* And you didn't call until *how* late? And once officialdom had humiliated her and picked her to pieces, she wouldn't even have Walter any more, animated or not.

After such a chain of heartbreak, she'd be, at best, alone.

In the bedroom, Walter looked exactly as he had earlier, when JJ had decided she was satisfied with him — no complaints, a sure thing, and the sex wasn't *that* much different . . .

JJ had become conscious of the cadence of her own breathing. Breathing works just fine until your brain meddles.

There was nothing to be done right away. No panic, no strife. She already knew Walter would patiently await her decision, and keep his mouth shut.

She washed him. It was done with invalids, a procedure called dry bathing. Sponge him off, turn him, spread towels, wipe, turn, done.

When she rolled him over she spotted the early dark smudges of dependent lividity marring his shoulder blades, his butt, his heels. She parted his hair. The back of his head was as black as a bad bruise. When she moved him back to his original position she saw that his abdomen now bore a greenish tint and his face was beginning to darken. In the soft bedroom light, it might have been mistaken for a lousy sun-lamp tan.

Walter's hair had been lush, thick, no splits, no male-pattern baldness, and only a thread or two of mild gray. If the myth was to be believed, his hair was still growing.

When she finished, Walter exuded a floral scent. His lips had thickened. She thought this made him look more sensuous; he had always had a mean, small, staple-shaped mouth.

She took a sandwich break. If you work a cleansing change, you must allow it time to stick. When she returned, Walter still smelled pretty, and another miraculous change had occurred.

The meanness was evaporating form his face. The old Walter was fading out. The lines of physiognomy she had associated with his worst traits were gone. His face had smoothed out; he actually looked well-fed. It was the bacteria inside him, expiring, forming gas to bloat him. His face inflated as his fluids sought gravity.

JJ knew this, and would admit it to herself later, but for now she wanted to celebrate the fleeting reality of Walter as she had forever idealized him — all hers, with the contrariness subtracted.

His penis was not dead flaccid, yet not useless either. JJ opened the tiny bottle of almond oil and another romantic scent was layered into the room. She lubed herself, then him, and straddled him, quick to climax because she was now astride the man she really wanted, and she wanted him because what she was doing held the tang of taboo. She whooped when she came, and Walter rose no objection.

As she fell asleep she noticed Walter's fingernails seemed longer. That made sense; Walter was unable to bite them, and he bit his nails whenever anything pestered him, which was, well, all the time.

Before.

For hair and nails to grow, they required nourishment from oxygenated blood. If breathing stops, if the heart no longer beats, nourishment is impossible and cellular life ceases. The reason fingernails appeared to grow on corpses was that the skin pulls back from the nails as moisture leaches from the body, exposing portions previously covered. JJ knew this.

She also knew that if the hamburger in the 'fridge smelled the way Walter now smelled in close-up, she would throw it away, outside, where it could not ferment.

She knew these things, but by the time she thought them through, she was wrapped up in satiated sleep.

A couple of days later, JJ got trapped into a long phone conversation with Cecily, hot for a payoff on her rain check.

Why? Only one reason — Cecily would be dying to talk about men in general, scumbags in specific, and her latest conquest, ole musky Cleve, in particular.

"When he put it *in*, JJ, it's like — I don't know. That *muscle* or something just snapped shut, like it didn't *want* him inside of me."

"Your sphincter."

Cecily paused; the gap felt uncomfortable. "Whatever. But I think I know what it was — it was like, well, all that courtin and chit-chat, all that winesippin and small talk, and he didn't care about *anything* we talked about; all's he cared about was whether he could put his thing in me, or not."

"It's a contest, and once the clothes come off, the contest is won."

"Yeah. Like that. Except . . . he didn't *fool* me into nothin. I wanted him in me, baby, by that time I *needed* him in me. You know how when you get to that point where you just *gotta* get filled up? And then you get to that point where he's gotta go faster, faster-deeper, then *boom?*" There was another pause, this one breathy, as though Cecily was turning herself on via instant replay. She was now being a *bad* girl over the phone. There followed a sound like a sigh. "Well. Anyway. You know, JJ. So — is Walter treating you right?"

"He's a changed man, Cecily. He's there for me."

"I'm glad *somebody out there has got a relationship that works.*"

"So what happened to your guy? Cleve?"

"Oh Well . . . he shot his stuff all over my comforter on account of my muscle thing. He's the kind of guy who'd think it was romantic or something if I licked it up and then frenched him. Eeuww, gross, I can't believe I just said that."

"It's all just protein, Cecily."

"Now *that's* truly gross." She giggled. "JJ? I thought your sphincter was, you know, up your butt."

"It is, dear." JJ called up her mini-lecture on feminine musculature. She felt extremely balanced; a woman with time, and a man to spend it on her. She'd learned the muscle arrangements from one of several books she'd acquired recently, all concerning the makeup of the human body. Yesterday she'd begun burning candles and cinnamon incense, and keeping the bedroom door shut, for privacy's sake, and because of the smell.

It was possible, she thought, to love a man until there was almost nothing left to make love *to*.

Cecily begged off with: "Golly, JJ that's . . . um, interesting." Or words to that effect. To JJ it was tone that mattered, and Cecily's tone said *I didn't know you were so into the icky stuff; gotta go.* Welcome to the real world, Cecily old pal.

Cecily would probably not call back for a week, minimum.

JJ was naked, oiled and scented. It had been a tasty jest, to chide Cecily with sexual anatomics while sliding around atop Walter in the dark. Walter himself was quite dark, so JJ kept the lights off. The candles burned. The incense smoked all vision to a haze. It was like a dream.

Maybe someday poor Cecily would discover a man like Walter.

"Happy anniversary, my love."

JJ sipped champagne in crystal. She dipped a finger into the flute, then eased it between her thighs to start things up again. Bubbly could make her so brazen.

She toasted the week that had passed since Walter had stopped breathing.

Her fingers moved to his lips, pushing the corners up to form a smile, which stayed exactly as she had arranged it. They made love every day, sometimes more than once, at all sorts of hours. Their shared bed had transformed into a domain whereupon JJ's sexuality had finally caught fire and burned hot.

Walter had grown warm again, all on his own. She could feel tiny movements, fervid activity just beneath the tight skin of his belly. His perma-plaqued smile asked nothing of her. It is an unspoken contract that lovers permit each other their humanity — their smells and body functions — so the stench in the bedroom was a minuscule cost.

Ignoring the insects, JJ wrapped herself up in the man of her dreams. And in her dreams, there were no insects, and everything was perfect at last.   Ω

THE POTTED FERN

I watched him pour his drink into that fern,
The fern that's growing in the giant pot.
I'm quite upset, it gave me quite a turn,
He should have asked me first, but he did not.
The fern's some unknown species that I got
Some years ago while it was very small.
In Africa I think, some place quite hot,
And since I've had it, it's grown rather tall.
When it was just a sprout, I built this wall
Wherein I'd drink and play with my pet rabbit.
The rabbit spilled my drink, then bones and all
Were eaten. Now the fern has got the habit.

I will admit this man was eaten quicker,
But I hate plants that cannot hold their liquor.

— John S. Davis

ONE FOR SORROW

by Tanith Lee

With thanks to Louise & Gary Cooper, and John Kaiine

1st FEATHER

Daisy saw the dress the way you see a light come on in a darkened window — sudden, surprising, to be expected.

She had been in the new flat a week, and was dutifully exploring the area, finding the supermarket and the green-grocers, the library and the off-license, then branching out into the back lanes of curio shops and antique dealers. Here she found a rewarding shop which sold china masks, and finally Vanities. Vanities sold clothes, not the kind for normal wear, but what you wanted as a little girl when you were dressing up. Creations of silk and satin, crushed velvet and lace, beads and sequins, buttons, hooks and eyes.

Daisy quickly located a pair of purple shoes that might have been made for her. As she was paying for them, she saw the dress.

It hung in a row of other dresses in incredible colours and shapes, and some careless hand or side had dislodged it, so it had, in a way, stepped out from among the rest. It was black and white, the thinnest silk, and marked just a little, just a little tarnished, by old age.

Daisy left her shoes and went to the dress slowly.

She could see at a glance there was no way on earth she could ever have squeezed into it, for although she was slim, the dress had been fashioned for a figure that was a wand. And it was fragile, too; to force oneself upon or into it would be to rend.

A long tight white underskirt fell to an invisible ankle, and over that a waisted tunic of black, cut in a gracefully jagged way, dropped to a vanished knee. A **V**-neck, with a tiny glimpse of white there too, and three-quarter-length sleeves, with white slashes, somehow described the absent body of the nymph for whom it had been formed. It was a magpie dress. And sure enough, above the right breast of the bodice flew a tiny embroidered magpie.

"It's an absolute curse," the fat woman said from the counter.

"I'm sorry?"

"That dress. The black and white. I'll swear it moves about. Half the time it's on the floor, or else it gets over into the hats."

"It's — beautiful," said Daisy, although she was not sure that beauty was quite the word.

"Like to buy it? I'll tell you now, only an anorexic schoolgirl could squash into that," said the fat woman. I measured the waist — eighteen inches. And an anorexic school-girl couldn't afford it. It's two hundred pounds."

"Neither can I," said Daisy.

Outside she put on the comfortable purple shoes, but after she had walked a hundred yards, they had begun to hurt after all.

Daisy thought the magpie dress was datable about 1912, which made it almost eighty years of age. Then again, it could have been a later copy.

She thought about the dress, actually, a lot; it was like someone she had met.

Who had worn it?

Daisy put aside her commissioned art-work, and made a drawing of the dress, and then a drawing trying to put a woman *into* the dress. But it would not come out in the right way.

As she was going to sleep in the new south-facing position of her bed, she thought: *With that cheque coming, I could probably afford it.* She had been going to have a long weekend at the seaside, and if she made it just two nights, instead of three, she could buy the dress.

But why should she buy the dress?

On the edge of oblivion, she saw a magpie flying round her bedroom. Fascinating birds. She had never minded only seeing one, although it was supposed to be, was it not, unlucky? What did they say? *One for sorrow —*

There was something about the dress, but it was not sorrow.

The next afternoon Daisy went back into Vanities.

"I bought a pair of shoes here yesterday, but they hurt a bit. I don't suppose you could recommend anything?"

"You should have tried them on," said the fat woman.

Daisy gave a mental shrug. She turned and went over to the dresses.

The magpie dress was not there.

"Oh — has someone bought it?"

"Bought what?"

"The black and white dress with the magpie."

"Oh *that*. No. Look, it's got up there."

Daisy looked where the woman pointed, and there the dress was, hanging up on a high rail, with its white tube of skirt depending and the black tunic fluttering a little, like feathers, in some random breeze.

"God knows how it got there," said the woman resentfully. *"I didn't put it there."*

"Does it have a history?" Daisy asked, still looking up. The breeze must be selective, for none of the other dresses were fluttering, but then the magpie dress was very thin.

"I expect so. You'd have had to ask Mrs Taylor, but she's retired."

"I can't then, can I," said Daisy.

"I don't know anything about it. I don't know anything about any of them. That's the only one causes trouble."

"Perhaps it flew up there," said Daisy.

But the woman only frowned.

Most afternoons, Daisy would walk to the shops, to give her body a change of movement from standing up before the drawing-board or crouching over it on the table. The illustrations had hit an unseen rock. She was having trouble with them she had not anticipated. She brooded on them as she shopped. She did not turn down the lane towards Vanities but, on the fourth day, she went into the mask shop for a present for Agatha Soames. And when that was seen to, there was Vanities, and Daisy walked in.

The fat woman was not in evidence. Instead a young fat girl was sorting through a pile of hats with speckled veils.

The magpie dress lay crumpled on the floor.

Daisy had an urge to run to it and pick it up, to comfort it, poor helpless thing.

"You'll never get into that," said Young Fatty, with vicious pleasure.

"No, I'm sure I shouldn't."

"They was smaller then," said Young Fatty, with slight fear.

Two cheques came in next morning's post, one for some drawings Daisy had done for a magazine which had folded. They had honourably and amazingly paid her for her work, although unable to publish.

Daisy examined the cheque, cautiously. It was for three hundred pounds.

"What would I do with it?" she asked the flat, to which she talked off and on, getting it used to her. "Hang it on the wall . . . like a carpet? It's stupid. I don't collect old dresses."

At two thirty she went out and walked to Vanities where, with her BarclayCard, she bought the magpie dress.

"I tell you what," said Old Fatty, "I think you've got a bargain. I think they underpriced this. Present, is it?"

"Yes," said Daisy, "for my anorexic niece."

The dress hung from a picture nail in the wall of the bedroom. It seemed composed and calmed. Being black and white it went with everything and nothing. Daisy kept coming in from her work, to touch it, look at it.

One for sorrow, two for joy . . .

What made for joy, though? What made you happy? Well, to be able to work at what you were good at, and to get paid for it; to have a few good friends. Maybe, one day, to meet a man she could have more than just a fleeting relationship with, but then he would have to understand her, how she worked . . . And any way, she did not mean herself, not Daisy. "What made you joyful, Magpie Dress?"

And what brought you sorrow?

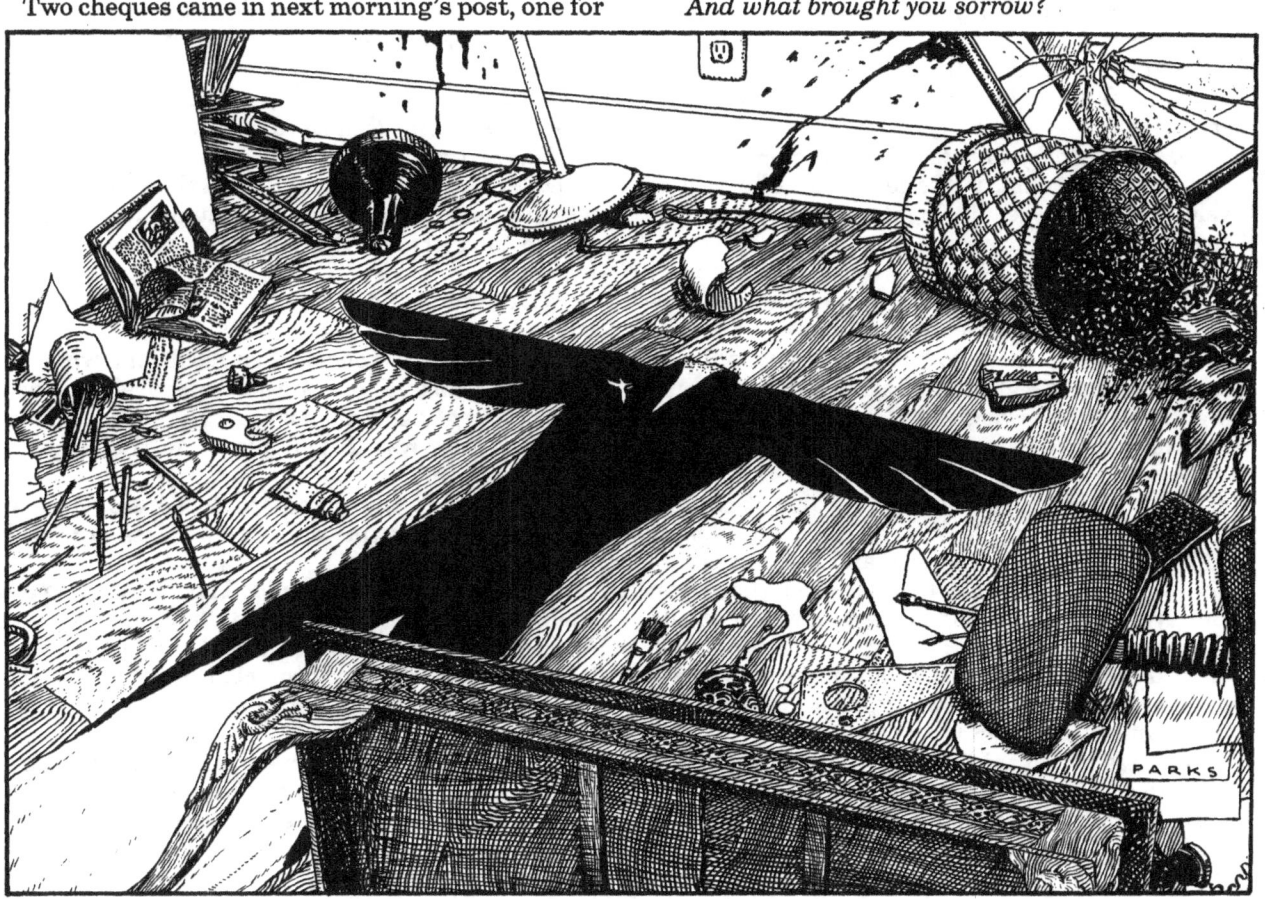

2nd FEATHER

Daisy was at a party, and she was sure she should not have come. Perhaps she had not been invited. Everyone wore wonderful clothes, even the men, for their evening wear was dated and ornate, starched shirt-fronts, tiny embroideries . . . And the woman were like flowers from a show, hot-house lilacs and roses of fire.

Before she could look down nervously to see what she had put on herself for this auspicious fancy-dress occasion, Daisy's eyes were attracted by a flicker of something up in the air. A magpie was flying round the room, round the quaint gas-fitments with their golden glow. But no. It was not a magpie. It was a woman on a wide stair.

She stood there with her hand on the gilded banister, looking down. To Daisy, the artist, she was the most beautiful thing, apart from an animal, that Daisy had ever seen. Her face was exquisite, and just touched by rays of colour and the gold of the lamps. And her hair was like white gold, the utterly pure shade of nature, and coiled back from the perfect tangle of her face into a gleaming shell on her long neck. And from her hair rose a black and white feather and on her slender perfect body was the black and white dress.

I'll have to tell her I've got it, Daisy thought. But of course, the woman was wearing the dress. How odd.

The woman was descending the stair now, without hurry. Some of the guests had looked up, and seen her.

She greeted them coldly, indifferently, and their faces were false. A few good friends — no friends were here.

I care for nobody, no not I, if no one cares for me.

Surely they would, if she let them. She was so lovely — but then, beauty frightened a lot of people, a threat to a man, a slap to a woman.

Daisy could not hear what any of them were saying and she realized she was dreaming, and now she wanted to wake up before the Magpie — for she *was* the Magpie — came to her. Because what could Daisy do, confronted by this dream creature? Would she have to explain herself? How could she, when there was no sound-track?

The woman moved nearer, through the crowd. Her eyes were dark. Her beauty was almost painful. She had the strangest look — as if she anticipated nothing, ever. As if she were old and dry and blind.

No wonder they hated her. To meet those gorgeous eyes and see nothing in them, nothing at all.

Daisy woke.

In the half-lit dark of the city night, she saw a little, enough to register the dress had fallen off its nail, leaving the hanger on the wall.

The dress lay on the bed, with its magpie sleeves wing-spread as if to fly.

"No, I don't want you to do this," said Daisy. "Get off." And wildly she kicked with her feet through the duvet, and the dress slid away on to the floor.

"Sorry," said Daisy, "but the carpet's quite soft. Don't spook me. We have to be nice if we're going to live together."

The following morning, one of Daisy's posters leapt off the living room wall with a flapping electric noise, making her jump, so she splashed paint where she had not meant it to go.

She thought nothing much of this, however, for she was no handy-woman, and even hanging up posters was some-times outside her range of skills.

Then she found the bathroom light was on. And later, the fire in the living room had switched on too, making the room very hot.

"Great," said Daisy.

She went and looked at the dress, and it lay there on its hanger, silent, still.

"I'm doing it," said Daisy. "Dotty Daisy."

Something went crash in the kitchen. She ran to see, and found a saucepan had come off the stacked washing-up and landed on the work surface across the room.

"Don't panic," said Daisy. She moved back into the bedroom and took hold of the tunic of the dress firmly. "Listen, lady, if this goes on you go *out*. Maybe you're used to that, if you are what I dreamed you were. But I won't play games. I mean it."

The rest of the afternoon passed peacefully. No lights or fires, nothing falling.

Daisy finished work for the day. She had not been shopping, working through, with salad in the fridge for supper. She opened a bottle of white wine, and went cautiously to look at the dress.

"You've been good. Don't think I don't appreciate it."

If I'd met her, she'd have hated me like she did everyone else. But then she didn't hate them, she just — didn't care.

Daisy sat on the floor before the open balcony window, looking out over geraniums and avocados to the long street, the big trees and on and off traffic.

What would it be like — not to have no one to love, but to love no one? *No one. Nothing.*

The wine had gone to her head and when she heard the smash, Daisy only got up gravely and went to look. In the bedroom a china cat her dead mother had given her was in four pieces on the carpet up against the wall.

"You bitch," Daisy said to the dress. And she threw the last of the wine in her glass across the front of it.

It swallowed the pale fluid. The mark was barely visible. How many times had they struck at the Magpie? Not physically, for it had seemed she was a lady, a society woman, protected, and yet certainly the blows had come in some schematic form, for she would incite them.

"I loved my mother. Fine, you didn't love yours."

Daisy pulled the Magpie off its hook, rolled it up — it was so slender it went to the thinnest, most flimsy coil — and put it into the built-in wardrobe under a box of shoes.

She slept with the light on. But nothing moved. There were no dreams.

"Oh this is just wonderful," Agatha cried. And she bore the white beaked mask before her like an offering. "What's in the other bag?"

"Chocolates."

"Evil, wicked weasel."

"And she's brought wine," said Tony.

"Also this." Daisy handed Tony the fourth bag. "I'm sorry, but I know you're brilliant at fixing things."

"It's Lettuce," he said. "Oh, poor old Lettuce. Did you drop her?"

"No. I've got a poltergeist and it threw her at the wall."

As they sat in the large room full of books and plants and statues of Egyptian gods, Daisy told them of the Magpie, and its deeds.

"It couldn't just be a coincidence?" asked Agatha. "The flat settling, or something."

"What, and turning on the fire?" said Tony. "No, she's got a nasty there all right. I think, love, you'll have to take the damn dress back to the shop."

"But how can she?" cried Agatha. "She's dreamed about the woman who wore it."

"Does that mean she owes her something?"

"She was so beautiful," said Daisy, "and so — awful."

"You've heard the expression," said Tony, "bored to death? It can happen. Sounds as if it did, to her." He drank some more wine, and then said, "I don't know if I ought to tell you. But you're getting there anyway."

"Tell me what?"

"You've never heard of the Magpie Fashion?"

"No," said Daisy. The hair rose sharply on her scalp and made her shiver. "Tell me now."

"About 1910, 1911. There was a vogue for black-and-white dresses for women, sometimes with feathers or feather effects. And little black hats with a feather sticking straight up. And magpie brooches. It was actually to do with the start of the cinema — everything in black and white."

"Why not pandas then," demanded Agatha, "or cats?"

"Magpies can fly. It was the element of flying in black and white."

Daisy mused. "I see. In the dream, she was the only one wearing a dress like that."

"Fashions come and go," said Agatha.

"That fashion didn't just go," said Tony. He looked uneasy and refilled their glasses and his own.

"Well?" said Agatha.

"Well," Tony said, "that particular fashion was *advised* to a stop."

"Advised — what do you mean?"

"The police advised that women, especially young, blonde women, should give it up."

There was a silence.

Daisy felt strangeness. She asked, "Why?"

"You've heard of Jack the Ripper," said Tony. "Have you heard of the Magpie Hunter?"

"Oh, you're making this up," said Agatha, with some pride.

Tony shook his head. "No. In the summer of 1912, there was a guy who used to go around a certain area of London, slashing to bits blonde women in magpie dresses."

"I feel weird," said Daisy.

"*Tony!*"

"No," said Daisy, "tell me some more."

"Not a lot to tell. He did it. Murdered about eight girls. Unlike the Ripper's, his victims were from all walks of life. Shop-assistants, house-maids, a couple of so-called ladies straying out on their own. And then the murders stopped. I can't remember if they caught him. I think — no, I just can't recall."

"But you do think she — I mean, the Magpie — ?" Daisy took a gulp of wine.

"She was blonde all right. And you said — *bored* to death."

They sat in silence again, looking at nothing.

Then Agatha got up.

"I'm going to inappropriately baste the chicken."

When she had left the room, Tony said, "Sorry. I didn't mean to make it worse."

"You haven't. But what do I do?"

"Take the dress back."

"Will that be enough? Maybe they won't accept it."

"Just dump it in between a couple of others when they're not looking."

"But what does it mean?"

"I don't know," said Tony. "But there is one thing."

"Yes?"

"She can't have been wearing it — I mean, not that particular dress. Not if he did get her. He used a knife, you see, and — sorry — just slashed. They, and their dresses, were in ribbons."

Daisy felt inured now. She sat demurely and said, "How odd."

Agatha returned with another bottle.

It had obviously been a relief to go out. Coming back at two in the morning, pleasantly tiddly and nicely tired, Daisy knew a slight sensation of fear.

The driver of the hired car watched her to her door, then drove off; and Daisy let herself into the sleeping house.

When she opened the door of her home, and switched on the light, she had only the violent first impression that she had entered the wrong flat. Then she know that she had not.

The worst thing had happened. Burglars had got in. The foulest type of burglar. They had thrown her ornaments and plants about the room — even thrown over her drawing-board and squirted coloured paint up the wall.

And then she realized it was not burglars.

For, no longer rolled up in the wardrobe, but on the carpet, neatly spread out with its wings unfolded, lay the Magpie Dress, the one quiet seemly object in the ruined space.

Daisy ran to the bathroom and lost Agatha's excellent dinner.

3rd FEATHER

When she was a child, Daisy could remember, it had usually been very quiet in libraries, but now there were constant comings and goings, soft and not so soft conversations, the buzz of electronic gadgets. Nevertheless she sat there doggedly at the long table, from ten in the morning until four thirty, and read the book they had found for her. She went out once and bought a sandwich, and ate it on the bench on the forecourt. All the time, the dress stayed coiled in her bag.

She had not slept the night before and her eyes were gritty. But even so, she read all the book. *The Magpie Killings* it was called.

At five in the morning, when she had finished as much of the cleaning up as she could manage, Daisy had spoken to the dress.

"I'm going to presume you want something. It isn't just spite. I'm giving you that chance."

The dress had lain quiescent where she had thrown it. It had not moved and it caused no further damage. It let her roll it up again and push it down in the bag, and take it out to the library.

At first they had said they had nothing on the subject Daisy wanted. And then someone had discovered the old book in their reserve stock. "I'm afraid all the plates are missing. Dreadful vandalism."

She was too stunned to care about the plates. She just wanted to know some facts.

Basically, the book was a list of the murderer's eight victims. There was a chapter on each one, how and why she had been in the notorious Faithways area, which the author, with inappropriate wit, had quickly re-christened the Black Whitechapel of the Magpie Ripper.

Of the murderer himself there was no proper information. He had been variously sighted and randomly described, sometimes as tall, dark, and gliding; and sometimes as stocky, squat, and creeping. He was alternatively a shadow, a ghost, a preying tiger, a lurching toad. Those who claimed to have caught glimpses never concurred. And so perhaps none of them had ever spotted the true murderer. What had become of him too was as much a mystery as his identity. As with Saucy Jack, the slayings had abruptly come to an end. The reason for his massacre was equally or more obscure. The author did not put forward any theories. Indeed, he smugly asserted that he had resisted them in the face of lack of evidence.

His concern was with the victims.

Daisy read the chapters with a slight sickness and a dim apprehension. The eight lives were very different, only similarly tragic because of their inevitable plunge on to the Magpie Hunter's knife — for, in each case, it really did seem as if they had been drawn to him, had almost sought him out. But was this one the owner of the Magpie Dress — or this one? It was impossible, horribly and frustratingly impossible, to tell.

And of course the plates could have — might have answered the question at once. For evidently,

judging by the table at the beginning of the book, there was a picture, although now and then, only a sketch, of each of the dead women. Plus certain other drawings and photographs, labelled:
THE FATAL ALLEY; A WEDDING AT ALL SAINTS CHURCH, FAITHWAYS; TWILIGHT IN FAITHWAYS;
and so on. The missing frontispiece bore the note:
A GLAMOROUS EXAMPLE OF A FASHION
WHICH KILLED.

At four thirty, when Daisy had completed the book and her pocket mirror told her her eyes were inflamed, she felt dissatisfied and uncomfortably anxious. She seemed to have learnt nothing, or nothing that might reflect on the enigma of the violent and evil dress. And conversely, Daisy had been swimming in blood, the blood of eight blonde girls, slashed from throat to groin, silk and muslin, cotton and voile, skin and arteries; bone.

"Excuse me." A plump and pretty and blonde young woman stood, almost perversely, at Daisy's side.

"Oh, are you closing? Sorry."

"No, not for another two hours, worse luck. But look. The van came over, and I was able to get hold of another copy of your book. This one's got *all* the plates."

Daisy felt a wave of nausea. The last thing she wanted now was to see — to *see* the whole forms of those women hacked to ribbons in the alleys and squares, in the very church porch, of charmingly named Faithways.

But the assistant had been diligent and kind, and it would be rotten and rude not to respond.

"Oh, thank you. That was good of you. I'll — just take that one then."

And so Daisy checked out and put the second copy of *The Magpie Killings* into her bag with the Magpie Dress, and went back to her flat.

The acrylic mark would not leave the wall unless she repainted. The red splotch on the curtain was never going to go either. Like a splash, of course, of blood.

Daisy tried to drink a glass of wine, could not; a cup of tea, could not; looked at her provisions of smoked fish and new potatoes with sadness. They were not going to be eaten.

Eventually she sat down, next to her bag, and withdrew the book.

Meticulously she turned to the first picture, the frontispiece. It was a dense black and white photograph; and it drained the vitality from her heart, which began to beat in slow loud strokes.

For the frontispiece — A GLAMOROUS EXAMPLE OF A FASHION WHICH KILLED — showed a slender, exquisitely beautiful girl on a stairway. Her hair was coiled shell-like on her neck and a feather rose from it. She wore the Magpie Dress Daisy had bought from Vanities. And she was the girl from Daisy's dream.

"All right," Daisy said aloud. "All right. I do believe it. Just — give me a minute."

Then she read the rest of the caption, under the photograph:

Margaret Shawn, a society hostess of the era, and said to be one of the most beautiful women of her day, dressed in an elegant version of the so-called Magpie Fashion, even to a feather in her hair. Margaret Shawn, although she defied police advice against such garments, was not one of the murderer's victims.

Daisy spread the dress out on her bed. She addressed it.

"Let's try. I'll trust you. But no tricks, Margaret Shawn. Or I'll burn you. And if that lets your demon out, then I'll find a priest. I'll stop you. Understand?"

Daisy rolled the Magpie up and put it under her pillow.

Then she drank some very hot tea with a little gin in it and swallowed two herbal sleeping tablets.

Would they work, against this sort of stress?

Let's hope so, Margaret Shawn.

Or Margaret Shawn might prove unhelpful. Margaret Shawn might pick up the bed and throw it through the window, and Daisy with it.

But no. That was not the way for Margaret Shawn to get what she wanted, whatever the Hell that was.

Margaret . . . it meant the same as Daisy, did it not . . . Pearl.

The room floated, and Daisy felt the dress stir under her neck, like a snake. But it was too late now —

—— : ——

She was wearing pale green tonight, *eau de nil*: Nile Water.

The man across the table from her, across the candles and the pyramid of fruit, the crystal and the wine, looked at her, could not take his eyes off her.

"Maggie, can we . . . It's been a long time."

"If you like."

"No, no, I'm sorry. I shouldn't have said anything."

He had been asking permission to make love to her, that was clear, and she had not refused, yet she had put him off. How could you make love to that beauty, any way, with those agates of eyes watching.

Then servants, came in, the ubiquitous dummy creatures of the big houses, always there, eyes and cars, and suddenly Margaret Shawn had got up.

The male port had arrived. Was that it?

Whatever it was, she was making some gracious, uncaring, flinty excuse, and leaving the room.

Up a stair, gas-lamps, a tapestry hanging, and smart pictures of long, long people with long, long dogs. Now a bedroom. Hers.

Margaret Shawn was sitting before her mirror in a lacy flounced gown, and one of the maids was brushing over and over that undone stream of lemon-gold hair.

"Tell me about it," said Margaret Shawn.

"Oh Madam — I can't. The Master said —"

"Never mind what the Master said. He knows I see the newspapers. He knows everyone is talking of it. I want to hear."

"But Madam. It's horrible."

"Yes it is. Horrible and fascinating."

"They say he does it because of the black and white dresses."

"I know. Lady Pane told me. But someone saw him, didn't they?"

"Oh, Madam."

"I shall be angry," said Margaret Shawn.

The maid flinched. And Daisy knew, as she had known about the refusal to have sex, that Margaret Shawn did not punish physically, but through the psyche.

"It was — it was Liza, Madam. Liza Meadows."

"You know her?"

"Yes, Madam. Sometimes on my afternoon she and I — well, she thinks she saw him. I mean, the murderer."

"Tell me," said Margaret Shawn. "No. Stop brushing my hair. That's enough."

And she got up, and walked to the long window, and there she stood looking down on to some interruptions of great trees, and beyond a square that had a garden.

The maid spoke. She said her friend, Liza Meadows, had had to go over to Faithways, to see her aunt. Unlike Red Riding Hood, Liza had not strayed from the path, but even so, in the onset of darkness, she had beheld before her a tallish figure swathed in the coming of night.

"He was dressed like a gentleman," said Margaret's maid, "only he hadn't a hat on his head."

This was strange to Liza, and made her check. And then she realized that she had put on her only good dress and jacket, which gave the effect, in twilight, of black and white. But she thought to herself, *Why should it be me?* And she went on gamely.

There was a street lamp which had been lit, and under it, he was.

"She said he was like a prince, Madam. I mean, from a fairy tale."

Liza, and Margaret's maid, did not have the words for it, yet it grew like a flower, out of the compost of dull sentences.

He was beautiful. So beautiful that when he looked at you — you were trapped. His hair was blonde, too, like the hair of the victims. His eyes a pale sere blue that gleamed. He seemed to hold Liza by a rope of fire, and she was drawn towards him now helplessly. And then she was under the lamp also, and he must have seen — her clothes were chocolate and pale green. Not black and white at all. And suddenly, as if the light itself went out, he turned his flame from her. And he was gone.

"Liza felt faint, Madam. She had to lean on a wall."

"Has she been to the police?"

"Oh, no, Madam. She had no business being there. Her Missus had warned her to keep away."

Margaret Shawn stood looking out on the busy square. A few autos came and went, like handsome insects. People walked. There too the gas-lamps had been lighted.

"It's all right, you can go," said Margaret Shawn, and her maid slunk out.

Margaret Shawn held the velvet drapes in both her hands as if she clutched at something, drowning. Yet her face was calm. Only her lips slightly parted. And her eyes rapt, wide.

Her husband looked at her like that, when he asked her to sleep with him.

But she wanted the murderer. She wanted the murderer of women. She wanted death. *That* death. The phallic knife the orgasmic scream —

It was in every line of her immaculate, frigid body. Blonde Virgo. For whom the magpie is a special bird . . .

And she asked the maid for news, the way the school-girl asks for stories, anecdotes, about the boy she has a crush on.

Out there, out there he is.

And Margaret Shawn let her curtains fall and turned to stare at her bedroom. She wanted nothing, disliked everything. Lusting for one thing only. Hair and eyes, the shadow, the hand and the knife.

I want to wake up.

Daisy shifted and half felt her flat about her and then she was down again, in the dark, with beautiful Margaret.

It was another place. A long street which Daisy knew at once, from the plates in the book that she had forced herself to see. Linden Avenue. Tall houses in the dark, and between, the greenish cat's eye glow of gas lights. And the turning — the alley. The Fatal Alley.

And Margaret Shawn walked into it.

She wore her black and white dress. No feather in her hair, just the pristine coiling. And she moved like a swan, the swan in the evening — over the lake.

Her face was avid, like the face of a madonna which works miracles if you go to it with pain and blood and tears.

Margaret Shawn walked through the alley, and back again.

It was a summer night. And nothing stirred.

How often had she come? Did she arrive by cab, perhaps, making the excuse to her ineffectual husband that she visited some non-existent friend, for friends she did not have. Only one potential friend — Him.

Margaret Shawn walked exquisitely along the alley again, and so across the avenue, and the square, where a great church brooded. Were there no police? She must have eluded them, or else the watch had flagged and she had taken advantage of that.

Death and the Maiden. She had gone out to find him. But he did not come to her. Coitus interruptus. Yes, her face was like that now, the lips a little slack, disappointed, a thin line between the brows.

How terrible. She had dressed for him, bathed and scented herself. And he had stood her up.

A blot appeared on the pavement. The lamps sizzled. Rain had fallen. Overhead, a rumble of thunder. Daisy heard as she had heard the conversation in the bedroom.

How often had she come here, Margaret Shawn, searching in vain, refused by death. In heat and in rain, fire and water. Jilted.

———:———

4th FEATHER

The phone was ringing.
Daisy woke. It was ten o'clock.
"Yes?"
She felt hung-over, which did not come from a single gin in tea and two herbal tablets. But she had been dreaming. What —?
"It's me."
Tony.
"Tony?"
"Are you okay? You sound odd."
"Overslept."
"Damn. Sorry to wake you. Only —"
"Yes?"
"I wondered if everything was all right? I mean, the dress."
"No. And yes. I suppose so. I suppose it has something to say. Can I call you back in five minutes?"
"No," he said, "call you in ten."
Daisy stumbled to the bathroom, relieved herself, cleaned her teeth and splashed water on her face. She came out and put on the kettle for Assam tea.
While it was brewing, Tony rang back.
"Sorry about that," said Daisy. I have a contact with Margaret Shawn."
"My God," he said, "she's in the book. Was it hers?"
"The dress — definitely."
"The thing is," Tony said, "I got intrigued. You know Martin over at Streatham? Well, I phoned him up and he had a book in the shop —"
"Not *The Magpie Killings*," said Daisy. "I've read it."
"No, this is older. Very small. About eighty pages. But you see, I sent it off to you. And now Agatha says I shouldn't have. Are you going to be okay?"
"Oh yes," said Daisy firmly, pouring and sipping the Assam, clenching her toes. Under the pillow she could see the edge of black and white. "I'm going to be fine."
"It'll probably arrive in your second post."
"Thanks, it was kind of you."
"Maybe you shouldn't read it."
"I think I'll have to."
"Look, if you need us —" he said.
"I know where you are."

The book came with the second post. It was a slender volume, black cover, white lettering. Its title was: *Sorrow*. Nothing more. Inside, on the title page, small lettering added: *Some speculations on the Magpie Murders*.
And under that was printed part of the old rhyme, not quite as Daisy had remembered. *One's sorrow, two's mirth.*
Daisy made toast she did not want and ate portions of it — not the crusts, *My hair won't curl* — and drank more tea. Then she sat down, in her nightshirt, to read *Sorrow*.
It was a strange book. Somehow intensely per-

sonal, as if the writer, whose name she kept forgetting, and which did not really matter, had become obsessed with the events at Faithways, and driven his obsession on into the realms of dream, and so the quasi-supernatural. In parts it touched poetry, and in others the prose was blunt and mundane. It mentioned the victims, not as individuals, like the other book, but as a sort of entity. Only to Margaret Shawn did it devote an individual section:
For Margaret Shawn, society hostess and celebrated beauty, was in fact also one of the Hunter's victims.
Testimony was quoted from Margaret's maid, Alice Dimpson, from her diary, and illiterate letters she had penned to friends. How 'Madam' had become fascinated by the murderer, and spoke of him constantly in private, such as when Dimpson was dressing her or doing her hair. 'It was as thow she had a lova,' wrote Dimpson, 'a fance man.' Dimpson indeed found her mistress's interest prurient, without knowing quite how or why. Then, when her mistress began to be absent from the house, saying she had gone to dine alone with Lady Pane-Rosythe, Dimpson realized that Margaret Shawn went to walk the alleys and streets of Faithways, in her black and white dress. 'Masta puts up wiv it,' wrote Dimpson, pragmatically. She believed he thought his wife was seeing another man. Dimpson herself was terrified by now. She reckoned Margaret would be 'sliesed up.' She did not dare to speak.
Faithways, said the author, whose name Daisy kept mislaying, was a corruption of the old Featherways, or Fetherwies. Featherways Lane had run on down to the river, and once there had been both a nunnery and a house of monks situated along its length. These religious buildings had been founded after the visitation of the Black Death.
The summer was erratic, and one night when Margaret Shawn was out walking, a massive storm took place, with torrential rain. Margaret returned about midnight, soaked through.
From this outing, apparently, she contracted a chest cold which swiftly turned to pneumonia.
Alice Dimpson believed Margaret Shawn had gone out courting the Magpie Murderer; instead she met Death in another form. A week later she succumbed.
"Not this way," the author of the book reported Margaret Shawn's dying words to be. "A straw death."
That was what the Vikings had feared, the book said, the 'straw' death — death in bed, as opposed to violent death in battle which would carry the warrior to Valhalla.
But Margaret Shawn had died through the Magpie Hunter as surely as if he had slashed her in bits; she too was his victim, the ninth. His choicest and most lovely, although he had never met her.

It was three in the afternoon. Daisy went and made coffee instead of tea. She returned to the book with a rabid reluctance.

The dress had not moved. Nothing had. A weird stillness enclosed the flat, into which the noise of traffic came from far away, as if through water.

Faithways, Fetherwies, was a haunted area. Halfway along it, in the fifteenth century, said the book's author, had been a statue of the Virgin. One night a priest from the monastery was found cut to pieces nearby, among the trees at the Lane's edge. He had been used to hear the confessions of the nuns.

Magpies, said the author, like nuns and monks, in black and white. Magpies, sacred to the Virgin, who had conquered the demon realm of darkness and the moon.

"No," said Daisy, "that's enough."

She shut the book on the last chapter, which was called 'The Murderer Vanishes.'

She went and had a bath. She felt exhausted. She ate cheese on toast and an apple.

The stillness had persisted. It was twilight now. The day had gone. Why had this book, so much smaller than the other, taken so long to read?

She was confused, too. Images of girls from 1912 in black and white and mediaeval nuns in black habits . . .

Finally she read the concluding chapter, propped up like an invalid in bed. The words blurred, came and went.

He did not keep his appointment with Margaret Shawn because he had had to escape.

Apparently the police had sussed the murderer, and he, getting word of it, fled. He ran from London, out into the rolling orchards and fields of rural Kent.

And so he came to a once notorious inn, which happened to be named The Magpie.

This must be pure invention, Daisy thought.

Yes, certainly, because —

At the inn, he was recognized. And in the night, the village people stormed his room and took him out. They took him to an old gallows across the square, and there they hanged him by the neck until dead.

And this was hushed up, remaining only as a rumour and boast.

The Magpie Inn had always, it seemed, vaunted a window which overlooked the gallows. The rich and curious had once paid to take it and watch the hangings of highwaymen. That night the room was empty. They were all down in the square.

They buried his body in an unmarked grave. There was no proof.

But, put down in black and white —

The phone rang.

"Sod it. I woke you again,"

"Hello Tony. I got the book. It's very peculiar."

"Martin says the writer was a known laudanum addict, who wrote under the influence. Most of it's — make-believe."

"What about the inn?" said Daisy.

"Oh that exists, I checked a Kent guide. A place called Asham."

"Sounds Indian." Daisy closed her eyes. Christ knew what she would dream now.

"Look, I'll call you again in the morning. Agatha's been giving me hell."

"It's all right," said Daisy. "Where's Asham?"

"You can get there from Charing Cross. Off the Dartford Loop somewhere. Should have told you."

"Isn't laudanum too late for 1912 . . . whenever."

"You mean the book? 1913. Apparently not. I'll call you at eleven."

Daisy said, "Got to go to sleep now. Night. Love to Agatha."

She depressed the cradle, and then left the phone off the hook.

Daisy touched the edge of the dress under the banked-up pillows.

"Be gentle. Don't kill me. Or I can't."

She did not recall putting out the light.

5th FEATHER

In the walled garden, the nun was standing with her arm up-raised.

The walls were high, but clad by roses. Roses like fat pink cabbages with red hearts. There was a small pool, and fish glinted there. Beyond, other higher walls. Grey, yet touched by sunlight.

In the sun, the nun's skin was young, and white as crystal. Despite the black garments and the pallid wimple, she was beautiful. And in her pale lifted fingers was a gob of raw and bloody meat.

Someone came through an arched doorway. Another nun. This one incredibly wrinkled, brown and warty. She turned to the beauty and tugged at her shoulder.

And the beauty turned her arrogant white perfect face.

Then they spoke.

Daisy could not understand a word. Well, maybe one word in twenty.

It's like Chaucer.

Just vision then, reading of faces, not lips. The young one was proud and disdainful, and the ugly one harassed and bustling; jealous.

Then there was the flap of wings and the beautiful one turned all her attention up into the air, as if at the approach of an angel. And Daisy knew she was saying, *Look! You see.*

The magpie dropped down. It was heavy and solid, black nun-mantle over white, and the wicked beak of a crow, and glowing sideways eyes. It landed on the white arm, where, Daisy now saw, there were already scorings from a hundred such landings.

It took the meat ferociously yet daintily from the girl's grip, and ate, standing there on her slender arm.

The old jealous one had drawn back muttering. She had even made a sort of sign that must be some version of the Cross.

With mouth sewn tight, she waited.

The beautiful one drew something up from under

her habit; it was a precious stone, greenish, maybe a beryl. She jinked it under the magpie's beak. She was saying, teasingly, 'Do you want it? Bright, pretty —' And the magpie seized the jewel and, green drop and shreds of bloody flesh dripping from the dagger of its beak, it flapped away. And the girl called after it, some name which meant a faithless lover.

The old one muttered. She told the girl — Daisy understood as if sub-titles were being printed in her brain — that the young one's brother was coming. And the young one said she did not care to see him. And then she told the old one to go away.

The daughters of the rich had sometimes been allowed to queen it in the nunneries. They must dress as nuns, but otherwise what they did was very much their own province.

And Beauty was of this order. Even to her jewels.

Now her dark eyes rested on the sky, where the magpie had gone. And she smiled.

She was not innocent.

Daisy saw the magpie, like a dot in heaven, wink out.

"No, it's getting muddled." Daisy lay in bed, talking to herself or the dress. "We had 1912. But what's this now?"

The book, *Sorrow,* lay on the floor.

What had the laudanum addict said? Margaret Shawn's broken 'appointment' with the killer?

Did Margaret Shawn look like the beautiful, dark-eyed nun?

"All right," said Daisy. "All right."

I'm not being rational.

She washed her hair and dressed, and when Tony phoned her at eleven o'clock, she was already sorting things out for her journey.

"I've got to go to Birmingham. It's a real nuisance. But they insist on seeing me, and they're paying expenses."

Tony sounded relieved.

"Well, it will give you a break . . ."

"Oh that. I think it's fading out."

When Tony rang off, she phoned British Rail. And then she packed a small bag and put the rolled-up Magpie Dress in at the top. And stuffed *Sorrow* down one side.

"Sorry about this," she said to the flat. "Take care."

She felt wild and light, perhaps the way the successful anorexic feels before the pain begins.

The train would take forty-five minutes. The long carriage was empty but for an elderly woman three or four seats further down. The windows were so thick with dirt the landscape outside was distanced, and though notices prohibited smoking, the space reeked of smoke. But perhaps it was only the pollution of the city.

London drew back. Old defamed tower blocks lined the horizon.

Daisy shut her eyes.

I'm not asleep.

Yes, but I was awake in the other dreams too. A fly on the wall.

It was a kind of walkway, with arches, and the beautiful nun was there, standing quite still. She was looking down.

In the stone yard below, a fat woman, also a nun, and with a golden crucifix on her ample bosom, was walking about with a priest.

He was tonsured, and Daisy felt a distaste for this. She sensed that Beauty did too. For the rest of his hair was thick and blond, shining in the summer light.

The important fat nun and the priest were speaking rapidly, and now and then a phrase of strongly accented Latin drifted up.

This time, Daisy did not take in any of the words, rather she seemed privy to the unspoken phrases of the beautiful nun's body. In her white throat the pulse, beating. And her slender hands grasping the stone of the arch.

Then she called. It was very respectful, addressed to the Mother Superior or whatever she was, but both of them looked up, the fat woman and the blond man.

The beautiful nun bobbed a sort of curtsy. She was trembling all over with suppressed laughter, and with something else.

The fat woman was disapproving yet restrained. Obviously, the beautiful nun came of a powerful family, which had granted a large beneficence to this house.

And the priest . . . He looked only arrogant, proud in the flawlessness of his vocation. If he saw Beauty, he did not show it. He might have been glancing at the stone.

He seemed about thirty-eight years of age, and so probably was in his late twenties, for Daisy imagined that Mediaeval maturity was evidenced early. In the same way Beauty, who looked twenty-five, was more likely about sixteen.

The priest was painfully handsome. Frighteningly so. And as he turned from the nun on the walk without acknowledgement, Daisy knew the heat of fire, the deep knocking of the excited heart, and the tingling awareness of its own loveliness which suffused the young girl's body.

"Have to get out here," said the station worker, sneering in at Daisy. "Unless you want to go back to Charing Cross."

Daisy got off the train, tumbled off, between two worlds.

She stood on the platform. Everything was grey. She had expected open fields and green hills, flowers and trees, but Asham was not like that.

She wanted him.

Oh yes, Beauty had wanted the priest all right. Daisy could recall those wonderful, awful feelings too well. They stopped you eating and sleeping, and working. But what happened if you were a nun sworn to chastity and he was at the cold-heat of religious devotion, given to his God, with no room for anything else?

Daisy walked out of the station.

It was a kind of village, but one which had sprawled and overbuilt and become a town. The rolling orchards of 1912 were only now the concrete suburbs of the nineties.

Wake up.

Daisy shook herself, actually and physically.

Above in the station foyer she bought herself a diet coke, the taste of her own time.

On the forecourt were three cars labelled as taxis.

"Do you know the — pub, The Magpie?"

"No. Try Jack."

She tried the second car. Jack said he had heard of The Magpie, but it was in Sidcup.

"No, it's at Asham. It's famous. They used to hang highwaymen on the square outside."

She expected him to look at her as if she was mad — maybe she was — but instead he shook his head. "That's in London."

Daisy took out the book, *Sorrow,* from her bag. She showed Jack the description of the inn.

By now the third one had got out of his car and come over. The first man had no interest and was reading a paper.

"That's the Old Mag you want," said the third man. "Blowed if I know where it is though."

Daisy drew in a deep breath.

"Would you be prepared to drive round Asham and help me find it? Whatever it costs, of course."

"Well," said the third driver, "I'll give it a go."

They gave it a go.

They drove through grey flat Asham, and finally they found the rolling fields after all, but they were cindery, and the trees looked scorched as London trees.

Besides, reaching the outer environs, the driver turned back. "It ain't out here. It's in the centre somewhere."

Back through Asham, up and down.

This pub and that.

The driver got out and asked at the Red Horse.

"We'll try up by the railway crossing."

They did so, to no avail.

Daisy felt contrite and determined. Any minute he might get sick of it and ask her to get out. But in fact the driver now seemed as questing as she. He only asked her if she was still all right to pay.

They found the Old Mag about four o'clock. The sky was heavy with summer overcast, and in a narrow street of dress shops and cafés, a timbered front appeared bulging out, and a sign — of a magpie in flight.

"Oh thank you," said Daisy, as if he had delivered her baby in the cab or rescued her cat from a tree or fed her when she was starving.

"I'm afraid it's twenty-two quid."

She gave him twenty-five and he drove off happy, pleased with victory and money.

The pub was shut. A board told her it would not open until six.

Daisy went into one of the cafés across the street.

She was disconcerted there was no square. As she sat there over her hot ham croissant and Spanish salad, she told herself the square must have been built on.

She drank a lot of tea, and when the café filled up at five-thirty, she removed herself for a nervous walk along the street, being careful not to wander too far from the elusive pub.

In this way she found that The Magpie backed on to a concrete apron, packed with tiny shiny Japanese cars. This was what the square had become.

At six sharp she returned to the pub door. She was the first customer.

6th FEATHER

"You say you're writing a book?" The woman was blowsy and aggressive.

"That's right."

"About the Magpie Inn."

"About the Magpie Murderer."

"Well — I don't know nothing about that. And George don't. We've been here six years, mind."

"It was really the room I was interested in."

"Well, as I say, we don't let rooms."

Daisy, on her second white wine, felt a deep hot desperation. And as the drink took hold, felt too the stupidity of her plight.

For she was in over her head. She did not know what she did. To bring the Magpie Dress to the Magpie Inn had seemed logical and sensible, actually consequent. But the dress lay limp, just a crumpled up bit of black and white silk, fragile enough to tear in two. As indeed had been its owner.

But what had Margaret Shawn, who courted death and died of the wrong brand, to do with the black and white nun and the arrogant priest?

Yes, thought Daisy, *I do know.*

An appointment. A meeting not kept.

"But would you show me the room?"

"I should think not," said the woman nastily, and then softened her voice a touch. "All our old junk up there, and stuff from the pub. Spiders, God knows what."

"What *is* all this?" asked George, coming up.

George was also blowsy, but genial. He liked a tipple and accepted Daisy's offer of a drink, as his wife had not.

After they had talked a while George said, "We could let her see the room, Rita. No harm."

"I don't think —" said Rita.

"Come on," said George to Daisy. He gave her another wine she had not asked for and waited for her to pay. Then he took her out the back, through a brown hall and up some floral stairs that creaked.

The landing was uneven.

"This is it, I reckon."

It was very low, the room, but the beams were long gone.

It was also, as promised, full of lumber, boxes and crates, a stag's head, skeins of cobwebs, and a window filthier than on the train. Which over-looked the concrete and the cars.

"The square was out there," said George. "I remember old Mick — he had the place before us — he used to say they had hangings there. People used to pay to have the room and watch, in private. Funny things people get up to."

"I'll pay," said Daisy, straight out, "to have the room tonight."

"What?"

"I know you think I'm crazy, but it would help my book."

"But — where'd you sleep?"

"That doesn't matter."

"God help us," said George. "Here, I don't think I can let you do that —"

"Fifty pounds," said Daisy. "In cash."

"Oh now look —"

"Seventy," said Daisy. "That's it."

Her mouth, despite the wine, was dry. She felt like a bad actor in a bad TV crime play.

George was a worse actor. He bumbled away to himself. Then he said, "Rita won't like it. And I'll tell you now, she won't do you breakfast."

"I don't want bloody breakfast," Daisy shouted, astonishing herself, "or a bloody bed. I want to sit in this horrible room for the night and I'm offering you seventy pounds to do it. *Yes?*"

"Just hold on —"

"Yes or no."

George hung his head. "It's your funeral."

"In fact not."

When he had taken the money and gone out, Daisy leaned on the wall the way Liza Meadows was supposed to have done after her brush with the murderer. Daisy too felt faint and weak. Then she drank off all the third white wine, and went to the bathroom she had glimpsed down the hall. Too bad if they did not want her to use it.

In the bathroom, which was puce, she found like a gift a hanger, and she took it because for seventy pounds a pee and some soap and water and a hanger seemed reasonable.

The dark was coming. It was nearly nine.

Down below noises came from the pub.

Daisy took out the Magpie Dress and smoothed it. She put it on to the hanger, and then hung the hanger on the window-frame. The dress faced out to the concrete apron, and the arrival of evening.

"Here we are," said Daisy. She sat down against one of the crates and began to cry.

After a few minutes, the pain left her.

She thought, *In pieces, but not broken.*

At ten she went down and bought a bottle off George, who stared at her guiltily, and some sandwiches from the bar which Rita did not want her to have, but what could she do, Daisy was the ultimate paying customer.

Then Daisy went back up to the room with the junk in it and the view of the cars.

She did not know what was the anniversary of the possible mooted hanging of the Magpie Hunter. But

even if she had, would it have been useful? The Earth shifted constantly, and time zones subtly altered. Greenwich Mean Time, daylight saving, leap years — all these would make havoc of exactitude. And if it would happen it would happen.

"Cheers," said Daisy to the Magpie Dress, and drank from the uncorked bottle.

7th and LAST FEATHER

Seven's for Heav'n and eight's for Hell,
And nine's for the Deil, his ain sel.

The noises in the pub went on until midnight, because Rita or George obviously had friends in, drinking after hours. Then Rita and George came to bed, and there were tooth-brushings and lavatory flushings, and a final door slammed. Daisy heard Rita say, "— Might be anyone." But no one came to the closed door of the junk room. No one came to disturb Daisy and the Magpie Dress. Daisy had drunk most of the bottle and long ago eaten the sandwiches, which had been, oddly, very nice.

The dress hung in the window, faintly glared on by the street lights of Asham as by the lamps of the capital. It looked thin and flightless.

Daisy thought, *I wish Agatha and Tony were here.*

Then she fell asleep. She was not surprised by what she found there.

Although the chamber of confession was not as Daisy would have guessed it to be. No, it was just a small room, lacking windows, with a crucifix on the wall, and a candle burning.

He stood there, the handsome priest. And he was beautiful. Yes, you would have to be insane not to want to possess him, or else, not a lover of men.

And she was, the girl. She had loved men before. She was stirred by their bodies. The gorgeous hardness, of muscle, of penis. Their hair and eyes that were like angels'.

And this one, this one —

The young nun spoke as she knelt there. And Daisy, hearing the words, knew them now not like sub-titles, but as if a parallel translation occurred within her inner ear.

"*Mea culpa.* I have sinned."

And he said nothing, only waited.

"I have sinned," said Beauty, her white face bowed, "because all I can think of is you. Not the Christ. You."

And then she stood up, and she looked at him. Her black eyes burned, but his eyes were blue and sere, cold as glaciers. He said nothing.

"Let me," she said, "let me touch you." And she crept to him and put her hand on his chest. "You have a heart," she said, "I feel it beating. Let me — oh, let me —" and she put her other hand on his face and tried to draw him down. But the handsome face of the blond priest would not allow it. Like a mask, it floated over her. He said, "You will damn yourself. You are giving yourself to the Devil."

"No," she said. "Only to you."

And then she slid her other hand from his heart and put it over his groin.

He moved then, away from her.

He had the face of a king confronted by the most abject and filthy suppliant.

"No," he said. "Hell has got into you. Kneel down."

"I die," she said, "I *burn* —"

"You will burn in Hell. On your knees."

And she lay on her face then, and she wept. She said, "I love you."

Then he lifted her and struck her across the cheek so that she fell once more. She lay on the ground again, weeping, and she pulled up her habit and her shift, black and white, and showed him the mound of her sex, which was covered with pure blonde hair, as on his own head.

"You are *here*," she said.

"And you are a demon," he said.

She sat up slowly. She was much paler than white. She whimpered. "Others," she said, "led me astray."

Then she confessed to him. How her brother had seduced her. How she had lain with grooms and soldiers. She said the Devil had come to her. She said she wanted to die. And all the while she wept, and her body, although covered up now, glowed like the flame on the shivering candle.

He listened like an icon. And when she was done he told her he must seek guidance. And then she was afraid, afraid in the midst of lust and love and agony. And she begged him not to betray her, he must not, the seal of the confessional protected her. Only he could save her from the dark.

No, he said. She was beyond him now.

Daisy went with her down a winding stair and up to a cell, in the shadow. Alone, the beautiful nun wrote a letter to her brother. Her tears fell on it like blazing acid not yet invented. The letter told how she had been forced to betray their fraternal secret. *Kill him,* the letter said.

And then Daisy saw the old rough track, Fetherwies, by night, no moon, the hard cold points of stars, and the priest walking there in the dark from which the beautiful nun had asked him to save her.

Near the statue of the Virgin, blanched and dry as a bone, the assassins came to him. There were seven of them but an unseen eighth — her brother — and an unseen ninth — herself.

"Do not forgive me Father, for I have not yet sinned —"

They stabbed and slashed with their blades, and he was cut in pieces, and broken.

His blood made a river under the trees.

When the dawn began to come, an angel did fall from Heaven.

It was the magpie.

It stooped above the carrion of the pale priest, it alighted on his breast. But then it only stared at him,

stared and did not plunder. And eventually it lifted up into the gilding sky and flew away.

Karma. They had lived then, died then, and were reborn. . . . She owed him her death, for his, since she had caused his death. And she had loved him. Had he gone looking for her, too, through the alleys and streets of Faithways in 1912? With a knife. Eight times he killed. And then he missed her, though she had gone to meet him. She had caught her death, had died — but wrongly, without his kiss. Margaret Shawn, the frigid nun, and her priest of the knife. *Lovers. Magpies.*

Daisy looked at the window of the junk room. Beyond the dress, there was no light. It was wholly dark, and dim, as if a fog had come and there had also been a power-cut. The room was abysmal.

She got up slowly. And walked to the window.

Outside was — nothing. Nothing at all.

Daisy was giddy. She backed away and sat down on a crate.

She put her hands together, held her own hand.

And then she heard them in the square that was no longer there. The crowd shouting as it pulled him along to the gallows. He had died twice. She heard the lurch and grind of wood. Then silence.

The silence was so thick.

I can't bear it.

But she must.

And then she felt the stirring through the air. Up out of time and night. A touch came on the window like the brush of a wing. And the dress quivered.

A slit shot through the window — and through the dress. Once — twice — again, again. Daisy felt the power of the air and of the dark. She fell sidelong on the floor, still holding her hand.

The knife — invisible — sliced through the dress over and over, over and over again. And in the air, soundless, the high orgasmic scream. Penetration, perfection, payment.

Then it was gone.

It was gone.

Daisy looked.

The glass was cut in shards, none of which had fallen out, like a pattern of strange frost.

And the dress was all in ribbons. Black and white. White and black.

"At last," Daisy said. She put her head into her comforting arms. Peace and quiet. And as the street lamp light of twentieth-century cities came back into the window behind the shreds of the slashed and murdered dress, she said again, softly, "At last." Ω